BOOKS BY TIM MCBAIN & L.T. VARGUS

The Violet Darger series

The Victor Loshak series

The Charlotte Winters series

The Scattered and the Dead series

Casting Shadows Everywhere

The Clowns

CELEBRITY SKIN

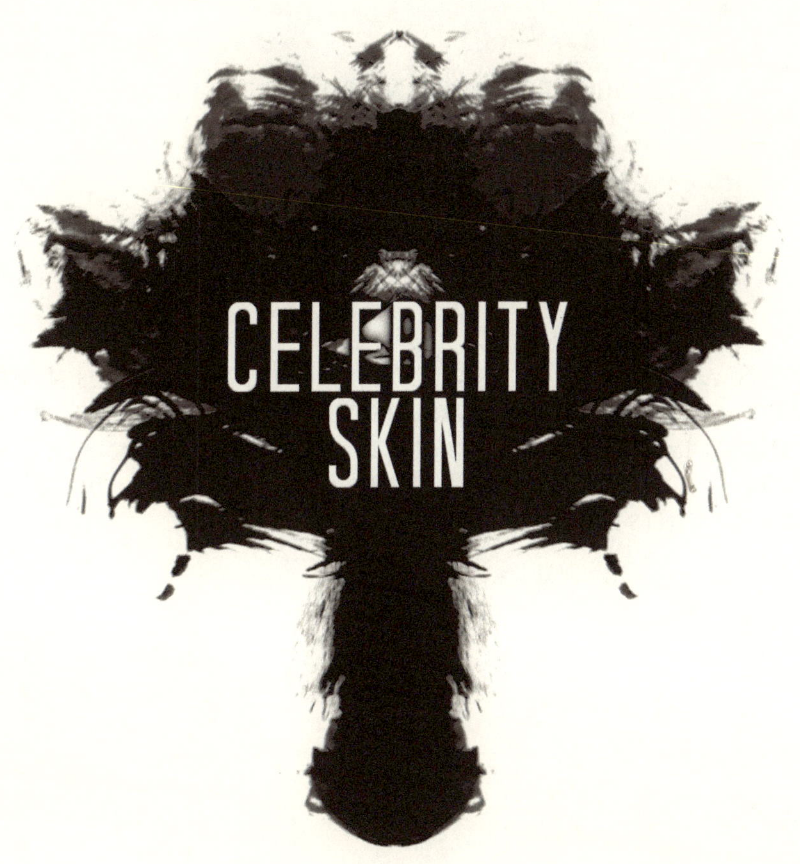

a Violet Darger novel

L.T. VARGUS & TIM MCBAIN

SMARMY PRESS

CELEBRITY SKIN

PROLOGUE

The compact car wheels into the long driveway, tires humming against the asphalt. A hatchback with peeling green enamel, shimmying and groaning like the whole thing might shake apart at top speed, the front end pointed at its destination like a missile.

The driver adjusts his hands on the steering wheel. Leans forward to see the buildings rising up beyond the windshield.

This is it. The big time.

It's all there just beyond the brim of his stupid Pizza Cottage hat.

The studio lot.

The hallowed halls, sacred ground practically, where so many movies and TV shows had been shot. All those dreams captured inside of a camera lens and then broadcast out to the masses or projected on a giant theater screen to become the shared fantasy of a whole culture.

He takes the reality in. Soaking up the details. Rapt.

It's all surprisingly… what's the word?

Shitty.

Up close, the buildings look like hell. Fifty shades of beige. Pockmarked like someone had flung gravel at the concrete exteriors over and over.

The drive snakes toward the buildings in the distance, tightly packed rows of plain buildings the color of sand, cement cubes that look more industrial than artistic. In a way, he supposes, they are.

These drab-looking dream factories crank out the sitcoms,

talk shows, movies. Not art really. Entertainment. Commodities with all the hard edges ground down. All the strong flavors sucked out. Everything reduced to something polished and bland that goes down smooth for the whole audience. Non-offensive even to the cranky church lady types, who are always squinting in an effort to see evil intentions everywhere they look.

The stack of cardboard pizza boxes in the passenger seat shifts as he rounds the gentle bend in the drive. He reaches out. Presses his hand flat to the top of the stack, sticks it there like a starfish suctioned to a boat's hull, and the stack of boxes goes steady.

He exhales. Feels a tremor in his breathing.

The toll booth takes shape around that curve in the drive — a glass box with the dark silhouette of the attendant vaguely discernible within. He pulls up alongside it.

The sunlight flares off the glass like a camera flash. Blinds him for a second.

And then the attendant's shape is moving inside the booth, and the window is sliding open.

"Pass."

He hears the monotone voice before the face comes into focus. Male. Early 30s. Stubble. Bags under his dead eyes. Could be hung over. The name patch sewn into the breast of his polo says "Cliff."

"Huh?"

"You got a parking pass?"

"Uh… I have these pizzas for the audition. The, um, Peter Angell audition."

Cliff's face somehow goes blanker as he interrupts.

"Look, I'm gonna need a pass to let you into the lot."

"I, uh… Wait. They gave me a code. Hang on."

"That'll work."

He digs a folded scrap of paper out of his left hip pocket, reads the code. Six digits.

The parking attendant types the number into a tablet. Finger smearing over the glossy screen in fast motion.

The driver's breath still feels shaky.

"I'm not seeing it…"

"Not seeing it?"

"The code. You're not on the list."

The driver turns his head. Looks over at the stack of pizza boxes. Swallows. He can feel the attendant watching him watch the pizzas.

"Shoot. I could take 'em off your hands. Call a page down to lug the stack up to the audition."

"The pizzas? No way. This is like $170 worth of pie. I need cash on delivery. Plus, I was hoping… I mean I figured a big movie audition… Peter Angell… Seems like I oughta get a decent tip, at least."

The attendant closes his eyes and huffs out a breath. Definitely hung over.

"Let me try to call up. Angell's office, you said?"

The driver nods. Watches the smart phone nestle against Cliff's cheek. Waits.

Cliff blinks a few times. Stares at nothing. Then he shakes his head.

"Phone system is fucked. I think they're doing maintenance or something."

He taps the phone screen to kill the call. Shakes his head again.

"So… like… what do we do?"

Cliff looks up at the driver, his eyes crawling to the Pizza Cottage hat and then the stack of cardboard on the passenger seat.

"Well..."

It sounds like he'll say more, but he trails off there.

Now the driver knows he has to seize the moment. Say the right words to get what he wants.

In a way, this is his audition.

"Look, I don't know how things work around here as well as you do, but I can hang out here all afternoon if need be. I figure a bunch of hungry producers won't mind. They've always seemed like patient and forgiving types to me."

The attendant rubs his knuckles at his eyelids. Blinks a few more times. Nods.

"Yeah. OK. I get it."

"So let me put the question to you a second time, Cliff: What do we do?"

Cliff holds up a finger. Digs around inside the booth for a second, ducking down out of view. He bobs back into the frame of the open window a couple seconds later, a flap of cardstock in his hand. He jots something on the back of the card in black ink, then passes it through.

"Here. It's a temporary pass. We, uh, don't use these much these days, but..."

"Desperate times. Desperate measures."

Cliff's arm jerks, his hand just out of view, and something clicks somewhere in the guts of the security booth.

The boom glides upward before the hood of the car, that metallic arm sliding away, and the threshold into the lot is suddenly clear.

The driver lets off the brake, and the hatchback creeps

forward again. Passes through the gate. Pulls away from the booth until Cliff is back to that indiscernible dark shape he'd been to begin with.

He toes the accelerator after that, and the vehicle lurches at his touch, engine coughing and then growling. A wide expanse of asphalt choked with luxury vehicles fills his field of vision now, those studio buildings rising up beyond them like rounded concrete mountains against the horizon.

Markings on the sides of the building guide him deeper into the lot. Letters and numbers coding the different soundstages. 32H. 33H.

He passes exterior sets along the way — strips of fake streets that snake between the concrete tubes. One set looks like a row of Brownstones in Brooklyn, at least the facade of such. Another sports the brick storefronts of a Main Street in some Midwestern burgh. A little utility shed surrounded by wispy foliage could pass for a lagoon setting if you blocked out the cement surrounding it.

It all appears small up close. Artificial in a preposterous way. Thin like the inch-thick cinder block tile they use to make the walls of a basement set look legit.

But that makes sense, he thinks. All that matters is what the camera sees. Angles and lighting can make even the phoniest backdrop appear convincing in the final cut.

He snugs the hatchback between a $300,000 Range Rover and a Hummer that looks like it could roll right over the other cars in the lot in a pinch. The compact looks ludicrous in this company. Cartoonishly small and shabby. He wonders if it sticks out too much, wonders if it will matter at all.

Will any of this matter?

He climbs out. Hoists the stack of pizza boxes. Crosses the

lot on foot.

An eerie hush seems to reach out over the asphalt. The tiniest whisper of wind moves here, tickling his arms, his top lip, the bridge of his nose.

He swallows. Looks over his shoulder as he nears the glass doors leading into the lobby.

In the distance, he can just make out the security booth and the shadow of a figure inside. A dark shape, shoulders more visible than anything. The edge of the building crops it out of view as he closes on the front door, that hard line of concrete sweeping over the booth like a curtain.

And he pushes through the glass panel, feels a faint suction, some pressure difference between the indoors and outside.

The shade inside washes everything out for a second. Blinding. And then he finds himself in a small foyer just shy of the lobby, another set of glass doors ahead.

He stops there. Surveys.

No.

Not here.

Not yet.

He pushes through the second set of doors. Enters a reception area. It smells vaguely herbal here. Something bright and green.

The woman behind the desk chatters into a headset and types on her laptop at the same time. Red hair. Pale eyes. A suntan that almost looks pink.

She blinks at him. Face blank. Staring.

And he turns on the big smile. Points an index finger at the stack of cardboard in his hand like she could have failed to notice. Then he points that same finger down the hall to his left and her right.

She blinks again. Nods and waves him through.

He strides down the hall. Finds it as empty and mute as most everything else around here. A row of doorways mars the wall off to his right.

And that herbal smell gives way to something more industrial. Fresh paint, he thinks. Maybe a hint of sawdust. They're probably building sets all day. He remembers reading that the soap opera sets are in motion 24 hours a day, backgrounds being built and scenes being shot into the wee hours of every night — the construction logistics perhaps more sophisticated than the actual scripts.

One spot of sunshine gleams into the box of white walls. He approaches the window and finds a potted plant huddling in a nook there. Some kind of yucca or palm, he thinks.

He strides toward it. Dumps most of the pizza boxes in behind the plant. One box peels open, part of a rounded pie sliding free of the cardboard flaps, a pale tongue exiting lips.

He keeps the bottom box — the last remaining box — steady as he glides on down the hall. Moves carefully with it.

He'd gotten the idea from a book about the making of *The Sopranos.* A would-be actor showed up in a Domino's uniform or something with a stack of pizzas to sneak into an open casting call. It jumped him past thousands of others in line and got him in the door.

Another story he'd read involved an actor getting his big break by posing as a UPS guy to get onto the set of a network hit. He not only got in, he landed a role and launched his career as a full-time TV actor based on the ruse — a career still thriving to this day.

He feels the air-conditioning touch the sheen of sweat now coating his face. Chilly and dry and harsh.

He ducks into the opening on his right.

☾

Back in the hall, panels of glass flit by on his left. Cutouts looking into some offices toward the back of the building, all of the panes blocked out by swaths of curtain.

And his reflection stares back at him, walking along with him, ghostly white from the creamy fabric of the shades.

He stares into the eyes of the double of himself. Something hollow in them. Unfamiliar.

He sees a face he doesn't recognize, a face no one recognizes. But that's the point.

Not so long ago, he had one of the most famous faces in the country. FBI's Most Wanted list. TV news segments that ran for months. His features boxed in a graphic pinned up over every news anchor's shoulder.

Plastic surgery has rearranged his visage. Morphed the features into something alien.

The scalpel and lipo vac pulled all the soft youthful bits into an angular jawline, square chin, masculine brow. Lean and hard. Riveted.

The procedure had left him a little mean-looking, a little empty-looking, even to himself. Like a crystal meth addict who somehow sucked on a glass pipe until they'd drawn most of that fleshy subcutaneous layer out of themselves, left only skin drawn taut over stringy muscle and blades of bone. Emaciated.

He'd read about the doctor somewhere in the guts of the dark web, where the eyes of decent folks never go. A plastic surgeon without scruples who would happily work for the highest bidder.

Even if the highest bidder was Tyler Huxley, apparently.

The serial bomber from the FBI's Most Wanted list.

Huxley trails deeper into the building. And suddenly he's not alone.

A security guard's thick frame fills the other end of the hall. Mustache the flat brown hue of a Snickers wrapper. Crew cut colored the same. He sips at a cup of Starbucks, moseying Huxley's way, a rolled up newspaper tucked under his arm.

Huxley stares straight ahead. Hears his own breathing go loud inside his sinuses as the security guard grows closer.

The big guy bobs his head as they come to within a few paces of each other. Grins like a friendly bulldog, a jutting row of bottom teeth somehow becoming more visible than the top.

"How ya doin'?"

Huxley's throat feels like some mess of tentacles pulling apart as he replies, turgid and tight.

"Hi."

And then the big lug is past. Trailing away down the long hall. No double take. No glance back. No problems.

But Huxley can feel his heart hammering in his chest. A rivulet of sweat cascades from the corner of his brow, and he dabs it away with the hem of his Pizza Cottage polo.

He rounds a corner. Comes, at last, to the bigger sets of steel doors marked the way he'd expected, the way he'd remembered.

Studio A. That's where they film the talk show where the awful host says rude things about his guests' appearances — not backhanded compliments so much as throat punches thinly disguised as praise. "Well, I think your new lips look great. Way better than those pink inner tubes they were before. Seriously. Bloa-ted."

Studio B. That's where they film the brain dead game show,

Ultimate Food Fight. While millions starve to death yearly, the American public watches idiots waste food by smearing themselves in kiddie pools of creamed corn and crawling through tunnels clogged with tapioca pudding and SpaghettiOs.

On and on it goes. The soundstages stretch out before him, all in a row. Mega-corporations churning out toxic swill, and the masses huddling around their screens to drink greedily from the poison well.

Finally he reaches the set he wants. Steps into the empty space. The posted filming schedule he'd seen online makes him confident that nobody will be here for some time, possibly hours.

He walks down the narrow aisle — a row of steps running through the theater seating. He moves into the open in front of the auditorium area and crosses the line where the shiny black floor gives way to beige carpet, stepping onto the stage.

He finds it surreal to walk among the living room furniture he's seen on TV so many times. So many one-liners and sarcastic comebacks delivered here.

It seems different up close, with that fourth wall wide open to the stadium-style seating. Naked. Peeled.

A fraud.

He kneels. Places the pizza box down on the shag carpet delicately. Holds his breath until the floor supports its weight fully.

There.

Good.

Then he squats before the couch like it's an altar — and he supposes that today it is. A sacred place to make his sacrificial offering.

He removes one of the couch cushions. Then he swallows and again smears his fingers at his soggy brow.

He opens the pizza box carefully. Peers at the gadgetry laid bare.

After two breaths, he starts to transfer his mechanism from the box into the couch. Slower than slow motion. Arms gliding. Gradually descending.

He rests the device on the flat expanse where the couch cushion should go.

Feels a breath come out all shaky.

Done.

Done.

Now he places the cushion over top. Slow to let it go, to let its weight free of his touch. Like a dad holding onto the bike seat for an extra second or two, he thinks. No training wheels now.

It's down. And his eyelids are fluttering. And a quiver runs through his whole body. Bubbles bursting in his chest, in his arms. Needles prickling in his thighs, along the top of his scalp.

Holy hell.

He tries to squelch the giddy feeling rising up from his belly. Even his body itself, the meat and bones of him, knows what comes next. Knows too well the big bang that's soon to arrive.

Hollywood loves a comeback. And Tyler Huxley's will be legendary.

CHAPTER 1

"If they die, it's on you. Their blood will be on your hands."

The inside of the SWAT van was stifling, but Violet Darger had more important things to worry about right now — like the phone in her hand.

"No one needs to die today, Justin," she said, keeping her voice calm and level.

She ignored the trickle of sweat running down the back of her neck, ignored the boom of her pulse in her skull, ignored the chuff of the news helicopters circling overhead like vultures.

She focused on only the phone, on the sucking silence shoved up to her ear. She adjusted her grip on the plastic case and waited for him to respond.

The man on the other end of the line was named Justin Leffew. Earlier that morning, Leffew had robbed a Dollar General store in Los Altos and then led police on a merry chase through the streets of San Francisco. The vehicular pursuit ended when a SWAT officer managed to shoot out the left front tire of the suspect's vehicle, but Leffew's crime spree hadn't stopped there.

Instead, the suspect fled on foot, ducking inside a nearby apartment building, and from there, 22-year-old Mindy Garza and her 15-month-old daughter, Leila, won the unlucky lottery. They'd been standing in the foyer of the building, collecting their mail, when the suspect burst in. Leffew saw his opportunity and took the woman and toddler hostage, directing them at gunpoint up to Garza's fourth-floor apartment.

SFPD's first act was to evacuate the rest of the building. The second thing they'd done was call the FBI to request a hostage negotiator. And that was where Darger came in.

The silence seemed to grow louder on the other end of the line. Darger felt oddly aware of the space there, conscious that she was listening to the inside of Mindy Garza's apartment, her right ear somehow granted access to the 650-odd square feet of efficiency living area which somehow sounded cavernous through the phone speaker just now. Empty. She pawed at the perspiration beading on her temple and checked the time.

Leffew and his hostages had been barricaded in the building for four hours now. Darger had been in communication with him for almost half of that span, but she'd yet to get him to agree to release Garza and her daughter.

A wail in the background pierced the quiet. Baby Leila was crying again.

"Shut that baby up," Leffew said, his voice slightly muffled, as if he had covered the mouthpiece to prevent Darger from hearing.

Not good. She wanted Leffew's attention on her, not the hostages.

Keep him talking.

Keep him calm.

She shuffled through the notes in her lap. Hastily scribbled details about Leffew's background.

"You have a sister, isn't that right? Rachel?"

The quiet stretched out again for a full second.

"What of it?" Leffew asked, and Darger could hear the uncertainty in his voice as he tried to wrap his head around the sudden change in topic.

"And a three-year-old niece named Caroline? Think of them, Justin. You wouldn't want anything to happen to them, would you?"

The phone's speaker fluttered in her ear as he exhaled.

"Of course not. But that's not… you still don't get it. No one respects me."

"You have my respect, Justin," Darger said, her tone soothing, almost a whisper. "And that's why I want to understand you. I think we've made some progress here. I've done my best to get you what you need. Would you agree with that?"

"I guess so. Except for the Xanax."

"And I told you from the start that there were certain rules. Things I can and can't get you. No drugs. No weapons."

He sighed again.

"Yeah, I know."

"I also think — and you tell me if you agree — that you don't want to hurt anyone."

"Of course not," he said, and Darger thought she heard the slightest waver of emotion blooming there. "Of course I don't want to hurt anyone."

"I can hear that in your voice, Justin."

"That's not what everyone else thinks, though. They think I'm a monster."

"Maybe that's true," Darger said. "But there's something you can do to show them you aren't a violent person. That you aren't a monster."

He sniffed.

"This… this can't go on forever."

"You're absolutely right," Darger said, feeling like she was walking a mental tightrope. "And I know there's a way everyone can get out of this unharmed, if you keep working with me, just like you have been."

"I just... I can't go back to jail, man. I can't do it."

The pitch of the helicopter's rotors changed overhead. The various choppers jockeying to get the money shot for tonight's newscast.

"Well, look... that's something we can discuss. But I'm not going to lie to you, Justin. That's going to be up to the prosecutor, in the end. So I don't know if I can promise no jail time. But I can promise you something else, and that's if you let Mindy and Leila go — right now — I will personally advocate for a lighter sentence on your behalf."

Leffew was silent for a few seconds. Darger thought that was good. He was considering it. There was only one possible soft landing here. He had to see that.

When he spoke again, his voice was low, confused.

"What the fuck?"

And then he erupted. Volcanic rage all at once.

"You fucking bitch! What have you been telling them?"

"Justin, you need to stay calm. I don't know what—"

"I knew it! I knew I shouldn't have trusted you."

There was a click, and the line went dead.

CHAPTER 2

Huxley's hands still hover just shy of the couch cushion when the door clicks behind him. A metallic snap that rings over the open soundstage and echoes back from the corners.

His mind freezes. The white noise of fear blotting out all the words, a tea kettle shriek filling his skull.

But instinct kicks in anyway. Lifts him to his feet. Shuffles him a few paces back from the couch.

Some part of him understands this, words coming unlocked in his head via a few fragmented sentences.

Need to get away. Away from it. *Like now.*

He turns just in time to see the security guard's eyes go wide.

"What the— Hey! Who let you in here?"

It's the one with the Snickers wrapper mustache. Those bottom bulldog teeth jutting out of the gap in his lips again.

No Starbucks cup or newspaper in his hands now. He juts an accusatory finger toward Huxley's chest, arm already trembling with adrenaline.

Huxley blinks once. Feet momentarily glued to the floor.

The big lug sneers. Mustache curling at the corners. He speed walks down the aisle toward the stage, shoulders hunched like a racoon's.

And then Huxley is running. Crossing that shag carpet floor of the fake living room and moving back onto the matte black of the studio floor. He bashes through a side door leading backstage.

The steel panel lurches out of his way. Bangs into the wall.

And another hallway opens up before him. A white tunnel of drywall. Names emblazoned on some of the doors.

He plunges down the rectangular tube. Feels almost claustrophobic after dwelling in the broad expanse of the soundstage.

Doors flit by one side of his field of vision like the dotted line in the middle of the freeway.

He picks up his feet. Builds speed.

Somewhere behind him, Mustache yells into a walkie-talkie. Voice coming out raspy. Out of breath.

"We've got a breach. An intruder exiting Studio C and moving into the backstage area. Over."

A voice gurgles out of the walkie-talkie speaker, but Huxley can't make out the words. Then Mustache speaks again, loud, practically shouting somewhere behind him.

"White male. Maybe early 30s. A frickin' pizza delivery guy. Or dressed that way, anyhow."

Huxley banks hard to the right. Another hallway says *ah* before him.

He needs to think. This is his chance.

Movement erupts down the corridor. A doorway leaping open. Another security guard takes shape there.

And Huxley jams himself into the nearest door. Closes it behind him.

Soundless. Sealed off in the dark.

Shit.

He doesn't think he's been spotted. But the two guards have got him pinned down in any case, whether they realize it or not.

He sweeps a hand along the wall. Finds a light switch. Flicks it.

The fluorescent bulbs flicker and then wink to life. White light floods the room.

Harsh.

Bright.

Confusing.

And then he sees.

Racks of clothes fill the space before him, an otherwise bare room not much smaller than a small grocery store floor.

The clothes seem sorted loosely by color. Reds to the right. Blues to the left.

This is the wardrobe room, or one of them. Another piece of the collective dream is housed and decided just here.

He flicks the lights back off. Takes a breath.

And then he steps forward into the darkness and submerges himself in the hanging flaps of fabric.

CHAPTER 3

Hands shaking with adrenaline, Darger redialed the number.

Come on, she thought.

It rang.

Pick it up, Justin.

And rang.

Pick up the phone.

Finally, she was redirected to a generic voicemail greeting.

"Shit," Darger whispered to herself.

Her gaze wheeled around the inside of the empty SWAT van as though the paneled walls might give her an answer to what had just happened. Blank white stared back in all directions, little gun portholes cutting circles into the contoured metal.

She moved to the back of the van, opened the door, and climbed out. Her skin was still dewy with sweat, and the blast of fresh air sent a wave of goose bumps up her arms.

Gregory Colfax, San Francisco's Chief of Police, read the look on Darger's face and frowned.

"What happened?"

"I don't know. I was so close. I had him on the brink of giving up the hostages, and then… he just turned. Started screaming about how he shouldn't have trusted me. He hung up."

"You tried calling back?" Chief Colfax asked.

Darger nodded.

"He isn't answering."

The radio clipped to the chief's vest crackled, and then a

voice said, "We've got movement at the window."

Darger tilted her head to look. It was a bright day, and the sun was at just the wrong angle so she had to squint and shield her eyes. She noted the chief doing the same beside her.

But yes, she saw it now. The curtains swished and swayed and then were shoved aside, exposing a narrow slit of window in the middle.

From a few yards away, Sergeant Barnes, leader of the SFPD SWAT team, brought his radio to his lips.

"Hold positions unless I give the word. We don't know if the person at the window is our target or one of the hostages."

Darger still couldn't tell what exactly was happening behind the curtain, but she knew one thing for certain: there was no way Leffew was stupid enough to stand directly in front of it. He was well aware they had snipers stationed on the surrounding rooftops.

Slowly, an inch at a time, the window slid upward. It stopped about four inches up, and then there was a flash of light and movement. A few seconds later, a distinct clatter rang out from the pavement below. Darger squinted at the ground, piecing together what she'd seen and heard with the small, black object now lying inert on the sidewalk.

"Was that the—" Chief Colfax asked.

"The phone." She sighed. "Yeah."

He'd just tossed the phone out of the window, fully cutting off their line of communication with him.

Chief Colfax scratched one corner of his mustache.

"Now what? We try to get another phone up there?"

Darger chewed her lip. The task force had determined it was too dangerous for any law enforcement to enter the building. The first phone had been delivered to Leffew by way of tactical robot, and the operation had taken forty-five minutes.

Her gut clenched at the thought of being out of contact that long. Too much could happen. She had to figure out what had set Leffew off in the first place and try to deescalate the situation.

She turned to the two men.

"Let's work on getting another phone up there, but in the meantime, do we have a bullhorn?"

"Affirmative," Sergeant Barnes said, toggling the button on his radio. "Abiko, we're gonna need to send another phone up. Lavilla, grab the megaphone from our gear and bring it out front."

Two minutes later, Darger had the bullhorn in hand. She took a few steps closer to the building.

"Not too close, Agent," Sergeant Barnes warned. "He's still armed."

Darger nodded and held the device in front of her mouth.

"Justin? It's Violet," she said.

Her voice sounded odd through the speaker. Thick and distorted. She hated it. But this wasn't about her.

"Justin, can you come to the window so we can talk?"

Seconds passed, and Darger was about to lift the bullhorn again when there was another flutter of activity at the window.

Behind her, she heard Barnes murmur into his radio.

"Snipers, hold for my word."

Fingers slid into view at the open gap of the window. They wrapped around the bottom rail, and the sash slid up until the window was fully open.

There was someone there. Standing directly in front of the window. Darger almost couldn't believe it. Leffew had to know he was putting himself directly in the line of fire. Was he *trying* to get shot?

Then she saw what Leffew was holding in front of himself.

A baby.

"You all get back," Leffew shouted. "Every one of you, or I'll drop her. You back the fuck off, or I'll do it."

As if sensing the threat, 15-month-old Leila Garza began to squirm and whimper. Darger's whole body tensed, terrified that Leffew would lose his grip.

She took a deep breath and spoke into the bullhorn, struggling to keep her voice in control.

"Justin, you can take Leila back inside. We're going to do exactly what you say. We're backing up now."

Darger held up her arms in a placating gesture and took several steps backward.

"You think he'll really do it?" Chief Colfax asked when she fell in line beside him.

"No," she said, glancing back at the window. "He's trying to intimidate us. The fact that he gave us an out — *get back OR I'll drop her*? He's still in a negotiation mindset."

"But you're still having us pull back?"

"It's too risky *not* to give him what he wants. If he so much as sneezes, he could lose his grip on the kid."

When they'd moved twenty yards back from their original position, Leffew whisked the baby back inside and shoved the curtains closed once more.

Darger exhaled and felt the faintest sense of relief.

"Justin, we've done what you asked," she said into the bullhorn. "What's next? What else can I do for you?"

His voice filtered out through the still open window.

"Fuck you, bitch!"

"I can hear that you're angry, Justin. I want to understand why."

"Fuck. You. Bitch."

Darger let the arm holding the bullhorn fall to her side.

At least the baby was safe.

For now.

CHAPTER 4

Darger watched two members of the SWAT team rig their little tactical robot up with another phone and wished the whole process could move about ten times faster. The clock was ticking.

Time slipped by in a slow crawl. Darger's heart seemed to be trying to pick up the pace, spurring things toward a gallop to no avail. The helicopters hovered above all the while, the rotors droning out an endless *whoomp-whoomp-whoomp* of their own.

Twenty minutes had passed since Leffew's outburst when Chief Colfax got a phone call. His posture went rigid when he answered.

"You've got what?" His eyes slid over to Darger. "OK. Just a minute."

"What is it?" she asked.

"It's one of our dispatchers. Apparently Leffew just used Miss Garza's phone to call 911, and he's asking for you."

Darger was already pulling one of her cards from her jacket pocket and handing it over.

"Have the dispatcher give him this number."

Colfax relayed the number and hung up.

The seconds stretched out again. Darger worried there'd been something lost in translation. Her phone rested in her palm, inert. She glanced from the phone to the open window and back again.

What if the dispatcher had written her number down wrong? What if Leffew simply decided that calling was one too many hoops to jump through?

Darger blinked and tried not to let her thoughts spiral. She'd just have to wait.

Heat wafted up from the asphalt in waves, the sun angled perfectly to reflect off the pavement in all directions. The warmth coiled around Darger's ankles, breathed on the backs of her knees. She focused on that sensation, staring at nothing, willing her mind to stay blank of everything but that rising heat.

When the phone finally rang a few seconds later, the buzzing from the vibrate function startled her so much, she nearly dropped it.

She hit the Answer icon and lifted the phone to her ear.

"Justin? Are you there?"

"Yeah, I'm fucking here."

"I'm glad you got in touch."

"Yeah right. You know, you're just like every other bitch I've ever met. You can't open your goddamn mouth without the lies just spilling out."

He was agitated. She had to calm him down. But she still had no idea what had set him off. What lies?

"I can hear how frustrated you are, and I want to help."

"Yeah, I'm fucking frustrated! Why wouldn't I be? You're letting them tell all these fucking lies about me!"

He was shouting now.

"Justin, I can't hear you when you yell at me."

His breath came in huffs. She waited. Seized on the word he'd used. *Them.*

"Who's 'them,' Justin? Who's telling lies about you?"

"Like you don't know. Like you're not spoon-feeding them this shit."

"I want to help you. But I can't unless you tell me who you're talking about."

"The fucking media. Who else?"

Darger whirled around. Let her eyes scan the rows of news vans spread up and down the nearest street. Each one of them jostling for the best angle of the scene. Each one wanting their piece of the drama unfolding.

"That cockroach, Vinnie Savage. He's saying things about me on the livestream. Saying I molested a 13-year-old. First of all, she was fourteen. And second of all, *she* seduced *me.* It was consensual, no matter what that fucking judge said!"

Darger knew Leffew's history. Knew he'd only recently been paroled after a six-year stint in prison for assaulting his 13-year-old neighbor.

But she couldn't dwell on who he was. What he was. She had to push down her genuine opinion about Justin Leffew and his crimes and remain in negotiation mode.

Law enforcement had explicitly kept the names of the suspect and the hostages from the media, but this Vinnie Savage guy must have figured it out somehow. A leak?

Darger shook her head.

That could be sorted out later. *Focus.*

Leffew was still ranting.

"...trying to make me out to be some kind of predator. A pervert. And that's not who I am. I mean... that's not how I see myself, OK? It's just not."

"I'm listening," Darger said. "I can hear the frustration and anger in your voice, Justin."

Leffew let out a bitter scoff.

"Yeah, well... I'm gonna start taking my frustration and anger out on this bitch and her stupid baby if you don't get that piece of shit reporter to shut up."

And then he hung up.

CHAPTER 5

Huxley waits. Encased in the blackness among the clothes.

The fabric hugs him. Conceals him. Smothers him in its fabric softener scent. *Moonlight Breeze* or *Lavender & Vanilla Bean* or some shit.

He hunches in a rack of dresses that reach all the way to the floor, shadows covering him from head to toe. That's good.

But did either of the security guards see him come in here?

He's not sure.

He swallows. Wipes his sweaty face into the breast of a satiny dress he thinks is red. Feels his heart punching in his chest. Blood squishing in his ears.

He runs his fingers over the plastic surgery scar just behind his ear. A bubbled piece of skin where his face now has a seam.

They'd pulled the skin taut from that point. Left a mottled scar where they'd stitched him up. He can only really see the mark if he stares straight at it in the mirror, but it feels rough against his fingertips. Textured like that point where the pizza cheese meets the crust.

He's found that something fundamental has shifted in him since his face was surgically altered. Another kind of identity has been stripped from him, another facade removed.

If you look in the mirror and you don't see *you* anymore, then who is this stranger on the other side of the glass, and who the hell are you?

Some deeper truth glimmers in that dysphoria, he thinks. Some vast and secret knowledge is laid bare when he looks upon that Other in the looking glass, a kind of sacred lesson that he is still trying to fully process.

All of the received wisdom is a lie, even the face in the mirror.

Nothing here has innate significance or weight.

The only meaning that's real is the meaning we give things.

Our choices.

He hears voices in the hall. Excited. Fast-talking.

"Did you see him?"

"Huh? Me? I didn't see shit."

One of the security guards lets out a big sigh. Something aggressive in it.

"God damn it. He came running right this way. Hauling tits, too. Son of a bitch left me in the dust, to be honest. Don't tell Morgan I said that."

"You think he was already past by the time I got out here?"

There's a pause. An *mmm* sound.

"Shit. I don't know."

"Well, he has to be close, right? We'll smoke his ass out."

Their voices swell in volume just a little as they converse. The loudness peaks; they're right outside the door.

And then the sound starts to roll back like a wave reaching its high-water mark and falling back. They keep going, and the voices seem smaller with every word.

"Was it paparazzi, you think?"

"Maybe. He was right on the set. Could have been trying to lift some memorabilia to sell on eBay or some shit."

They're moving away. For now, at least.

Huxley waits in the darkness. Thinking. Breathing. Fingering that blistered spot behind his ear where the scalpel left its mark, where his old face died and he became something new.

The voices fade to quiet. The seconds seep past.

When the voices have been silent for nearly seven minutes, Huxley steps out of the rack of dresses and moves back toward the light switch. He searches the wall for it. Snaps it on.

The glow hurts again. Worse than before. White and hard and artificial. Stabbing his pupils like roofing nails.

He looks out through slitted eyelids. Watches that smear of colors firm up into shapes and textures as his eyes adjust.

And then he moves deeper into the room, keeping low as he traverses the racks of garments.

His eyes crawl over the clothes all around him. Costumes. Lots of soccer mom-looking stuff. Scrubs. Police and military gear. A whole rack of lumberjackesque flannel shirts that he thinks must be from that sitcom about the carpenter and his zany family, *Household Renovation.*

He finally sees something that makes sense to him, and a little smile curves some of the hard angles around his mouth.

He plucks the Pizza Cottage hat from his head. Tosses it into the back corner of the space like a Frisbee. It disappears behind a rack of fringed suede jackets and pants that he finds mildly disturbing.

Network TV storytelling operates on a strict structure to fit the commercials. This is the big cliffhanger at the act break, no?

It's time for a costume change.

CHAPTER 6

Darger used her phone to search the reporter's name and blew out a breath when she found it.

"Oh for crying out loud," Darger said.

"What is it?" Chief Colfax asked.

"Vinnie Savage. He's not even a real reporter. He's broadcasting on *The Daily Gawk* livestream."

"*The Daily Gawk...*" Colfax repeated. "That's like one of those TMZ-type tabloid sites, right?"

Darger bobbed her head once, remembering her first run-in with the site. It was years ago, the original case she'd worked with Loshak in Ohio. Some teenagers had broken into the local morgue and taken video footage of a victim of the so-called Doll Parts Killer. *The Daily Gawk* had paid good money for the video, spreading the clip of the headless woman far and wide on social media, and Darger had taken all the heat from her superiors.

"Yeah."

She tucked her phone in her pocket and strode off toward the edge of the police barricade.

"What are you going to do?"

"The only thing I can," she said. "Try to talk some sense into this guy."

She stepped around one of the blue sawhorses stenciled with the message, "POLICE LINE — DO NOT CROSS."

The street beyond was choked with vehicles emblazoned with the logos of every conceivable media outlet, local and otherwise. Aside from the reporters and camera operators, civilian onlookers huddled close as well.

Despite the crowd, it wasn't difficult for Darger to locate Savage. In the video she'd seen online, she recognized the building he was standing in front of during his broadcast. Beyond that, the tabloid reporter had dyed silver hair which was swept up into a messy quiff style that reminded her of a cockatoo. He wasn't exactly inconspicuous.

She'd spotted the spray of silver hair right where she'd expected, just in front of the steps of the library across the street. He had his phone on a tripod and was angled so the barricaded apartment building was in view over his shoulder as he spoke into the camera.

"—and you could actually see this occur just a few moments ago, that harrowing moment as the demented criminal, Justin Leffew, dangled an innocent child — a baby — out the window, perhaps as some sort of threat."

Savage was still yammering on when his gaze flicked over to Darger. A beat later, his eyes bulged a little.

"Hold up, guys. Insane development happening live, right now. I've got eyes on a legendary FBI profiler, a bona fide true crime celebrity, and she's heading my way." He yanked the phone off the tripod and came jogging toward her, shoving the camera in her face.

"Special Agent Violet Darger, everyone! Agent Darger, can you give us any insights on what's happening inside that building now?"

Darger thrust her hand out, blocking the camera.

"I'd like if we could talk. Off camera."

"Sure," Savage said, crossing his arms so the phone was tucked against his chest, camera lens partially concealed but facing outward.

Darger raised her eyebrows.

"I can tell you're still recording."

Savage flashed two rows of bright white Chiclet teeth.

"Can't blame a guy for trying," he said, making a show of turning the camera off and placing the phone in his jacket.

"Where'd you get the name of the alleged suspect?"

He snorted.

"*Alleged.* That's great. And you know I'm not going to reveal my sources."

Darger shook her head.

"Fine. I don't actually care how you got the name. I just need you to stop talking about the specifics until we have the hostages safe."

The reporter's chin ticked upward, eyes alight with something like glee.

"So you're confirming that the man inside the building is indeed Justin Leffew?"

"I'm serious, Savage. You're putting those people in danger and undermining our attempts at negotiating a peaceful surrender."

His mouth puckered and contorted as if he were eating a piece of candy. Literally chewing on what she'd said.

"What do I get in exchange?" he said finally.

"Exchange?"

His eyelids fluttered.

"For doing what you ask. I'm going to need *something.*"

And there she was, negotiating again. Her mind whirred. What would someone like Savage want? What would be juicy enough to get him to drop the Justin Leffew bone?

When she landed on it, her first instinct was to hold it back.

Not that. Anything but that.

But she knew it would work.

"An interview," she said, trying to conceal how off-putting she found the whole idea. "With me."

Savage got a hungry look in his eye.

"Really."

"Yep. Right now. What do you say? I give you an exclusive interview, and you dial back the commentary on the alleged suspect."

He couldn't get the phone out fast enough. He reattached it to the tripod and made a few adjustments to the angle, making sure they were both in frame.

Before he started recording, the reporter pulled out a small pocket mirror and adjusted the silver tuft on top of his head.

"OK, we're live in 3... 2... 1..." He stood up a little straighter and fixed his gaze on the camera. "I'm standing here with Special Agent Violet Darger, FBI profiler extraordinaire, and she's agreed to give me an exclusive interview."

He swiveled sideways to face her.

"Agent Darger, how dire is the situation here?"

"I think it's very dire. That's why SFPD and I are doing everything in our power to negotiate a peaceful resolution."

"A peaceful resolution..." He cupped his chin in his palm. "Do you think that's even possible with someone like Justin Leffew? A deviant, child-molesting ex-con?"

Darger ground her teeth together. She knew what Savage was trying to do.

"First, I'd like to make it clear to you and to your viewers that we have not released any names in relation to this case, so I'm answering this and any further questions with the understanding that the suspect in this case is an as-yet-unnamed individual."

Savage nodded, his face a mask of phony solemnity.

"But to answer your question," Darger went on, "I believe it's possible to negotiate with just about anyone. And one of the keys in a successful negotiation is to avoid making assumptions and judgments."

She gestured at the building.

"The man in that apartment is a human being just like you and me. He wants the same things we do. Understanding, compassion, validation."

The reporter's face scrunched into a skeptical expression.

"Well, he might want *some* of the same things we do, but I have to say, I've never wanted to fondle a middle schooler."

Darger gave him a warning look. Did he actually think she was going to continue the interview if he kept this up?

"Again, until law enforcement decides to release the name of the individual, I can't comment on any question or statement that makes an assumption of his identity."

Savage laced his fingers together.

"What about the fact that Justin Leffew's own mother described her son as, 'deranged,' 'sick,' and 'an all-around garbage human'? Can you comment on that?"

Darger reached out and plucked the phone from the tripod. Stopped the recording.

"What the hell are you doing?" she demanded.

"Pandering to the crowd, Agent. Look, I don't like it any more than you do," he said, sounding about as sincere as a door-to-door salesman. "But I have to do my job. Just like you have to do yours."

He held out his hand, palm up.

"Now, can I have my phone back?"

Darger got a sudden flash of the gears at work in the

reporter's head. It occurred to her that a leech like Savage might not want a peaceful surrender. A bloodbath would drive more views, more engagement.

He was still holding his hand out. Darger made no move to hand the phone back.

"Are you, as a member of federal law enforcement, denying me my right to free speech?"

"No. I'm asking you to be a decent human being. You can say whatever the hell you want about whoever the hell you want… *after* we have the hostages safe."

Savage gave her a condescending smile.

"You realize you have no power over me, right?"

"Yeah. I do."

Darger made to hand the phone back and instead dropped it on the ground.

"Oops."

He glared at her and bent over to pick up the phone. Before he could, Darger gave it a little kick with the toe of her boot. The phone went skittering over the blacktop and disappeared down a storm drain.

Darger winced and pasted an expression of mock sheepishness on her face.

"Gosh, I'm so clumsy!"

Savage's face went the shade of cranberry juice.

"You fucking bitch. You did that on purpose!" Spittle flew from his lips. "I'll sue you. I'll sue the whole FBI. You're denying me my first amendment rights!"

"Calm down, Savage. One of the fire crews can help you fish it out of there. After this whole thing is resolved, of course."

Darger turned and walked back to the police barricade with

the reporter still yelling at her back.

CHAPTER 7

Darger stalked across the grass, planning her next move. She may have stopped Vinnie Savage from dropping any further bombshells, but the quote from Leffew's mother was bad. Really bad.

All-around garbage human…

Jesus.

Thankfully, *The Daily Gawk* livestream was on a delay. Which meant she might be able to distract Leffew from seeing the worst of it.

"How'd it go?" Colfax asked when she returned to their position.

"Well, the bad news is that Savage threw a few more cans of gasoline on the proverbial fire before I could stop him. The good news is that he won't be broadcasting anything else for the time being," she said.

"So he listened to reason after all?"

"I mean…. something like that."

Darger dialed the number Leffew had called her from before. She tried three times. But he wasn't answering.

The bullhorn was just where she'd left it. She hoisted it in her hand.

"Justin?"

She waited, squinting up at the window. But there was nothing.

"Justin, it's Violet. Can we talk?"

She moved closer to the building. From behind her, she heard Sergeant Barnes call out to her.

"Agent Darger..."

She kept walking until she was just below the window.

"Agent Darger," Barnes said again. "You're too close. Please move back."

She ignored him. It wasn't that she was worried Justin couldn't hear the bullhorn. She wanted to be so loud he couldn't ignore her.

Bullhorn in place, she addressed the man inside the building.

"Justin, I want to help you, but I can't do that if you won't talk to me."

Something white flitted behind the window and then thudded against the glass. It was a piece of paper with the words, "FUCK YOU" scrawled in black marker.

A smile tugged at the corners of Darger's mouth. She'd rather have him talking out loud, but this was something, at least.

"OK, you're still angry. I can understand that. Whatever you have to say, I'm willing to listen."

There was silence again. And then finally, Leffew's voice came from the open window.

"You don't really care about me. No one does."

Darger checked her phone again. Her interview with Savage was just beginning on the stream. Christ. She had to keep him from hearing that quote from his mother, especially in his current state of mind.

"That's not true, Justin. I absolutely do care. I wouldn't be standing here if I didn't."

"Bullshit."

She wracked her brain for something, anything she might use to get Leffew's full attention on her.

"I know someone else who cares about you, too. Your sister, Rachel."

"Yeah, right. Rachel doesn't give a shit about me. My whole family hates me."

"That's not true, Justin. I just talked to her, and she's very concerned about you. About this whole situation."

As the seconds ticked by, Darger worried she'd miscalculated. Made the wrong move. But then her phone rang. It was him.

She nearly fumbled the phone as she hurried to answer, adrenaline making her movements jittery.

"You… talked to Rachel?"

There was a shift in his voice. A note of hope she hadn't heard before.

She swallowed, considering her next move. The truth was, they *had* tried to get in touch with Leffew's sister, but so far they'd had no luck tracking her down.

"I did. Unfortunately, our call was cut short because she was in an area with bad reception. We're trying to get her back now. When we do… would you consider talking to her?"

Darger hated lying during a negotiation, hated making promises she wasn't sure she could keep, but she was running out of options.

"She said she'd talk to me?"

He sniffed. He was crying.

"Yes. Though like I said, we have to get her back on the line again first. Maybe you could tell me what you'd like to say to her."

"I'd say…"

Leffew sighed and then whimpered.

When his voice came back it had changed again. There was

an edge to it that hadn't been there before.

"I'd say, *I fucking warned you.*"

There was a clatter, and at first Darger thought he'd hung up again. But when she glanced at the screen, she saw the call was still connected.

"I told you! I fucking told you what would happen!"

His voice sounded more distant now, and she realized he must have set the phone down. He was shouting so loud, she could hear him through the open window, but she kept the phone pressed to her ear, focusing on the other sounds she was hearing in the background.

A hollow thud. A crash. It sounded like he was destroying the apartment. Throwing things around.

Darger swallowed. She hated not being able to see what was happening.

She picked up the bullhorn.

"Justin, please keep talking to me."

In answer, something came flying out the window, and Darger scrambled back. A TV crashed to the ground. Splintering on the square of sidewalk where she had just been standing.

"I'm garbage? You're fucking garbage! You're all fucking garbage!"

Well, that answered her question. He'd seen the interview. Heard the quote from his mother.

Damn it.

A few seconds later, a lamp with a clear glass base came flying out the window. He was just tossing things at random now. A grown man throwing a tantrum like a toddler.

"Justin, I need you to calm down so we can talk," she said into the bullhorn.

"Fuck you, I'm done talking!"

A potted plant in a ceramic planter tilted over the window ledge and smashed to the ground, an explosion of soil and pottery shards.

Behind her, Darger heard Barnes giving the order for the snipers to be ready. Leffew was getting reckless now. Coming much closer to the window than he had before.

A high-pitched keening joined the cacophony Darger could hear over the phone. The baby was crying again. And then she heard a woman's voice.

"No! Please!"

It was the first time she'd heard Mindy Garza speak. Leffew had refused all requests to let Darger talk to her.

The woman's voice sounded shrill and small. Something powerless in it. Something very scared.

She didn't know what Leffew was doing, but whatever it was, Darger had to stop it. Had to act. Had to draw his attention away from the hostages.

"Justin—"

Movement at the window again. More frantic this time. The curtains thrashing.

And something came tumbling out of the window. No electronics this time. Something pale and irregularly shaped. Blobby, almost.

Laundry? He'd thrown out a wad of clothes?

But the clothing looked solid. Compact. Tumbling end over end.

And then Darger's mind put it together.

The baby.

He'd tossed the baby out the window.

CHAPTER 8

Huxley slips down the hall once more. He almost wants to laugh looking down at himself.

Tight Wranglers hold his hips and thighs in a denim grip, flaps of red and black flannel dangling to about crotch level. Seems like he should go line dancing at some honky-tonk dive in Branson, Missouri, or otherwise lament his Achy Breaky Heart.

But the bulky tool belt focuses the image. Cordons the shirt from the pants in a way that tells the story he wants it to tell, the dangling hammer pulling the leather cuff down on the right side so the whole belt rests cockeyed on his waist.

He's just one of the endless crew members here to help construct the sets, see? Another drone to help sell the endless dream that broadcasts in stunning HD each and every night. A worker bee. That's all. The queen lives in an office somewhere up high downtown, he figures, but that's all above his pay grade, man. He just measures twice and saws once, ya know? Doesn't get to flex his brain so much and doesn't want to.

Who would have thought that *Household Renovation*, the lowest of lowbrow comedies, would come to his rescue? All that flannel and even the tool belts hanging there for the taking.

He adjusts the trucker hat cupping his brow. Keeps it low. His eyes shadowed.

Something flutters at the end of the hall. Two figures turn a corner there.

A man and a woman. Both speed walking toward him.

Not security. Crew members.

The woman stares at the clipboard in her hands, eyebrows furrowed. Her dark red hair sweeps back from her forehead and reaches almost to the middle of her back, somehow looking not of this century.

The man chatters into the mouthpiece of the headset wrapped around his thinning hair. He pushes big glasses back up onto the bridge of his nose.

Huxley struts toward them. Something going loose in his gait, in his shoulders — a swagger like a puppet with the strings left a little slack, that hammer swinging at his right hip. Some internal message tells him that played-up nonchalance will serve him well here, and he obeys the instinct.

The two crew members rush past. Never giving him a direct look.

He turns the corner, and another hall stretches into the distance. He peeks into some of the rooms as he passes.

So many doors leading to all these make-believe places. Set after set. Phony living rooms and talk show desks and emergency rooms and court rooms. It all looks endless. A bottomless well of fictional spaces. Meaningless.

No one else shows in the corridor. He walks alone.

Thin carpet muffles his footsteps. The quiet here seems shocking. Somehow at odds with the sets he peers in on.

He presses into the stillness. Tense now. Waiting for the scene to turn.

He forces himself to breathe. To not rush.

And then he sees it.

The red glow shimmers in the distance — an exit sign hung above a steel door.

A big breath rolls out of him. Makes the bottom of his field of vision go shaky for a second.

The end is in sight.

Two security guards poke out of one of the rooms ahead then. One barks into a walkie-talkie.

"We're entering the northwest hall now. No sign of him."

He recognizes the other as he steps fully into the hallway, that candy bar wrapper mustache hanging just a little crooked over those jutting bottom teeth.

The big lug forms a human wall between Huxley and the exit door. Hands on his hips like he's consciously trying to make himself as wide as possible.

Both security guards look around. Heads swiveling and seeming to stick in unison as they look him over.

Neither one moves. Totally locked in on to the carpenter-looking guy headed their way.

Huxley keeps strutting. Feet kicking a little.

Body calm. Mind screeching like a dying cat again.

A voice crackles on the walkie, and both of their heads snap toward the bulky black radio. Distorted chunks of dialog spew forth, but Huxley can only make out every fourth word or so.

He keeps going. Slides right alongside them, hugging against the right side of the hall to squeeze through the skinny opening there.

He tries to pick up more of the walkie-talkie chatter as he gets close, but the internal tea kettle shriek keeps him from discerning what's being said. The voice sounds like a crackling growl of nonsense syllables. Wordless and clicky.

Both security guards lurch into motion. They rush the way Huxley has come in a hurry.

His head goes fizzy again, but he keeps advancing. Moves toward the door. Pushes the bar and hears the telltale click of metal on metal.

The steel slab of the door wedges out into the world outside.

And sunlight floods the shady corridor — the orange flares of that perpetual California sun stinging his eyes for a second. He steps out onto the concrete, feels the faint breeze touch his sweat-dampened cheeks, sees the palm fronds swaying on the trees deeper in the parking lot.

Almost done.

Almost over.

But then the twirling lights catch the corner of his eye off to the left. Red and blue smears over the asphalt, over the sandy concrete walls.

Police here already. LAPD.

Three security guards and a pair of uniformed officers huddle there talking near the mouth of the lot, standing between the booth and those swiveling police lights.

His eyes zoom in on the scene. Spot the fateful detail.

The rear end of the LAPD cruiser blocks his car into its spot.

Shit.

His jaw flexes in little bursts. Makes gritty sounds when his molars grind together. Tiny *scritches* that remind him somehow of melting ice cubes settling at the bottom of an otherwise empty glass.

Movement draws his eyes back to the right. Pulls his head that way.

Someone else on foot, moving deeper into the lot. First he just sees the shape of her — slight shoulders draped in a black blouse, dyed red hair that reaches down to the middle of her back, the darker roots visible along the scalp, something scrawny about all of her in an unhealthy way. Probably a smoker, he thinks. A lot of those too skinny girls are heavy smokers, it seems like.

It's not until he sees the clipboard in her hands that he recognizes her from the earlier encounter. The production person he'd passed in the hall.

How she got back out here when she was seemingly headed the other way, he doesn't know. Doesn't care.

She presses into the throng of cars, and he follows. Closes on her.

When he's to within four paces, he fishes a hand into his beltline at the small of his back. Frees the dark bulk there. Porcelain to get past metal detectors.

They move to a small EV tucked in a shaded spot between a couple of bigger SUVs.

Cover.

Good.

The producer tucks the clipboard under her arm and opens the car door. Oblivious.

Huxley lifts his voice.

"Excuse me..."

Just as she turns her head, the Glock brushes up to line up with her temple.

The barrel extends into the empty space between them. Looks impossibly long with the silencer screwed onto the end of it.

He squeezes the trigger. Hears the gun lisp one syllable not quite as loud as a firmly closed door.

Thuff.

Something about the noise is almost backward, a sucking sound like the gun is inhaling the bullet.

But no.

That smooth plane of her face somehow bursts, too fast to really see, and the whole head flings to the side. He can only vaguely make out the red venting from the opposite temple. A blur.

The ragdoll body falls into the car, crumples over the driver's seat. Dead weight. Floppy.

The clipboard falls from that grip under her arm as the rest of her goes down. Clatters to the blacktop. Almost as loud as the gun — not very.

He pushes closer. Doesn't dare a look at the cops across the lot. Not yet.

He lifts the legs and wheelbarrows her torso over the center console. Drapes the small figure across the passenger seat.

Blood jets from the twin holes in her head. Gushing and slowing before his eyes. Scarlet puddling onto the seat around her.

Then he climbs in. Rips the keys out of fingers already going a little cool. Then realizes he doesn't need them and drops them in the cup holder at his elbow.

A push button starts the vehicle, which doesn't growl or rumble in any way. There's some vague sense of electric current coming to life — maybe an almost inaudible hum. It sounds like he's starting a laptop instead of a car.

He huffs one breath in and his chest squeezes it out almost at once. An involuntary clenching of the muscles there.

Finally he lifts his head. Looks.

The police and security guards still stand around talking. All their feet set just a little too wide apart — like strapping cop outfits onto their doughy bodies must turn them into superheroes or something. Funny.

He pulls in another big breath and manages to hold onto it

for a moment this time.

He shifts the car into gear. Eases out of the parking spot. Banks to the right.

He rolls past those rows of vehicles again. Moves toward the police — no choice.

But they seem to be paying him no mind.

He puts the window down a crack to try to hear a snippet of their conversation. He doesn't dare look that way to see who is speaking.

"He took off. Kind of think he got away, if I'm bein' honest."

"Probably just trying to sneak into an audition. Fuckin' loser."

"Or maybe he was trying to get scripts. Spoilers are worth a bunch of money. Like this guy at one of the networks made over $500k selling spoilers to the tabloids back in the day. We all have to sign waivers. NDAs, you know. They come after your ass if any of the employees sell that kind of thing, but an outsider? Hell, an outsider could waltz right in here and…"

The voices trail away as he moves for the vent of the lot. Passes the little glass box of the security booth.

His body trembles as he spills out into the endless murmur of the Hollywood traffic. He turns a corner and disappears into the crowd.

A little smile curves the edges of his lips.

Nobody knows. Yet.

CHAPTER 9

Darger didn't think. Her body moved of its own volition. An animal instinct driving her forward. Some kind of primeval autopilot.

The phone and bullhorn fell away from her all at once. Discarded. She lurched for the building.

Arms extended. Neck craned. Vision aimed at the blurry object plummeting toward the blacktop.

In some detached part of her brain, it dawned on her that there was no sound in this moment. Her mind had blocked out everything but the visual of the plummeting child, turned the flickering stream of images into a silent movie.

The streaking comet came straight down at the concrete. Darger didn't flinch.

She shuffled into its downward path. Made a basket out of her arms and belly. Movements fluid and precise.

One last breath vented from her nostrils, and her lungs went still.

She bent at the knees, fielding the toddler's body like a punted football.

There was a violent thud as the child's torso connected with hers. Felt like a bowling ball slamming into her sternum.

The breath woofed out of her. Knocked her back a step.

And water flooded her eyes. Added a rim of soft focus to her already motion-blurred vision.

The small body crumpled against hers and slid down, down, down. Speed maintained. Barely any change in momentum.

And for a split second, everything was out of control.

Darger staggered. Feet skittering over the bits of gravel littering the sidewalk.

The baby was still falling. Plunging head first toward the ground.

The cement at Darger's feet lay in wait. Hard and gray. Rough texture like acne-scarred cheeks.

Darger squeezed her arms around the bulk. It felt like hugging a heavy pumpkin with limbs to her chest.

The kid kept falling.

The agent got one foot jammed down into a craggy section of sidewalk, and finally her legs steadied beneath her. She cinched her arms as tightly as she could. Felt the little body constricting against her chest.

And then it was over.

The world around her evened out and came back into focus.

There.

Got her.

She reached down and flipped the toddler upright. A pair of bright brown eyes stared back at her in something like awe. And then the child's mouth opened, her head tilted back, and she let out a howl worthy of a banshee.

Darger gazed into the squalling pink face and let out a strange little laugh.

The kid was OK. Terrified, but OK.

Darger took a breath. Turned and gave a thumbs-up to Colfax and Barnes.

Colfax gave a nod. But Sergeant Barnes wasn't looking at her. His eyes were still on the window.

She couldn't hear the words he spoke into his radio. His

voice was too low, and she was too far away. But she could read his lips.

"Take the shot."

She glanced back up at the window just in time to see the sniper's bullet shatter the skull of Justin Leffew.

CHAPTER 10

Darger sat toward the back of the open ambulance doorway. Her legs dangled into the sunlight, but she was happy for the little bit of shade here. Or maybe it wasn't just the shade. The shelter. Shelter felt good.

"This is where the pain is?" The EMT jabbed at the front of Darger's chest where a mottled bruise was already forming. "Right here?"

Darger flinched away from the woman's probing finger. Her pulse still pounded in her ears, and she felt vaguely nauseous.

"Yes."

The EMT nodded, her black ponytail bobbing slightly.

"Probably a bruised sternum, maybe even a fracture. We should take you in for an X-ray."

"No, thanks," Darger said.

"Well at least let me give you something for the pain."

Darger shook her head. Felt a bit dizzy with the movement. "That's not necessary. I'll be fine."

"Ma'am, I really think—"

The woman was interrupted by Sergeant Barnes and a few other SWAT guys coming over to praise Darger again for "saving the day."

"I was telling the boys, we should get in touch with the 49ers. See if they've got a spot for a wide receiver on the roster."

Barnes clapped her on the shoulder hard enough to rattle her ribcage, and Darger tried to cover her wince with a smile.

"Made me nervous as hell, having you so close to the

building, but thank God you were. If you hadn't been standing right there, this thing might have ended a whole different way."

An uneasy twinge radiated out from Darger's gut. Two images played in her mind on repeat. The first was Leila Garza's tiny body plummeting through the air. The second was Justin Leffew's corpse splatting on the pavement at her feet — the aftermath of being shot by one of the SWAT snipers. Her brain had begun overlaying one image on the other, so that it was the child's body hitting the ground instead.

She heard the sickening thud. The crack of bones.

Icy tendrils of adrenaline slithered from Darger's fingertips up into the meat of her arms. The crisis was over, but her limbic system didn't seem to know that.

She shivered, then glanced around in a panic. She needed to find Leila. Needed to see her. To be sure.

Her eyes scanned faces in the crowd. Flitted past the various members of law enforcement littering the street in a way that reminded her of football players convening haphazardly on the field to shake hands after a game.

There.

Leila was just across the parking lot, being checked out at another ambulance. They'd bundled her in a blanket, and she was being cradled by her mother as the EMTs talked to her.

Leffew was the one who'd died. The baby was safe.

It was over.

But even after confirming this fact with her own eyes, Darger couldn't shake that feeling of dread.

She knew why, of course. It was like Sergeant Barnes had said.

If you hadn't been standing right there, this thing might have ended a whole different way.

It was a fluke that Darger had saved Leila Garza. If the scenario were replayed 100 times, 99 of those times, Darger wouldn't have been in that exact position under the window. Wouldn't have caught the girl.

The sounds came again.

Thud.

Crack.

A thick ribbon of blood oozing from the nose. Spilling onto the rough concrete. Forming an ever-spreading pool.

If that had been Leila Garza instead of Leffew…

If Darger had been standing just a couple yards to the right…

Stop it, she thought.

Stop catastrophizing.

She inhaled deeply, trying to calm her nerves. At the apex of her breath, a bright bolt of pain shot through her chest. She grimaced and bent over, coughing, which only made the pain worse.

Darger tried to speak, managed to get out one strangled word.

"Fuck."

The EMT crossed her arms.

"You should let me give you something for the pain."

Darger's jaw clenched. But this time she nodded.

"OK. Fine. Whatever," she wheezed, taking shallow breaths.

Her eyes watered at the sting of the needle puncturing her flesh, though it was nothing compared to the ache in her sternum.

There was a flash of cold at the injection site, and then the analgesic effect washed over her in a wave. Endorphins flooded her system and beat the dread back into its hole. Finally.

Darger's heart rate slowed. Her breath began to even out.

She leaned her weight against the side wall of the ambulance and stared across the parking lot at the baby.

Safe.

She was safe.

They were both safe.

Darger's eyelids began to droop. Fluttering for a moment. Narrowing a little more with each passing second.

Finally, she let them fall closed and drifted.

CHAPTER 11

The studio audience files down the aisle and packs into the theater seating. Fresh off the tour bus, they gawk and gape and crane their necks. Highly impressed.

This evening's crowd splits, fairly neatly, into two groups. They all do.

Some are straight tourists — fanny-packed folk from Iowa or one of the Dakotas. Most of this group has never seen the show they're about to form the laugh track for. They're here on the promise of free pizza and a look inside one of the studios where all their favorite 80s and 90s sitcoms got made. They're here for the spectacle more than the content.

The second group are the die-hards — the super fans who join the tours just to watch their favorite stars perform the show live. They will hang on every joke, watch the episodes over and over some months later when they air on TV, parsing the material for new layers.

If it's a good crowd, the laughs heard on TV will be legitimate. If it's a bad one, the sounds of a laugh machine will be blended with the real audience reactions. In the latter case, it's technically not a "laugh track," as it's usually referred to, which would suggest old recordings of actual laughter, but a machine that produces wholly artificial laughter. No human involved on that side of things.

The two groups mix in the rows of seats. Restless as they wait a few minutes for the whole thing to start, their differences somehow erased as the ritual of the stage lords its power over them equally.

By the time the warm-up comic has cracked a few jokes, an excited thrum seems to waft through the little chunk of stadium seating. The lights change, going down in the seating area and up on stage, and that sense of anticipation sharpens to a fine point.

A bit more waiting. Silence hangs over the whole soundstage now, the crowd slightly breathless.

Crew members zip around the equipment down in front. Cameras and cue cards angled at that living room without a front wall, the lone glowing space here, like it's the only thing that's real.

The little sign over the stage lights up. Red letters glowing in all caps.

APPLAUSE

The response is thunderous.

☾

The stolen car rockets south on the freeway. Huxley grips the wheel, knuckles and jaw about equally clenched.

No destination in mind. Just go south and figure out the rest later.

He's driven like this for over an hour already. Due south. Slowing only when the traffic thickened around him near some of the busy entrance ramps.

Thankfully the highways had mostly complied. Stayed open for him. No traffic jams today. Early enough. And he'd switched routes to avoid some of the worst of it.

A jacket now lies over the corpse in the passenger seat. He'd found the garment in the backseat.

He'll need to ditch that sooner than later. The body. The car, too, he supposes.

The thought makes his tongue lick out over his lips. Involuntary. A touch nervous.

He probably has a little time yet. Before the detonation. Maybe an hour. Probably less.

In any case, once that happens, law enforcement will pounce quickly. Put together the pieces.

No, he should ditch the car now. As soon as possible.

His tongue flicks again. Wets the pink rim of skin around it.

He hates to leave the comfort of the road, the reassurance of constant movement.

But he starts eying the exit signs anyway. Better to be smart than comfortable.

Green signs with white lettering fill his vision. Small blue signs with fast food logos popping up in the foreground now and again.

When he finally finds the right exit, he veers that way. The little electric vehicle loops around a ramp and off the highway like its falling through the cracks in the asphalt.

Then it melts back into the city traffic.

☾

Good crowd tonight.

Sam, the warm-up comic, watches from just offstage, tucked back in the shadows with some of the crew members. He swivels his head now and then, turning away from the gleaming spotlights and looking out at the dark silhouette of the crowd.

The "Is it bigger than a bread box?" double entendre callback lands. Another big laugh ripples through the theater seating, something almost percussive about the way it turns on and off all at once. Reminds him of audio of Nazi soldiers marching through conquered streets of Paris.

Between rehearsals and sitting in on a table read, he's heard most of the jokes multiple times already, had all of the flavor and punch sucked out of them like a long-chewed piece of gum. But he doesn't mind.

It is somehow more scientific to observe from the sterile position of already knowing all the material, all the beats and punch lines. Clinical. Like doing it this way, he's transformed into a comedy pathologist, or maybe a coroner, dissecting this script's corpse to see why and how it works.

The warm-up jokes are merely a side hustle to earn a few extra bucks. Learning this craft, comedy screenwriting, inside and out is his real purpose here. He'd landed a dream gig — assistant to the head writer on the show. If he did gopher duty for a couple years, making Starbucks runs and delivering rewrites to the cast, he'd get a shot at a staff position sooner or later, and then the sky would be the limit.

Hank, the goofy next-door neighbor, enters through the back door and slides in socked feet over the strip of kitchen linoleum into the living room. Just this tiny flourish of physical comedy gets another big laugh from the crowd.

Jesus. Really good crowd tonight.

The audience always gets that doe-eyed reverence once the stars come out and do their thing — some primordial vestige playing out over and over, the ritual of human beings watching performers on stage.

But it's an especially electric feeling in the room tonight. Sam has watched thirty-six episodes filmed live. Some were better than others, no doubt, but it's never felt as… *alive* as this.

He finds himself drawn into the scenes against his will.

Watching the three stars thrust and parry their insults at each other. He even realizes that he's chuckling along with the crowd.

These sitcom casts become like a machine, usually sometime late in the first season or early in the second. It's unbelievable how they can turn it on at the sound of a bell, week after week. Always getting the shots they need, getting the laughs every single time.

They will run through the episode two to three times this week and edit together the best takes, but this, their first draft, is good enough to air. They nail it, as always.

On stage, the main characters, Mitch and Tammy, are confronting the zany neighbor, Hank, about his latest scheme. After deflecting their earlier attempts to talk him down, he now seems to be accepting reality.

"So you're saying my Pumpkin Spice Steakhouse fast-casual chain is not a hundred-billion dollar idea?"

Tammy sucks her teeth before she replies.

"Hank. It's not even a twenty-dollar idea."

Defeated, Hank sinks back toward the couch, falling like he's been physically wounded. He floats, torso limp like a toddler in hysterics, above the cushion for just a second.

His weight thuds onto the cushion.

And then he explodes.

☾

A high-pitched tone rings over everything. An endless screech. Daryl's blown-out eardrums offer only this shrill noise over the chaos around him.

He blinks. He can feel the crowd swirling alongside and behind him. Everyone panicking, tumbling, thrashing in that near silence. It seems wrong.

His wife, Maggie, is still there, sitting right next to him in the front row. But he can only see her out of the corner of his eye.

When he looks straight at her, the pink blotch floating in his field of vision blocks her out.

But she's there. He knows she's there. That's the important thing.

OK.

OK.

We're going to be OK.

No need to freak out.

We'll live through this, and we'll be back home tomorrow.

He breathes. Feels the shock loosen its grip on his chest just a little.

He knows. That pink spot? That's where the blast was, where it burned itself into his retinas. Searing brightness like a thousand camera flashes at once.

And now there's only a cratered couch on stage in that spot. Black smoke rolling out of the burned-out hole where the cushion used to be. The whole room smells like melted polyester and chemical smoke. Gloomy fog rolls over the set and out into the crowd.

A body lies on the carpet before the mortally wounded couch. A tattered, blackened thing that used to be the actor, Tom Malone. It looks like a lot of him is gone. Vaporized along with the couch cushions.

One of the other actors is face down near the kitchen. Daryl can't tell who.

Part of his mind keeps telling him that none of this is real. That it can't be.

But he knows otherwise.

And then Maggie is jerking next to him. Shoulders bobbing. Chest quaking. Like she's trying to cough. Like she's…

Choking.

He turns toward her again. He can just see her through that fading pink blotch now.

She's in shock. Probably most everyone here is.

"Breathe, baby," he says, his voice sounding tiny in his own ears.

But she hears him. Turns toward him. Eyes wide. Scared.

And as she cranks her head fully his way, arterial spray jets out of her neck. A clean spurt that reminds him of a ketchup bottle squeezed hard.

Holy shit.

His eyes drift down. Find her throat.

The wound gapes at him. Flaps of neck open wide. Red. So open he can't even tell what he's seeing.

Shrapnel?

Jesus Christ.

Maggie took shrapnel in the neck.

And Daryl's head goes light. His face is hot, and he's ripping off his sweatshirt, pressing the balled-up fabric against the wound.

He can feel blood saturating the fabric in pulses. So hot it seems impossible. The heat inside of her pouring right out into his hands.

Words rush through his head.

I need to call 911.

But no.

That'll take too long.

We have minutes. Maybe seconds.

He looks around the room. Sees the panicking crowd all congested at the doors. Both exits that way blocked.

A flash of memory interrupts. Their wedding day. Maggie smiling, the sun shining on her cheeks.

Everyone else in the room is moving away from him and Maggie. They're on an island at the front of the seating area. Alone.

There has to be a medic on set.

He yells that.

"Medic!"

His voice sounds louder now. Stronger. He yells again.

"We need a medic over here!"

But no one is coming. He knows as soon as the words are out of his mouth.

Another memory hits. The day Jack was born. Maggie holding the tiny bundle, smiling. Exhaustion had actually changed her facial features, or so it seemed, pulling her eyelids and cheeks down into something drooped. She'd looked so happy and so tired at the same time.

He squeezes Maggie tighter. Tries to will some of his life into her.

He pushes his face into the side of hers. Whispers near her ear.

"Hold on, baby. Just hold on."

But she only goes cold in his arms. Icy.

And twenty-two seconds later, she's gone.

CHAPTER 12

Darger's consciousness bobbed to the surface in stages. She had the sense that something was happening around her. Movement. Excitement. Something important.

"...just got word from the Los Angeles field office," someone was saying.

That voice. She knew that voice.

Loshak?

No. That was impossible. Loshak was at a criminology conference in Seattle.

The voice came again.

"...can be there in a few hours if we hurry."

OK, that was definitely Loshak.

Darger tried to open her eyes. It felt like her eyelids were made of concrete. Heavy and stiff.

She managed a weak flutter, caught a glimpse of the blurry interior of the ambulance before they snapped shut again.

As the darkness closed in on her, she felt herself drifting once more. The stillness rising up.

Minutes separated her thoughts.

She wondered in a half-detached way at hearing Loshak's voice.

Realized the most logical explanation was that she'd dreamed it.

Christ. What the hell kind of horse tranquilizer had the EMT given her?

"...so far they're saying two fatalities and several more wounded."

That got her attention.

She fought against the swimmy, numb feeling. The weight of the drugs holding her under. She had to wake up.

She lifted her arm. Felt around until she found something to grab onto. Pulled herself upright.

Her head cleared a little as she sat up, and this time, when she opened her eyes, they weren't so quick to close again.

But her thoughts still came at a sluggish pace. Only able to process one thing at a time.

She was still in the back of the ambulance.

A blanket draped across her shoulders.

The sun was still bright and high in the sky. Not much time had passed since the EMT had injected her with the knockout juice. She was pretty sure of that.

Her thoughts stretched beyond the here and now. Dredged up what she'd heard before.

Loshak.

Fatalities.

Wounded.

She blinked and lifted her chin. Squinted at the group of silhouettes standing a few yards away from where she sat. One of the men drifted into focus. Instant recognition.

Loshak *was* here.

Darger's skull felt like it weighed about a hundred pounds, and she bowed her head as she took in this development. Wondered what it might mean that Loshak had come here in person. Her eyes fell closed again as she pondered it. A case, obviously. Something important. Dire.

"You think it's really him?" Chief Colfax asked.

"No one's saying anything for certain right now, but between you and me, my gut says yeah. It's him," Loshak said and then uttered a name.

Synapses fired. A series of flashbacks detonated in Darger's mind, one after another. The destroyed mansion of an up-and-coming actor. The melted flesh of a starlet's face. The bone-rattling boom of an explosion caving in a subway tunnel.

Her head snapped up, eyes wide now.

Tyler Huxley.

CHAPTER 13

The name echoed in Darger's mind the entire ride to the airport.

Tyler Huxley.

It reverberated again and again as they stood in the security line.

Tyler Huxley.

As they milled around at their gate.

As they boarded the plane.

As they sat on the tarmac waiting to taxi to the runway.

Tyler Huxley.

Even now, with the engines of the plane humming as they rocketed southward at 160 miles per hour, the name pulsed in her brain. Throbbing like the beat of a heart.

Tyler Huxley. Tyler Huxley. Tyler Huxley.

The serial bomber who earned worldwide infamy after targeting a series of entertainment industry-related public figures in New York with his homemade explosives.

Darger glanced over at Loshak slumped in the window seat. One of those dumb neck pillows cupped his drooped chin, a little drool collecting at the corner of his mouth.

She didn't know how he could sleep at a time like this. Her own mind was whirring with all the unanswered questions. It felt like someone riffling together a deck of cards in her skull, shuffling all the pieces of information around.

Of course, there was also the fact that she'd chugged a 24-ounce gas station coffee on the drive to the airport in an attempt to fight the mix of painkillers and sedatives the EMT had dosed her with. She was more than a little wired now.

She could still feel some lingering effects of the meds in her system duking it out with the caffeine. The combination left her somehow jittery and deadened at the same time.

Darger plucked a pretzel from the tiny bag the flight attendant had handed her. Shoved it in her mouth.

The pretzels tasted like cardboard. They didn't seem to have any salt on them. Was that on purpose — some kind of low sodium nonsense — or was this a bad batch? Either way, they were nearly inedible, and yet she kept eating them for some reason.

She washed the flavorless crumbs down with a sip of Sprite and ran through a CliffsNotes version of the case she and Loshak had put together for one of their lectures at Quantico.

Tyler James Huxley. 31 years old.

A narcissist who believed society had held him back from achieving his dreams of stardom, Huxley got his revenge by creating an elaborate and deadly scavenger hunt involving cryptic clues, ciphers, and bombs hidden in the homes of celebrities.

"A sort of histrionic Unabomber, if you will," Loshak had said during one lecture. The line had earned a decent laugh.

But all the faces went grim again when it came time to discuss the victims.

Ricky Fuller had technically been the first — a patsy Huxley had used in a ruse to fake his own death. Unlike Huxley's later victims, Fuller's death was less personal than the others. Huxley needed a stand-in to play a dead body, and Fuller fit the bill. There'd been no symbolism. No underlying message in Fuller's death. To Huxley, the victim was little more than a prop.

Gavin Passmore was the first to be targeted with intention.

The B-list actor had his face blown off when he opened a mysterious package at his estate in the Hamptons.

Then there was Amelia Driscoll, an up-and-coming starlet who'd been permanently disfigured and left partially blind after discovering an acid bomb in her upscale apartment.

The task force had managed to thwart Huxley's attempt to blow up his next target — a game show host named Dirk Nielsen.

Darger had a momentary flashback of riding in the back of a van with the guys on the Counter-IED team, essentially the FBI's bomb squad. They'd been in high spirits. Each attack came with its own little puzzle meant to help them prevent the next one. A psychotic scavenger hunt designed by Huxley himself. The fourth bomb was meant to be the last. If they defused this one, they'd be in the clear.

And they'd done everything right. They'd solved Huxley's riddle. Determined his final victim was Oscar-winning director, Lucio Mancini.

But Huxley hadn't been playing fair, after all. The fourth bomb was booby-trapped, and the detonation killed Special Agent Michael Dobbins instantly.

It was shortly after the loss of Dobbins that Huxley revealed himself to be alive. They tracked him back to his mother's home in Queens, but Huxley managed to flee into the subway tunnels beneath the city. Darger and a team from the FBI's Critical Incident Response Group followed him, only realizing too late that it had been another trap — Huxley had planted more bombs in the tunnels. Three men died in the blast, another was maimed for life.

Another reel played in Darger's head now. Bodies crumpled under falling slabs of concrete. Black smoke engulfing everything in dark. Agent Fitch lying in the rubble, his leg mutilated, bleeding out. The choice she had to make: stay with Fitch and try to stop the bleeding, or follow Huxley.

In the end, she let Huxley go.

By the time the task force had regrouped, the bomber had disappeared. For the next two years plus, he'd stayed underground. Scuttling about like a cockroach. She'd known in her gut that it wasn't over, that they hadn't heard the last of Huxley. And now here he was again. In the flesh.

Or so it seemed.

So far, there was no solid proof that this was Huxley's work. No taunting message posted online. No cryptic note found at the scene. But who else would detonate a bomb on the set of a sitcom, targeting an actor?

The revolution will be etched into celebrity skin.

Darger checked her phone for any updates, but there was nothing yet. She found herself skimming through the photos of the Los Angeles crime scene again.

The set pictures were first. It was hard to tell what she was looking at in some, the destruction was so complete. Destroyed couch. Blackened upholstery and carpet. Cracked and cratered concrete below.

The set looked like a living room. Well, almost. Three walls of a home. The fourth wall gaped toward rows of theater seats.

Some of the angles of the photographs laid the artifice bare. There were fake tree branches visible outside the kitchen window. A lighting rig there meant to simulate the sun shining down outside.

The artificial touches added to the wrongness of the scene, this cardboard cutout of a house. Something was off in all the details, so that even at a glance, she could tell it wasn't real, wasn't right.

She imagined there were dozens of sets like this one, all in a row, a slew of buildings packed with them on this studio lot. The cast and crew drove in every day and wound up shut inside these big cement blocks all day, pretending in faux living rooms and the like before a live studio audience. A fake world totally encapsulated inside a warehouse in Hollywood.

The white noise of the flight seemed to swell and fill the space around her. It somehow added to the sense of unrealness in the photos. Too quiet. A prickle ran down her spine, causing the hairs on the back of her neck to stand at attention.

She hesitated to thumb through to the next set of photos. She'd looked through them enough by now to know what was coming next.

The actor's body. Tom Malone. The 6'6" goofball with curly blond hair. He'd been a sitcom regular for coming up on twenty years now, flitting from network to network, from hit to hit. The tall doofus who kind of only really played one character, even if he was technically in four different shows during that span.

Darger still associated him with one of the catchphrases from his first sitcom. He'd transitioned to playing the goofy neighbor on his new show, but she still thought of him as the *What did you do?* dad from all those years earlier.

In the photos, he was unrecognizable, of course. A tattered thing. Almost shredded. The strips of a flannel shirt draped over gaping meat holes.

Thinking about the order of events, Darger considered one thing that wasn't photographed here. One of Malone's costars — Morgan Beasley, who played the matriarch, Tammy, on the show — had flecks of shrapnel embedded in her face and a deep laceration in her leg. She'd been rushed to the hospital before police had even arrived, so her injuries and general role in the scene hadn't been documented to the same degree. From what law enforcement had been told, she would live.

Darger kept flipping, and the photos changed.

Now she looked on the second corpse, an audience member who'd taken a big chunk of shrapnel — possibly a piece of couch spring — right in the throat. Maggie Logan, the 56-year-old woman from Pierre, South Dakota, had bled out in the front row of the theater while her husband tried to stanch the wound with a balled-up sweatshirt.

And for just a second Darger could feel the chaos that must have overtaken that room. The blast. Two actors down — one dead instantly and one wounded — the entire crowd running for the doors, screaming and whimpering, a mass of humanity flexing to squeeze through that tiny pinprick of an opening that would lead them away from here.

An electronic ding came over the speaker system and shook Darger out of her trance. A second later, the pilot's voice flitted on the intercom.

"Good afternoon, folks. We're beginning our descent. The temperature in Los Angeles is 68 degrees. Local time 4:38 P.M. We'll be touching down just in time for rush hour. Ha-ha."

Loshak stirred as the plane swooped toward the ground, seeming to unfold to his full size all at once. He sniffed and looked around. Blinked at the phone in Darger's hand just after they'd landed.

"Any news?"

"Nothing yet."

LAPD was crawling all over the crime scene even now, employing UV rays and metal detectors and every other high-tech fine-tooth comb they had at the disposal, but so far they hadn't found a note.

Darger didn't get it. This was Tyler Huxley's work. It had to be.

So why didn't he leave a note?

CHAPTER 14

They picked up their rental at the airport and slogged through stop-and-go traffic to the LAPD headquarters downtown. All the while, Loshak bemoaned the fact that they wouldn't have time to stop for donuts.

Darger still remembered the LAPD HQ from her last case in town. It looked like a large mirrored cube surrounded by a triangle of concrete, shimmering in the late afternoon sun almost like the shiny surface was on fire. The reflections morphed and changed shape as they walked up to the doors.

At the ground floor kiosk, a desk sergeant directed them to a fourth-floor conference room where the task force was convening.

Loshak turned to her as they rode the elevator up.

"When I talked to John Bullock earlier — he's the SAC for the L.A. field office — I requested Luck be on the task force. Turns out, our friend is heading up a task force of his own at the moment."

"Oh yeah?" Darger said.

"Some white-collar crime thing. Agent Bullock couldn't give any details, as it's still very much an active investigation." Loshak shrugged. "Anyway, it's nice to see Luck doing so well for himself, though I would have loved to have had him on this."

Darger nodded, though inside she was secretly relieved Luck wouldn't be working their case. If she had it her way, she'd put a great distance between Tyler Huxley and anybody she cared about.

As soon as they stepped from the elevator, Darger stared dumbfounded at the broad-chested man striding toward them. The last time she'd seen Agent Fitch, he'd been in a wheelchair. How was he walking upright? A beat later, the obvious explanation came to her, but he'd already seen her reaction.

"Didn't recognize me with two legs, eh?" Fitch said, the corners of his lips curling just a little.

He bypassed the handshake for a bear hug, his heavily muscled frame nearly crushing Darger's ribcage. She bit down on her cheek to keep from crying out. How long did the EMT say the chest pain would last? Two to four weeks, and that was if it was just a bruise. Eight to twelve weeks if it was fractured. Lord have mercy.

"Of course I recognized you," Darger said.

"Bullshit! I saw the look on your face. Did a total double take. Am I right, Loshak?"

He kept one arm clamped around her, and she had to use her elbow to give herself an inch or two of breathing room.

"You look good, Fitch," Loshak said, shaking his free hand — the one not still wrapped around Darger's shoulder.

Fitch lifted his pant leg. Rapped on the prosthesis with his knuckles.

"Carbon fiber with a titanium pylon. Still trying to see if insurance will cover one of those blades. You know, like that Oscar Pistorius guy. How fuckin' sweet would that be? Can you imagine me chasin' down a perp with a bionic leg? Bet half of these mopes would shit their pants at the mere sight of it."

Without taking a breath, he was waving over a man in the dark blue, nearly black, LAPD uniform.

"Chief Cattermole, this is the lady I was telling you about. My guardian angel, Violet Darger. Saved my frickin' life!"

His grip on Darger's shoulder tightened, and he gave her a jovial shake. Her head snapped from side to side, loose as a ragdoll, as if her spine had transformed into a wet noodle. At least he wasn't compressing her aching ribcage anymore.

"I believe you worked with my predecessor on the serial arson case a few years back," the chief said as he shook Darger's hand.

"That's right," she said and tried to shove the memories back into the mind-closet they threatened to tumble out of.

For a brief moment, Darger heard the crackle of flames, felt the burning in her throat and lungs. The blistering heat on every inch of exposed skin.

To distract herself, she cataloged Chief Cattermole's appearance.

Judging by the crow's feet around his eyes and the flecks of white in his dark hair, Darger figured he was in his late forties or early fifties. Average height and build. Skin tanned from the California sun. Crew cut and that uptight military posture that always made Darger feel slouchy.

She tried to stand up straighter, which tensed the muscles of her chest. She winced at another bright jolt of pain and rubbed her sternum as Cattermole led them down the hall and into the conference room.

They must have been waiting for Darger and Loshak to arrive before beginning, because the room was already packed with officers. The chief walked straight to the podium and cleared his throat.

"If I can have everyone's attention, I think we're ready to begin." He nodded at one of his men. "Most of you already know our lead on the case, Detective Rohrbach. He's going to walk everyone through the crime scene again. McGuin, can you hit the lights?"

With the lights dimmed, Rohrbach moved to the podium. He was in his late 30s, with reddish hair and a face Darger imagined would look more jovial under better circumstances. He drew their focus to a projector screen on one wall. He brought up a photo of a security booth.

"What we've put together so far is that the bomber gained access to the scene by posing as a pizza delivery guy. Usually the delivery drivers have codes to get onto the lot, and our guy provided one that didn't work. From there he managed to talk his way past the guard, which gave him free access to the entire studio lot."

He clicked to the next photo, showing a generic waiting room with chairs, potted plants, and stacks of magazines.

"He made his way from the security booth to Soundstage 34H, where he entered via the front lobby. He passed the secretary and dumped the pies in an alcove here before proceeding farther into the building."

The pizza boxes had been dropped hastily enough that some had slid off the pile at an angle, revealing grease spots staining the cardboard.

"As you can see, the pizzas are from Pizza Cottage. We're working on figuring out which specific restaurant, but there are easily twenty-plus locations within plausible driving distance of the studio lot, so it's going to take time to dial in where he bought them," Rohrbach said, then paused to let out a heavy sigh. "OK, folks. Brace yourselves."

A photo showing the violent aftermath of the explosion filled the screen. Then another. And another.

"This here is the set for the sitcom, *Dysfunctional Family*. Ground zero for the explosion."

Something clicked deep in the detective's throat, his eyes flicking back and forth like marbles in his head as he studied the photos. The fact that Darger had already seen most of them before didn't make them any less disturbing. She thought the same went for Rohrbach.

He was silent as he ran through the worst of the photographs, apparently feeling that the horror in the images spoke for themselves.

"There's video footage, of course," he said, swallowing. "The, uh, incident was captured on five cameras filming the TV show. I kind of figure… I mean, anyone who wants to see it can see it, but uh… We don't need to all watch it here, I don't think."

No one spoke to the contrary.

"OK, here's where we get something useful, maybe. Let's go back to what happened immediately after he planted the device."

The screen switched over to black and white video tinted green. The resolution was decent enough, but the footage had a low frame rate, which gave it a choppy, stop-motion quality.

"Instead of leaving the way he came in, the perpetrator rushed into this rear access hallway to avoid security, heading into the backstage area." Rohrbach clicked to the next point of view, where the bomber sped around a corner and then entered a door. "After ducking into a doorway, he stays off camera for six minutes and 47 seconds. When he reappears, he's changed into a flannel and jeans with a work belt, a baseball cap as well. More or less the standard uniform for the construction crew who build all the sets on the lot.

"He works his way to one of the exits at the back of the building. That's unfortunately one of the dead spots for the camera setup, so we lose him shortly after he exits the building. Somewhere in the parking lot, he comes across Kathryn Smith, a producer. We found her Nissan Leaf ditched thirty miles to the south in a Burger King parking lot just off the freeway. Miss Smith was found draped over the passenger seat, deceased. He'd covered her body with a jacket.

"At this juncture, we're not sure if he took Miss Smith hostage for a time or if he killed her immediately. Either way, we suspect he had another vehicle waiting in the restaurant parking lot. No cameras, unfortunately, which is probably why he picked that location."

The video screen switched to a different camera again as Rohrbach talked, still playing footage of the perp walking the halls in the studio even though his narrative had moved on. In his new disguise, the bomber walked straight toward the lens. His body language looked calm, though Darger doubted he'd been as cool as he looked. A good actor, then. Ironic, given his choice of targets.

He kept his hat low and his head down, so his face stayed shadowed and out of focus on the screen. Just when she'd given up hope of getting a look at the man's features, his head suddenly bobbed up.

Rohrbach paused the video, and the face froze there. In full view. Exposed.

Except it didn't look like Tyler Huxley.

CHAPTER 15

"Is that him?" Darger found herself asking out loud.

A murmur spread through the room, and Rohrbach cleared his throat.

"We were kinda hoping that you would be able to, you know… confirm or disconfirm?"

He brought up a photo of Huxley that Darger recognized from the FBI's Most Wanted website.

"Here are the two images side by side."

The spacing of the eyes looked right, but the nose and chin were all wrong. Angular in the security footage, rounded in the Most Wanted shot.

Loshak kept his voice low as he spoke to Darger, but the room was quiet enough she was sure everyone could hear him.

"Forget his facial features for a minute… his build looks right to me. The posture. The body language. You?"

Darger blinked. Until she'd seen the bomber's face, there'd been no doubt in her mind that it was Huxley.

She nodded once but felt a twinge of the same blend of conviction and uncertainty she'd felt on the plane, looking at the crime scene photos.

Her mind spun like a hamster wheel, something frantic in its attempt to make the pieces fit.

Could this be a copycat?

No, that didn't feel right.

An accomplice?

And then an obvious explanation popped into her head.

"He's into all that special effects stuff. He could be wearing makeup."

Loshak blinked, and Darger could tell her suggestion had rattled something loose.

"What if he did something more… permanent?"

Darger pondered this. Realized what he meant.

"Plastic surgery," she said, her head bobbing up and down. "It'd be a drastic move, but after all the run his face got in the media, I don't doubt that he'd go that far."

"It's what I would do if I were on the Most Wanted list," Loshak said. "When John Dillinger was on the lam, he got the cleft removed from his chin and his cheeks tightened. That was all the way back in 1934. I imagine you could get a whole new face these days."

"Wait. What kind of doctor would be willing to do surgery on this turd?" Fitch asked. "I mean, the guy's a mass murderer."

"There are certain… let's say, less-than-scrupulous surgeons who do this kind of thing for the mafia and cartels, if the price is right. A lot of them operate in places like the Bahamas and Caymans, but some work stateside."

"That doesn't sound like an angle we'd be able to pursue, then," Chief Cattermole said. "At least not easily."

"Doubtful," Loshak agreed. "There are other methods we might use. I know a gal who's developed software that can identify someone by gait with something like 98 percent accuracy. I can give her a call, but it might turn out to be unnecessary."

"How so?" the chief asked.

"The thing about this type of perpetrator is that they almost always claim credit for their crimes. In many ways, they are serial killers turned histrionic. Instead of hiding in the shadows, they demand the spotlight. I predict that it's only a matter of time before we hear from the bomber, and that will tell us everything we need to know in terms of whether it's Huxley or not."

"That sounds like as good a segue as any," Cattermole said, gesturing that Darger and Loshak should take over. "Everyone, this is Agent Loshak and Agent Darger from the BAU."

CHAPTER 16

Loshak stepped to the podium, one hand thrust in his pocket.

"Well, given that there's still some uncertainty as to whether today's attack is the work of Tyler Huxley, let's take a moment to quickly compare and contrast the details of this bombing and those from Huxley's original spree."

He raised his arm in the air and used his fingers to count off each point on the list.

"I'll start with the similarities. In both cases, the perpetrator used homemade explosive devices, and they both used disguises to deliver the device by hand. In the original spree, Huxley posed as various deliverymen — flowers, parcels, etc. — which is not unlike what we saw here with the 'pizza guy' ruse. And finally, both perpetrators targeted victims in the entertainment industry, though in both cases, there's a clear disregard for the safety of innocent bystanders."

"Isn't that kind of a given when you're using a bomb?" Detective Rohrbach asked. "I mean, if one of these sickos wants to be certain that only their target gets killed or injured, a bomb seems like the worst possible choice."

Loshak pursed his lips before he answered.

"For many bombers, you're absolutely right. The total destructive power of the bomb is often used to do as much damage as possible rather than singling out specific targets. But there are deviations. For example, Ted Kaczynski — the Unabomber — was quite distraught when one of his bombs killed a bystander. So I think it's worth noting that in Huxley's previous spree and the attack today, there was no attempt to mitigate the danger to bystanders. It's a significant similarity."

"Point taken," Rohrbach said with a nod.

"That brings us to the differences," Loshak went on. "Most obviously, we have a change in geography. All of Huxley's original bombings occurred in the state of New York — most in the city with one upstate. Of course, he's been off the grid for some time, so there's no reason to think he couldn't have relocated here to Los Angeles. Probably the most perplexing anomaly is that Huxley always left notes and clues at the bombing scenes, and he posted most of his missives on the internet as well. Now, as I said earlier, I expect the bomber will communicate in some form or fashion, but until that happens, it's a discrepancy that can't be overlooked."

From his position in the corner of the room, Chief Cattermole stepped forward.

"I have a question about the notes, actually."

"Go ahead."

"As I understand it, Huxley's notes included clues not only for where he'd hidden the bombs, but also how to disarm them."

"That's correct," Loshak said.

"Why would he do that? Isn't he working counter to his own agenda?"

"It would seem so, but something you have to understand is that attention is the primary motivator here. In many ways, bombers are serial killers turned histrionic. In Huxley's case, the killing is secondary to the attention he gets for it. Period. He can't resist leaving notes, because he wants to be absolutely certain that everyone hears what he has to say. Which explains why he even goes so far as to post the messages on the internet. The more people reading his words, discussing his motives, speculating about him, the better."

The room fell quiet for a beat, everyone digesting that bit of info. Then Loshak went on.

"There's another element to the notes, which is the fact that Tyler Huxley is incredibly narcissistic. He invited us to play a game with him, believing that he would win no matter what. And even though we did manage to disarm some of the devices, he made sure we wouldn't win them all by booby-trapping one of the later bombs. The ensuing explosion resulted in the death of Agent Dobbins, one of our C-IED bomb techs."

Again, a quiet tension swelled to fill the gap in Loshak's monologue. The agent took a breath.

"Now, given the similarities and my personal gut feeling that today's attack was indeed committed by Tyler Huxley, Agent Darger is going to give you a rundown on his personal background."

Darger took a quick drink of water before swapping places with Loshak.

She brought up a screencap of Huxley from a video he'd released online during his original spree.

"This is the last image we have of Tyler Huxley from before he went into hiding. He's now 31 years old and grew up in a working-class family in Queens. We found no evidence or secondhand reports of violence or trauma in his childhood. He was neither popular nor ostracized in school. According to his brother, Tyler was somewhat of a pathological liar, often telling stories or making promises to classmates to make himself seem more important or impressive than he really was."

Darger skimmed down her page of notes.

"One noteworthy incident from Huxley's past is the fact

that he apparently did well on a standardized test in elementary school and was invited to some sort of special school for gifted children. The family didn't end up sending Tyler to the school, and nothing in the rest of his academic history is particularly noteworthy. I highlight this episode, as it might go some way to explaining the idea that there had been some hope of greatness from Tyler that never came to fruition. When that didn't happen, he grew resentful."

Darger clicked to a screen that showed Tyler's face alongside a few other notable killers.

"This is not an uncommon trait for mission-oriented killers. Where serial killers may be angry at a singular type, like prostitutes or women who physically remind them of a prominent female figure in their life, bombers are often angry at a broader segment of society. Ted Kaczynski blamed tech and industry. Timothy McVeigh blamed the federal government. Tyler Huxley blames the entertainment industry."

Next, Darger showed a scan of one of Tyler's high school journal pages, outlining one of his movie ideas.

"Tyler's obsession with the entertainment industry began early. He dreamed of making it big as a filmmaker, going as far as conning his classmates into contributing money and time to his 'movie project.' Despite all of this planning and fantasizing, from what we can tell, Tyler never shot so much as a single scene."

Rohrbach raised his hand and spoke up.

"So from what you're saying, it's like the guy didn't even *try* to make it, right? It's not like he had a budding career that got squashed. Did he just expect success to fall into his lap?"

"More or less. Another hallmark of a bomber's psychology is a sense of entitlement. They believe they are inherently special, and in their mind, that specialness should be rewarded. Kaczynski, at least, had the intellect. But in my opinion, he's an outlier in that regard. These are generally very mediocre men who have a belief in their own talent and genius that is nothing short of delusional. And instead of taking responsibility for their own failings, they blame someone else for their lack of success."

Darger held up a finger.

"However, I wouldn't let his inflated ego fool you into believing our bomber is stupid. He is highly motivated and willing to cross boundaries most people would never dream of. The irony with Huxley is that if he'd applied half the initiative to genuine creative pursuits that he's put into his violent spectacles, I think he might have been very successful indeed."

She paused and shook her head.

"But I'm getting off on a tangent. Mission-oriented killers generally live very stable lives. They are not psychotic — they know exactly what they're doing. This type of killer chooses specific victims and plans out each murder with meticulous precision. And they do not stop on their own."

She paused and crossed her arms over her chest.

"The takeaway here is that this is a very dangerous man. He is crafty. He is resourceful. He is angry. But despite all of that, he does have a weakness."

A photo of one of Tyler's journal entries filled the screen now.

"He simply can't resist going public with his plans. This desire to espouse his philosophy and disseminate his so-called manifesto to a large audience serves his desperate need for attention, but it also creates an opening for us. Even if his words are carefully chosen to lead us where he wants to lead us, to tell us what he wants us to hear, he's giving us information. And there's a reason one of the tips the best poker players in the world tell newbies is to *stop talking so much.*"

"So you think we'll catch him this time?" Rohrbach asked.

This time.

She didn't think the detective had meant it as a dig, but she couldn't help but feel a painful twinge of guilt at what the words implied.

Because you didn't catch him last time.

"Yes," Darger said, her tone firm and confident.

But the truth was, she didn't know.

CHAPTER 17

Traffic cluttered the streets all the way to the studio lot. That bright L.A. sunshine glinted off several lanes' worth of rear windshields before them, the vehicles packed together in a way that reminded Darger of a herd of elephants — hulking shapes set shoulder to shoulder, moving forward in fits and starts.

Rohrbach weaved his Camry in and out of the mess, fighting his way forward the best he could. Loshak made chitchat from the passenger seat, with Fitch chiming in from the spot behind him, but Darger couldn't focus on the words.

She reclined as much as she could in the backseat, the back of her skull lolling onto the headrest. She found her innards awhirl with a mix of feelings.

Part of her was anxious to see the scene up close and in person. Experiencing the crime scene that way had a way of making the place fully concrete, fully real, and seemed to aid her somehow in working a case.

Another part of her, however, was equally queasy at the thought of walking through that destroyed sitcom living room. The blood going tacky. The shredded couch and walls. The flecks of debris strewn about like rice after a wedding. She shuddered when she thought about stepping into that reality.

Rohrbach jerked the sedan hard to the right, and there it was. The single lane of the curving driveway shuttled them closer and closer to their destination.

A pair of towering palm trees bracketed the entrance of the studio lot, which was partially blocked by an LAPD cruiser. Beyond the police barricade, Darger spotted the guard booth from the file photos.

Two uniforms stood in the street, directing civilian traffic away from the studio entrance. One of the unis gave a nod of recognition to Rohrbach and waved at the gate attendant. The gate arm swung upright, and Rohrbach's car cruised through.

The lot was a seemingly endless grid of round-topped warehouse-style buildings, all colored the same shade of beige. They reminded Darger of something that could sit on a farm, a storage building of some type off to the side somewhere. The huge roll-up garage door of the nearest soundstage stood wide open. A gaping mouth, empty and still.

In the security videos, the lot had been packed, and it felt strange to see the place so desolate now. Empty craft services tents. Cast trailers with the doors left hanging ajar. A sea of open parking spots. Not a single person in sight.

Rohrbach steered the car around a golf cart that had been marooned in the middle of the lane. The more Darger looked, the more she saw signs of people stopping in the middle of a task and fleeing. A circular saw paused halfway through ripping a sheet of plywood down the middle. A tangle of PVC pipes hastily dropped in a pile.

"Guess they evacuated the entire lot," Darger said.

"Yeah, and it was kind of a clusterfuck, to be honest," Rohrbach said. "The lot itself is over 60 acres. Something like 5,500 employees, depending on the day. It was like evacuating a small town. Trying to get everyone out of here in an orderly manner, without causing a panic? Well… let's just say it was no easy task. And that was only the beginning. When the bomb squad finished with Soundstage 34H, they moved onto the adjacent buildings. We called in reinforcements from five neighboring jurisdictions, plus your Counter-IED guys, and it's still probably gonna take them a whole 'nother day to sweep the entire lot."

They zigged and zagged between the various buildings. Moving past what must have been some sort of prop storage, Darger spotted two ancient-looking cannons sitting beside four vintage refrigerators of various makes and models. They turned a corner, and the stillness dominating the rest of the lot evaporated.

Here, there was action. Techs in white suits flitted back and forth between the soundstage and the cluster of vehicles parked alongside.

Rohrbach parked next to a firetruck, and they exited the car.

"The side door here leads directly onto the set, but I figured you'd want to follow Huxley's actual path. The formal entrance is around front."

Darger had to skirt around a pile of cables, all neatly coiled and arranged in a stack. One coil spanned about three feet wide and looked heavier than what anyone could carry.

They passed a craft services tent laid out with an array of deli meats, cheeses, fruits, and vegetables. The hotel pans swarmed with flies.

There were two vehicles parked haphazardly near the entrance of the building. The first she recognized as the little hatchback Huxley had used to gain entry to the grounds and abandoned. Techs surged around it now.

The second vehicle looked like a golf cart on steroids. Five rows of seats and a logo on the side that read, "Super Star Tours."

Everyone else skirted around the cart, which sat between them and the door, but Darger stopped, thinking.

Loshak glanced back and raised an eyebrow.

"What is it?"

Darger licked her lips. Looked back in the direction they'd come, spotting the guard booth in the distance. It was a long, circuitous path to get from there to here. It would have been easier to target one of the soundstages closer to the entrance, but Huxley was the type who wasn't satisfied with a random victim. His targets were specific.

That meant planning. He would have needed to know not only how to get to this exact soundstage, but where to go once he was inside.

Darger gestured at the tour cart.

"I'm wondering how often they run the tours."

She saw the gears turning in Loshak's head. Knew by the slight twitch of his mouth when the realization hit.

"You think he took a tour himself. That's how he knew where to go."

Darger nodded.

"And I suppose these tours would require registering for tickets," Loshak said.

Darger nodded again.

"Obviously he wouldn't have used his real name, but knowing what alias he might be using would be something, at least. And if he used a credit card to book the tickets, that could give us an address."

Loshak's gaze was glued to the tour cart.

"We need to get the names of anyone who's been on a tour in the last month or two."

Detective Rohrbach nodded and pulled out his phone.

CHAPTER 18

They milled around outside while Rohrbach put in a call to the task force hotline. It wasn't an especially hot day, but the lot was one giant sheet of blacktop. It felt like the Sahara the way the heat radiated up from the ground.

Finally Rohrbach hung up and filled them in as they headed inside.

"Specialist Nahali is going to contact the tour group company immediately to get the names. She's one of yours. Seems sharp."

There was another uniformed officer stationed inside the airlock that led into the reception area of the building. He greeted Rohrbach and held the glass door open for them.

"Tanaka wants everyone fully suited up before entering the scene," the uni said. "There's gear on that table over there."

"Thanks, Reese."

They paused there and slipped into bunny suits, booties, and gloves before continuing on.

"You probably recognize this from the crime scene photos," Rohrbach said as he banked left toward a hall. "Bomber entered here. Moved down this hallway. Dumped the pizzas in the alcove here."

Indeed, the pizza boxes still sat behind the potted plants, a yellow evidence marker next to them. Just before she slipped her mask over her face, Darger caught a whiff of congealed cheese and tangy tomato sauce. Usually the fragrance would make her hungry, but the thought of gloopy cheese and red sauce conjured a memory of the carnage she'd seen in the crime scene photos. She swallowed against the sudden constricted feeling in her throat.

Rohrbach led the way deeper down the hall. The front office facade morphed into something more industrial. Darger peeked into the open doors along the way, looking into mostly dark, cavernous spaces where the ceiling went up at least forty feet, crisscrossed by catwalks and lighting rigs hanging from cables and chains.

The building, like the lot, was eerily empty, though a lone tech streamed past now and then.

The space was so huge that Darger was surprised their footsteps and voices didn't echo more. Must be some trick with the acoustics.

And despite the lighting rigs blazing down on a few of the sets they passed, it felt dark. Shaded and cool like a cave.

They rounded a corner and peered in at a set in the early stages of construction, just unfinished plywood and bare framing. The next doorway exposed what was obviously the set of a daytime talk show. A massive semicircular blue modular couch took up most of the stage. Behind the couch, faux windows looked out on a generic cityscape in silhouette.

Detective Rohrbach glanced back at Darger.

"That's where they film *The Riley Murphy Show*."

When she shrugged, he frowned at her.

"You know, the 'Treat yourself good!' lady."

"Not familiar," Darger said.

"Count yourself lucky, then. I can't stand the woman. Got a voice on her like nails on a chalkboard. But my wife is absolutely gaga for her and her stupid 'Treat Yourself Tips.' Half of 'em are crap like, 'Stop and smell your coffee before taking the first sip!' So obvious it almost seems like a joke, right? Then the other half is 'Splurge on this designer bottle of nail polish!' or 'Buy this thousand-dollar massage chair!'"

He shook his head.

"Just a great big racket where they try to convince people to buy even more garbage they don't need. But all dressed up like it's some positive, quasi-spiritual experience."

The next set looked like a small downtown area but painted in bright candy colors. Clearly some kind of kids show.

"Oh hey! This is the set for *Bigsby & Friends*!" Fitch said, whipping out his phone and handing it to Darger. "Snap a photo of me, would ya?"

Darger obliged, waiting for Fitch to get in position. He lowered his mask so his face was visible and gave two thumbs up.

"Big fan?" she asked, handing his phone back.

He laughed.

"Not me. My kids. *Bigsby* is one of their favorite shows. Bigsby is this big purple turtle. No wait. He's a *tortoise*. They always correct me when I call him a turtle. Anyway, Bigsby and his friends solve mysteries and sing songs about it. But the music director is that guy from The Buttcrusts. You know, that band from the 90s? So the music in the show kinda slaps, actually."

Next, they bypassed a wardrobe room, which was essentially a walk-in closet the size of Darger's entire apartment.

As they trekked farther into the building, Darger was suddenly glad they had Rohrbach with them. She was certain she would have gotten lost without a guide.

Fitch paused in front of a large glossy poster marking the entrance to *The Tom Giovanni Show*. It featured a large photograph of an overly tan man with dark hair and perfect teeth.

"Oh hey… that's the guy, isn't it?"

Rohrbach looked slightly disgusted when he answered.

"Yeah. That's him."

"What guy?" Darger asked.

"You know," Rohrbach said. "The entitled little shit who crashed his Bugatti going like 100 on the freeway? Killed his friend who was riding shotgun? Had a blood alcohol level of like point-two-five? He went to prison and everything."

Darger only shook her head.

"Well, that was like thirteen years go, but he's one of those guys that's just constantly in the tabloids. After he got out of prison, he was in and out of rehab. Supposedly he did so much heroin that his colon exploded. Then *The Daily Gawk* got footage of him scoring drugs in Skid Row, and when he yelled at the cameraman, it became clear that he had about three teeth left."

Darger tried to square these details with the photograph of the smiling man on the poster with the biggest, whitest teeth money could buy.

"Anyway, I guess he was able to clean up his act. His talk show was number one the last two years."

"Talk about a comeback," Fitch said.

"Yeah, well… I guess most people figure he paid his debt to society," Rohrbach said. "But I have to wonder how you can ever truly pay back a debt as big as killing someone. Seems wrong to me, personally. Guess I should be glad my wife is into that Riley Murphy and not this schmuck."

Finally, they reached the set where the bombing happened, and once more the stillness was broken with frantic movement.

At least a dozen techs were still busy bagging, documenting, searching.

They entered near the control room, positioned behind the rows of blue velour theater seats where the live audience had been seated. Darger felt her eyebrows climb her forehead as she spied the puddle of blood lying in the front row, just off center. She swallowed hard, her throat tight enough to make the act difficult just now.

They followed the sloped aisle down to the set. It was built to look like the interior of a suburban house — an open-concept living room and kitchen, a stairway that surely led to nowhere, all of it opened on one side and facing the stadium seating. The windows looked out on flat, two-dimensional exteriors, and from Darger's slightly elevated POV, the lighting rigs and backdrops were visible. The effect of all those bits together was disorienting and somehow unsettling.

Even more unsettling was the smell. Despite her mask, an acrid chemical stench of scorched polyester and black powder assaulted her nostrils.

Her eyes snapped to the point of impact. What was left of the couch — part of one arm, mostly — looked like it had melted into the floor. Exposed springs and splintered wood surrounded by foam and batting that looked like they'd liquefied and congealed into some new substance that was something in between liquid and solid.

The concrete floor itself had been cratered, a roughly medicine-ball-sized divot a few inches deep showing exactly where the detonation occurred, all the carpet leading outward from that point singed black.

Holes punched inky spots into the wall — chunks taken out where the shrapnel had hit. And the floor was littered with what looked like some kind of confetti but was actually shredded bits of fabric and lumps of drywall.

She was glad the body was gone — the photos had been grisly enough — but evidence of the bloodshed remained. Bloodied gauze and bandages in a pile where the EMTs had worked on the wounded. A lone shoe spattered with gore.

"You never really get over it."

Darger didn't realize she'd said it out loud until Loshak responded.

"What's that?" he asked.

"How much damage a bomb can do. It's…"

She shook her head, at a loss for words.

Loshak put his hands on his hips, following her gaze to the hollowed-out place in the center of the living room floor.

"Yeah."

CHAPTER 19

Darger's eyes scoured the set. Up and down, back and forth. An inch-by-inch scan of the place made more difficult by the fact that it was still bustling with activity. She kept having to step aside for a tech photographing this or bagging that.

She took a few steps back from the destroyed couch and felt an odd sense of relief. Something about the number of people jammed into the space, and the constant movement, and the windows to nowhere… the combination was giving her a claustrophobic feeling.

She floated farther away from ground zero, until she was standing amid the audience seating. Looking down on the set as a whole, she seemed to have fresh eyes with which to study the scene. But what she saw only disheartened her further. It was clear the techs had already torn every inch of this place apart, and they still hadn't found anything from Huxley.

No note.

No clue.

Nothing.

She fell into one of the theater seats. Then she folded her hands on the back of the seat in front of her and rested her chin on top of her knuckles.

If it was truly Huxley behind this, if he'd gone to such trouble to orchestrate this whole thing, then surely he'd be playing the same game as before. So where was the note?

Just asking herself the question seemed to unfold an empty feeling in her gut. Hopelessness gnawing there like a tapeworm.

There was an inevitability to all of this. Huxley coming

back. The bombings resuming.

A true Hollywood comeback.

An irony too irresistible for Huxley to pass by.

Loshak joined her then, lowering himself into the seat behind her.

"You OK?"

"Yeah. Just thinking."

"It's weird to see one of these sets in person. Doesn't look quite so artificial on TV, you know? I mean, if you really pay attention, a lot of times you can tell that the walls wobble a little when they slam a door. Or you can see that the brick isn't real brick. But to see it all together… it's like a dollhouse blown up to human size. Kind of eerie-looking, you know?"

As he went on, Darger found she was only half-listening. Something else was nagging at her mind again.

"A couple months ago, I saw pictures of the set from the original *Addams Family* TV show — the one from the 60s. It showed what the set looked like on TV — which was in black and white — side-by-side with photos of the set in real life. And it was all these bright colors. I'm talking cotton candy pink wallpaper and bright yellow velvet curtains."

Darger ran back through their conversation, feeling the familiar itch of precognition.

Was it what Loshak had said about the set looking fake?

No. That's not it.

Before that.

What had she been thinking about when Loshak walked up?

When it finally hit her, she leaped up so quickly her seat slammed back into its folded position with a *thunk.*

Loshak frowned as she ran past him and up to the top row

of seats. When she shoved through the doors that led to the production booth, she heard his voice.

"Where the hell are you—"

His words cut out as the door of the studio snicked shut behind her.

The hallway was eerily quiet as she retraced their steps from earlier. The booties on her feet scuffed against the floor, made tiny swishing sounds that somehow made the silence here seem bigger, stronger.

She continued back down the winding passage that ran from one set to another. Her head whipped from side to side, scanning the doors.

Then she spotted it. Up ahead.

The Tom Giovanni Show.

She pushed through the steel door. Just like the sitcom set, this door led first past the production area and then into the audience seating. Below, a stage spread from wall to wall. Thick velvet curtains hung as a backdrop on one side. Two plump leather chairs and a desk with an executive office chair sat clustered on the other.

Darger moved forward, her eyes casting about the space. The set was equally as large as that of the sitcom, but it wasn't as cluttered. If she was right about this, that meant there were only so many places it could be.

She considered the rows of theater seats. The plush armchairs. Then her gaze landed on the chair where the host would sit.

The Comeback King himself.

She hustled down to the stage and crossed to the desk. Her fingers skimmed the back of the chair, about to roll it back into the open, when she froze.

Loshak and the others had caught up to her now, and they were fanned out across the stage, watching her.

"They've cleared this set?" she asked, suddenly wary of some kind of booby trap.

"Yep," Fitch confirmed. "This whole building is clear."

Still feeling a sense of trepidation, Darger gently scooted the chair out from under the desktop. Got down on her knees and looked underneath.

She prodded at the folds in the leather. Jiggled the height adjustment lever. Tipped it from one side and then the other to poke at the wheels.

When the chair proved fruitless, she nudged it away and crawled into the space under the desk. Used the light on her phone to illuminate the underside.

Nothing. Stained wood.

She wriggled back out. There were no drawers on the desk, so that was out.

She sighed.

It had to be here. Had to be.

She was still on her knees, eyes level with the surface of the desk. Six inches from her nose rested a mug printed with the show's logo.

She imagined the host sipping from it. Grinning behind it with his slick Hollywood smile.

She snatched it up by the handle. Lifted it over her face.

There she spied the folded piece of paper taped to the smooth ceramic bottom.

Darger plucked the note from the mug and unfolded it to read the words scrawled there in blood-red ink.

CHAPTER 20

Greetings piggies,

Guess who's back?

You know how Hollywood is. The first set of bombings [My debut?] was such a blockbuster. The demand for a sequel was too much to deny.

It looks like we've got the makings of a full-blown franchise on our hands, folks. Hopefully I can negotiate a piece of the Huxley toys and, of course, the Saturday morning animated series.

Speaking of toys, I've made a whole slew of new gadgets and scattered them throughout the city. Violent things. Ready and waiting for someone to come play with them.

You all know the game by now.

Find my journals. Solve the clues. Maybe save some lives.

But never forget the rules. The winner takes all, you know?

They stand tall, above it all, looking down on the rest. Champions of this city of light. Shining as bright as bleached teeth, even in the dark.

And second place? Oh, you don't want second place in this game.

The consolation prize is a fiery thing, you could say. Raging. Melting faces.

Work quickly. If you're too slow, the game will claim more lives, more bodies, more faces.

Every twelve hours. It begins at midnight tonight.

Darger's pulse thundered in her ears as she read the note. She felt almost lightheaded.

Because she knew that handwriting on sight. Spiky. Aggressive.

Tyler Huxley's handwriting.

She supposed, of course, that it could have been faked. Given the publicity the original bombing spree had received, someone else could have made an effort to copy the angry-looking scrawl.

But it wasn't just the handwriting that was spot on. It was the voice.

Huxley's voice.

Snippets of the old notes echoed in her mind.

If we burn out the old way, we can build something new on the ashes. We can remake the world in a new image.

The old idols will topple. Die off like the dinosaurs. Reality will pierce the veil of tinsel at long last.

Kill the stars. Kill the dream.

The revolution will be etched into celebrity skin.

When it hit her what it truly meant to be hunting Huxley again, her mouth went dry.

Now it was her own words replaying in her head — something she'd said at the task force meeting.

This type of killer chooses specific victims and plans out each murder with meticulous precision. And they do not stop on their own.

Part of her struggled to believe this was really happening, and she found herself thrust right back into those feelings she'd had working the Huxley case in New York. It was an off combination of déjà vu and dread.

Déjà dread.

She read the note again. Studied the pen strokes. Red ink on plain white paper, two horizontal creases like it was about to go into an envelope, and then another fold down the center.

"Agent Darger?" a voice said from beside her.

She turned. Evelyn Tanaka, the lead crime scene investigator on the task force, stood at Darger's shoulder, gloved hand outstretched.

"The note?"

"Oh," Darger said. "Right."

Her fingers felt numb against the page as she took a quick photo of the note, then handed it off to Tanaka to be officially entered into evidence.

The area around the desk was brimming with techs now, and Darger moved off to the curtained side to make room. There, she huddled around her phone with Loshak, Fitch, and Rohrbach, studying the photo of the note.

She was particularly interested in Loshak's assessment — was eager to know if his gut said the same as hers — and the tension of waiting for him to finish reading made her clench her teeth.

His eyes zoomed from left to right and then back again, and then finally they snapped up to meet hers.

"Well?" she asked, and the thudding of her pulse in her ears made her voice sound strangely muted.

"It's him. Definitely." He put his hands on his hips, the bunny suit crinkling. "Of course, we'll send it to the analysts at the lab. Get confirmation on the handwriting and the linguistics, but I think we know they're going to tell us the same thing. It's Huxley."

"That confirms it, then," Fitch said and glanced down at his prosthetic leg. "It's him, but shit. Not sure if that's a good thing or a bad thing."

"We're not starting from scratch. That's something," Loshak said.

Darger held her phone up.

"And we finally have a clue."

Fitch made a frustrated sound in the back of his throat.

"More of his cryptic bullshit, you mean."

"I figure the 'stand tall' part has gotta be a reference to a building, right?" Rohrbach said.

Darger's eye traced over that paragraph again. Stopping on certain phrases.

Above it all.

Looking down on the rest.

City of light.

Shining as bright as bleached teeth, even in the dark.

A sharp breath sucked in between her teeth.

Loshak's eyes bored into hers.

"You know where it is?"

She nodded.

CHAPTER 21

A queasy feeling bloomed in Darger's stomach as they wove up into the hills, the road narrow and steep, with twists and turns that followed the natural topography. Once again she sat in the back of Rohrbach's Camry with Loshak riding shotgun. Fitch was already on the scene with his C-IED team, ready to defuse any explosives should they find any.

Rohrbach drove aggressively. The detective seemed content to whip around every hairpin turn as they ascended the slope. The constant centrifugal shifts didn't help Darger's stomach any, but at least the traffic wasn't so bad out here.

She kept her gaze fixed out the window where lush green now dominated most of the view. She somehow always forgot how mountainous the terrain was in Los Angeles, how rustic things got in the hills. Most of the houses up here had little in the way of back or even front yards. The land was too sharply sloped.

Instead, the spaces between houses often featured retaining walls and hedges of bamboo and ficus. Bougainvillea and creeping sedum spilled over the tops of the concrete and stone barriers, with dappled sunlight filtering through a canopy of pine and eucalyptus. It made the road feel enclosed. Jungle-like.

Some of the houses were more classic Mediterranean style, with stucco walls and red tile on the roof. Others leaned more modern — boxy concrete structures with glass walls and black metal accents.

The drive took them past Lake Hollywood and through the old Hollywoodland neighborhood with its fairytale houses.

And all the while, their destination loomed over them. The big white letters looked stark set against the green of the hills, jutting out of the land. The sign seemed to get taller as they closed in on it, the sheer size of the thing only truly discernible up close.

HOLLYWOOD. The iconic sign was lettered in all caps, perhaps for emphasis, like the hill was yelling it.

Darger had seen the sign on TV and in movies probably thousands of times. And she'd driven past it in real life, too. But she'd never been this close before.

Finally, they got to within a half mile or so, and the foliage blocked her view of the sign, the treetops along the roadside screening the slice of sky where the thing had been visible. Somehow losing sight of those white letters made Darger's heart pump faster.

They passed a row of road signs warning "DEAD END" and "NO ACCESS TO THE HOLLYWOOD SIGN."

"What's with the signs?" Darger asked.

Rohrbach found her eyes in the rearview before he answered.

"Ah, well… the sign can be a pretty big draw for tourists, and they'll stop wherever. Blocking driveways. Clogging up the roads back here, which, as you can see, are pretty tight. The additional traffic has been a pain for the residents, and there's also been some concern about first responders needing access during fire season. Needless to say, neither the locals nor the city wants a whole bunch of people parking up here to get to the sign."

"Is the only way to reach the sign by foot?"

"Oh, there's a road, but it's closed to the public. Secured by a gate that's locked 24/7 and only accessible by city personnel, unless you have a special permit."

"That's surprisingly strict," Loshak said.

"You think that's strict, just wait 'til you hear about security around the sign itself. We're talking fences, infrared cameras, and at least one security guard stationed in the vicinity at all times. If someone hops the fence, sometimes they send out a helicopter to chase them away."

"And somehow Huxley managed to get around all of that?"

"It's not the first time. Every so often, someone gets through. Few years back, someone pulled a prank. Changed the two O's at the end to lowercase e's, so it said 'HOLLYWeeD'."

"I guess it would be a beacon for vandalism," Loshak said. "A landmark that famous. And that visible."

"I think the other reason for the security measures is that it's pretty dangerous. You can't always tell when you see it in movies or photos, but the terrain is steep and rocky. If the public was allowed to just gallivant around up here, it'd be a disaster."

They reached a fork in the road with one side partially blocked by an LAPD cruiser. The officer waved their mini motorcade through, and they proceeded further into the hills.

They rounded a sharp bend in the road. As the trees and vegetation thinned, Darger caught a fresh glimpse. The gleaming white letters thrusting out of the hill above looked all the brighter up close, almost blinding against all the green around them.

How had Huxley described them?

As bright as bleached teeth.

And there was something about them that reminded her of the artificially white smiles that seemed ubiquitous in this city. Big and fake.

Two more police vehicles were positioned at the gate Rohrbach had mentioned earlier. Again they were ushered through.

They turned a corner, and the sign disappeared again. The serpentine path of the road continued up and around the east side of the peak. The soil here was a bright orangey-red, the foliage low and scrubby. Darger suddenly had a flashback of the last time she was in this type of chaparral landscape.

Klootey. The fires.

A prickle of unease crept up her spine, and for just a moment, she swore she could smell smoke.

Loshak's phone emitted an electronic chime. He glanced at the screen.

"Ah. There we go. Huxley's note is online."

Darger frowned down at her own phone, wondering why she hadn't received whatever update he had. And now that she thought about it, Rohrbach's phone hadn't dinged either.

"How do you know?" she asked.

He held out his phone.

"I set up a Google alert with some of the phrases from the note."

Darger's eyes narrowed to slits.

"Since when do you know how to set up a Google alert?"

"I have my ways," he said, looking entirely too proud of himself. "Anyway, it's already getting attention. 274 comments and counting."

Rohrbach took one hand off the wheel and adjusted the rearview mirror.

"We're following the assumption that Huxley is releasing the notes himself like last time?" he asked.

"More than likely," Darger said.

"I know you said this guy likes attention, but it seems to me that going public like this increases the likelihood that the puzzle will be solved. I mean, it said in the old case file that at least one of the clues was solved by a civilian, right?"

Loshak nodded.

"I don't know if he minds us solving the puzzles, as long as he causes a stir. It was a media frenzy last time, and that was no accident. Whether a bomb goes off or not, he knows people are scared. But they're fascinated, too. It's a win-win for him."

"I also think he likes the idea of getting the public involved on a deeper level," Darger added. "Audience participation, I guess you could say."

The road up the mountain finally deposited them just above the sign and near a radio tower. Some of the units Chief Cattermole dispatched had already arrived, and a pair of uniformed officers were setting up a line of barricades to keep the civilians back.

Tanaka had divided her techs into two groups — those who would stay and continue collecting evidence at the soundstage, and those who would begin the search at the Hollywood sign.

Units had also headed to the Mount Lee Drive gate, Bronson Canyon, Sunset Ranch, and Wonder View, as well as shutting down the trails. With that level of security cordoning off the park and dissuading any and all comers, in addition to the remote location, Darger hadn't imagined there'd be an issue with gawkers up here.

But she had been wrong.

Already, there were at least a dozen people gathered behind the barricades. Rohrbach had said it was a big tourist draw, after all.

Most of the bystanders appeared to be twenty-somethings

in retro sunglasses and trendy-looking athletic gear, jackets and hoodies tied around their waists. Cameras out and filming the action. Some probably had no idea what they were seeing, just that it was *something*.

A barbed wire fence enclosed the radio tower and the cluster of buildings surrounding it. Rohrbach steered them through the open gate and parked in a large concrete lot alongside several other law enforcement vehicles.

They climbed out and marched back to the stretch of road immediately behind the sign. The white letters exceeded Darger's expectations yet again — at least as tall as a three-story building — but it was the view that really caught her attention.

Los Angeles sprawled before them, a gridwork of houses and city streets as far as she could see, stretching on and on until it shifted into bigger towers dotting the horizon. An unbelievable expanse. It all lay at the bottom of the hill, and it felt to Darger like the whole world was at her feet.

"We're lucky. Smog isn't so bad today," Rohrbach said, looking out over the city as well.

Movement near the giant white letters drew Darger's eye back to the sign. Four legs and a flash of fur. Her first thought was there was a coyote down there. Then she saw the man in black tactical gear come into view and realized it was one of the bomb-sniffing dogs and his C-IED handler.

She spied Fitch leaning against the fence that ran along the road. His gaze was focused on his team down below.

As she approached, he brought a radio to his mouth and murmured something into it.

"How's it going?" she asked.

"Clear so far. Once they finish sweeping the 'D' and give the word, we can begin the search in earnest." His jaw clenched.

"Well, I say 'we' in the collective sense. As much as it chaps my ass to admit it, I think this terrain is too much for Rusty."

He leaned and rapped his knuckles against his artificial leg.

"You named your fake leg?"

Fitch's glacier-blue eyes grew uncharacteristically serious.

"It's called a prosthesis, Darger. The word 'fake' is frowned upon in the amputee community."

"Oh. Sorry."

His mouth stretched into a grin, and he swiped at her shoulder with one of his bear-like paws.

"Ah, I'm just pulling your leg! Get it?"

The radio in Fitch's hand crackled.

"Fitch, you there?"

"I'm here. What's the status?"

"It's all clear down here."

"Good job, boys. Bring the dogs back up."

With the search site cleared of imminent danger, Tanaka's team headed down to the letters. The rest of them formed a huddle with Chief Cattermole at the front. A uniform passed out bunny suits and gloves.

"Agent Tanaka is setting up a grid down below. We've got a lot of area to search, as you can see. Each of those letters is approximately thirty feet wide with the total length of the sign coming in at 350 feet. Needless to say, this is an all-hands-on-deck situation. Everyone suit up and stand by for assignments."

CHAPTER 22

The sun slid down toward the horizon, blushing full red as it touched the sea in the distance. It was beautiful in a way, how the scarlet reflected off the top of the water, but Darger couldn't help but see it as great plumes of blood saturating the Pacific.

The techs had set up a dozen lighting rigs to illuminate the search area. The bulbs were harsh and bright white, gleaming on the surface of things and casting hard shadows in relief.

Darger and Loshak skulked beneath the mammoth letter "Y." They angled their flashlights along the dirt and grass there, around the pilings anchored in the ground, snaked the beams up the steel support beams. Seeking anything that seemed out of place.

Darger paused and ran her hand across the face of the Y. From a distance, the surface of the letters appeared flat and smooth. But up close, they were ridged like a corrugated roof.

She thought back to such scenes during the first Huxley case in New York. Her mind shuffled through the fractured images. Pictured searches in parks, in a dock area along the bay, in a living room, in a parking garage. This area felt right to her, mostly. It matched up well enough with some of the prior locations, but…

He'd buried most of his previous clues, to be sure, but that didn't mean he'd continue doing that.

"What if he didn't hide it near the sign at all?" Darger said, thinking out loud. "Maybe the reason he didn't trigger any of the cameras or anything is because he stayed on the other side of the fence."

"And resist the urge to bypass the security as an extra little 'fuck you'?" Loshak said. "No way. It's down here, one-hundred percent."

"Are you trying to jinx it, or what?"

"Jinx it? Please. That's superstitious nonsense."

"There's a fine line between confident and cocky, you know," Darger said.

"Well let me just go ahead and cross that line. Because not only am I certain the clue is down here, I bet I know which letter he chose as the hiding place."

Darger squatted near a clump of sedge and made sure there was nothing concealed in or around it.

"OK, smart guy. Which letter?"

"H. Obviously."

"H for Huxley."

"Exactly."

Darger found herself annoyed that there was a certain logic to Loshak's theory. Why hadn't she thought of that?

A sudden crescendo of voices arose from the next letter over. Rohrbach zipped past, headed that way.

"They found an area of disturbed ground near the W," he said.

Darger raised her eyebrows. Looked at Loshak out of the side of her eye.

"It's nothing. You watch. Probably a gopher hole or something," he said, crossing his arms.

They abandoned their post and trudged through tall scrubby grass to join the crowd forming near the W. Darger could feel the excitement even before she reached them.

Techs stood shoulder to shoulder with heavily armored C-IED guys, everyone trying to get a peek. Darger elbowed her way to the front of the pack.

Camera flashes strobed against the dusk, documenting the area. Before they started digging, they brought one of the bomb-sniffing dogs back down, just to be sure. The hound put his nose to the ground and wove back and forth over the area.

Darger doubted Huxley would booby trap the first clue, but it was always better to be safe in a case like this. Always.

Once the dig site had been cleared, the techs used trowels to excavate the area one small clump of dirt at a time. The scrape of metal on dirt rang over the scene in a slow and steady rhythm. A gritty drumbeat in Darger's ears. It counted down the passing seconds.

The soil they removed went straight into a bin with a screen over the top so the larger pieces could be sifted out. After several minutes of digging, all they'd found were rocks, a plastic bottle cap, and a glass marble.

Just like that, the excitement waned some. The crowd had already thinned, parts of it drifting off to other sites.

Then Tanaka's radio sputtered to life.

"Might have something near the H."

Loshak gave Darger a haughty look. Eyebrows up. Lips pursed.

"It's probably just another gopher hole," Darger said.

Loshak followed Tanaka over to the other site, but Darger stayed. It was petty, she knew, but if she abandoned the W now, it'd be giving credence to his prediction.

She started to lose patience when the next fifteen scoops of dirt revealed nothing but more rocks. Then the next several brought more of the same.

Well... shit.

She sighed to herself and then glanced around. Finally, with great reluctance, Darger crunched through the dry weeds over to the H to see what, if anything, had been found there.

The bomb tech was just leading his dog away from the area. Tanaka was down on one knee almost perfectly centered between the two legs of the giant H. She jabbed a soil probe into the ground.

"Oh yeah, there's something down there for sure. Something solid," she said, marking the spot with an orange flag.

"Could be a boulder," Darger muttered so that only Loshak would hear.

Tanaka and one of her techs worked at the spot in the same painstaking manner. One meager handful of soil at a time.

And that familiar thump and scrape grated over the hushed setting. It felt like Darger could hear every little grain of sand screeching against the trowels, a choir singing out of tune.

The red light of the dying day glinted over it all, the last light slowly sinking behind the hill. The day bleeding into night little by little.

With the sunlight fading fast, the hole itself seemed to stretch out of the reach of the lights, a gaping maw of blackness. Darger tried standing on tiptoes to better see into that wounded spot in the soil, but it didn't help.

She felt a combination of impatience and dread in her gut as she watched them burrow into the earth. She squinted, strained her eyes trying to sense something, anything, emerging from the dark pit.

Tanaka froze, her face oddly calm. She shuffled closer to the lip of the crater.

The tension in Darger's belly swelled. What was it? Had Tanaka spotted something?

Then Tanaka turned her head, eyes slightly wider than normal, and Darger saw the triumph and excitement there.

Her voice sounded slightly raspy when she finally spoke.

"Got something."

CHAPTER 23

Vinnie Savage, tabloid reporter extraordinaire, snugged his Porsche into the spot behind the Chevron. He took a breath. Smeared his sweaty palms on the thighs of his jeans.

He'd hated every second of easing the sports car over the craggy asphalt of the parking lot, navigating around potholes deep enough to do fender damage on top of fucking the tires. Anyway, it was over. Now the wait could begin.

Savage scanned the area.

The cinder block building shielded this part of the lot — kept it clear of cameras and streetlights, clear of any visibility from the traffic going by. It even screened most of the noise, cut the roar down to a dampened drone.

He stared at the wall in front of the windshield — matte white paint smeared over concrete blocks, grooved lines gridding the whole thing into rectangular cells. A drooping Bud Light banner flapped against the top edge of the wall, a sun-bleached thing that had probably been strung up there since Obama's first term at least.

A sheet of dark glass interrupted the cinder blocks — a window covered over with inky contact paper. Finger smudges covered the pane — enough marks to suggest it hadn't seen Windex in this century.

Savage let his gaze drift over the lot. He found the back half of the craggy expanse empty. Just a bunch of puddles from the car wash runoff gaping at the heavens gone freshly dark.

Something chewed deep in his gut. Nerves, he supposed.

The other car — an electric blue PT Cruiser, of all things —

wasn't here yet.

Shit.

He checked the time on his phone. He was a couple minutes early.

Fine. That's OK. Whatever.

He balled and unballed his fists. Drummed his fingers on the steering wheel for a second. His eyes drifted back to the concrete wall, to the window set within it.

A warped version of the Porsche's reflection stared back at him from that black mirror. A purple sports car. Fancy and curved, though not as cartoonish as a Lambo or Bugatti that some 'roided-up action star might drive.

A 911 Turbo still had some class. And even if everyone else on the road didn't know the specific retail price — starting at $184,350 for this year's model — they had a pretty good goddamned idea, didn't they?

He could just faintly make out his own reflection there in the driver's seat. A faceless blot roughly the shape of a man framed behind the windshield, all the fine details lost to the finger smears. The blurred shape looked gray, drab next to the vivid purple sheen of the car, like the life had been sucked out of him somehow.

Bled white.

Something about buying the Porsche made him realize what he had really been lacking in life, what he had always been missing.

He'd made millions plying his trade, digging up celebrity dirt, unearthing the juiciest details from autopsies and sexual harassment complaints and divorce proceedings, whipping up social media's furor over and over. Turning all that misery and scandal and controversy into stacks and stacks of cash — an exponentially growing number in his bank account.

He'd thought money had been the driving force for him all along. That the security and luxury of wealth would fulfill his every desire, every need. That a big enough number with a dollar sign in front of it could make his life make sense permanently.

And the money had been pretty great. No doubt about that. It had a way of whipping open any damn door that got in his way.

But once he'd bought the six-figure sports car in a lurid, glowing shade of enamel and found himself driving up and down the strip in it hoping to get noticed, he learned something new about himself.

He wanted to be seen. To be known. Maybe even to be loved.

Money couldn't buy that. Not now. Not ever.

He didn't think it was *credit* he wanted so much as a kind of acceptance.

As a tabloid star, a decent number of people knew his name, and a few even knew his face from all the livestreams he'd started doing. But for the most part, he was a byline that was skimmed over. People read about the stars they loved and hated, reveled in his work in the process, and nevertheless had no clue who he was.

He'd thought that the money could be the meaning, the purpose, the source of his endless joy in and of itself — like he could become Scrooge McDuck swimming in a vault of gold coins about twelve feet deep and living in some eternal bliss in the process.

Instead, as a rich man he felt more empty than before. A rudderless ship adrift in an angry, deeply uncaring sea.

But after this? After Tyler Huxley came out to L.A. and fell right in his lap?

The whole world would know Vinnie Savage. His name *and* his face. Once and for all.

The electric blue PT Cruiser wheeled into the lot. Thudded over potholes and parked three spots to the Porsche's left.

Savage took a shaky breath and climbed out of the car. Dry wind circled him as he walked the few paces to the aging Chrysler and climbed in the passenger side door.

The man in the driver's seat gave a crooked smile. Hissed out a little laugh. Eyes hidden by sunglasses that covered half his face, greasy hair hanging down to his chin in strawberry blond strands to cover another twenty percent or so of said face, blotting out most of his cheeks.

Savage knew this person only as Kav. A one-word name like Bono or Rihanna or Slash. No first or last name, though he wasn't sure which was missing.

"Hola, amigo. Any big plans for the weekend? Fourth of July is coming up."

Savage swallowed hard. Mind empty. Caught off guard.

"Uh… I mean. Not really."

Kav hissed again, his cackle morphing into a wheeze.

"I'm just fucking with you. Jesus Christ. We both know why you're here. You got the money? You sick fuck. Like I care about your long weekend or whatever the hell."

The reporter extended his hand, some wad of dollar bills palmed there. Sweaty by now. Damp.

Kav pressed his own hand into Savage's. Fingers cold and dry.

The currency left his fingers, slid somehow into Kav's like being sucked through a straw, and a hard little nub came back instead. Savage held up the little black object, saw the colored glow from the dash glint off the metal edge.

"Don't tell me what you're planning to do with that," Kav said. "I don't want to know. Believe me."

Savage looked at his own reflection in Kav's sunglasses. Then he looked back at the little object and shoved it down into his hip pocket in a rush.

Kav laughed again.

"Hey man. The heart wants what the heart wants. I ain't one to question. So long as you pay up."

Savage nodded.

"So… later."

"Yes, indeed. Later on, Vinnie, my boy. I know you'll be back."

The reporter climbed out of the PT Cruiser and back into that dry wind. Crossed the pair of empty parking spaces on legs gone numb.

He clawed open his own car door and plopped down in the Porsche's driver's seat. He felt oddly hollow as the door closed and blocked out the breathy noise outside.

And then a big rush swelled inside his skull. Endorphins. Giddiness.

He peeled the thumb drive out of his pocket. Imagined the horrors contained on that little memory stick, how many views the footage would get.

And he knew just how to play it.

Holy shit. I'm going to be fucking famous.

CHAPTER 24

Plastic crinkled as Agent Tanaka peeled open the Ziploc bag. With a gentle shake, a bundle of folded pages slid onto a metal tray. Tanaka used a pair of tweezers to unfold and separate the pages.

Darger felt a sense of déjà vu when she got her first glimpse of the top page. It was a block of jumbled capital letters. A cipher.

Underneath that, she spotted pages of handwritten text. Huxley's so-called "journal."

So he was sticking to the pattern he'd begun with his first bombing spree. A cryptic clue at one bombing site pointed them to a second location where they'd find a coded tip for the next target, plus a selection from his manifesto.

The slight annoyance Darger had felt when Loshak had been right about where they found the clue was superseded by the fact that they'd successfully found the first section of the journal and the cipher that would point them toward the next bomb. They were making headway.

Darger resisted an urge to grab the pages and start reading, but this was Tanaka's domain. She had to wait, let procedure run its course.

Tanaka took the top page with the cipher and handed it off to one of her techs.

"This needs to be photographed immediately and sent to the FBI cryptanalysis lab. Agent Loshak can tell you exactly where to email the files."

Photos were taken of the rest of the pages as well and

distributed among the task force. Darger began downloading the images on her phone so she could start reading when Loshak interrupted.

"I think we ought to take this operation back to headquarters while we wait for Agent Remzi and his team to decrypt the cipher. Otherwise, we're going to be stuck on top of this mountain with everyone else, trying to get back down to civilization on the same one-lane road."

Darger gazed around them at the sheer number of vehicles. Between the FBI, local police, the C-IED team, the state crime lab, and ATF, there were at least thirty vehicles crammed into the small parking lot next to the radio tower.

"OK. Yeah. Good idea."

"Chances are that HQ will be more centrally located, too," Rohrbach said. "For whenever we figure out the next target."

On the ride down the mountain, Darger found herself intermittently losing her internet connection, which made downloading the journal pages a frustrating endeavor. Each page was a massively high-res photograph, and she'd only managed to download two by the time they reached the gate of the private road.

She sighed, which triggered a spasm of pain in her chest. Probably about time to take more meds.

She plunged her fist into her purse, rifling around until she found the pill bottle with the tablets of ibuprofen that looked big enough for a horse. She tossed one in her mouth and grabbed for her water bottle, realizing too late that it was empty.

With some effort, she was able to swallow the pill dry. A mistake. The sensation of the giant tablet slithering down her esophagus inch by inch was far from pleasant. Its hard edges scraped all the way down, felt like a small brick. She could still feel it worming its way ever deeper into her gullet when Rohrbach suggested they stop off for food.

It was late enough that the pickings were slim. They opted for Jack in the Box. When it was Darger's turn to order, she asked for a large Coke.

"Nothing to eat?" Loshak asked.

Darger shook her head. The crawling sensation of the pill stuck halfway between her throat and her stomach was making her vaguely nauseous. That brick seemed to have slowed somehow.

"Just the drink."

The instant the cup was in her hand, she took a long drink. After several gulps, she felt the pill finally get washed all the way down.

She relaxed back into her seat, took a deep breath, and checked her phone. The last photo had finally loaded.

Darger began reading.

CHAPTER 25

I'm in L.A. now — a city with a plastic soul. Doing recon for the mission.

I'm renting this house in Hollywood tucked back from any road, way up a hill in a nest of other homes. There's a parking area some few hundred feet down the vertical face of the hill, a series of garages down by the street. And there's an elevator that takes you from the parking area to up near the house. Otherwise, you have to walk it, and it's a couple miles by way of the sidewalk path. A maze of stairways and steps leading to the various homes. The scenic route, you could say.

It's truly a strange spot. Unique. Still fairly central to the city, even despite the kind of remoteness the lack of street access gives it. Probably a multi-million-dollar property due to the land itself, too, but the house is a dump, probably should be condemned, so the rent isn't too bad.

Anyway, it will serve me well enough as a base of operations. For the next few weeks, I will get everything in order. The next chapter in my story, it will take shape here, and then it will be inflicted on an unsuspecting public.

Shock and awe.

Soon.

From the back deck, I can look down the hill and see part of the city. A slice of the urban sprawl. At night all the lights flick on down there. Neon and fast food signage and street lamps and the gleaming bright of windows that all look utterly hollow from way up here.

I look down at where all the people roam, and I can't help

but think about the bloody trail I'll cut through it all.

Slicing, ripping, gashing.

There's just something about plastic explosives. Hell, what could be better suited for that city with a plastic soul?

☾

Out of sleeping pills. I hadn't planned for this. My hookups, of course, are many miles from here. Not like I can go get a prescription, being one of America's Most Wanted or whatever the hell.

My face might not be so recognizable these days, but I don't want to chance getting someone's full attention, especially a doctor. They're more observant than most, I think.

No. Better to keep my distance.

I could probably order what I need from some kind of online black market pharmacy or something like that, but it'd take time to get here, and it, too, may put me on someone's radar, even if it's not too likely.

Shit. I think I have to rough it. Sleep won't come easy. But I'm so close to the end of the journey now, the end of the road. Maybe it's just as well.

What does it say about that world we've made that so many millions, me included, need pills to sleep at night?

☾

Traditionally, when something goes wrong in a factory farm of the poultry variety, when disease spreads through the flock, they smother all the birds simultaneously.

Sometimes they do it with foam, sometimes by pumping the building full of carbon dioxide. An egg farm fearful of avian flu infection recently roasted 5.3 million chickens alive to cull the disease.

Mindless violence. Brutality. Handed down by society's ultimate parasites — the rich who only look to suck all the wealth they can out of everything around them.

And what about you?

Wouldn't the corporate ticks love nothing more than to sink their heads into your flesh until their bodies were plump with your blood? Until they suck you dry? Wouldn't these companies happily roast you alive if there was a profit to be made in it?

Can't you see?

Don't you get it yet?

The whole world is a factory farm. Funneling the people down the chute to the killing floor. Grinding the bodies up.

A great rending machine. Squeezing out every last drop of oil.

Sucking. Slurping. Drinking greedily. Drinking deep.

What good are people if those in power can't get something out of them?

They use you. Spend you. Put your bodies on the gears, on the cogs. You keep the machine running.

Hitler wanted to turn the earth into a prison planet. That was his ultimate vision. Everyone made his slave. Crushed under his boot.

Where does that desire come from? Not to live a peaceful life in pursuit of one's desires but to enslave the entire world.

And why is the evidence of that everywhere? All around us. Crushing us under tank treads and locking us in cages and channeling us into dead-end jobs just the same way they channeled us into schools as kids.

Celebrity Skin

Power. The ultimate corrosive force. The one ring, stronger than the rest, a poison thing that warps all those who come near it. Corrupts absolutely.

Hitler's prison planet is the final expression of what power is, how it works. The logical conclusion.

Because exerting control over someone else only becomes power if those controlled are not willing participants. That's the trick. It becomes power when that boundary is crossed, when consent is withheld.

So it ultimately has to be a prison, and it has to be everyone. That is total power. That is the end point.

And terror is the fuel that keeps the power going. Fear is inextricable from dominance, the other side of the coin.

That is their primary tool. They tell us what to be scared of, to vote out of our fears, bombard us with it.

The concentration camps were an awful lot like factory farms, were they not? Herds of human beings huddled in tight spaces. Fed next to nothing. Then filed away to gruesome death.

Every condition dialed in as though to maximize suffering. Efficient in creating misery.

That's what our culture produces, what it has always produced.

Is something wrong with me that I want to blow it to pieces? Watch it fall?

Or is something wrong with you — with all of you — for walking into the prison of your own free will? For growing so desensitized you see it as normal?

School shootings every few days? Normal.

Opioid overdoses in the thousands? Normal.

Homeless people sleeping on slabs of cardboard laid out on

concrete? Normal.

15,000 murders a year? Normal.

Living under the threat of nuclear missiles flying out of Russia at any second? Normal.

Perfectly normal, perfectly healthy.

And I'm supposed to be the crazy one?

Does what I do invoke the same terror as those I oppose? Of course it does.

You can only fight fire with fire. Strength is the only language the people in power understand.

You don't reason with a bully. You throw him on the ground and kick him in the fucking teeth until he stops moving. You make him know, by sheer force of violence, that if he comes back, he'll get it worse next time. You change the power dynamic permanently.

Because if all they know is strength and weakness, one of you has to live in fear. Him or you. You write it with your fists, with your kicks. Scrawl it in purple marks, broken bones, shattered teeth.

I dare to fight back, and now the whole world wants to crucify me? So be it.

Nail me up.

Power is not optional. Someone possesses it and someone else doesn't.

And we can never get away from it. Not entirely.

Even when we rip the parasite free from our flesh, the head of the tick remains under our skin. Burrowed. A sucking tube with little notches that prevent it from being pulled free. A dark hard speck inside of us that slowly infects the blood, turns it sour.

This is what rules the earth.

Parasites. Restless creeping things. All around us.
They never sleep. Never rest.
Always out for blood.
Yes. Yes.
Fire.
You kill a tick with fire. It's the only way.

☾

I haven't slept in a week. I think at some point, you get used to it, mostly. The insomnia. Mentally, you get used to it. Your thoughts move slower, almost like they get snagged sometimes and then catch up a few seconds later. Like a laggy spot in a streaming video.

My eyes sting most of the time, though. Gritty and glassy. They can't get used to the lack of sleep, it seems.

But my mind burns so bright now. A filament in there I can never turn off, glowing white hot. Hissing and spitting and kicking off heat and dreams. Blinding.

There is a low-level depression to this walking dead state — while part of my mind burns brighter than ever, the dimmer switch of joy has been turned down in my skull. Just a brown flickery light left as the max pleasure I can feel, the bulb guttering to nothing and bobbing back like a candle flame in the wind.

I've experienced it before. Learned to grow sensitive to it. So much so that I don't really feel it as a negative. Just a different state.

It's only been after I finally get sleep that the depth of this altered state comes clear. All those neurotransmitters finally being replenished, the brightness and alertness returning to a shocking full force. It makes me go, "Oh, *this* is what normal feels like."

Sometimes I wonder if one of these times, I won't get back there, if I will get stuck in the zombie mode. Would a walking corpse be able to carry out the plan?

I don't know.

Maybe it won't matter for long.

☾

You're at war.

Whether you like it or not.

War.

It's already here.

CHAPTER 26

I've been in L.A. for ten days now. Driving everywhere in a beat-up car.

The sun shines down all the time here, it seems like. Bathes the concrete in lemon yellow light in the morning. Paints everything in pale shades — mutes the fast food signs and the foliage in the hills and the bright enamel of the cars.

It all looks washed out like something in an old movie. The color all sucked out so it appears bloodless. Ashen. Almost veering toward those sepia tones in ancient photographs.

But the daylight slowly goes orange over the course of the day, all those bleached colors growing saturated and rich as the natural light morphs in the sky. Deep reds and greens shine out of the once-faded setting. Vividness leaping to life as the sun goes down. High contrast.

Pedestrians mob the streets out on Hollywood Boulevard. I drive back and forth and watch all the people passing by. And I see little snippets of their lives, the expressions on their faces, the light shining out of their eyes, and I try to make sense of all those meaningless shards, though I know I can't.

It's a little Disney-ish during the day, if I'm being honest. Touristy and plastic, you know? The bums dressed as superheroes are, ironically, the only blot against the wholesomeness, I think. Poverty flecking the shiny veneer like rust spots in the paint job. The homeless Avengers pose for pictures to get their little slice of the tourist trade.

But after dark, you can kind of see what the city used to be, what it wants to be.

Seedy. Dangerous.

Something frantic and feral gnawing under the surface of all those faces. Wary, too.

Restless and full of dread about the violence lurking around every corner and maybe not even unhappy about it.

A city that lives for that adrenaline rush that only fear can provide. The real thing.

Maybe it's better that way. Better than being bored.

The animals creep out in the dark, and the silhouettes all look different in the shadowy places that the streetlights just barely touch. No more doughy tourist bods. No more fanny packs jutting out from pot bellies and love handles.

At night, you can see all the hard edges, the angular physiques. Lean. Hungry. Something aggressive in their postures, in the sway of their gaits.

Stalking figures that make you want to turn the other way. Militant. Scary.

All that Disneyland shit is long gone after dark. Even the superheroes go into hiding.

The shadows come out and try to swallow the city whole.

☾

We all choose what we worship. We all choose how we spend our lives, spend ourselves.

We dedicate our beings to a time and a place, to an activity. Whether it's working, golfing, whatever.

Sleeping. Waking. Producing and consuming.

We serve something. Even if we do it without much thought, without much care, we all serve something.

You don't get the time back. You spend it, one way or another, for better or worse. You spend it, and then it's gone.

So what do you worship?

Who do you serve?

How will your life be spent?

Do you care at all?

These are only the most important decisions you will ever make.

Do you even give a fuck?

☾

I sit alone in a ramshackle house in Hollywood. Floors stripped to bare subfloor in much of the building. Holes punched in the drywall in every room, the wounds ranging from finger-sized to bowling ball-sized and everything in between, a few of the roughed spots crudely spackled over — the uneven white somehow reminding me of a tooth with a cheap filling.

It looks like someone went at the wall in the bathroom with a pick axe. Tiles split and splintered. Walls opened wide enough that you can see the studs. Probably trying to rip out the copper pipes there, though they seemingly gave up just shy of the finish line on that.

But I sit at a dining table and work on my craft. Huddled over explosive devices day and night. Wiring in the dark. Soldering in the light.

Chasing a dream can be a lonely existence. Even someone like me can feel that.

And I wonder: do all our dreams carry us away from each other? Pull us apart from everyone? Does striving for greatness require us to be so obsessive as to become singular in all parts of our lives?

Separate.

Lonesome.

I can walk out on the deck and see the Hollywood Bowl in the distance — some outdoor venue where the crowd congregates, where some music act plays just beyond what I can see. Thousands of people. Acting out that ritual of holding up their lighters like torches during the ballads toward the end of the set, the little orange triangles flickering in the dark emptiness just above the mob.

It feels weird to see so many people just down the hill.

So close and so far away.

☾

My eyes burn all the time now. Sand gritting behind my eyelids. Tiny grains. Scritching at the soft flesh. Tearing and stinging and itching. The whites gone bloody red. Snaking vessels leading from the irises back into the sockets, red streaks trailing back into my skull.

Everything comes with a price, I guess.

The plan will cost me everything. I know that now.

I push myself. Spend myself. Express myself, my being, my life so completely.

But is there joy in it?

No. None.

Only emptiness. Pain. Loneliness. Doubt.

It feels, sometimes, like no one else is even really here. The planet is teeming with humanity, people flooding city streets, on foot on the sidewalk and in the cars racing endlessly past, but they live a distracted life.

They flit around without purpose. Something half-assed about everything they say, think, do. Shallow. Convenient.

Fast food people in a fast food world.

No one sees what I see, feels what I feel. They're only

halfway here, halfway real.

There is distance between us. Between me and everyone. Cold space. Hollow.

And whatever I do, that distance will remain.

☾

You are a part of this world.

You are.

You can't nope out of responsibility for what is happening here. There are no sidelines to sit on.

You are here. You are living here. All that happens, happens on your watch.

One way or another, someone wields power, exerts control, shapes the world as we know it. And when they lead us to ruin, it's up to us, all of us, to step in and set things right. It's up to us to change it.

They have made a world where the suffering is endless.

Violence. Hunger. Despair.

These are the idols we worship. We build altars to them in the factory farms, in the homeless shelters, in the morgues where we lay out the daily sacrifices to these dark gods. The death cult in power demands it.

Suicide. Overdoses. School shootings. Homelessness. All occurring in record number.

Meanwhile we kill billions of animals in slaughterhouses built just like concentration camps. Our landfills become mass graves of chicken carcasses.

This is the legacy we will leave behind. A fossil record of chicken skeletons in the billions. I read about this idea, I can't remember where, but in thousands of years, will those who excavate our buried history think birds were the dominant species here? Or will they see us for who we really were?

And all the while those dark gods demand more sacrifice. More suffering. More death.

That is what our culture produces. That is what we exalt.

Day in and day out, the suffering grows, compounds like interest. The machine demands more bodies, animal and human alike, to consume, to render, to grind up into gristle and bone.

The misery only intensifies, and those dark gods are exuberant. Their shadows swell to consume the globe.

So what do you do?

What do I do?

You are part of it. You can't sit and do nothing.

In dark times, the light shines the brightest. It fights off the gloom, beats back the dark forces, lays bare the truth.

And what light shines brighter than flame?

CHAPTER 27

Darger paced around the fourth-floor conference room, rereading Huxley's journal pages for a third time. The bomber's words seemed to worm into her head and spread an iciness over her, which surprised her.

There was anger in these pages. Fury. Graphic threats of violence on a mass scale. Fantasies of the same. But somehow the forlorn feeling in Huxley's lonely passages affected her more — the melancholy crawled right under her skin and stayed there.

A passage flitted through her mind, interrupting her reading. Huxley's voice speaking in her head. Uninvited.

There is distance between us. Between me and everyone. Cold space. Hollow.

And whatever I do, that distance will remain.

She blinked and another quote came to her.

It feels weird to see so many people just down the hill.

So close and so far away.

She closed her eyes. Tried to clear her mind. Tried to make the bomber's voice stop.

But it didn't.

In dark times, the light shines the brightest. It fights off the gloom, beats back the dark forces, lays bare the truth.

And what light shines brighter than flame?

Darger thought about what might come of these pages, how law enforcement might turn the information here to their advantage. They had units up in the hills now, trying to pin down the location of the rental home Huxley had described.

Rohrbach had known what neighborhood he'd been talking about immediately.

Her gut didn't trust that anything would come of it, though. Oh, they might find the house he'd been staying in, but he had a fairly precise timeline for when these pages would be found, and he'd clear out well in advance. She was sure of it. Huxley was many things, but a fool wasn't one of them.

"Whoa, check it out!" Fitch pointed at a stack of bakery boxes. "Cupcakes!"

Darger's stomach gurgled. Taking the ibuprofen on an empty stomach had been a mistake. Her belly felt sour and acidic now, which only made the idea of eating sound worse than it had when she'd had the pill lodged in her throat.

"Hey, there's a note here. Says, 'To Darger, Loshak, and the rest of your team. I stopped in to say hi, but you were out. Hope these will keep you going through the night. Best of luck with your investigation, Casey Luck.'" Fitch flipped open the lid of the top box. "I don't know who this Luck guy is, but I like the cut of his jib."

"A real mensch," Loshak said.

Fitch selected a cupcake and offered Darger the box. She shook her head.

"No, thanks."

"You sure about that?" Fitch asked. "These are gonna go fast once the rest of the crew gets back. It'll be like piranhas in a feeding frenzy. You'll be lucky to get even a crumb."

"I'm good."

"OK, but I'd like it on the record that I think you're making a big mistake," Fitch said.

He extended the box to Loshak, who took some time to study the contents.

"Hmm… red velvet or— Oh! Is that lemon?"

Darger went back to reading, trying to ignore the burning sensation in her gut. In the background, she could hear the others smacking their lips and licking their fingers.

"I think the frosting is cream cheese with lemon zest. Delightful."

"Fuckin' tasty," Fitch said.

Darger focused on the words in front of her, blocking out the chatter. And then a half-eaten cupcake appeared in her peripheral vision.

"You gotta try this," Loshak said. "Just a bite."

She recoiled.

"No."

"Come on. I know you haven't eaten anything since the little bag of pretzels on the plane."

She got a whiff of the sugary lemon smell. Under normal circumstances, she was sure it would make her mouth water, but just now, it sent a wave of nausea rippling through her.

"Get that thing out of my face."

Loshak frowned and looked almost hurt.

"Sorry," she said, feeling like a dick. "My stomach is—"

Her words were interrupted by a clatter of footsteps in the hallway.

Detective Rohrbach raced in, phone held high like an Olympic torch. His mouth twitched into a grin.

"The feds just cracked the cipher."

CHAPTER 28

Greetings from Hell.

Every comeback should start with a bang.

Lights. Camera. Action.

Ka-BOOM!

I hope the reviews are kind. I suspect the critics will be blown away. Such excitement.

We're just getting started, though. And the best is yet to come.

Here's the big-budget sequel. Huxley takes Los Angeles.

God, I'd love to erase the whole vapid city from the map. Cleansing fire to burn it to the ground. Or biblical floods to gush down the city streets, to wash it all away.

At least in NY we have the decency to acknowledge our dark side. We embrace the filth, because everyone knows you're only ever a few steps away from the gutter.

But this place? They dress it up.

Fake teeth, fake lashes, fake tits.

Voila! The metamorphosis is complete. A junkie whore dressed up in couture.

But the glossy facade can't hide the blood on the city's teeth. All the thousands this place has chewed up and spit out. The fallen stars. The washed-up has-beens. The bums sleeping on the streets.

Welcome to Los Angeles, where dreams go to die.

No one cares about the little guy. No one cares when a bug gets crushed.

If you want the attention of the world, you have to kill one of the pretty people, one of the celebrities. So be it.

I came back for a reason. My work here isn't done, and I mean to do whatever it takes.

The stakes couldn't be higher. It's always darkest before dawn.

And the degree of difficulty ratchets up this time. You'll have to be sharp to save them.

Who will live, and who will die? I suppose it's all up to you.

When Darger finished transcribing the note from her phone to the whiteboard, she took a few steps back and gazed upon Huxley's message.

"'Fake teeth, fake lashes, fake tits,'" Fitch read. "That hardly narrows down the potential victim pool. I'd say it describes just about half of the city's female population. Maybe more."

But it was a different line altogether that caught her eye.

The stakes couldn't be higher. It's always darkest before dawn.

She drew an invisible line underneath it with her finger.

"This line? He used it last time, except it was 'always *dirkest* before dawn' because the target was Dirk Nielsen."

"You think he's targeting Nielsen again?" Fitch asked.

Darger's face scrunched up, like she'd caught a whiff of something unpleasant.

"Maybe, but it almost seems…"

"Too obvious," Loshak finished. "Too easy. And I'd expect there to be more here to point us that way. Last time he included Nielsen's catchphrase."

"Didn't he, uh… include instructions for disabling the bombs before?" Rohrbach said.

The room held quiet for a few breaths. Processing.

"'The degree of difficulty ratchets up this time,'" Darger quoted the clue. "I guess he's not going to be quite as helpful as he was the first time around."

Loshak closed his eyes and shook his head. It looked like he was about to say something.

But Rohrbach's phone rang, interrupting. The detective picked up after a cursory glance at the screen.

"Hey, Chief."

Darger could only hear Rohrbach's end of the call, but it was enough to pique her interest.

"They what?"

There was a pause and then, "Well, how'd they get it?"

Another pause. "Jesus. Yeah. OK."

His face was grim as he ended the call.

"What is it?" Darger asked.

"*The Daily Gawk* somehow got their hands on a video of the *Dysfunctional Family* bombing. It's online."

Wordlessly, Darger pulled up *The Daily Gawk*'s website on her phone. It didn't take long to find the video. It was featured on the front page.

She clicked the link, and the video rolled.

First, she saw an unexpected face and grit her teeth. That familiar smirk seemed a touch diminished perhaps, but the gray hair swooping back from his forehead looked just like it had earlier today.

"This is Vinnie Savage with a word from *The Daily Gawk* about the video you're about to see. The content is potentially disturbing and neither appropriate for younger viewers nor the faint of heart. We think the public has a right to such material, so we present it to be viewed at your discretion."

He probably paid top dollar for this footage. He wants to

make sure to brand himself with it, to milk every possible bit of visibility out of the tragedy.

Savage's face cut away all at once. The color palette of the video shifted from the natural sunlight streaming through the windows in Savage's office to the artificial lighting of a TV studio set.

Big Tom Malone stood center stage on the *Dysfunctional Family* set, all six-foot-six and two-hundred and thirty pounds of him looming over the living room couch in stunning HD resolution. The crystal clear image made even the faint stubble around his chin and jawline visible, and the saturated colors displayed an almost ludicrous juxtaposition between his deeply tan skin and bleached-white teeth. Beyond stark.

Though the edited video cut off the line prior, the context seemed clear enough — Malone's character had just been struck with some stunning verbal blow. Defeat flashed over his features, softened his eyes. The audience was already laughing even as he let himself plop onto the couch.

A bright flash filled the frame. And a boom popped and blew out the speakers. Distorted wind. Sounded like a stand-up comedian eating the mic, breathing right into it.

Even through the flash and the smoke, Darger could see the actor, Malone, coming apart. The violence foggy and in fast motion and somehow all the more disturbing for it.

Malone's backside burst like a struck piñata. The couch cushion exploded right up through him, a spray of his torso and haunches fanning outward from the point of impact. Impossible. Disgusting.

The cloud of black smoke filled the screen and blotted out the grisly image then. Gloomy coils enveloped the broken body, fluttered over it violently like a mess of trapped birds.

Then came the screams.

The audience moaned and shrilled and whimpered in the background. That familiar, joyous laugh track turned to something profane in a fraction of a second. Something wrong.

The smoke fluttered and fluttered. Black spirals muffled the screen for several seconds that felt like an eternity.

When the smoke finally cleared, Darger could see the carnage left behind.

A gaping hole yawed where Malone had sat down, smoke spewing from the charred pit freshly poked into the concrete. Bits of torn couch foam soaked in blood laid out around the only part of Malone Darger could see — just his tattered legs — in the foreground.

And now the stillness of the image grew eerie. Nothing moved there but the remnant of pluming smoke. All else held motionless, lifeless. That little sitcom living room paralyzed.

Somewhere off-screen, a woman just continuously screamed, louder than the rest. The raspy tone made Darger cringe — so much anguish in that voice. The screamer paused only briefly, probably to take a breath, before screaming some more.

Then the image blinked out. A smash cut to black, to silence.

The video was over.

CHAPTER 29

Darger gazed into the black screen for a few seconds. Then she sucked in a big breath, felt a strange tingle in her chest, pins and needles pricking there like her lungs had fallen asleep. She could feel the muscles in her eyelids spasming, blinking fast, somehow in time with the fear shuddering through her.

She remembered the first thought that had occurred to her after seeing the video earlier that day: *No one can ever see this.*

Her eyes landed on the view counter in the corner of the screen. Over fifty thousand views already.

Too late.

The room had gone silent around her, and it was Fitch's voice that finally broke through the dead air.

"Well," Fitch said. "Fuck."

"Yeah."

Darger's gaze flicked to the clock in the corner of her screen. It was almost ten. They'd made zero progress on the clue, and now this.

She felt slightly panicky at the thought of being trapped in another one of Tyler Huxley's perverse scavenger hunts.

Deep breath. Getting hysterical won't help anything.

Darger inhaled, her chest still quivering and prickling.

"Holy Christ," Fitch said. "Some of these comments on the video. 'Looks so fake. I can't believe you idiots are buying that this is real, lol. But I guess sheep gonna sheep.' Here's another one. 'Yawn. If you really want to see something sick, watch Man vs. Chainsaw.'"

"What's 'Man vs. Chainsaw'?" Rohrbach asked.

"A video of a guy being attacked with a chainsaw," Fitch explained. "I strongly urge you to *not* Google it. Like, seriously do not."

Darger couldn't take the gnawing feeling in her gut anymore. She'd thought that avoiding food would be the best course of action, that in time her stomach would settle, but that didn't seem to be the case. She felt worse now than before.

She walked over to the bakery boxes, where a few cupcakes still remained. She snatched up a chocolate with sprinkles and shoved it in her mouth.

"I think Darger's got the right idea," Fitch said. "We need a little help here. Something to jump-start our brains."

He stalked over to a black duffel bag at the back of the room.

Darger heard the *zzzzzzzzzz* of a zipper unzipping. Then a metallic clanking sound.

Fitch straightened, hoisting a black and green case of Monster energy drinks.

"Thankfully, I came prepared."

He set the box on the table and ripped open the side, handing out the drinks.

The other three cracked open their cans one after another, the little snicks filling the empty space and echoing. They drank.

Darger was still studying the can in her hand. She didn't like Monster on a normal day and was dubious that this would help anything, least of all her stomach.

Fitch stared her down.

"Come on, Darger. Drink up. We're gonna need that profiling gourd of yours in tip-top shape if we're gonna solve this thing."

Darger took one last look at the can.

Fuck it, she thought.

She pulled the tab and tipped her head back. Fitch chuckled and then began chanting her name as if she were doing a keg stand at a frat party.

"DAR-GER! DAR-GER! CHUG! CHUG! CHUG!"

She guzzled a third of the can before coming up for air. Already she felt the faint buzz of the caffeine and sugar entering her bloodstream. Or maybe it was just a placebo effect. Either way, it was invigorating. Fitch had been onto something, after all.

"Who's ready to solve a fucking puzzle?" she asked.

Fitch grinned and pumped his fist in the air.

"Hell yeah! Let's do this!"

CHAPTER 30

Darger peered across the room at the decoded clue scrawled on the board. She'd been staring at it so long and hard that her vision was starting to blur.

She blinked. Squeezed her eyelids shut.

From somewhere behind her, there was a familiar chime. She recognized it as Loshak's phone. It had made the same notification sound when Huxley's first note was posted online.

She craned her neck to look at her partner.

"Let me guess. The journal's up?"

"No," Loshak said, frowning down at the screen. "Worse."

Darger straightened, her mind whirring through the possible bad scenarios and landing on the worst.

"Please tell me the bomb didn't go off early."

"OK, it's bad but not *that* bad."

He held up his phone, and Darger could see *The Daily Gawk*'s letterhead.

Oh no...

"As if posting the video of the bombing wasn't bad enough, that hyena from *The Daily Gawk* just posted an open invitation to Huxley, asking him to get in touch for an exclusive interview."

He played the video, and Darger's mouth dropped open. Vinnie Savage talked into the camera again, addressing Huxley directly.

"Tyler, if there's even a chance it could help curb the violence, we want you to be able to tell your side of the story, to reach millions of people through *The Daily Gawk*. Consider this an open invitation to an interview or whatever alternative way you think best to reach the public."

He started listing the various ways Huxley could reach him.

"This is that Roger Dirtbag guy again?" Fitch asked.

"Uh… his name is Vinnie Savage," Darger said.

Fitch shrugged.

"That's exactly what I said."

"You know him?" Loshak asked, looking at Darger.

"You could say that. He was in San Francisco. At the hostage scene. I literally talked to him this morning."

"So you could ask him to take this down," Rohrbach said.

Darger winced.

"We're not on what I'd call the best of terms. He was interfering with the negotiation, and I… sort of kicked his phone… into a sewer grate."

Fitch let out a high-pitched cackle and squeezed her shoulder.

"See, now that's what's great about my gal Darger here. She does *not* fuck around."

"You could still try, even if it's a long shot," Rohrbach said. "Worst case scenario, he says no, right?"

Loshak was nodding.

"Rohrbach is right. We have no idea what might happen if someone actually gives Huxley a legitimate platform."

Darger let out a little cough.

"*The Daily Gawk* is legitimate now?"

"You know what I mean. The last thing we need is the media getting more involved than they already are."

Darger inflated her cheeks with air, then let it out in a slow stream.

"Alright. I'll try."

Savage had just listed a variety of ways Huxley might get in touch, so it was easy enough to get a message to him. She sent an email with her phone number, asking him to please call her.

It didn't take long. Darger's phone rang less than five minutes after she hit send.

"This is Darger."

"Well, well, well." Savage's voice was cloyingly glib. "We meet again."

"Hello, Vinnie."

"What can I do for you?"

"This video, the sort of open letter you posted to Tyler Huxley — I need you to take it down."

He tittered.

"I have to ask, is this how you behave in all of your day-to-day interactions? You make demands and people just... comply? I mean, with all the media attention you've received over the years, I imagined you'd be a little arrogant, but this 'ultimate authority' act borders on narcissistic."

Darger closed her eyes and pinched the bridge of her nose. He was trying to bait her. To get a reaction. Probably because there was a non-zero possibility that he was recording this call.

"I'm not demanding anything," she said steadily. "I apologize if that's how it sounded. I'm making a request. And if you want my advice, I think it's in your best interest."

He was quiet for a few seconds, and when he came back on the line his voice had gone harder.

"That almost sounds like a threat."

"You misunderstand me, then. I don't know if you've thought about the risks of what you're doing, Vinnie. Tyler Huxley specifically targets the media. *You're* the media. Posting this letter is like painting a giant bull's-eye on your back."

"Well I'm flattered, frankly, that you think I'm of the same caliber as Huxley's victims. But I'm just a guy with a camera. Anyway, I'm going to pass. On your request-slash-advice, I mean. It's a hard no. Thank you, though. It's truly touching that you're worried about little ol' me, it really is. But I can take care of myself. Goodbye."

There was a click and then silence.

The hand holding the phone fell limply to Darger's side.

"Sounds like that went well," Loshak said.

"Yeah, he basically told me to fuck off."

"So… what do we do now?" Fitch asked.

"I don't know if there's anything we *can* do," Loshak said. "It's probably too late, anyway. We know Huxley is watching the coverage of his crimes. If I had to bet, I'd say he's seen Savage's stunt already."

Something squirmed in the back of Darger's mind. A wriggling worm of precognition.

She froze. Cleared her thoughts. Let her subconscious mind do its thing.

Seconds ticked by, and it was Loshak's words that echoed back.

If I had to bet…

Betting.

Stakes.

She snapped her fingers.

"'The stakes couldn't be higher,'" Darger read. "What if it's a casino?"

Loshak sucked in a breath. Pointed to the previous line.

"'You'll have to be *sharp* to save them.' That's a gambling term. A sharp is basically a professional sports bettor." He rubbed his hands together. "I think we might be onto something."

"What about—" Rohrbach started, then stopped himself. "Never mind."

"What?"

"Nah, forget it."

"Sometimes the best ideas are the ones that seem stupid at first," Loshak said. "Your right brain is faster at problem-solving than your left brain, but it doesn't always have the reasoning ability to say why. And without a 'why,' your left brain wants to tell you all the ways it's wrong. So humor us."

"It's just the line, 'The best is yet to come.'" Rohrbach explained. "It's a song title. An old Frank Sinatra number. And I was thinking that he's kind of associated with the casino lifestyle, right? But I always think of him as more Vegas than Hollywood."

Loshak shook his head.

"No way. I'd say Sinatra is equal parts Hollywood and Vegas."

"OK, so how many casinos are there in the immediate area?" Darger asked.

"Half a dozen, at least," Rohrbach said.

"There must be something else here that will help us narrow it down," Loshak said. "Are any of the casinos owned by anyone famous?"

Rohrbach cupped his chin in his hand, thinking.

"Larry Flynt owned Hustler Casino and The Lucky Lady. But he's dead."

A pensive quiet settled over the room. Darger read the lines again, parsing each word.

It was Rohrbach who broke the silence.

"Wait a minute…"

"Yeah?"

"Well, maybe ten years ago, there was this actress who died at the Beachside Resort & Casino. She fell from a balcony on the top floor of the hotel. Shit… what was her name…" He clicked his tongue a few times and then held his finger in the air. "Melanie Lawson! That was it. Anyway, she was married to Erik Manuel, the CEO of the resort. He's kind of a big shot around town. Always canoodling with celebrities, walking red carpets and whatnot."

"Hey, I remember this," Fitch said, bobbing his head up and down. "It was headline news in the tabloids because her death was ruled an accident, but there was all this talk of her husband's many affairs and money troubles, which led to speculation that her death could have been suicide or even murder. Life insurance or something."

"Right. Manuel ended up suing a couple of the newspapers for some of the so-called rumors they printed. Don't remember if he won or if they settled out of court or what. Anyway, I'm thinking that maybe 'fallen stars' could be a reference to the Lawson death."

"So we're thinking Manuel is the target?" Loshak asked.

Rohrbach shook his head.

"Not him. His fiancée. She lives in a penthouse in the hotel."

"Another actress?"

"Brazilian supermodel. And there's something else."

Rohrbach stepped up to the whiteboard and jabbed his finger at one of the lines.

It's always darkest before dawn.

"Her name is Dawn. Dawn Barboza."

CHAPTER 31

Outside, it smelled like ozone and salt, and the lights of the city glittered on wet asphalt. It must have rained at some point while they were inside working the clue.

Fitch hopped into the CIRG van that was ready and waiting near the door. Two squad cars pulled up to lead their caravan, lights already flashing.

"We're right behind you," Rohrbach said, pointing at his vehicle parked at the curb.

"See you over there," Fitch said and pulled the van door shut.

They closed in on Rohrbach's car and climbed in. Darger barely had time to shut her door before they were lurching forward. Plunging down a Los Angeles boulevard like a bowling ball barreling down the lane.

Rohrbach drove with one hand on the wheel and the other clutching his radio, coordinating with dispatch as they rushed down the darkened streets.

"Find the closest fire station to the resort. Get them on the horn and have them start evacuating the building ASAP."

The deep voice of a dispatcher responded, bassy enough to make the Camry's speakers rattle faintly.

"We're talking with LAFD now. Crews from Station 23 and Station 69 are already en route."

Neon lights glowed in the windows of bars and clubs and restaurants, casting pinks and blues and yellows on the shimmering sidewalk. Something about the glowing scene looked nautical just now, like the streetside was underwater.

Fitch's voice came over the radio.

"My GPS says our ETA is seventeen minutes. It's going to be a tight one — again — but I think it's doable."

Rohrbach brought his radio to his lips.

"We have units from LAPD and LAFD converging on the scene as we speak. They'll initiate the evacuation protocol and hopefully have the place cleared, or close to it, by the time we arrive."

"Roger that."

They merged onto the freeway, and for a moment, Darger spotted the skyscrapers mostly gone dark along the horizon. Giant towers of steel and glass. They glimmered golden in the daylight, all warm notes, but at night they looked cold. Like great castles made of ice.

With the road open in front of them, the Camry built speed rapidly. The dotted line in the middle of the highway flicked past. Something about the image and the speed reminded Darger of the Millennium Falcon performing a hyperjump, all those stars smearing past on the windshield when Han or Chewy punched it.

And then, just like that, they were spiraling onto an exit ramp. Descending that curved lane back into the city. Leaving the freeway behind.

Exiting the freeway, they passed into a residential neighborhood with bungalows packed tightly together. Darger thought about how weird it was that much of L.A. was comprised of single-family homes. Totally unlike most other urban centers where big apartment buildings were the norm. But this city was just an endless sprawl of houses outside a few scattered "downtown" areas.

And even after dark, there were people out and about.

Gathered on corners. Lounging on porches. Smoking outside of bars or convenience stores or on their front stoops.

Too many people. With a population density of something like 8,000 people per square mile, it was a natural choice for someone like Huxley. Maximum potential victims. Maximum damage.

Darger pressed her fists into her thighs and prayed they'd evacuate the casino and hotel in time.

CHAPTER 32

The lights on the casino twinkled in the dark, visible from some distance away. Darger thought back to the neon signs they'd passed earlier. This was like that on steroids.

"He's going bigger this time. More public. Maybe bigger bombs. More..." Loshak trailed off, staring out at the flickering lights on the building.

"More victims," Darger said.

Loshak didn't adjust his gaze to meet her eyes. Only nodded.

The street leading to the casino was barricaded, with fire engines, tape, and orange and white reflective sawhorses blocking the way. Rohrbach pulled to the curb about a block and a half away, and they got out.

The crowd of casino and hotel guests streamed past, being directed to "keep moving" by a handful of uniforms scattered along the evacuation route. Despite these commands, some people slowed or stopped, phones out and focused on the shifting mob and then at the upper floors of the building.

Darger looked at the glowing phone screens for a second, small rectangles of brightness shining in the dark, before the meaning occurred to her. She pointed.

"They're focused up high... like they know the penthouse is the target."

Loshak sighed and pulled out his own phone, finger already scrolling and swiping as he walked.

"Probably the internet ghouls solved the clue. Again."

They found a gap between two sawhorse barriers and sidled

through. Darger caught a whiff of cigarette smoke as they passed one of the SWAT teams milling about outside of their armored truck.

Loshak made a clicking noise out of the side of his mouth and nodded to himself. The rectangular reflection of his phone screen glowed in each of his eyes.

"Yep. They solved it alright. The fallen star bit. The casino hints. They got it all."

Rohrbach led the way up to the entrance, which was flanked by a planting of red aloe vera and blue agave. The scattered palm trees were individually lit by colored spotlights.

A current of people still flowed out of the building, and Darger felt like a salmon struggling upstream. She wove around hotel guests in silk pajamas and women in cocktail dresses. Then there was a high-pitched whistle and someone called her name.

It was Fitch. He was standing at an inconspicuous side door which was propped open with his foot.

"Over here."

Their group veered away from the torrent of people exiting the building and ran toward that glowing wedge of exposed doorway. Darger felt a little better as soon as she got away from the crowd, but then she remembered what they were up against and her gut clenched like a fist.

A bomb. A bomb hidden somewhere inside the very building we're walking into. A bomb that will blow in a little over an hour if we don't find and disarm it first.

She shivered a little at the thought, but she kept moving.

The door Fitch ushered them through led into a stark hallway lined with empty luggage trolleys. A few dark marks smeared the walls where the trolleys had bumped into them.

Some kind of side entrance for employees only, apparently. None of the glitz of the main lobby here.

"This is Arnaldo Pacheco, security director for the Beachside," Fitch said, gesturing at a heavily muscled man wearing an expensive-looking suit and a wireless earpiece.

Pacheco stepped forward and shook hands with everyone.

"If you follow me, I can take you down to our control room."

With Pacheco in the lead, they proceeded down the corridor and through a set of double doors into the lobby. A cavernous space opened before them with gleaming marble floors and soaring ceilings held up by stonework pillars. A massive blown glass chandelier formed the centerpiece of the room, with thousands of iridescent spheres hanging from it on invisible strands. It gave the impression that a cloud of bubbles was hovering overhead.

The last of the guests had finally made it outside, and the vast space felt eerie in its emptiness. Every footstep, every sigh and clearing of the throat, echoed throughout the chamber. Coupled with the artificial chill courtesy of the air-conditioning, it felt like walking through a brightly lit tomb.

It didn't smell like a tomb or even a cave, though, Darger thought, giving a sniff. It smelled like… well, it smelled like the beach. Sunny and salty and fresh, with just a hint of coconut.

She remembered that many casinos and high-end resorts hired companies to create one-of-a-kind scents to pipe into the ventilation systems. Just another way to titillate the tourists, to sell them the dream.

They crossed to the main casino pit, and the floor transitioned to carpet in a bold art deco pattern of red, gold, and purple. An old Vegas theme rose up to dominate here, very retro compared to the modern-looking lobby. The whole room glowed with the amber light streaming from a dozen mid-century-style globes with a gold sunburst design.

Clusters of slot machines strobed and beeped out endless gibberish. Burbles and tinkles and whoops. Each grouping had some sort of motif with sounds to match.

One batch of patriotic machines had an ear-piercing "screeching eagle" sound effect layered over a music box version of "Battle Hymn of the Republic."

Another group of machines sported logos that read "Gods of Fortune" and appeared to be decorated with images of vaguely Norse-looking gods. These machines had a flashing lightning effect followed a beat later by a rumble of thunder.

Adding to the digital cacophony was the music being piped in overhead. A mix of bland Top 40 hits, with many of the songs fitting the gambling theme. "Poker Face" by Lady Gaga was shifting to "The Winner Takes It All" by ABBA now. Darger could imagine "The Gambler" by Kenny Rogers got very heavy rotation here, though she personally was more of a "Just Dropped In (To See What Condition My Condition Was In)" fan as far as Kenny went.

Loshak leaned in as they walked.

"You ever read that Ray Bradbury story, 'There Will Come Soft Rains'?"

"Is that the one about the guys who crash on a planet where it never stops raining, and it drives them all insane?" Darger asked.

"No. That's 'The Long Rain.' 'There Will Come Soft Rains' is about this futuristic, automated house," Loshak went on, his eyes traversing the space around them. "All the household tasks are computerized. It cooks breakfast. Washes the dishes. Makes the beds. Even recites poetry for the residents. Except that the residents are dead. Everyone's dead. It's post-nuclear war, everything is destroyed, except for this one house. And it just keeps mindlessly going on, as if everyone is still alive."

Darger was already nodding, understanding exactly why this story would have occurred to him just now.

"There's something very unsettling about an empty casino."

Darger had never been in an empty casino before, and she realized how much ambient noise the people added. Without the ambient noise of people — voices babbling, coughing, laughing — the gaming floor felt even more artificial than usual. A weird empty spaceship of blinking lights and bleeping machines.

They kept going, past the semicircular swaths of green felt of the blackjack tables, past a smaller set of oval poker and craps tables, past the roulette wheels.

At the back of the room, Pacheco used a key card to unlock a door partially concealed by an array of potted bird of paradise plants. Beyond the door was another unassuming corridor. Clearly another "employee-only" area.

There was an elevator at one end. Pacheco pressed a button on the wall and the stainless steel doors slid open.

They stepped inside, and the doors whooshed shut.

Darger's stomach lurched faintly as they began their descent. She took a breath and checked her phone.

They had 58 minutes until midnight.

CHAPTER 33

For the first few seconds, no one spoke as they rode the elevator down into the bowels of the casino. Then Loshak piped up.

"How often do you catch card counters?" he asked.

Pacheco raised his eyebrows.

"Depends on what you mean by 'catch.' We get plenty of people who *think* they can count cards. They read a book or watch a tutorial online and know the very basic principles, which they mistakenly believe gives them an edge. The thing is, even if a player manages to net a profit at the table, by the time you factor in food, drinks, tips, a room, we've usually come out ahead. So we're actually quite fond of your average self-proclaimed 'card counter.' The guys who can actually do it and have the bankroll to really cause some damage? They're exceedingly rare. In fact, I can only think of one in my twenty-two years on the job."

The elevator came to a stop, and the doors parted. Unlike the ultra-modern lobby and glitzy gaming floor, the basement of the casino was pure utility. Commercial vinyl flooring, beige walls, gray steel doors, buzzing fluorescent lights.

Pacheco kept talking as they disembarked from the metal box.

"On a day-to-day basis, most of the security incidents we handle are of the more mundane variety. People who have had too much to drink. People getting pissed off about losing. People who think being in a casino means they can act like zoo animals. Then there are the deaths. Several times a year, we have a retiree from Iowa or Indiana who just drops dead in front of a slot machine. Heart attack, usually."

"That sounds like it'd be bad for business," Rohrbach said.

"You'd think so, but I'd say 90% of the guests barely bat an eye. Just keep on churning through their chips as if there isn't a corpse a few feet away."

They came to a door at the end of a long corridor with a sign that read, "Security." Pacheco scanned his key card again to unlock the door. Within the security wing, he used his card one last time to access the control room.

Inside, a dozen workstations were arranged in two rows, about half of them still occupied. Each desk had three monitors on swivel arms showing various feeds from inside the casino. The walls beyond held a further thirty or so screens with additional camera angles.

There were various cameras showing the casino floor, the surfaces of the gaming tables, the cashier cages. Another set showed the lobby, the elevators, the floors of the hotel. The cameras focused on the parking lot showed it was emptying steadily, headlights sweeping toward the camera on one screen, a line of taillights trailing away on another.

Darger studied the screens. High-definition. Full color. Crisp. Not the average grainy surveillance footage they were often forced to work with.

Fitch whistled.

"This is quite the set-up."

"We redesigned the whole control room a few years back," Pacheco said, and Darger heard the unmistakable lilt of pride in his voice. "State of the art. Spent about three million dollars on it, but we wanted the best."

He gestured at the wall of screens.

"We've got about 2,100 cameras, all backed up to both DVR

and the cloud. Biometric software to identify players on the banned persons or self-exclusion list."

"Self-exclusion list?" Darger asked.

"People who have problems setting limits for themselves can voluntarily request that we ban them from the premises."

"So… gambling addicts," Rohrbach said.

Pacheco displayed a forced smile.

"We try to avoid using that term, but… essentially, yes."

"What happens if someone on the list tries to sneak in?" Fitch asked.

"They are escorted off the premises and reminded that they are trespassing. We take self-exclusion very seriously."

A tiny woman with dyed black hair and a thick band of eyeliner around her eyes got up from her work station and approached Pacheco.

"I think I have something you should see," she said.

Pacheco nodded.

"Show us what you've got, Lucy."

She led their group over to her workstation, scrambled into her swivel chair, and hit play on a video she had cued up in advance.

The video showed an elevator bay somewhere in the hotel. After a few seconds, a man appeared on-screen in a brown uniform and baseball hat carrying a cardboard box.

"As you can see, there was a delivery to the penthouse at 6:06 P.M.," she said. "He came in through the main lobby and then used the private elevator."

Pacheco's face was grim.

"So he had a key card for the penthouse elevator."

"No," Lucy said.

"That doesn't make any sense. How else could he get up to

the penthouse?" Pacheco demanded. "It can only be accessed with a key card."

"You'll see."

Pacheco made a little noise, clearly annoyed at having to wait.

The man stepped into the elevator, and Lucy switched to the feed from inside.

The elevator camera was angled toward the door, and Darger leaned in, hoping for a better look at the man's face as he entered.

Unfortunately, his hat was pulled down so low on his brow that the brim threw a deep shadow over his eyes and nose. What the hat couldn't hide was the faint smile curling at the corners of his lips.

I know that smirk, Darger thought, *even if the face around it has changed.*

Tyler Huxley had clearly found some way to alter his appearance, but the curve of his lip was the same, as if even a surgeon's scalpel couldn't remove his innate smugness.

Huxley stepped to the call buttons, thrust his free hand into his pocket, and then inserted something into the control panel.

"What was that? What did he just do?" Pacheco asked.

Fitch whistled.

"Oh shit. I think our boy's got himself a K-01 key."

"A what?" Darger asked.

"It's a universal elevator key. Gives access to all floors, even restricted ones. The keys are supposed to be exclusively for the fire department and emergency services, but if someone wanted one badly enough, I'm sure they could find one on the black market."

"He might not even need to do that," Loshak said, shaking

his head. "The last time I needed a key cut, the locksmith had me text him a photograph of the key I wanted copied. All you'd need to get your very own universal key is a high-res photo of one. Hell, seems like the kind of thing you might even be able to 3D print these days."

"Fucking technology," Pacheco muttered.

"There's something else," Fitch said, and Darger didn't like the note of concern in his voice.

"What?"

Fitch pointed at the cardboard box on the screen.

"Look at the way he's handling the package. Straining a little, right?"

He shook his head.

"Whatever's inside that box is bigger — and I mean significantly bigger — than anything he's made before."

CHAPTER 34

Darger blinked. Tried to process the new information.

Huxley's new device looks to be bigger. Significantly bigger.

That makes sense. Fits the profile. He'd want, above all else, to raise the stakes, to heighten the spectacle.

But we cleared the building. At least there's that.

Her eyes flicked over the other security monitors around the room, all of the screens strangely empty now that the building had been evacuated. There was something ghostly about all those vacant rooms, cameras peering into blank spaces, watching nothing. Utter stillness. She couldn't help but wait for the jump scare to arrive, for something horrific to lurch into the frame on one of those monitors, but nothing happened.

I watch too many horror movies.

While the rest of them were left to digest this new revelation, Fitch wasted no time springing into action.

He unclipped his radio from his belt.

"Lasko, this is Fitch."

"What do you need, boss?"

"What's our current evac distance?"

"We're at, oh… about fourteen hundred feet."

"OK. Well, it's looking like we've got potential for a 50-pounder, something like that. We need to move the evac zone back another 500 feet or so."

"I'm on it."

Fitch nodded to himself and spoke into the radio again.

"Where's Marsh?"

Another voice crackled out of the speaker.

"I'm here, boss."

"Get suited up, if you're not already," Fitch said. "You're heading up to the penthouse."

"Heard."

Back on the screen, the elevator doors peeled open again, letting in bright sunlight from a windowed hallway. Huxley stepped forward and walked out of the frame.

Lucy switched feeds, this time to a camera in the antechamber outside the penthouse suite. There was a small velvet sofa in navy blue and a console table with a vase of tulips. Huxley stopped at the door, lowered the box to the ground, and pulled something from inside his shirt.

The object looked like a large sheet of paper, but it was stiffer and slightly translucent. The bomber got down on one knee and slid the sheet under the bottom of the door. He then wiggled the sheet around the corner until it was between the door and the frame, guiding it upward with a back-and-forth sawing motion. When he reached the height of the door level, he gave the sheet a little jiggle and a downward tug, and the door popped open.

Pacheco's jaw dropped.

"That's not possible. Our locks are supposed to be shim-proof."

"He didn't shim it. Look."

Lucy rewound the video to the point where Huxley first produced the flat sheet-like object.

"With a shim, the goal is to simply slide something flat between the latch and the strike plate, right?" She paused the video and tapped the screen. "But there's something else going on with this tool here. See that hole cut in the corner?"

In unison, everyone squinted and moved closer to the monitor.

Lucy was right. There *was* a hole cut in the sheet.

"So what's the hole for?"

"For the door handle. I mean, most hotels use the storeroom-style locks, right? Essentially always locked from the outside, but never locked from the inside."

Darger nodded slowly, realizing how often she'd taken this detail for granted. To get into a hotel room, one had to use a key. But to get out? Unless the security latch was engaged, it was as simple as turning the handle.

"Storeroom locks seem extra secure, since they always revert to the locked state. But they have a major weakness in that if you can access the interior handle from outside, they're basically already unlocked." Lucy shrugged. "Anyway, from the design, my guess is that his tool can work as a shim, too. It's kind of a two-in-one deal. Pretty clever in its simplicity."

Pacheco clenched his jaw so hard the muscles quivered. Darger didn't think he was in the mood to give any praise to someone who had so easily defeated the hotel's most basic security measures.

This time, Lucy let the video play through. After opening the door, Huxley disappeared inside the penthouse.

"He was inside for around twelve minutes," she said, skipping forward in the video until he reappeared in the antechamber. His hat wasn't pulled quite so low now, and they got a better look at his face.

"Can you pause it there?" Loshak asked.

Lucy stopped the video.

They spent several seconds studying the screen.

"I can see it now," Loshak said. "He did something to his

nose and his chin, but it's him."

"Yep," Darger agreed.

No surprise. She thought of what Fitch had said earlier, about not knowing if it was a good or bad thing that they'd confirmed Huxley's identity.

One of the screens mounted on the wall caught her eye. The cameras in the parking lot.

"You said he came in through the main lobby," Darger said. "What about before that? Did he park in the parking lot or…?"

"I haven't tracked his movements outside of the building yet. We can do that now."

They watched the man backtrack through the hotel. First riding the elevator down to the main floor, then sauntering back through the lobby. When he exited the building, Lucy switched to a new camera feed.

"Let's see… I think Camera 403 will give us the best angle of the promenade."

She pulled up a feed showing the landscaped entrance to the hotel, skipping around until she found the right time stamp.

"There he is," she said, pointing out the figure in the delivery uniform.

They watched him cross the screen.

"Looks like he's heading for Parking Lot C. We've got a few options there. Just a second."

Lucy typed a command that divided her screen into four quadrants. She filled each with a separate camera feed showing rows of cars parked outside the casino. She cued up the correct times and played each video in turn, following the man's course through the lot. They hit pay dirt with the footage from the third camera: a clear shot of the man climbing into a tan minivan.

"Looks like a Toyota Sienna. Maybe a 2016 or so," Rohrbach said.

Loshak murmured in agreement.

"I wonder if there's an angle where we might see the license plate. Front or back."

They watched as Lucy sifted through the various parking lot cameras. They found several shots of the vehicle exiting the lot, but the motion blur made the plates illegible. As it finally turned out onto the street, the last three numbers came clear: 278.

"Hey, it's something."

"Maybe," Loshak said. "I mean, we can put the information out there. Maybe even suss out the full plate number and put the word out to find this exact vehicle."

"I sense a *but* coming," Fitch said.

"Huxley drove a little hatchback to the studio and ended up ditching the car there. Then he stole an EV from the lot and ditched that a few miles away."

"You're thinking he has multiple cars at the ready."

"He must. So I doubt, even if we find this Sienna, that the bomber is anywhere near it."

The room fell quiet for a second.

Then Rohrbach pointed at the live feed from the penthouse elevator. Someone in a bulky black bomb suit was maneuvering into the enclosed space, bobbing in a way that reminded Darger a little of astronauts walking around in the low gravity on the moon.

"Looks like C-IED is about to start the show."

Darger checked the countdown on her phone again. They had 36 minutes.

CHAPTER 35

The control room went silent. All eyes latched onto the monitor where the bomb tech in the EOD suit exited the elevator.

The tech's bulky armor looked like a perfect cross between a spacesuit and a fat suit. He sort of waddled out of the elevator, taking trudging steps, slow and labored.

Fitch was seated at one of the workstations. The laptop screen in front of him showed the live feed from the helmet cam worn by the bomb tech. The audio feed between the tech and his partner sounded tinny through the small speakers.

"Exiting the elevator. You copy me, Advani?"

"Loud and clear, Marsh. The penthouse is to your left. The same key card you used for the elevator will open the door."

"Roger that," Marsh said.

It looked like Marsh was moving in slow motion as he scuttled up to the door and swiped the card. The light on the door blinked three times and then turned green. Marsh caught the handle with his heavily mitted hand and pushed down. The door swung open, and he shuffled inside.

Everyone shifted closer to Fitch's laptop now that Marsh had moved beyond the realm of the hotel's surveillance cameras. The helmet camera was a bit of a step-down in terms of video quality, and the shakiness of the feed gave Darger a faint feeling of motion sickness almost immediately. Still, she couldn't tear her eyes from the screen.

Marsh swept slowly through the foyer. Darger spied two doors to the left, probably the bedrooms. To the right, a kitchen decked out with matte black cabinets and gleaming white marble countertops. Straight ahead was the living room with glass walls looking out over Topanga Beach.

Beyond the windows, Darger caught a glimpse of a balcony with a hot tub and deck chairs.

Marsh proceeded through the penthouse, peering behind curtains, under furniture, and inside cabinets. The decor was fairly minimal, clean, which helped speed up the search.

"Living room is clear," Marsh said. "Moving on to the kitchen and dining area."

Marsh's movements echoed through this part of the penthouse, the sound seemingly amplified by the hard surfaces. Sharp. When he finished in the kitchen, he moved into the master bedroom, the camera shaking a little with each lumbering footstep as he passed through the doorway into the new space.

Pink and champagne shades adorned the interior design here. A crystal chandelier hung over the bed. Half of the square footage of the master suite was dedicated to a generously sized walk-in closet and a bathroom with enough open space to do a gymnastics floor routine.

"Why do they have to make these places so fuckin' big?" Marsh asked rhetorically.

"I'm just glad it's not the same size as the Nielsen penthouse we had to search in New York," Loshak muttered.

Darger nodded. She'd been thinking the same thing. What they were looking at was big, no doubt, but Nielsen's penthouse had been obscene.

Marsh cleared the bathroom first, then began scanning the closet. Racks filled with a small boutique's worth of clothing on one side. Shelves of designer shoes and luxury handbags on the other.

Dawn Barboza's bag collection was eclectic. There were the more ubiquitous Louis Vuittons and Birkins, but Darger spotted several with more novel designs in unique shapes. A sheepdog. A stack of pancakes. An old Volkswagen Beetle. A beaded sphere designed to look like a globe and a three-dimensional butterfly encrusted in rhinestones.

Over the next ten minutes, Marsh made his way through the second bedroom and two additional bathrooms.

"I think we might need to bring the dogs in," Marsh said. "Because so far, I haven't found shit."

"Wait," Pacheco said from behind them. "There's one place he hasn't searched."

"Where's that?" Fitch asked.

"There's a utility closet off the foyer. Gives access to the HVAC controls and the on-demand water heater. The door is mostly concealed unless you know where to look."

Fitch opened a screen with a schematic drawing and zoomed in. He studied the screen for a moment before pointing to a small room toward the center of the schematics.

"This is it?"

Pacheco bent down to get a better look before nodding.

"Yes. The door is a push latch. He just has to press on the right side, and it should pop open."

Fitch toggled a button on his headset.

"Marshy, can you hear me? It's Fitch."

"I copy."

"I've got one last place for you to check out. There's a small utility room accessible from the foyer."

"Not a problem," Marsh said, hobbling back through the penthouse toward the entry.

"Position yourself as if you've just walked into the penthouse, and it should be at about one o'clock or so."

Marsh followed the instructions, approaching a section of wall decorated with vertical wood slats.

"The section on the far right should open with a push," Fitch said, relaying Pacheco's instructions.

Marsh's gloved hand came into view on the laptop screen. He felt up and down the door with suit-plumped fingers, applying pressure until a faint click could be heard.

"Got it," he said. "Entering the utility closet."

As the panel swung outward, a light flicked on automatically overhead, illuminating a stark white room with ducts and pipes snaking over the walls.

Marsh took one step forward and stopped.

"Got something."

He angled his helmet cam down to the floor. There was a suitcase on the floor, up against one wall.

Marsh began to speak but stopped.

"I—"

A ragged, sibilant sound came over the speakers. It took Darger a moment to realize it was the sound of Marsh breathing. He was… sniffing?

"Marsh?" Fitch said. "What's happening?"

The only answer was silence. Tension thickened in the air, and Darger had a bizarre urge to scream. She bit down on her cheek and kept still.

"You still there?" Fitch tried again.

When Marsh finally answered, his voice sounded hollow in a way that filled Darger with dread.

"Oh shit."

CHAPTER 36

The feed from the helmet cam spun and blurred. Choppy steps seemed to carry Marsh over the floor, the camera jumping forward like he was running. When the picture steadied and came back into focus, the bomb tech was in the vestibule outside of the penthouse.

"Smelled like rotting apples in there. You hear me, Advani? Like acetone."

"Mother of Satan," Advani said.

"Yup. He's got the device positioned right against a support column running up the side of that closet. Probably hoping for maximum damage. You compromise that beam, even at the top? You could be putting the whole building at risk."

"What are they talking about?" Rohrbach asked.

"TATP," Fitch explained. "Triacetone Triperoxide. Also known as 'Mother of Satan.' Has a telltale fruity acetone smell."

"That's the stuff that was used in the bombings in Paris and Brussels?" Loshak asked.

Fitch nodded.

"Only the looniest of 'toons would even consider messing with this stuff. It's extremely volatile. I like to say that just looking at it wrong could cause it to detonate."

Darger's attention went back to the laptop.

"We're gonna need the Talon for this, then," Advani was saying. "You might as well head back down now, Marshy."

Marsh scoffed as he dragged a potted plant from the corner of the anteroom and used it to prop the door open.

"What the hell do you think I'm doing? I'm just trying to

make things easier for you."

"I could have opened that door with the Talon."

"Yeah, well, we don't exactly have time for you and your precious robot to fuck around with a key card, OK?"

"Speaking of time," Fitch said, breaking in. "We're at under twenty minutes. I think we're going to have to go with a controlled detonation at this point."

"Got it, Chief," Advani said. "I'll get the Talon set up."

Fitch spun around in his chair to face the group in the casino's control room.

"Right, so we're dealing with an HME — homemade explosive — built with an extremely unpredictable primary explosive. Given our options, I'd rather not take any chances with it." He aimed a thumb over his shoulder at the laptop. "Our safest bet at this point is to use our explosive ordnance disposal robot to collect the bomb from the penthouse and bring it down here to our mobile total containment vessel or TCV. Once it's inside the TCV, we can safely detonate the device."

Fitch pushed himself to a standing position.

"Secondly, we've seen what we came to see in terms of the security footage. It's my recommendation that those of us here in the control room vacate the building before we start moving this briefcase around."

"Actually, this place is essentially a bomb shelter," Pacheco said. "Kind of has to be with the earthquake risk."

Fitch's gaze ran the length of the room.

"Oh, I don't doubt that. The thing is, I don't particularly want to be trapped down here if, say, the building were to collapse on top of us."

Pacheco's Adam's apple quivered.

"Point taken. Let's go."

The elevator ride back up to the ground floor was significantly more crowded with the additional bodies from the security control room added to their party.

Pacheco led them through one of the employee-only areas of the building to the nearest exit and outside. The night air opened up around them, the sky a vast starry expanse overhead. Darger thought it felt a little more humid than it had when they'd gotten there, that thicker night air settling in with the darkness.

They followed Fitch to the CIRG van, where they huddled around the open side door and watched what was happening inside the casino via the laptop screen.

Marsh's helmet cam provided their first look at the remote-controlled bomb disposal robot as it rolled across the lobby. The Talon was roughly the size of a push lawnmower. It moved on tank-style tracks instead of wheels and had various arms, posts, and antennae sticking out of it. It reminded Darger a little of a Dalek from *Doctor Who.*

It was equipped with four cameras: front, back, left, and right.

At the elevator, the Talon rolled inside. Marsh stepped in behind it, scanned the key card, hit the button for the penthouse floor, and hurried out before the doors could close him in.

Then Marsh's voice came over the radio.

"Going up."

The feed from the robot held on the four angles of the elevator interior for what seemed like an eternity. No one spoke. Finally, the doors popped open with a pleasant-sounding *bing*, and Agent Advani guided the Talon out of the elevator and into the hallway of the penthouse floor.

Marsh joined them outside the van then, and Fitch helped him out of the blast suit.

The helmet came off first, and Marsh let out a sigh of relief. His sweaty cheeks plumped as he smiled.

"Nothing worse than a blast suit that smells like other people's B.O."

"You saying you like it when it smells like your own B.O.?" Fitch asked, handing him a towel.

Marsh mopped at his face.

"I mean, if it's a choice between my own stank or someone else's? Heck yeah, I prefer mine."

Fitch grinned and clapped him on the shoulder.

"Well, thankfully the stank wasn't so strong that it prevented you from sniffing out that TATP. Good work in there."

"It would have been hard to miss."

"Talon is entering the penthouse," Advani said, putting an end to the banter.

"How fast is the robot?" Loshak asked.

"About five miles per hour," Fitch said.

Advani cleared his throat.

"It's actually five-point-two."

"OK, Rain Man," Fitch said. "The really cool thing is how versatile it is when it comes to rough terrain. Works on sand, snow, and water. It can even climb stairs. Thing is a beast."

The robot zipped across the foyer and into the utility closet. Advani brought the Talon to a stop and adjusted the front-facing camera until it was centered on the briefcase.

"Engaging the HME," he said and took a deep breath.

An articulated arm with a claw-shaped grabber at the end

flexed into view on the camera. Something about it reminded Darger of Arnold Schwarzenegger's exposed android arm in *Terminator 2*.

The robot arm extended outward until it was nearly straight, while the claw end swiveled and opened wide. Advani finessed it into position and clamped it tight around the briefcase.

"Moment of truth," Advani said.

A bead of sweat rolled down his forehead.

"Initiating lift."

He gave one of the joysticks on his control pad an upward nudge.

Darger held her breath.

CHAPTER 37

The suitcase rose slowly.

"Yes!" Fitch hissed.

"HME secured," Advani said and directed the robot backward.

It rolled out of the closet, through the foyer, and down the hallway to the waiting elevator. As it crossed the threshold into the stainless steel cabin, the briefcase bounced and swayed. Darger grimaced and squeezed her hands into fists.

"OK, let's move the TCV in place while the bot is coming down," Fitch said into his radio.

An engine rumbled closer, and Darger turned her head in time to see a truck pull into view, halting in front of the hotel entrance. It was towing a trailer with an apparatus on the back. A large silver sphere in a cube-shaped cage.

"That's good, Peterson. Go ahead and unhitch, then clear the area."

The driver hopped out, unhooked the trailer, climbed back into the truck, and drove away.

Fitch chuckled to himself.

"Had to remind him to clear the area because when we do demos with the TCV, Peterson usually just sits right there in the truck when we detonate."

"Isn't that… dangerous?" Darger asked.

"Nope. That's the beauty of the TCV. As long as you're not touching the enclosure when the blast occurs, you could stand right next to it and be completely fine. Assuming you're wearing proper hearing protection, that is."

"And if you *did* happen to be touching it?" Rohrbach asked.

"Well, the fella that trained me on the TCV told me the shockwave would pulverize all the bones in my arm."

Rohrbach winced and looked sorry he'd asked.

"Not sure if that was literal or figurative, and I don't care to find out. Though, one time we put a coffee mug on top of the sphere during a demo, as an experiment. Blew the thing into a thousand pieces."

Fitch made a bursting gesture with his hands, fingers flicking outward.

"Anyway, we can afford to be a little lackadaisical when we're doing demos since we always use C4. Stable as hell. Shoot it, light it on fire. Stuff won't blow." He nodded at the building. "This TATP, though… until it's secured inside the TCV, I'm treating it like it could go off at any second."

It was silent as they watched the bot churn through the lobby and out the front doors.

Darger stepped away from the screens and watched from a distance as the robot chugged down the promenade to the waiting TCV trailer. The briefcase looked so small from this distance. Almost inconceivable that such a small package could be so dangerous.

The Talon trundled over to the trailer. The hatch on the device was already open. A circular mouth waiting to be fed.

The robot wheeled closer. There was another tense moment as Advani maneuvered the briefcase inside the chamber and released the claw mechanism.

"HME is in place."

Fitch got on the radio again.

"OK, Peterson. Initiate the containment sequence."

"Copy. Initiating containment sequence."

The hatch swung shut and a wheel handle similar to those Darger had seen on old submarines began to spin.

"It's all automated?" Loshak asked.

"Yep. Saves us from having to get anywhere near the HME."

There was a blinking yellow light on the side of the TCV. It stopped blinking and turned green.

Peterson's voice came over the radio.

"Containment sequence complete."

"When you're ready."

From a distance, Darger heard Peterson's voice calling out through the night.

"Fire in the hole! Fire in the hole! Fire in the hole!"

The same words came over the radio on a slight delay.

There was a cracking sound and the TCV jerked and shivered. A split second later, smoke hissed out of a valve on top of the sphere. More clouds roiled out from underneath.

The C-IED guys all whooped and hollered and celebrated. It wasn't until the hatch door on the TCV swung open a few seconds later that Darger realized that was it. They'd done it.

Fitch saw her face and laughed.

"Kind of underwhelming, huh? All that build up and then, *psssssssssssst.*" He mimicked the sound of the smoke. "But that's good! Underwhelming means we did our job right."

If only catching Huxley could be so simple, Darger thought, but she didn't say it out loud.

CHAPTER 38

The celebration was short-lived. With the clock already ticking on Huxley's next bomb, the sooner they found the clue pointing them toward it, the better their chances at thwarting another one. Everyone understood that without speaking it.

While C-IED began a precautionary sweep of the penthouse with the bomb-sniffing dogs, the rest of the crew gathered in the lobby and geared up.

"Let's talk logistics for a moment," Chief Cattermole said. "There are two elevators. The private elevator goes directly from the ground floor to the penthouse. We're reserving the first two trips on that elevator for Agent Tanaka, her people, and their equipment."

They were huddled together near the entrance to the casino floor, and the jingles and whoops from the slot machines sounded incongruently cheerful paired with the sober faces in the crowd.

"There's a second service elevator that stops one floor below the penthouse. A set of stairs will take you the rest of the way up. Obviously, we can only fit so many people at a time, so there will be a wait. Lastly, if you're up to the physical challenge, you can take the stairs now."

Darger and Loshak were toward the back of the horde, and by the time they reached the service elevator, it was already full. Darger bounced from one foot to the other, watching the digital display over the elevator slowly count upward. After about thirty seconds, she huffed out a breath.

"Screw this," she said. "I'm taking the stairs."

Loshak raised an eyebrow.

"You'd rather climb twenty-two flights of stairs than just wait another whole minute for the elevator?"

Darger shrugged.

"See you up there, then," he said.

Darger pushed through the doors and started to climb. The thud of her footsteps reverberated around the cavernous stairwell.

Loshak was such a grump. This wasn't so bad.

Around the fourteenth floor, she started to have regrets. She was totally winded, and her calves were on fire. But she'd already made it more than halfway. And she couldn't let Loshak be right.

When she finally reached the penthouse, she was sweaty and exhausted. Her bruised ribcage throbbed along with her heartbeat.

She paused at the top and leaned one arm against the wall, trying to catch her breath. She waited until she was no longer gasping for air and pushed through the door.

Even with the crowd of people milling around the penthouse, the noises they made were softened by the furnishings. It was an odd contrast to the harsh echo of the stairwell.

Everything about the penthouse was bigger than it had looked on the various cameras. The other thing that struck her was how sterile it felt. All the shiny, expensive furniture and decor couldn't seem to hide the fact that this was still essentially a hotel room.

Darger wove through the various clusters of law enforcement personnel already searching the place. She spied Loshak in the kitchen, and he waved her over.

Despite an expansive white marble island and a generous amount of recessed lighting, the kitchen felt oddly dark. Shaded. Something about the flat black cabinet faces seemed to eat up all the available light.

She and Loshak rifled through the drawers of the island. One drawer held a set of black ceramic-coated knives. Another held silverware. A taller door on the end concealed a wine fridge.

Darger turned to the range and used the flashlight on her phone to check inside the stove and up under the stainless steel hood.

Each place they searched that turned up empty caused the uneasy feeling in Darger's gut to ratchet up another notch. Some valve there squeezing tighter and tighter.

They'd never be able to search this whole penthouse.

She stopped.

"This is stupid."

"What is?"

"Rushing in here and searching blindly like this. It never works."

Loshak ran a hand through his hair.

"What do you suggest?"

Darger was already flipping through the files on her phone. "We need to go back to the clue."

CHAPTER 39

Darger found the decoded clue and read it again.

Greetings from Hell.

Every comeback should start with a bang.

Lights. Camera. Action.

Ka-BOOM!

I hope the reviews are kind. I suspect the critics will be blown away. Such excitement.

We're just getting started, though. And the best is yet to come.

Here's the big-budget sequel. Huxley takes Los Angeles.

God, I'd love to erase the whole vapid city from the map. Cleansing fire to burn it to the ground. Or biblical floods to gush down the city streets, to wash it all away.

At least in NY we have the decency to acknowledge our dark side. We embrace the filth, because everyone knows you're only ever a few steps away from the gutter.

But this place? They dress it up.

Fake teeth, fake lashes, fake tits.

Voila! The metamorphosis is complete. A junkie whore dressed up in couture.

But the glossy facade can't hide the blood on the city's teeth. All the thousands this place has chewed up and spit out. The fallen stars. The washed-up has-beens. The bums sleeping on the streets.

Welcome to Los Angeles, where dreams go to die.

No one cares about the little guy. No one cares when a bug gets crushed.

If you want the attention of the world, you have to kill one of the pretty people, one of the celebrities. So be it.

I came back for a reason. My work here isn't done, and I mean to do whatever it takes.

The stakes couldn't be higher. It's always darkest before dawn.

And the degree of difficulty ratchets up this time. You'll have to be sharp to save them.

Who will live, and who will die? I suppose it's all up to you.

"'Fallen stars,'" Loshak said. "We figured that was a reference to the actress who died, right?"

Darger pointed at him, her eyes stretching wide with comprehension.

"The balcony."

They jostled their way through the penthouse and out onto the expansive balcony.

Potted bamboo and cannas divided the space into two halves. One side featured a set of chaise lounges and a hot tub, the other contained a large circular outdoor sectional with a stone fire table in the center. Pyramid-shaped patio heaters were strategically placed throughout.

Even in the dark, Darger couldn't help but admire the view. The sky was a dusty eggplant color, and a serpentine line of lights stretched out to either side, following the contours of the coastline.

She stepped closer to the steel and glass railing, and her stomach lurched as she gazed downward. It was a long way down, and a hell of a long way to fall.

The rhythmic sound of the surf crashing into the beach

below was almost hypnotic. A crushing, sloshing sound and then a sizzle, rolling in and out like breaths.

They checked the upscale patio furniture first, shuffling between the various pieces, lifting cushions and peering underneath. When that revealed nothing, Darger poked around in the mulch and under the leaves of the potted plants while Loshak pried the access panel off the side of the hot tub.

More nothing.

There were several outdoor carpets laid out on the ground, and Loshak began lifting the corners and shining his light under. But Darger was beginning to doubt her balcony idea. Something wasn't right.

Darger pulled the note up on her phone again, and this time, it was a new line that caught her eye.

Wait, she thought.

Wait.

"'The metamorphosis is complete,'" she said.

Loshak stopped and squinted over at her.

"Huh?"

"Like a butterfly."

They ran back inside.

CHAPTER 40

Loshak caught up with Darger in the closet off the master suite. She pointed at the glittering bag on the top shelf.

"There. The butterfly," she said. "'Metamorphosis.'"

His eyes bulged.

"Yeah. OK."

Darger spun in a circle, eyes searching.

"There has to be a step ladder or a stool somewhere."

Loshak gazed up at the bag that sat just out of reach, hands on hips.

"Hmm… yeah. I'm sure we can find something like that."

There was a small trash can in the bathroom, but it was made of flimsy plastic, and Darger didn't trust it to hold her weight.

"Let's go see if— What are you doing?"

Darger had begun to use the bottom two rows of the floor-to-ceiling shelves like a ladder. Loshak rushed forward and braced his shoulder against the entire unit, apparently worried it might topple over. Darger climbed to the fourth shelf and was able to reach the bag.

"Got it!" she said, hopping down with her prize secured in her hand.

"You know furniture tips over and crushes people all the time," he said, frowning at her. "It's a thing."

"I was fine," she said. "This thing is bolted to the wall."

"You couldn't have known that."

Darger shrugged as she fiddled with the clasp on the bag, trying to get it open.

"It's California. They have to worry about earthquakes. And this isn't exactly the same as a private residence. The hotel could probably be held liable if something like that happened." She pawed at the locking mechanism on top of the bag. "How the hell does this stupid thing work?"

Loshak crossed his arms, ignoring her struggle.

"That's crap. You didn't think about any of that before you started climbing. You made an impulsive, split-second decision, like you always do."

"Well, yeah, but..."

Darger twisted the clasp and the bag sprang open.

"Yes!"

She held the open bag between them. There was something tucked inside.

Darger knew what it was on sight, her heartbeat thrumming faster in her chest like hummingbird wings. Neither she nor Loshak spoke.

She snapped a few photos first to document the bag as they'd found it. Then she pulled the note free with a pair of tweezers and they both read.

The time grows short. The gloom rushes in, black as night. The game races to its climax, to its finish.

Just as all the flowers die, this, too, will cease to exist soon enough.

Split in two. Slashed down to nothing.

The body laid out in that death pose. On the slab. In the coffin. Posing for that final image.

But the mind? The mind is endless.

And in a way, I'll always be here. Living on eternally. Grinning from ear to ear.

CHAPTER 41

Back in the conference room, the bulk of the task force worked the clue in silence. A fresh tension had settled over the room within seconds of their arrival, something leaden in the atmosphere.

Darger's phone sat on the table in front of her, the glowing screen looking minuscule on the shiny slab of wood. She stretched, pointed her head up at the drop ceiling, and felt something pop in her neck. Then she went back to reading the clue over and over. Even though someone had beamed a giant version of the text of the clue onto the wall with an overhead projector, she preferred the handwritten version on her phone.

Loshak bounced a racquetball as he did the same with his own phone. The muffled thump of the rubber hitting the carpet made for a backbeat to the tension, to the work. Darger was surprised that she didn't find it unpleasant.

Nothing in the clue jumped out at Darger on the first read, or the tenth read, or the twentieth read. But somewhere between the thirtieth and fortieth pass, she felt an itch deep inside her skull.

She recognized the feeling right away. Her right brain was responding, getting a twinge. Some instinct kicking in. She knew… something. It felt like it was right there on the tip of her tongue.

But whatever intuitive connection was happening there in the muck of her subconscious, she couldn't get a grip on it, couldn't haul it up to the surface of her mind. She remembered reading in a study that intuitive flashes in the right brain take about eight minutes to be communicated to the conscious mind on average. Sometimes longer.

She clenched her teeth. Closed her eyes again.

The racquetball stopped pounding the floor all at once.

"If anything sticks out to anyone, throw it out there," Loshak said without looking away from his phone. "There are no bad ideas at this stage, and you never know what might set off the sequence of leaps that will solve this thing. Seriously, don't be shy."

Eyes shifted around the room, but no one else spoke. Darger wanted to say something, but what?

I'm getting a feeling over here.

Stupid.

"I was stuck on 'all the flowers die,'" Loshak said after a few seconds. "Thought it seemed familiar, but I Googled it and... well, nothing useful came up."

He looked around the room after that, clearly hoping to elicit some response, get a dialog going. Still, no one chimed in.

Loshak went back to bouncing the ball off the floor over and over. The quiet resettled over the space.

Darger got to her feet and pushed through the doorway out into the hall. The corridor held even more quiet somehow. Maybe it was the lack of that racquetball thump, or perhaps it was the total vacancy. Nothing even moved out here.

She walked some thirty feet into the stillness, the echo of her own footsteps sounding eerie just now. Then she stepped into the restroom.

Gray tile surrounded her like cave walls. Fluorescent bulbs buzzed and cast harsh white light everywhere.

At one of the sinks, she leaned down and splashed cold water over her face, like the jolt of it might loosen that twinging instinct, help it get home to her. After a few handfuls, she stood half upright and watched in the mirror as the beads of water rolled down her cheeks and drizzled off her jaw.

The chilly fluid felt good on her eyelids and on her nose, but her mind remained blank.

Well, that didn't work. So um...

Food.

I could eat.

A candy bar or something to get my blood sugar up. Maybe that'd help.

Back out in the hall, she moved for the vending machine, fishing a dollar bill out of her wallet as she did. She already knew what she wanted.

Snickers.

When she was a kid, she used to get a king-sized Snickers and a Pepsi most every day after school — the perfect combination of sweet and too sweet that only the palate of a twelve-year-old could truly appreciate.

The quiet hallway held its breath again as she passed through. She rounded a corner, and then the glowing machine was there in front of her.

She stood just shy of the glass, dollar bill in her hand, all those brightly colored logos gleaming at her. Skittles. Starburst. Reese's. Butterfinger.

And she changed her mind.

The candy didn't sound good at all now that she was face-to-face with it. She could only imagine the sugar coating her tongue. Sticky and filmy.

She shoved the dollar bill down into her jacket pocket and walked back to the conference room. When she pushed open the door, she found the earlier silence shattered.

Fitch and Loshak were talking fast and swiping frantically at their phones. Other voices hissed whispers around the room, some excited sibilance filling the space.

"Whoa. *Cease to Exist* is another reference," Fitch said. "A song he wrote that the Beach Boys recorded as *Never Learn Not to Love* in 1968."

"Holy shit," Loshak said.

That whispering around the room seemed to intensify.

"What's going on?" Darger asked, trying to catch up.

Rohrbach leaned close to her and spoke much more calmly than the others.

"There's a line in the clue. '*The mind is endless,*'" he said. "It's a Charles Manson quote."

CHAPTER 42

The conference room bustled around Darger. The task force thrummed and jostled and lurched, so many moving pieces, seemingly all of them animated and loud.

Rohrbach coordinated the guts of the operation with Fitch and some of the other LAPD detectives, each of them taking turns pointing at the map hung up on the wall. With three clues tying the clue to the Manson murders, they'd do the obvious. They'd start a search at the most famous crime scene related to the case: the former Sharon Tate house.

"The house is here in the hills," Rohrbach said, tapping at the map. "So far all of the journals have been hidden or buried outside, out in the open. Way I figure it, we'll want to get the dogs out there and clear the grounds right away. Then the real search can begin."

"Hell yeah, I'm on it," Fitch said.

He lifted a walkie to his lips and started handing down the orders to his team.

"We're starting with the Tate house, focusing on that," Loshak said. "And I think that makes perfect sense given her history as an actress and the way that ties into Huxley's history. But the Manson murders did involve another crime scene, the LaBianca house on Waverly, and there was also the killing of Gary Hinman about a month before that. Less famous, but still relevant. A Manson deep cut, if you will."

Now he traced his finger over the map, gliding from one location to the next.

"I think we should prep to search the Tate and LaBianca

sites up front and be ready to pivot if we don't turn anything up."

He kept talking, but Darger tuned out his words, tuned out all the sound and fury swirling around her. She held still in the center of the storm, kept looking at the clue glowing in black and white on her phone screen. Reading it over and over.

Something still nagged at her. Something felt wrong.

Whatever gut feeling that had been itching in her skull before all of this? It wasn't satisfied. Not yet.

She blocked out everything else, the noise outside overpowered by the quiet inside. Her focus sharpened on just those letters on the screen.

Certain lines leaped out at her as she took another pass. Her eyes jumped right to them, one after another.

The time grows short.

The gloom rushes in, black as night.

Just as all the flowers die...

Split in two. Slashed down to nothing.

The body laid out in that death pose.

Grinning from ear to ear.

She blinked a few times. Closed her eyes.

That quiet inside seemed to strengthen. Darger leaned into the stillness. Accepted it. Surrendered to it.

And her mind whittled the list of lines down further, rattled off just the keywords.

Short.

Black.

Flower.

Slashed.

Split in two.

Death pose.

Grinning from ear to ear.

Blood pounded in Darger's temples, keeping time with the rapid beat of the words in her head. She could feel the blood vessels quaking, quivering the surface of her skin.

And then it was there. The whole understanding arriving all at once.

At last she saw what her right brain had seen all along. All the pieces snugged together, pointed to one solution.

Elizabeth Short.

The Black Dahlia.

Darger's eyes snapped open, and a big breath whooshed into her. The noise in the room swelled back to full volume.

"Stop," she said, her voice loud and hard to be heard over all.

The room went quiet at once. Everyone stopped what they were doing and turned to face her.

"He's describing the Black Dahlia murder."

All eyes swiveled back to the clue in that glowing box on the wall coming from the projector. The quiet elongated, filled the space.

"Elizabeth *Short*," Loshak said, almost under his breath. "Flowers."

"Split in two? Death pose? Grinning ear to ear?" Darger said, offering up more of the connections to him.

In what ultimately became one of the most famous murder cases in the world, Elizabeth Short's body was found severed at the waist in a vacant lot in South L.A. Her corpse had been bled white and posed, the torso about a foot away from the lower half with the intestines tucked carefully beneath the buttocks and hamstrings. The horrifying crime scene photographs had spread across the world even in the pre-internet era.

Loshak now had his phone in his hand. He read from one of the popular crime sites, picking out a part of the description of the crime.

"'Short's lips had been slashed at the corners, sliced almost from ear to ear, a wound commonly known as a Glasgow smile.' Sounds like a match for that 'grinning from ear to ear' bit."

"Glasgow smile? The hell is that?" Fitch asked.

"Apparently in Glasgow it was fairly common to be attacked that way in the 1920s and 30s, to have your lips slashed to your ears. It leaves scars in the shape of a smile, as you can imagine."

Fitch gaped.

"That was *common*? Jesus. Remind me to never go to Glasgow."

Loshak brought the focus back to interpreting the clue.

"So do we think the Manson clues are there to throw us off, like last time?"

In New York, Huxley had purposely confused the police with one of the later clues. It seemed to point to a Jack the Ripper connection, but instead the clue had been found at Strawberry Fields, in an homage to the murder of John Lennon by Mark David Chapman.

"Maybe," Darger said. "We should probably check both. To be safe."

Loshak gave a single nod in response to that, and then the room surged back into action. The plan came together quickly.

They'd split up. Dogs and techs would be sent to all three locations. Darger and Fitch would head to the lot where they'd found the Dahlia. Loshak and Rohrbach would go to the former Tate mansion to search the grounds there. Chief

Cattermole would lead a team to the LaBianca scene. They'd keep in constant contact to best pour their resources into whatever scene looked the most promising.

When it was all settled, Fitch was the first to move for the door, speaking over his shoulder as he did.

"Let's roll."

CHAPTER 43

Vinnie Savage squats in the corner of his living room, which serves as his home office, huddling over his laptop. The apartment, otherwise fairly upscale, smells vaguely like cream of mushroom soup. It tends to do that in the warmer months, though he can never figure out the source of the odor.

For now, the smell doesn't rise fully to the reporter's conscious mind. He stares at the glowing rectangle facing him, mind blocking out all other stimuli. Entranced.

He touches the keyboard, fingers settling over the home row keys, two thumbs hovering just a couple millimeters above the space bar. His middle finger finds the F5 key. Jabs it.

His inbox splashes over the screen, refreshing before his eyes. The dark mode's black background is striped with tiny white lines like filaments, each row populated with bright text.

No new messages. No word from the bomber.

He takes a breath. Refreshes again. And again.

Nothing.

He needs to think. Needs to…

He leans back in his chair. Stares up at the apartment ceiling. A spider plant hangs in the foreground, reaching green tendrils down like it means to touch his face.

He closes his eyes. Grits his teeth. Clenches the muscles in his brow.

And he tries to will inspiration to come flowing out of him. Tries to force it, wrestle it under his control, choke it. Like his brain is a toothpaste tube he can get something good out of if only he squeezes hard enough.

It's all right there in front of him. Fame. Recognition. The dream.

He has the world's attention — the video of him inviting the bomber to reach out to him personally has twenty million views and counting. Almost as many as the bombing video itself. And both of them are still piling up thousands of views per minute even now, in the middle of the night.

The public knows his face. Finally. But he needs to keep that attention if he's going to fully capitalize. Needs to make all of this pay off.

Fifteen minutes of fame isn't enough. He wants more.

His cat trills. Walks across the back of his desk, rubs her left hip along the top edge of the laptop screen.

Savage opens his eyes to look at the beast, but his attention stays inward.

Is there some way he could win the bomber over? Change the narrative? He has to think.

Words have always been his tools, his weapons. They've gotten him what he's wanted in this world. Put a roof over his head. Put money in the bank.

If he can come up with the right set of words now, the way before him will come unblocked. Some perfect turn of phrase working like a key, snicking the deadbolt out of the way, opening the door to a future so bright it's blinding.

He closes his eyes again. Takes a deep breath. And now he loosens all those clenched muscles in his face, in his neck. Instead he lets his mind drift.

His words have never been more important than right here, right now. He needs to pick the right ones. Something inspired. Now or never.

He opens the word processing app. Stares at the blank

screen. Gleaming white that seems brighter after all that time staring at the black background of his inbox.

He leans over and snorts the blue line crushed out on the mirror on the edge of the desk. Just a bit of Adderall to clear his thoughts, sharpen his mind. He hasn't touched the harder stuff in years, though he wants it so bad right now, he can actually taste that cocaine post-nasal drip.

With speed, getting the dosage just right is key. He knows the way. With two fat lines, he will find total confidence in his abilities. Unending internal strength.

But the two lines disappear up his nostrils, and the reporter chops another. Some beam in the air tells him to.

With three lines, it can get iffy.

Savage means to toe right up to the edge. Find that sweet spot where he can sense the delusions of grandeur the speed gives him — can stay aware of them without necessarily obeying their unhinged whims.

If he crosses the line from confidence into amphetamine-induced incoherence, it will doom his plans before he even starts. If he lets the delusional impulses take over, he'll likewise fail.

No manic episodes tonight. No phone calls to ex-girlfriends. No jaunts down to the strip to chat up strangers at a bar, gibbering a mile a minute.

Focus. Only focus.

He lowers his face to the mirror. The last line spirals up his right nostril. Stings faintly somewhere deep in the sinus cavity.

He takes another breath, chest filling and expanding, tingling at the apex, and then he slowly lets the wind come rolling out.

OK.

Go time.

He leans forward and starts to type.

CHAPTER 44

The Tate house had once been a 3,200-square-foot luxury home in Benedict Canyon, built in the 1940s in a French Country style. Loshak thought it looked understated in a charming way in the photos he'd looked at on the ride over. Rustic and sided with wood panels stained red, it resembled, in some ways, a really nice barn.

But that house — the house where the first wave of the most infamous Manson Family murders had been committed — had been torn down in 1994. What stood on the land now, with a fresh new street address sans the brutal history, bore nothing in common with the old home.

The new mansion was over 21,000 square feet with 9 bedrooms, 18 bathrooms, and a potential price tag of over fifty million dollars, according to a quick internet search.

Loshak didn't spend much time dwelling on the new home's details, as he didn't feel they'd be pertinent to their cause here. No. This newer building held no significance to that violent American folklore that seemed to be Huxley's obsession.

What interested Loshak, what he thought might be of value to the investigation, was the 3.6-acre lot surrounding the home. That still made this landmark a piece of history, albeit a disturbing one.

Techs had set up bright lamps everywhere here. Harsh spotlights shining so bright over the grounds that this one little slice of L.A. looked as though it were broad daylight even at coming up on 4 A.M.

Loshak took a few steps into the yard, detected the green smell of the freshly cut grass, and then turned to let his gaze drift over the land in all directions.

Palm tree fronds seemed to burst open in set intervals above the driveway, but the tropical touch faded out immediately as he looked farther out on the property, the foliage shifting to something more usual compared to most of America. It reminded Loshak of a fact he'd heard — that 25,000 palm trees had been planted in L.A. in the late 1920s so the city would seem more exotic for the 1932 Olympics. Then 40,000 more palm trees were planted as part of a public works project. Though the two were often associated in modern times, there was only one species of palm tree that was native to California, and it was naturally occurring in the desert, not on the beach.

Dense woods cluttered the outer rim of the acreage, a vibrant riot of branches, leaves, and needles reaching for the sky. It formed a barrier of plant life between the house and the rest of the world. Loshak realized that he felt very sheltered standing on this island of luxury.

That hadn't kept Sharon Tate safe way back when, he reminded himself. *Maybe it hadn't kept Huxley out either.*

The lot was a big enough expanse to worry him. Three-point-six acres sure seemed a whole lot bigger when you had to search every inch of it. He wondered how they could winnow this down into something manageable. What clue or insight would tighten their focus, tell them where to look?

He didn't know. Movement in the distance shook the thought away.

The dogs wove through the heavily wooded parts of the plot now, heads down and snuffling along the ground all the while. The black-clad handlers jogged along a few paces behind the beasts. The C-IED guys all had the upright posture of soldiers. In a lot of ways, that's what they were.

The team cleared the area near the house first. The hounds quickly chewing up the open grass of the yard and moving on. No explosives. Nothing there to offend their sensitive noses.

The techs then swooped in to begin the search in the cleared area. One mussed stretch of exposed soil, a wounded spot in the sod, was being troweled now, but the owners had supposedly had a dead tree ripped out there a few weeks earlier. Loshak didn't figure the disturbed land was likely to be related to Huxley. He'd never make it so easy on them.

The agent walked across the yard and stepped into the edge of the woods, planted himself in a place where the dogs had already come and gone. The scent around him changed, that cut grass tang dying back, replaced by the smell of trees and dirt. Not the sharp pine odor you'd get at Christmas time, but the sweet smell of earth, leaves, and decay.

Footsteps crunched up behind him, dead leaves crushed under dress shoes. Loshak turned in time to see Rohrbach arrive next to him.

"Do we know where the old house was on the lot?" the detective asked. His words came out fast, excited. "I'm thinking maybe Huxley would want to leave his clue in the place most directly tied to the murders, ya know?"

Loshak blinked. Considered it.

The exact spot. That could make sense.

"That's smart, Rohrbach. Certainly better than digging at random. I have no idea where the old house would have sat relative to the new one, but I bet we can find out."

He swiped at his phone and brought it to his ear.

CHAPTER 45

When Elizabeth Short's body was found all those years ago, the lot on South Norton Avenue had been practically barren. The old crime scene photos showed a cluster of police standing just where Darger stood now.

Back then, scraggly grass poked up everywhere save for the strip of sidewalk running through. A stark line of telephone poles ran along the back of the empty space, trailing away into the distance.

Today, a bevy of small homes choked the same piece of land. The exact lot where they'd found the severed body accommodated a beige and brown bungalow where all that tall grass had stood.

Rather ordinary, Darger thought. Looking at it now, nothing about the structure suggested anything exciting. Thousands of people had probably driven right past, not knowing about the lurid history.

The neighborhood as a whole gave off an unassuming vibe in Darger's opinion. Small, tightly packed houses mostly dating to the 1950s. The shallow front yards were divided up by thin strips of pale cement that formed the driveways. The houses looked well-maintained, and the streets were clean. Otherwise, this could pass for any of the countless blue-collar, industrial neighborhoods that had cropped up in the mid-20th century. Darger thought this section of town wouldn't look out of place in Scranton or Boise or Atlanta or the outskirts of Chicago. Take out a few palm trees, and you could put it pretty much anywhere in the country.

Movement in the lot brought Darger's attention back to the scene. She cupped her hand over her brow to block out the rack of lights over her shoulder.

The dogs had done their job, and now the techs swarmed in to take over. Darger and Fitch watched as they began their work, snapping photos and walking the perimeter of the grounds. One CSI had what Darger was pretty sure was a metal detector. Another used a device that was supposed to reveal any solid objects underground. She didn't know if it'd help so much with something as thin as a few pages of journal.

At first glance, at least, there wasn't much to go on here. The grass had been mowed recently and there were no identifiable footprints or other obvious trace evidence presenting itself.

They walked toward a female tech with short hair and a no-nonsense look in her eyes. Darger recognized her from the studio crime scene, remembered hearing someone calling her by her last name, Simmons. It wasn't until they got closer that Darger realized what the CSI was doing.

A yellow measuring tape snaked across the ground in front of Simmons. She knelt to double-check the measurement, then she gave a nod to another tech standing back by the hydrant, a stoop-shouldered man with a mustache and a pouchy face that reminded Darger of an aging pug. He let the end of the tape go, and it zipped back into the dark bulk clutched in Simmons's left hand.

"This marks 54 feet north," she said.

Darger remembered reading in the original coroner's report that the body was found 54 feet north of the fire hydrant and a few feet west. Simmons was trying to find the exact spot where Short had once lay.

The tech turned and walked a few paces into the yard then pointed down at the wedge of grass between her feet.

"This would be 'a few feet west,' yeah?"

Simmons turned and looked back at the pug-faced tech who shrugged his shoulders in a way that reminded Darger of a marionette. When he spoke, he sounded a little like Droopy.

"I mean… I guess so."

Darger strode up to get a closer look at the spot in question, standing right alongside Fitch and both techs. They all stared at the ground at Simmons's feet.

Thick sod carpeted this area, a healthy head of green hair, though it cut off in a hard line where it met the concrete edge of the driveway on one side. Darger let her eyes trace over and over the little patch of ground. Nothing looked obviously disturbed.

The female tech poked her toe at the grass a few times. Took a step farther into the yard and poked a few more times. Then she turned back with her eyebrows raised.

"So what do you think? Do we just start digging here?" she asked.

Darger squatted down and started running her fingers along that seam where the grass met the edge of the driveway. She hooked her fingers into the bottom of the grass and tried lifting, like she meant to pop off the ground's toupee. The grass moved a little, but it seemed secure.

She shuffled a couple steps forward and tried again. Felt the tips of her fingers dig into the dirt and matted root system. She tugged. The grass peeled up easily this time — too easily — a whole section coming up as one piece, reminding Darger somehow of a big piece of sheet cake being spatulated out of a pan.

Her breath caught. Her heart thumped. And icy needles prickled over her scalp right away.

He was here.

He was right here yanking up this grass just like I did.

Hiding something here.

The backs of her knuckles brushed against something cool and smooth then. Plastic. She could already picture the journal pages there, wrapped in a Ziploc bag, though she couldn't see anything yet.

She went to talk, but her throat sort of clicked instead. Her breath still frozen in her throat.

"What is it?" Fitch said, just behind her, his voice low and gravelly. Expectant.

Darger blinked hard, and black dots strobed over her vision for a second. She took a deep breath, and then she finally got the words to come out.

"I think… I think I've got something here."

CHAPTER 46

Great day today. I spent all day at a… well, let's just call it a special location. I think I finally have the final phase of my plan worked out. The details came clear out of nowhere. The murky concepts congealing into a full-blown vision in my head. It felt like a message beamed into my skull from somewhere outside of myself, like something just meant to be. Divine.

I could see it. All at once, I could see it.

The footage rolled in my head. Violence. Mayhem. The great spectacle, where my whole life has led me all along. I could walk down the aisles and see it.

A grand finale. A crescendo.

It will be glorious.

I could elaborate, but… you know, that would be telling.

Fear not. Good things come to those who wait.

☾

Power is force. It is a blunt tool wielded. Inflicted. A heavy thing that bludgeons, traumatizes.

The force is inextricable from the rest, mandatory. Power requires one pressuring, compelling, dominating another.

Control without force is merely influence. Not power. That might sound like a small difference, but the distinction is key.

It's only when a boundary is crossed, when one person's will overpowers another, that it becomes power. There has to be a loser for there to be a winner. Two sides of the coin.

And somehow this desire for domination is baked into our

nature. We don't create sports where both teams can win, do we?

Instead we revel in crushing the opponent. Take pleasure that borders on sexual in a blowout victory. There is no sweeter joy than to run up the score and humiliate the other side. We can't be truly dominant without their shame, without their pain.

Power and pain. Dominance and submission. Two sides of the coin, like I said.

I read about this high school football incident. Later on in a 48-0 blowout, the backups went into the game for the losing side, including some younger players. A couple of linebackers for the winning team got a puny sophomore quarterback on the ground, ripped off his helmet and stomped him, breaking ribs, puncturing both lungs, lacerating other organs.

Think about that desire. The game was in hand, and their team had won. But that intense desire to see themselves as powerful persisted. The only way to be even more dominant was to cross another line, go a little further. It's only in inflicting injury that they could try to sate that lust swelling in their hearts.

Power and pain.

Dominance and submission.

Wherever people are, the air is thick with it, a palpable energy that can be felt even when it isn't seen. Everywhere you look, it's there: a heavy, oppressive presence that lingers in the corners of rooms, creeps out of shadows, and swirls in the air like smoke.

Power.

This is the key to understanding human nature.

Another spectacle. A way to make the message stand the test of time.

The world will feel it, feel what I feel. The hate that's etched into all of us. The raging seas just beneath the surface.

And once this is all over, I will be everywhere.

A red shimmer in the air. Almost like a mist you can only see out of the corner of your eye.

Every time some lone wolf crashes a van into a sidewalk crowded with pedestrians, I'll be there.

Every time a brick flies through a storefront window, I'll be there.

Every time rioters tip over a police car and set it on fire, I'll be there.

Every time a gunman shoots up a mall or night club or school, I'll be there.

Every time.

Everywhere.

Huxley everywhere.

That will be your brave new world.

☾

Two weeks.

For two weeks I've been without the pills that make me able to sleep at night.

I still lie down in the dark. Wrapped in a blanket. Body gone still. I open my eyes from time to time to stare out at nothing.

But sleep won't take me. Doesn't want me.

And that hamster wheel keeps turning in my head. Spinning out thoughts.

This buzzing noise keeps rising up in my ears — a flock of

mosquitoes squeezing into the little canals there somehow. I know it's not real, but…

☾

Escalation. Building to a crescendo. That's the shape that a story takes. A blockbuster movie in particular.

You have to raise the stakes in the second act if you want to keep the audience on the hook.

Of course, I don't think this game of ours will have any trouble keeping the mob tuned in. We're serving up the red meat they crave, aren't we?

This I've learned: The audience loves nothing more than a violent spectacle. Blood and bone. Destruction and death.

The three-second burst of shock that real violence creates is the strongest drug in the world. They stare and gasp and shake their heads. Enthralled and denying it all the while, aroused by it yet somehow seeing themselves as above it.

Frantically licking at the blood on their teeth. Savoring it.

You're all here, aren't you? Reading this.

☾

I can't sleep, so I walk the streets at night. Zigzagging through the city blocks, veering at random intersections, cutting through alleys. Getting lost in that endless sea of concrete.

I get away from the downtown shit and end up in that endless expanse of small homes. Mile after mile of suburban sprawl. Little boxes blotting the landscape as far as the eye can see.

It's mostly quiet out in the residential areas, at least after dark like this. A dog barks in a backyard once in a while. A car zips past every couple minutes. Wind whistles through bushes and small trees. That's about it.

There are streetlights everywhere fighting the darkness, pools of yellow light sheening on the asphalt, glowing spheres everywhere even as you move away from the big buildings. Garage lamps join in the skirmish, along with the occasional floodlight tripped by my motion, bigger and brighter than the rest.

And I find that I move away from the light by instinct, gravitate toward the darker places. Every night I take a different route up into the hills. Tonight was the darkest yet. The quietest, too.

And I know, all the while, that there are people all around me. Millions and millions of people tucked away into all these little boxes, put away for the night. So many, many people. Eighteen and a half million souls in the metro area. I could walk all night and never reach the end of them.

Too many people.

But I can't really feel any of them there, and I know they can't feel me, either. Detached, you know. Separate.

In certain spots, when you're up in the hills, you can look down and see the busier streets down in the city below. Headlights streaming past, even into the wee hours.

Again, I think about all the people out there, sailing across the black sea of the city in their SUVs, all of them going nowhere fast.

But me? I'm not a part of that. Walking my own path. Walking alone. Walking into the unknown.

So I keep heading deeper into the darkness, stepping off the sidewalk and into a chunk of wilderness, finally leaving the streetlights behind. The woods thicken between the houses as I get up in the hills.

Tonight I found a spot tucked away in a valley, hidden from everything. The night sky was so clear here that the stars seemed to stretch all the way down to the ground.

The air smelled like cold wet dirt, and wildflowers bloomed in silvery patches of moonlight. The crickets were loud enough that it felt like they were keeping pace right along beside me as I went. Following me.

I came across an old willow tree and sat beneath it, letting my feet rest in the grass while I looked up at the starry night sky and dreamt of what might be beyond this world.

It seemed like the darkness between me and those stars was just never-ending. Made me feel real, finally. Made me feel alive.

It's funny, you know? Only when I'm alone in the dark do I really feel alive.

But loneliness is the only thing that's real. At least for people like me. I feel like I've finally accepted that, embraced it.

I've surrendered to that ultimate truth.

And now, finally, I can finish my work here.

☾

The time is short. That's the tricky thing to grasp.

The days are long, but the years go by like nothing. And soon enough it's over for each and every one of us.

Life is spent, one way or another, like I said. We all end up the meat on the altar. We all end up the hollowed-out, empty vessels laid out on the stainless steel slab.

And most of the time, most of the people, they get lost along the way. Awash in the thrum of the day-to-day activity. The buzz of the daily routine fills their head, drowns out all other thoughts. Drags them along in a trance.

Only now and then do they even ask themselves how they are spending their time, spending their life. The most important question anyone could ask themselves, and it comes up, what? Once a month? Once a year? Once a decade?

It all passes them by. The world just uses them up.

Don't let it be you. OK? Because it's all happening right now.

Not yesterday. Not tomorrow.

Now.

Never forget it.

CHAPTER 47

Back in the conference room, Darger studied the fresh journal pages. A hard copy this time, the white printer paper laid out in a stack before her. Her eyes stung now, and she couldn't stand reading off of her phone screen anymore.

Once again, Huxley's words tangled strands of rage and hatred and self-pity into weirdly compelling journal entries. The images leaped off the pages. She couldn't help but picture him alone in some dumpy house in Los Angeles, writing these notes to himself as much as anyone else.

She took a break from reading to rest her eyes. Stared at the clock on the opposite side of the conference table. Slowly watched the hour and then minute hand sharpen into focus. Finally she could even see the red sliver of the second hand slowly spinning.

A quick glance around the room showed a whole mess of task force members likewise reading the journal text over and over. Loshak sipped a Fanta while he worked. Fitch kept shrugging his shoulders and twitching his nose and brow like he couldn't quite get comfortable. The movements reminded Darger of a horse jiggling its muscles to shoo flies away.

When she looked back down at the journal pages, a memory blotted out her field of vision. She remembered the packet coming out of the ground, sliding out from under the sheet of sod. Rich black soil clouded the plastic bag at first, clumps of it falling away as Simmons lifted the thing, dark smears still smudging it where moisture had adhered a fine layer of black speckles to the sheet.

Even so, the top page became visible beyond the smudged plastic. Another cipher presented itself there. A cryptic grid of symbols, black shapes almost like hieroglyphics, stark against the white paper.

The image of the cipher made Darger wince; those symbols still held creepy connotations from their connection to the Zodiac case along with the first set of bombings.

The cryptanalysis team worked at cracking the cipher even now back in D.C. After speaking to Agent Remzi, Loshak had seemed hopeful enough that they'd have the clue soon.

In the meantime, Darger riffled the pages of the journal in front of her, moving back to the start and tapping the pile on the table to neaten the stack.

She began reading again.

CHAPTER 48

The minutes stretched into hours, but the cryptanalysis team never got back to them. The sun crept over the horizon, a dim light barely reaching over that black edge at first.

Darger found herself in a trance-like state. She stared at the journal without really seeing it, though that didn't really matter. She had the words more or less memorized by now. Random lines flashed into her head, her imagination trying to look through the text and stitch some deeper meaning together.

Every time some lone wolf crashes a van into a sidewalk crowded with pedestrians, I'll be there.

Loneliness is the only thing that's real. At least for people like me.

A strange wheezing sound coming from the corner of the room finally broke the spell.

Darger turned and saw Rohrbach slumped over. Snoring.

When she glanced around at the rest of the team, she saw slack faces and red-rimmed eyelids. It was time to start thinking about some kind of rest rotation.

She got up and nudged Rohrbach awake. He startled a little at first, eyes wide and scared as if he wasn't quite sure where he was, and then he blinked groggily at Darger.

"Shoot. Sorry about that."

"Don't apologize. Go home for a few hours. Get some sleep."

He stretched and shook his head.

"Nope. No way," he said, rubbing his eyes. "I'll tell you what I will do, though. I'm gonna go down to the locker room, take an ice-cold shower, maybe have a cigarette, and I'll be right as rain."

As Rohrbach left the room, Loshak perked up.

"There any more coffee?"

Darger drifted over to the refreshments table and lifted the pot. Less than a quarter-inch of muddy brown liquid sloshed around in the bottom of the carafe.

"Nope, but give me a minute."

She ducked out of the conference room and into the ladies' room across the hall. It took a few rinses and some vigorous scrubbing with a paper towel to get all of the condensed coffee sludge out of the carafe, and then she filled it back up with cold water.

Back in the conference room, she set about making a fresh pot, water glugging out of the carafe as she refilled the reservoir on the machine.

Darger's mind drifted as she went through the almost mindless task of preparing a pot of coffee. Something about her hands being busy seemed to stimulate her thoughts, focusing her on a few of the phrases from the journal.

The footage rolled in my head. Violence. Mayhem. The great spectacle, where my whole life has led me all along. I could walk down the aisles and see it.

Darger took a second to ponder the word that stuck out there.

Aisles.

He's walking down aisles in that quote. Could that be a clue as to where he'd go next?

She opened the filter compartment and tossed the old filter and grounds into a nearby garbage can, and then another quotation came to her.

But loneliness is the only thing that's real. At least for people like me. I feel like I've finally accepted that, embraced it.

I've surrendered to that ultimate truth.

And now, finally, I can finish my work here.

For Darger, it was hard to ignore the fatalism in that passage. Something final about it. Almost funereal. But was it truly significant? She didn't know.

She measured three scoops of Maxwell House into a new filter, then pressed the button to start the brew cycle.

And for just a second, the panic welled up in her. The time was racing past. The cryptanalysis team hadn't even cracked the cipher yet.

What if they don't?

What if we have nothing?

What if we can't stop the next bomb?

The first jet of coffee spurted into the carafe, sizzling when it hit the glass that was already hot from sitting on the warming plate.

No.

No.

The cryptanalysis team will solve the cipher. They have to.

In the meantime, keep working the journal. It's all you can do.

Darger whispered that turn of phrase again, *loneliness is the only thing that's real*, as if saying the words out loud might help her make some further leap of logic. It did not.

Her jaw flexed. She was close to something. She could feel it.

The coffee machine gave a final gurgle and went quiet. After filling her own cup, Darger did a circuit of the room, replenishing the cups of her comrades like a waitress.

She'd just set the carafe back in place when clattering footsteps echoed in the hall. The door of the conference room burst open hard enough to bang against the doorstop, which let out a wobbly *twaaaaaang.*

All heads turned to stare at a moist and disheveled Detective Rohrbach standing in the doorway.

From the look of him, he'd been halfway through getting dressed when he ran up to the conference room. Barefoot. Rust-colored hair still wet and going in all directions. Shirt half-buttoned.

He licked his lips before he spoke.

"Ready for another shit show? Check out *The Daily Gawk.*"

CHAPTER 49

Fitch loaded the tabloid site on the laptop connected to the projector. A second later, the livestream started playing in that glowing box on the wall.

Vinnie Savage's face filled the frame, the faintest smile touching his lips and eyes. His silvery hair was perfect as ever.

"—can promise you that neither I nor our producers were expecting something like this to happen today," Savage was in the middle of saying. "I mean, we put our invitation out there, but… I guess you never really expect it to happen."

Something about his dewy, tan skin reminded Darger of a gas station hot dog.

"For those of you just tuning in, we have quite the development. We've got the bomber, Tyler Huxley, live on the line now."

"What the fuck," Fitch whispered under his breath.

Savage yammered on, the excitement clear in his voice.

"Mr. Huxley, are you still there?"

Darger held her breath and waited for the answer. There was a staticky sound of someone exhaling.

"I'm here and losing patience. Can you or can't you get me what I asked for?"

The voice was oddly distorted. Probably a voice modulation app of some kind.

"And just to reiterate, what you're asking for is to speak with the attorney Howard Barclay," the host said.

An annoyed huff.

"I know you have to repeat and rephrase everything I say to

make sure the dumdums tuning in can actually follow along, but I have to tell you, Vinnie, it's starting to get annoying."

Darger leaned back against the table and closed her eyes, focusing on trying to identify the voice as Huxley's, but whatever the caller was using to alter their voice made it impossible to tell.

"But just so no one is confused: yes, I want to speak with Howard Barclay."

"OK, Mr. Huxley. Very well. My producer is on the line with Mr. Barclay's law office as we speak. Rest assured, we are doing everything we can to get him on the line. But while we work on that, there's something I'm desperate to understand, and I'm sure our viewers are as well. Why are you doing this?"

No one in the conference room moved. All eyes locked on that image of Vinnie Savage blinking on the screen, waiting for Huxley's response.

The bomber sighed a little into the phone's microphone. Then he spoke.

"Why am I doing this? Calling you? Livestreaming on your awful tabloid's website? Well, I was hoping you'd bore me to death with dumb questions like this, of course. Why else would I do it?"

Savage gaped on the screen. Then he smiled.

"I meant to ask why you're committing the bombings, but I like your answer. Your bluntness is refreshing."

"Ah. The bombings, yes. Everyone wants to know why. I write page after page explaining just that, detailing it down to the fine points, and still they all wonder how they might get a clue. But that's what people are like, in my experience. Always ignoring what's right in front of them. Always looking for something else, something more. Mankind is a restless beast.

Never satisfied."

Huxley fell quiet for a moment. Vinnie Savage made a face — what he must have thought would seem like a serious news anchor expression, though to Darger he looked more constipated than anything.

The bomber went on, sounded a little exasperated.

"Really, honestly, I'd just like to talk to Howard Barclay if you can make that happen. You offered help. I'm taking you up on it. It's that simple, Vinnie."

"We're working on Barclay now, like I said," Savage said. "Let's take a quick break and come back when we get him on the stream. I don't think I need to say this, but stay tuned."

The screen flicked to a commercial for some kind of medication.

Fitch tapped a button on the laptop to mute the ad, and then he turned away from the glowing projector image.

"So this Howard Barclay guy… does he represent celebrities?"

"Oh yeah," Rohrbach said. "He's a big deal. He represented Charlotte Ainsworth when her lifestyle company sold that anti-wrinkle serum that gave a bunch of people chemical burns. He was involved in the Tiffany March/Andrew Reed divorce case and also the big defamation suit that came after. Actually, the trial that really put him on the map was the Tom Giovanni drunk driving manslaughter thing way back when."

"The guy with the talk show? Where we found the first clue."

"One and the same," Rohrbach said.

Darger hopped to her feet. One of Huxley's earlier lines echoed in her head.

And still they all wonder how they might get a clue.

"We need to go back and watch this from the beginning."

She felt everyone's eyes on her as she extended two fingers and pointed them at the projector screen like the barrel of a gun.

"The cryptanalysis team has yet to solve the latest cipher. What if it's unsolvable on purpose? Like the two remaining Zodiac ciphers?"

She blinked hard before she finished her thought.

"What if this call *is* our clue?"

CHAPTER 50

The drug dealer, Kav, sits in Savage's Porsche, the bucket seat cupping his moist body, his aching lower back. His phone is jammed to his ear. Fat beads of sweat grease his forehead so that slice of skin glistens like a rotisserie chicken in the rearview mirror.

He lights a new cigarette off the one he just smoked down to the butt. Exhales more smoke into the clouds already scudding across the car's ceiling and roiling there.

The plastic burner case sits on the passenger seat. A clam shell all ripped along the top edge where he took his keys to it to get it open. Punctured it and tore at the side like he was shucking an actual oyster.

The laptop rests on his lap. The script Savage wrote for him glows there on the monitor. The words went down in a speed-induced blur last night; Kav could tell that when Savage made the offer, talking way too fast, and he can tell it now as he reads the fevered text on the screen.

One hundred thousand dollars in crypto. That was the offer Savage made. Kav took about two seconds to accept.

This phony call into the livestream is the plan. Pretending to be the killer. For better or worse.

"I'm here and losing patience. Can you or can't you get me what I asked for?"

☾

Up in his apartment, livestreaming, Savage looks away from the camera for just a second while the distorted voice launches into a fresh monologue that is a kind of rambling word salad of Huxley quotes stitched together. The reporter gazes out his office window, looking down at the Porsche in the parking lot. He can only kind of see Kav there, sitting in the passenger seat.

What he can really see is smoke rolling out of the open window. He'd told the son of a bitch, specifically, not to smoke in his fucking Porsche.

No matter.

The call will make the few weeks of lingering Camel smell more than worth it.

The call will change the narrative. Grab even more headlines. Perhaps set the stage for the bomber to reach out for real. It's worth the shot, he thinks.

Huxley ultimately strikes Vinnie as an opportunist above all. Shrewd in the ways of publicity. A storyteller. A narcissist. With something like this, he'd want to wrestle back control of the narrative, wouldn't he? And maybe in that way he could be pulled into the media sphere, use the tools made available to him.

The bomber would see this publicity stunt as an opportunity, a wide open door to capture the public's imagination all the more. The cliffhanger serial killer call-in. All the soccer moms and office dads edging up to the edges of their seats. Rapt. Hypnotized.

And would he really be able to resist the chance to interject? Savage is betting he will not. That's the gambit.

The distorted voice wraps up its monologue.

"The revolution will be etched into celebrity skin."

A direct quote from the real Huxley. A little heavy-handed, maybe, but the public will eat it up.

☾

Kav lets the line trail off. Breathes into the phone mic — the sigh part aggressive, part mournful.

He's got a rag over the mouthpiece of the phone — totally unnecessary with the voice changer app distorting his voice, albeit subtly, but something about the flap of fabric makes him feel more confident, more concealed. A spider tucked out of sight, watching its victim get tangled in the filaments of the web.

"I'm going to go now. But I'll get in touch again soon. Get it all off my chest."

Savage lets the silence linger. Lets the tension stretch out. Finally, the fake killer goes on.

"I don't know. I just…"

☾

Savage licks his lips, and the motion pulls his eyes to the mirror just off camera, the one he uses to fix his hair before he goes live.

He watches himself there. Feels suddenly distanced from the moment, from the call. Like this is a tense scene in a movie he's watching. He's one step removed.

The character smiles a little on that small sheet of glass that has momentarily become the silver screen. The daring scoundrel, neither hero nor villain, something clever and amused detectable in the corners of his lips.

Savage watches himself projected there in the center of the frame and finds it exhilarating.

CHAPTER 51

While the live video kept playing on the overhead, Darger opened her own laptop. It was easy enough to drag the cursor back on the progress bar to watch the beginning of the phone call. Even better, the video had real-time transcription, which meant she could look at the text as well.

Darger scanned through the first page of the transcript.

HOST: You're *the* Tyler Huxley? The man responsible for the bombing attacks in New York and now here in Los Angeles?

CALLER: The one and only.

HOST: There are rumors a bomb was found at the Beachside Casino and Resort last night. Can you confirm that?

CALLER: Yes. I thought the bimbo supermodel who lives in the penthouse there would look so much better in pieces, so I left her a little present. The police found it before it went *boom*, but that's OK. I'm only getting started.

Darger glanced up at the version of the video playing on the wall, trying to keep track of what was happening live. There was scrolling text at the bottom of the screen now.

"BREAKING: *The Daily Gawk's* Vinnie Savage chats live with Tyler Huxley, streaming now."

Vinnie Savage put his hand to his ear and sat up straighter.

"I just want to give everyone a quick update on the situation here. I'm told Mr. Barclay is in his office now and will be joining the stream within minutes. During the last commercial break, I had the opportunity to talk a bit off the air with Tyler, and I put forth a proposal. Would you mind if I shared that with our viewers?"

"Do whatever you want," the strange voice said, sounding amused.

"Fair enough. I asked Tyler if he would consider some sort of quid pro quo arrangement. If we got Mr. Barclay on the show, Tyler would give us additional information as to where the next attack is going to take place. Are you willing to honor that agreement, Tyler?"

The room went silent as they waited to hear the answer.

"Yes. *After* I talk with the lawyer."

"'Course he's gonna say that," Rohrbach said, seeming to address the TV more than anyone in the actual room. "He wants his big moment with Barclay."

Darger moved on to the second page of the transcript, which began with Savage asking, "Why are you doing this?"

HOST: OK, Mr. Huxley. My producer is on the line with Mr. Barclay's law office as we speak. Rest assured, we are doing everything we can to get him here. But while we work on that, there's something I'm desperate to understand, and I'm sure our viewers are as well. Why are you doing this?

CALLER: Because we're living in Hell.

HOST: "Living in Hell"? What does that mean, exactly?

CALLER: A child dies from hunger every ten seconds on this planet. In many cases it's not long after they're born in the first place. They're born to die, you could say. That's it. Meanwhile, you have the Dirk Nielsens and Dawn Barbozas of the world living in multi-million-dollar penthouses. Gorging themselves however they please. Why? Because they look good in their underwear.

HOST: I—

CALLER: This is what normal looks like. This is the pinnacle of humankind's progress. Every step of evolution working to lead us to this reality. Mass death. Suffering. Cruelty. Brutality. Misery. Hell is already here. We made it. We are living it. They call it the American dream, but it's all bullshit. So kill it. That's why I'm here, why I was born. To kill the dream one celebrity at a time.

Darger read the last line and jumped out of her chair.

"What is it?" Loshak asked.

She was too busy shuffling through the hard copy of the Huxley file they'd brought along to answer. When she found what she was looking for, she set it down in front of Loshak.

"This is part of the journal we found in New York. Read this line here."

Loshak's brows scrunched together as he read the text out loud.

"'That's why I'm here, why I was born. To kill the dream one celebrity at a time.'"

Darger pointed at the corresponding line of the transcript.

"They're the same," Loshak said. "Word for word."

A beat later he raised his eyes to meet hers, and she knew he was thinking the same thing she was.

"The call is fake."

Rohrbach swung around to face them.

"Wait. What?"

"Huxley wouldn't recycle old material," Loshak explained. "It's a screenwriting rule, right? No repeated beats. He's a better storyteller than that."

"Not to mention that he's too much of an egomaniac to

half-ass something like this," Darger added. "He's a planner, remember? He has a script for every attack with meticulous timing. And this call feels like someone doing improv. Trying to keep the call going as long as he can. If Huxley did something like this, he'd have a big reveal in mind. He'd get to the point, and then he'd get out."

Fitch was bobbing his head.

"The more I think about it, the more sense it makes."

"If the call is fake, we're back to square one, and we're running out of time," Rohrbach said, rubbing his eyes.

On the livestream, Howard Barclay's face now filled half the screen as he joined the broadcast via Zoom. His chiseled features and broad, tan face made him look younger than his 66 years, though the white hair revealed the truth.

Savage smiled like a wolf as he welcomed the lawyer on-screen.

"We really appreciate you getting linked up with us so quickly," he said. "Tyler, are you there? I assume you're watching and can see that we've done what you asked. Mr. Barclay is here."

Barclay nodded from his half of the screen.

"Hello, Mr. Huxley."

"Mr. Barclay. I've been so eager to meet you."

"So I hear. Now, I'd like to say something before we go any further. I'm not sure if this discussion is business or personal, but I imagine you're aware of something called attorney-client privilege. If you're calling to retain my services or even just ask for legal advice, I would be remiss not to suggest that we do so in private so that our conversation could remain confidential."

Savage, looking suddenly panicked, sputtered out something like a cough.

"I don't think we need to—"

The caller chuckled.

"Relax, Vinnie. I was just about done here, anyway. Growing bored." He sighed. "I appreciate your concern, Mr. Barclay, but I want everyone to hear what I have to say."

The line held silent for the length of a few breaths. When the fake Huxley's voice sounded again, it seemed louder, deeper, right on top of the phone mic.

"The revolution will be etched into celebrity skin."

Then the dead air resumed. The silence straining. The faux Huxley's voice softened this time.

"I'm going to go now. But I'll get in touch again soon. Get it all off my chest."

Darger and Loshak looked at each other. Even if the call was fake, it held some genuine tension, fascination. Someone out there was doing this, for whatever twisted reason.

"I don't know. I just..."

There was a click, and then the line went dead.

CHAPTER 52

After the phone call was over, the conference room grew grim quickly. Darger could feel the dread swell in the space, a palpable negative wave in the air.

Loshak called the cryptanalysis team, but they still had nothing. She could see that etched on her partner's face even as he listened to Remzi on the other end of the line.

He didn't even say anything when the call was over. Just shook his head.

The cold, hard reality caught up with Darger all at once.

They only had 90 minutes or so until the next bomb should go off, and they still didn't even have a clue to work with, let alone a location.

Oh my God.

We aren't going to make it in time.

We just aren't.

Somewhere out there in the city, the bomb was waiting. Ready. Tucked away.

And they were powerless to find it, powerless to stop it.

Darger clenched her teeth. The overwhelming dread made her feel like she'd either vomit or explode from it sooner or later.

Loshak and Rohrbach both appeared listless and exhausted. Long faces, utterly blank for the both of them.

In the opposite corner of the room, Agent Fitch looked like a little kid about to cry. He couldn't stop blinking.

And the clock only seemed to speed up.

CHAPTER 53

The sports car idles just shy of the gate. A curving black lane curls out of view into the woods beyond the boom bar, with just a hint of the mansions poking up through the trees there.

It's getting toward lunchtime, but the air retains a touch of that morning crispness. A little heavy.

Trent Carter leans out of the driver's side window to punch in the code, the stainless steel buttons cool against the tips of his fingers. The bar slides up as he settles back into the bucket seat, and then the Bugatti glides through the opening.

Should he ever feel self-conscious about driving a $900,000 car around Los Angeles, rich and rough parts alike, that feeling evaporates as soon as he passes through these gates.

Here, in Sand Piper Country Estates, an ostentatious display of wealth is far from the norm. The gated community nestles a smattering of full-blown mansions into the wooded terrain of the hills, multi-million-dollar estates hidden in the trees; others that look like Frank Lloyd Wright side projects lay themselves bare up on the hilltops, posed provocatively there like the architectural equivalent of pin-ups. Showing a little art glass here and pier-and-cantilever structural system there. All 15,000 square feet of each home sprawling for the centerfold shot.

The ball of his foot presses the accelerator, and the car thrums at his touch, building speed. After he rolls through the first wave of mansions, the more modern part of the neighborhood crops up — newer construction, still huge homes but lacking the class and character of their earlier counterparts. All gaudy things set in the hills way back from the road. Tons of glass and brick. Fussy.

The clumps of unkempt woods give way to expanses of manicured sod in this part of the subdivision. Looks like the Disneyland version of what being rich might be like. Somehow phony and cutesy.

For a second, he can't remember why he wanted to live here.

But then he does. Exactly. The memory comes clear all at once.

The closing on the house was just three weeks after his show hit number one. He was so high at the title office that he nodded out before they could place the papers in front of him to sign. With his sunglasses on, nobody could tell at first. Then he drooled, and the title agent, a bony woman in her late 40s, nudged his elbow. All the real estate people gawked as he signed the papers, and then he never saw them again. Never so much as thought of them until now.

Before his acting career took off, he used to go to open houses in neighborhoods like this, looking for pills in the medicine cabinets and nightstands. A few percs here. A few oxys there. Xanax. Fentanyl. Vicodin. Demerol.

One time he pilfered a few Klonopins and sloshed them down as soon as he was back in his car. He didn't remember anything that had happened for the next 60 hours. He woke up two days later in a dingy motel in Bakersfield, 50 miles from home, some kind of smoky mesquite barbecue sauce smeared on the frosted glass of the shower stall door like the maroon blood of some George Lucas or James Cameron creature.

Anyway, those memories of filching prescription drugs are what planted the dream in his head, he thinks. In neighborhoods like this, there is no pain. It can't exist. Every medicine cabinet is filled to the brim with tablets created to eradicate hurt, to flush it away, to overpower it with an all-you-can-eat endorphin buffet.

And if he could live there full time? The bliss would never end.

The Bugatti hugs along the row of shrubs that marks the edge of his property, and then it's his house rising up over the trees.

More glass and brick and absurd architectural flourishes. Shards of sunlight refract off the expansive windows and twirl over the harsh angle of the single-sloped roof.

More tacky and modern than the Frank Lloyd Wright shit, he must admit. He hadn't only been high when he signed the papers. He'd been high when he toured the place, high when he made the offer, all of it. Only later, with a clear head, could he see how it looked over the top enough to be the kind of place where Pablo Escobar might spend the winter months. Even the bathroom looked like the place where a 1980s drug dealer would hang out — jet-black toilet with a gaudy chrome inlay.

He cranks the wheel, and the sports car climbs the sloped driveway. His eyes bug a little when he sees it.

A plain cardboard package rests on the doorstep. That's the one. Fresh from India where the pharmacies are only really strict about the money part.

He can taste the bitter pills just looking at the box. That stripe of medicinal harshness trailing from the back of his tongue all the way down his esophagus, somewhere in there transitioning from a flavor to more of a feeling.

And he thinks about how weird that is. That the body learns all the little details around a reward like drugs, how that wired connection grows and blooms until he has learned to not just enjoy that awful pill taste but to fantasize about it.

It makes him think about an article he'd read about psychological tests performed on rats. Rats given jolts of dopamine for pressing a button will eventually lose interest in food. They just chase that dopamine rush relentlessly, mindlessly, no longer willing to cross the cage to eat, no longer caring about anything else but pressing that button, even their own survival.

Nature's flaw, maybe, but he understands it. He presses the button with pills, and it feels good. It feels so fucking good.

He parks in the driveway, eschewing the garage as it'd take those few seconds longer to get to the little box on the porch. Nothing else matters now.

He strides up to the front stoop. Sighs as he bends to pick up the rectangular brown package, the cardboard smooth and cool against his fingers, against his palms.

Even before he heads inside, he strangles the box under one arm and punches a house key through the layer of scotch tape. Pierces it right where the two flaps of cardboard meet. Then he fingers the hole, gently prods, trying to get enough of a hold to peel it open.

Too much tape. He can only get about one knuckle deep, fingernail scritching beyond the threshold but to no avail.

He sighs and heads inside. Stands in a foyer reeking of a $200 candle that's supposed to smell like lavender but reminds him of toilet cleaner.

He lets his eyes adjust to the shaded interior. His gaze traces over the console table just beyond the door until the knobs protruding from it come clear.

He takes a letter opener shaped like a cutlass from a mug

there. Fumbles with it for a second. Jams the pointy end into that film of packing tape and rips to the side.

The tape gives. Parts.

The box seems to exhale. Cardboard easing some in his hands like those knotted muscles in the lower back finally letting go.

He peels the thing open, so ready to free the payload, to let that bitterness trail over his lips and tongue and down his gullet. A faint moan of ecstasy is just barely audible somewhere deep in his throat.

He paces into the living room and sets the box down on the desk. Reaches into the shadowy cardboard opening.

Something pops inside the box, a crack that almost sounds electrical. Sharp.

The noise makes him jump just a little, shoulders shaking, feet shuffling. Something clenches in his gut.

And then orange leaps from the cardboard flaps. A fireball. Too bright.

The heat swells to overtake his face.

CHAPTER 54

Sharon is drying her hands on a kitchen towel when she hears the muffled whoosh and hiss ring out over the neighborhood. A tiny thundercrack that rolls for two seconds and cuts out. Close, though.

For a second she is still. Towel motionless in her hands. Processing. Listening.

Then she leans over the stainless steel crater of the kitchen sink to press her face close to the window there. Head scanning left and then the right.

The suburban scene holds motionless beyond the glass. A vast sheet of grass interrupted here and there with high-end landscaping flourishes. An uneven row of mansions stretching away from that, partially obscured by trees, shrubs, the pale wooden planks of privacy fences.

No movement.

Must be nothing.

Right?

"Did you hear that?" she calls out.

She can hear Steve's shoes shuffling in the next room, but he fails to respond to the question.

"We're out of Joe-Joe's," he says, and for just a second she pictures the Oreo knock-offs. The chocolate cookie image strikes her as absurd given the explosion somewhere outside.

She doesn't dare leave this screen looking out at the neighborhood. Instead, she asks again, sharpens the tone of her voice to cut through the walls.

"Did you hear that, hon?"

"Sounded like an explosion or something. But a weird one. Oh! That reminds me."

His footsteps clop closer, something in the gait reminding her of an excited dog getting ready for its walk, and then his figure fills the kitchen doorway to Sharon's left.

He's a slightly stooped version of what he once was. Shoulders broad but just that little bit rounded. Stubble gone white crawls up to his cheekbones like a thin layer of snow. But she can still see the man she married there. Something masculine in the big jaw and square chin, even in the gray eyes. And the tie-dyed shirt and cargo shorts give him that leisurely California retiree look that fits his true personality even if the age showing in his face doesn't.

He rattles his keys against the leg of his cargo shorts as he talks.

"There have been reports all over the country of these explosion sounds in the atmosphere. Unexplained shit. Hang on."

He plops the keys down on the quartz swath of the kitchen island and goes back to scrolling on his phone.

"Multiple reports in Utah. Idaho. Binghamton, New York. Grand Rapids, Michigan. Jacksonville, Florida."

They fall quiet. Steve studies the phone screen another few seconds before he speaks.

"Could be aliens."

Sharon wrenches her face away from the window to glare at him.

"What?"

"I'm just saying. It could be aliens. These mysterious explosions."

Sharon doesn't say anything. She glides past him into the

living room. Moves to another window and looks out at vast seas of green, the hills rolling away from her like waves.

"Look, they're out there, Sharon. More likely than not. You ever read about the stuff in Muskegon?"

But she's not listening. She's got her nose jammed to within a quarter inch of another glass pane. Watching the side yard now, the corner of the McCluskey house in the middle distance.

"On one night in 1993 or '94, they had hundreds of calls of sightings of, uh, UFOs, you know. Muskegon. Holland, Michigan. All the way down the coast of Lake Michigan to Chicago. And the National Weather Service tracked the things on the, whadaya — radar or whatever. Crazy story. There are recordings of it all, weather service phone calls with law enforcement and the military. I'm not sure why it's not household knowledge, to be honest. It's like maybe *someone* doesn't want us to know."

Something twitches outside. A dark thing lumbering and disappearing behind a thick barrier of bushes.

Sharon gasps.

Steve looks up from his phone. Eyes wide. His voice comes out as a thick croak.

"What?"

Sharon jabs a finger at the window. Thrusts it a few times.

"It was close. Right up alongside the house off to the left, moving toward the front yard, toward the..."

"What was?"

But she's off again. Running to the front of the house. Pressing herself to yet another window, the big bay window at the front of the living room.

Quiet. Both hands touch the glass, fingers kind of clawed

there like she might try to climb through it.

She angles herself to try to peer into the front left corner of the yard, to try to see what she can. Her field of vision stretching that way like a camera panning.

Nothing.

The suburban sprawl has fallen quiet again. A painting of an upper-class landscape at rest.

And then the thing lurches toward her from just next to the window. A black and red smear. Frantic.

A bloody face thrusting itself toward the glass.

Sharon's arms retract into a Tyrannosaurus rex pose against her chest. But she can't look away, can't step back. Can only take in the details.

Blackened rumples pucker around the mouth where the lips have been shriveled. Red teeth looking wet beneath that. Laid bare.

Exposed bone punches through charred flesh where the brow ridge protrudes. Bleached-white lines gleaming over the orbits of the eyes.

One eye looks melted shut, puddled flesh covering it over.

The other eye is opened wide. Alarmed. Panicking.

The rest of the face looks blackened. Skeletal. Blistered in patches.

Seared dry meat like beef jerky connects the cheekbones to the jaw. Fibrous filaments that flex and lurch and bunch.

The horror presses right up to the window in front of her face. Thuds as it makes contact. Smears its red on the glass there.

And Sharon screams.

CHAPTER 55

The victim's home was located in a gated community, an area of Beverly Hills known as Sand Piper Country Estates, Rohrbach informed them on the drive over.

"Median home price is something like ten million bucks. Can you imagine paying over forty grand a month for your mortgage? Makes my ass clench just thinking about it."

Gentle curves and even gentler slopes bent and tilted the streets here. A few of the houses sat on smaller hills, but most of the community sprawled on fat expanses of sod. Compared to the winding roads and dramatically placed homes in the hills leading up to the Hollywood sign, this was awfully straight and orderly. A little manicured, Darger thought. A little tame.

She thought about the clue on the ride over. The cryptanalysis team had managed to decipher it with minutes to spare. Too late for them to solve it, let alone do anything.

She read the text off her phone again. Even though they already knew where to go, even though the bomb had blown, she wanted to find the answers held there, wanted to understand it.

Lights. Camera. Action.

Now we approach the final climax. The cameras zoom in for the kill shot. Follow my path to glory.

(Ain't it grand?)

It's justice in a way. Rough justice, to be sure. Not the kind society hands down typically.

But this is in service of something bigger, something better.

We can make a better world. If you want it. If you will it.

In the straight world, justice is rarely blind.

Especially here in Babylon, where everyone worships the cult of beauty.

By the time they arrived on the scene, the street Trent Carter lived on was so clogged with first responders that Rohrbach had to park at the end of the block, and they all walked up to the house.

Neighbors gathered at the edges of the yellow tape crisscrossing a sidewalk shaded by rows of eucalyptus trees. Older ladies with coifed hair and expensive-looking shoes. Men in thousand-dollar sunglasses and overly tailored jeans. Gawking wasn't just for the unwashed masses, apparently.

Darger couldn't stop herself from imagining absurd versions of suburban complaints. *Um, homemade explosives are in direct violation of the HOA guidelines. What do I even pay the fees for, if they're not going to enforce the rules?*

She didn't have to ask which place belonged to Trent Carter. The front lawn was already dotted with task force members in white suits.

The house itself was a modern monstrosity, all glass and brick and jutting angles. A gaudy, exaggerated caricature of a Beverly Hills mansion. A paved bricked driveway surrounded a cluster of king palms and a jacaranda tree. The yard was lush and green.

Probably costs a small fortune to keep it watered, Darger thought.

The front door stood open like a yawning mouth. And a clear trail of evidence markers ran from the door, over the lawn, across the street, and through one of the neighboring driveways. The small plastic tents appeared to stop beneath a window of the neighboring house near a planting of white roses.

As they get closer, Darger began to see exactly what the tiny yellow tents were marking. Blood.

Flies buzzed and flitted in the sticky puddles of liquefied tissue.

Agent Tanaka handed them each a set of PPE and gave a summary of what they'd found so far.

"It appears there was a package left outside. The victim took it in the house and opened it. After detonation, he ran out here. As you can see by the evidence markers, he took a kind of meandering path from his front door over to the neighbor's house across the way."

"So he was still conscious after the explosion?"

"We think he was probably in and out, operating purely on fight or flight. He probably had some instinctual urge to flee, maybe even seek help. But it was more automatic and reflexive than deliberate. Thus the confused, zigzagging route."

It wouldn't be the first time Darger had seen someone sustain a traumatic injury and somehow stay on their feet. Some desperate animal impulse keeping them moving.

Chief Cattermole approached, phone in hand, face grim.

"That was the trauma surgeon from Cedars-Sinai. She assured me they're doing everything they can, but the vic sustained severe burns to a significant portion of his body. The tissue damage is… extensive."

Everyone went quiet for a moment, waiting to see who'd ask the question that was on all of their minds. It was Loshak who broke the silence.

"Do they think he'll make it?"

The chief shrugged, and the Tyvek material of his white suit crinkled with the movement.

"She said it's touch and go for now, but he has a chance."

Darger's gaze went to a clump of sedge just off to her left. The long yellow-green leaves were dappled with tiny red dots that glittered in the sunlight.

She stared at the glistening droplets of blood and felt cold all over. An innocent man had suffered because they couldn't get here fast enough, and now he'd either end up dead or scarred for life because of it.

They couldn't let it happen again. They had to be faster. *She* had to be faster. Better.

And that meant finding the next clue. Now.

On cue, Loshak interrupted her internal stewing.

"You ready to take a look inside?"

She took a breath, nodding, and they swished through the grass toward the open front door of Trent Carter's mansion.

CHAPTER 56

The foyer of the victim's house opened into a circular room with a floating stairway following the curved wall. There was no handrail, and just looking at it gave Darger vertigo. A chandelier with black tubular pendants hung in the center of the space, and what appeared to be a live potted hibiscus tree stretched nearly all the way to the vaulted ceiling.

The fabric booties over Darger's shoes swished as they passed a dining room walled off by a glass-enclosed wine cellar. The hallway leading to the living room featured a series of framed posters for projects Carter had worked on, and suddenly the clues in the cipher made sense.

There was one for his hit TV show, *Blind Justice* — a courtroom drama in which he played a visually impaired lawyer. Another was for Lucio Mancini's war epic *The Path to Glory.* If Darger remembered correctly, it had been his big break. His role was small, but everyone agreed he stole the few scenes he was in.

In the straight world, justice is rarely blind.

The cameras zoom in for the kill shot. Follow my path to glory.

Finally, they reached the living room. There was a grand piano in one corner, and arched recessed niches in the walls displayed various sculptures: a statue Darger could only describe as "Mickey Mouse on acid," an oversized figurine of a businessman with the head of a wolf, a small-scale reproduction of Venus de Milo, with her naked torso covered in graffiti.

The decor was a mix of modern and traditional that Darger found she didn't totally hate. But the real focus of the living room was the bank of sliding frameless windows that opened onto a courtyard. Beyond the glass, Darger spotted a small oasis complete with a pool and hot tub, walled off from the neighbors with orange trees and a massive pride of Madeira shrub with big purple flower spikes.

Permeating everything was the acrid smell of burned plastic. Half a dozen bunny-suited figures clustered just inside the room, near a row of built-in bookcases. One column of shelves and the wall above was singed black. A pair of mid-century chairs with Lucite arms and legs were partially melted. The floor was still wet and puddled with grungy water from where the fire crew put the blaze out.

One of the white suits peeled off and came toward them.

"Agent Haslett," Loshak said, putting his hand out. "I was hoping they'd bring you in."

Haslett was the top chemist with the Scientific Response Analysis Unit at the FBI and had assisted with the first Huxley investigation.

"Flew in on a red-eye this morning." Haslett glanced back at the charred area of the room. "Just in time, it appears. Although I hear I missed a bit of fun with a TATP device last night."

"That's right."

"Truly nasty stuff," Haslett said and shook his head.

"You know it's bad when even the C-IED guys are spooked," Darger said. "Is that what he used here?"

"No, and there's frankly very little of the device remaining. But from what I've observed myself and what the witnesses described, I think this one was more of an incendiary device than a traditional bomb. Something like a thermite grenade, which wouldn't produce so much an explosion as a ball of fire hot enough to melt steel. We're talking 4,500 degrees Fahrenheit. It's how they weld railroad tracks."

Loshak cupped his chin in his hand.

"How advanced is this? It seems like he's getting more experimental this time."

Haslett inhaled and adjusted his glasses.

"Assuming he did indeed use thermite, it's actually quite simple to make. Basic thermite is just aluminum powder and iron oxide. In case your chemistry is a little rusty, remember that aluminum is significantly higher on the electrochemical series than iron. And the greater the distance between the two metals, the more intense the reaction will be when combined.

"So you get the aluminum and iron oxide ground down into nice fine powders so that when you mix them up you have lots of contact. The second you ignite that mixture, there's a vigorous transfer of oxygen from the iron oxide to the aluminum, resulting in an immensely exothermic reaction. Pretty much instantly turns into molten iron."

He pointed to a clump of something that had melted clear through the rug and into the wood floor. Darger had assumed it was either human tissue or plastic from one of the oozing chair legs, but now she saw that it was shiny. Metallic.

"Wait. That's metal?"

Haslett nodded.

"Slag. When the fire department came in, it was still glowing red."

"Jesus," Rohrbach said.

"In chemistry lab in college, we used to make thermite all the time, especially if we were doing some kind of demo for a high school or wanted to impress a girl or something," Haslett said. "We'd combine glycerin and potassium permanganate as a sort of self-lighting fuse, maybe a magnesium ribbon for luck, and *WHOOSH*! Produces a really impressive fireball. Looks like the surface of the sun.

"In this case, he likely constructed it with some kind of electrical ignition. I'd expect something similar to his other devices. More precise than the improvised igniters we used in the lab, since he had to make sure it would go off when he wanted it to go off."

Agent Fitch stepped forward. He'd been listening in from the doorway behind them.

"I've heard it's actually standard procedure when a US embassy is overrun, like in Benghazi, to use thermite grenades to destroy sensitive documents," the big CIRG agent said. "They'd set up a paint can-sized grenade on top of a filing cabinet and let it do its thing."

Darger couldn't help but picture the scene, some cold twinge of déjà vu accompanying the images in her skull.

Trent Carter opening the package. A molten fireball enveloping his face in brightness. Singeing hair. Melting skin.

And the bits of slag hitting the chairs, the carpet, the books. Fiery orange. Catching. Spreading.

Flames licking and lurching up the wall. Blackening patches of drywall. Blistering paint. Reaching higher and higher.

Darger's gaze landed on the solidified puddle of slag on the floor, and she tried — and failed — to *not* imagine what something like that did when it came in contact with human flesh. A prickle of revulsion crept up her spine.

She was thankful when Rohrbach broke the silence.

"Guess we should join in the search for the next clue." His

eyes scanned the room. "Any idea where we should start?"

Darger's mind leaped to the most recent cipher, and before she'd even fully worked through the conclusion, her feet were moving.

CHAPTER 57

Vinnie Savage hunched over the wheel of his Porsche once more. He'd crisscrossed Los Angeles over the course of the day, plumbed the guts of the city, slashed right through the heart of the thing, and now exhaustion was settling in.

His legs and back ached. Muscles twinging in that plane where his spine and legs connected.

Still, the fake Huxley call had been streamed 59 million times and counting — a new *Daily Gawk* single-day record. In the right company, he'd admit to having watched it a couple times himself, marveling at the image of his own face as it broadcast out over the whole world in bold, saturated HD color.

He'd spent the afternoon shuttling around L.A., filming at key locations — the Tate house, the suburban lot where the Black Dahlia's body had been found — and now he was heading to Trent Carter's mansion to wrap things up.

For today, he'd let the Huxley call remain the star, let it rake in views without stepping on its momentum. The video he was working on now, featuring him standing outside of Sharon Tate's house and so on, would go live tomorrow morning. He'd walk people through all the scenes involved in the Huxley investigation, give those grim backstories of Tate and the Dahlia, all the graphic details to get the public's blood up.

He'd be ready to keep the hype going, keep making himself part of the story, front and center. The publicity beast was hungry anew every morn, and Vinnie Savage had more red meat, ready to feed it.

CHAPTER 58

Darger's intuition carried her back to the hallway, where she halted in front of the framed posters they'd walked by on their way in.

"'...justice is rarely blind.' And '...follow my path to glory,'" she quoted, pointing at each poster in turn.

Loshak nodded.

"Both lines from the cipher." He licked his lips and quirked his head toward the frames. "Shall we?"

"Let's do it," Darger said, stepping closer to the wall.

She grasped the sides of the *Blind Justice* poster and lifted it from its hanger. It was over three feet tall with real glass glazing, which made it surprisingly heavy. Gingerly, she lowered it to the ground and flipped it face down.

Loshak did the same with the *Paths of Glory* poster.

There didn't appear to be anything tacked to the back of either frame, so they bent the tabs on the backing board and began dismantling each frame. They sifted through the various layers of backing and mat board and finally the posters themselves.

Darger's shoulders slumped.

"There's nothing here."

"Nope. Looks like a dead end," Loshak said, scratching at the stubble bristling along his jawline. "Read the cipher again?"

She read it out loud, and this time, it was Rohrbach who perked up.

"How about the piano?"

"What about it?" Darger said.

"That line… 'Ain't it grand?' Made me think of the grand piano in the living room."

Propping the still-partially-dismantled frames against the wall, they returned to the living room, spreading out around the piano. Rohrbach lifted the fallboard while Loshak shone his penlight inside the lid. Darger got down on all fours and crawled under the thing, using the flashlight on her phone to check the various nooks and crannies.

There was more going on under the piano than she'd expected. Similar to the undercarriage of a car, the underside was open, exposing a grid of wooden slats. She had a flashback to slithering under Dirk Nielsen's yellow Porsche and hoped she'd have similar luck finding a clue here.

She poked into the various corners and crevices, feeling around for anything that seemed out of place. A plastic baggie or a piece of paper. But after a thorough frisking of the bottom of the piano, she hadn't found a thing.

"Anything?" she asked the two pairs of legs she could see standing next to the instrument.

Loshak stepped back from the lid and ducked down to make eye contact.

"No. You?"

She shook her head and scooted out from under the thing, staying in a sitting position on the floor. She woke her phone and read the clue again.

"Let's think about this," Loshak said. "The first letter he left during the New York attacks was in plain sight. Taped to the wall of his basement. The next attack was the acid bomb left in Amelia Driscoll's brownstone. The clue was inside the Blu-ray player in her bedroom."

"Right."

"Then came Dirk Nielsen, and the clue was—"

"—tucked into one of the wheel wells of his car," Darger finished.

"OK. Then came the Mancini mansion in Lake Placid and…"

He trailed off then, probably remembering the explosion that had killed Agent Dobbins.

"And he didn't leave a clue there," Darger said, pushing away the grisly images that had been burned into her brain. "It was all a big 'fuck you' prelude to his big reveal."

"Wait…" Rohrbach said. "You're not suggesting that he didn't leave a clue here, are you? Wouldn't that be, like… cheating?"

"Oh, don't let him fool you into believing that he won't cheat, Detective Rohrbach," Loshak said. "He intends to win this little game one way or the other."

"Schrödinger's clue," Darger muttered mostly to herself.

"What?"

"Until we either find it or know for certain there's nothing here, the clue both does and does not exist."

The suggestion that they may be searching for something that didn't exist sent a wave of giddiness through her, and she let out a giggle that sounded more than a little unhinged in her own ears.

Loshak stared at her, apparently unamused by neither her observation nor the absurdity of their situation.

"Sorry." She shrugged. "I think the exhaustion is catching up with me."

He stuck out a hand, intending to help her up.

"Either way, we have to keep looking, don't we?"

She took the proffered hand, catching a whiff of something

as he pulled her to her feet.

She sniffed the air, frowning, her nose following invisible scent lines that led to Loshak's hand.

She leaned in.

"What?" he asked.

Before she could stop to think about what she was doing, she snatched Loshak's wrist and snuffled at his hand.

He yanked his arm away, fully glaring at her now.

"What the hell are you doing?"

"Why do you smell like a hippie?" Darger demanded.

Loshak blinked.

"Excuse me?"

"You smell like patchouli."

Loshak lifted one hand to his nose and inhaled.

"Huh. Must be the soap I used."

Darger wrinkled her nose.

"Now what?" Loshak asked.

"I hate patchouli."

"Christ. You're like a bloodhound. It's, like, the *faintest* aroma." He turned to Rohrbach and offered his hand. "Here. You smell."

Rohrbach's eyes narrowed to slits.

"You want me to… smell? Your hand?"

Loshak dropped his arm to his side.

"No, I do not." He shook his head and gave Darger another disapproving look, like it was her fault he'd asked Rohrbach to smell his hand. "Let's just… stay on task."

"Guess we're all getting a little loopy," Darger said.

"No, I think it's just you." He waved his hand at her. "C'mon. We gotta keep looking. Read the clue again."

But Darger didn't need to read it again, and instead recited it from memory.

"'Especially here in Babylon, where everyone worships the cult—'"

She stopped.

"Oh…"

"What? Cult of what?" Loshak asked. "It's 'beauty,' isn't it? That means something to you?"

Darger extended an arm toward the sculpture in one of the wall niches.

"Venus. Goddess of love and beauty, right?"

They crossed the room and huddled around the statue. It was approximately thirty inches tall and made of ceramic. The toga draped over the bottom half was glazed to look like aged marble, but Venus was nude from the hips up, and her skin was a mottled rainbow of neon colors with stark black letters in a graffiti-inspired font that spelled out words like "Sex" and "Love" and "Lust."

Darger glanced at the other two. Rohrbach gave her an encouraging nod.

"Heavy," she said, hefting it with both hands.

She turned it this way and that before finally flipping it upside-down. There was a faint rattle, which she felt more than heard.

Loshak clicked his tongue.

"Well, look at that."

There was a dime-sized hole in the bottom of the sculpture from when it was slip cast in a mold.

"Perfect hiding spot if I've ever seen one," Loshak said, waggling his eyebrows.

"Check this out."

Darger flipped the statue sideways and shook it. The rattle

was audible this time, though just barely.

"Hear that?"

"Holy shit," Rohrbach said. "There's something inside."

"Something soft, too. Like a wad of paper, maybe."

She held the sculpture out to Loshak, her arms stretching over her head.

"Here, hold it up like this."

The statue traded hands, and Darger peered up into the hole on the underside.

"Can you see it?" Loshak asked.

"No." Darger jabbed her pinky in the hole and wiggled it around fruitlessly. "The hole is too small. We need a chopstick or something."

Rohrbach jogged over to one of the crime scene collection kits set up in the room and returned with a pair of tweezers and a screwdriver. They took turns trying to loosen whatever was rattling around inside with no luck.

Loshak pointed his penlight at the hole and squinted inside.

"I don't see anything, but it kind of narrows at her waist. It must be wedged all the way into the upper half."

Darger inflated her cheeks.

"I think we're going to have to break it."

"Whoa," Rohrbach said. "Did you see the artist's signature on the bottom?"

He exposed the bottom and tapped a finger against the name scrawled into the clay.

"This is a Doctor Pixel."

"A what?"

"You've never heard of Doctor Pixel? The guy is massive. People are calling him the next Banksy. Partially because he has the whole enigmatic, secret identity thing going on. Always appears in public wearing one of those creepy Ronald Reagan Halloween masks, so no one knows what he looks like. But also one of his paintings just sold for like twelve million bucks."

He set the statue down and brought up a photo of the painting on his phone. It appeared to be a still life of a McDonald's Big Mac rendered in oils.

"Clearly these Venus statues of his are at least semi-mass-produced, but they've still gotta be worth a pretty penny," he said.

"Sure, but… we're talking about life and death here," Darger said.

Rohrbach's thumbs pattered against the screen of his phone.

"Ah ha. What'd I say? Here's a different version of the statue listed at $20,000. Says here that each one is one-of-a-kind."

Darger was still staring at the dollar sign followed by all those zeros when Fitch sauntered back inside.

"What'd I miss?"

Darger, Loshak, and Rohrbach exchanged a three-way glance.

"We think we found the clue," Darger said.

"Sweet. Where is it?"

Darger inclined her head toward the statue at their feet.

Fitch bent down and took hold of it.

"Rohrbach doesn't want to break it because it's valuable," Darger explained.

"Well, that's not exactly what I said." He crossed his arms. "It's just… what if it was Van Gogh's *Starry Night*?"

"Art aficionado, I am *not*," Fitch said, rotating the Venus in his hands. "But this ain't no *Starry Night*. And besides that, if we're talking about saving lives, then hand me a match and some lighter fluid, and I'll torch *Starry Night*, *The Mona Lisa*, and *Whistler's Mother* all in one go."

"That's what I'm saying," Darger said.

"And Loshak?" Fitch asked.

Loshak cocked his head to one side.

"Can't really put a price on it, can you? Maybe if we had more time, we'd have the luxury of finding a more delicate solution. But time is of the essence."

"That's three-to-one." Fitch's face broke into a devilish grin. "Majority fuckin' rules."

He raised the Venus above his head and let go.

CHAPTER 59

Venus de Milo crashed head first into the wood floor and burst into pieces. The sound of the shattering ceramic was almost musical. A loud jangle followed by the smaller tinkling of shards skittering in every direction.

Silence followed, each of them processing what had just happened.

"Well..." Loshak said. "I guess that solves that."

Fitch shrugged.

"You said it yourself. *Time is of the essence.*"

With that, the four of them squatted down and began sifting through the shards. They sorted anything that was an obvious pottery fragment to one side, and when they were finished, only one thing remained.

"What is it?" Rohrbach asked.

"I think it's a ball of aluminum foil," Darger said, picking it up and rolling it between her gloved fingers.

Fitch's tongue flicked over his lips.

"You think there's something inside?"

"Only one way to find out."

The ball was so tightly compressed that Darger had to use the tweezers again. Finally, she found a loose edge and was able to slowly pull the layers of crinkled foil apart. The glittering silver transformed from a tight sphere into a wrinkled, uneven sheet. And inside?

Nothing.

Darger flipped the foil over several times, certain she was missing something.

Finally, she sighed and locked eyes with the others.

"Well. Crap."

☾

After the debacle with the broken statue, the search in Trent Carter's mansion stretched out for hours. Darger and Loshak referred to the cracked cipher over and over, but they'd run out of promising leads.

Meanwhile, the techs and task force members tore up the house, inside and out, working together.

They pulled everything out of closets and cabinets, spread it over the floor and sifted. They checked the frames of the dozens of photos and paintings on the wall. They even ripped up the carpet in Carter's bedroom, exposing pale planks of wood.

Darger spent quite a bit of time out in the yard. Though he clearly had left the box on the front stoop, there was no evidence that Huxley had gained entry to the house. That meant the clue being left in the landscaping was plausible.

She poked through bushes, shrubs, tufts of decorative grass. Then she dug through the beds around some of the flowers, gloved hands peeling up handfuls of red woodchips.

Nothing.

Nothing.

Nothing.

Somewhere in there, as the afternoon melted into evening, Darger forced herself to eat. Fitch had brought sandwiches from a place not too far away. Deli meat.

Darger had an Italian sub doused with some kind of potent vinaigrette. In normal circumstances, she thought she'd probably love it. Right now, it tasted dry and strange in her mouth. Sour, maybe.

The conversation dried up as the sun started to set. Loshak and Rohrbach and even Fitch fell silent. All their faces went grave.

And Darger couldn't stop the stream of negativity from raging in her skull. The words came to her while she went through Trent Carter's luggage for a second time, phrases repeating over and over internally like a mantra.

There's no clue.

He's fucking with us.

There's no clue.

He's fucking with us.

The next time she stood up and looked out the window, it was already dark outside. The streetlights had come on, LEDs bathing all that sod out there in harsh yellow light.

The clock was ticking.

And they had nothing.

CHAPTER 60

The apartment is dark, but the fridge light spills out over cluttered countertops. Glints on empty cans of SpaghettiOs and drained bottles of domestic beer crammed together in tight clusters.

Vinnie Savage leans his head back and dumps Bud Light down his neck. Feels the fluid's chill seep into the flesh of his throat all the way down to his stomach, the effervescent tingle of the bubbles fizzing over everything inside him.

He pads out toward the darkened living room in socked feet, toes aching as they flex over the carpet. Finally free after some fourteen hours encased in a pair of shoes that were just a bit too narrow.

This is his nightly routine. Getting his shoes off and half a beer downed before he even flips on the light.

He hovers in the doorway. Takes another swig and looks around.

He's only half able to make out the details in the half-light creeping in through the windows.

Newspaper clippings spill out of the sides of folders, all of the research material piled high on the coffee table. A box of moonlight creases along the edge of a bookcase in one corner, the silvery glow revealing two rows of true crime books with lurid lettering on every spine, blood red.

And then words ring in his head. An urgent stream of language assailing him.

He sets the beer down on a clear section of the table and fumbles to get his phone out. Swiping and pressing buttons to get the thing recording.

And then he's speaking into it. His voice filling the darkened room, a little shaky from the excitement. Another nugget for an article spilling out as fast as the words can occur to him.

"Can we truly know Tyler Huxley? Can we understand him? Should we try? I think we can. I think we should. I think we might find he's a lot more like us than we probably first think."

More content. Red meat for a hungry public. Gotta feed the beast.

He takes one step toward the TV and stops talking midsentence.

The darkened room falls silent at once. Somehow naked without his voice there to cover the quiet.

He listens. Stares down the darkened hallway leading to the bedrooms. Blinks a few times.

Something is off here. He feels it. A cold twitch in the muscles at the base of his spine.

He takes a step to the side. Extends his arm. Flips on both light switches there.

The glow arrives a fraction of a second later. Three bulbs burning in the fixture over the couch. Another leaping to life in the kitchen off to his right, the doorway shimmering.

He thumbs the record button and his phone makes a little noise as the recording stops. Then he holds still for a second. Looking. Listening.

He doesn't see anything, doesn't hear anything. Still, that icy feeling won't flee his lower back.

He grabs his beer off the coffee table. Dumps six more ounces of sour Bud Light into his digestive tract, and now the bottle is empty.

OK. It's nothing. Forget it.

He gets himself another beer and moves to the snack bar to sift through today's pile of mail. No packages or anything like that. Just bills. A couple offers for sweet mortgage deals and another for a rewards card. Yay.

With the mail sorted, he cracks another beer. Laughs quietly to himself.

Weird night. Jesus. I guess even a dead-inside hack like me can still get scared of nothing.

Another sip of beer. He can feel his pulse in his neck, slow now, normal, pumping that slow drip of alcohol all through his body.

And then something thumps in the back bedroom, and he drops the beer.

The bottle smashes on the linoleum. Suds froth over the shards of brown glass.

But his head snaps toward the hallway where the thuds persist.

Footsteps. Headed his way.

Savage bumbles with the phone in his hand. Tries to swipe the screen, but it's like his fingers won't work. Curled-up claws that smear at the glass without having any effect.

Panic.

Breath stuttering. Heart leaping in his chest.

Panic.

His feet shuffle under him. Socks soggy with spilled beer.

Then the number pad is there on the screen and he dials, but it's wrong. All wrong.

9-9-1

Shit.

God damn it.

Needs to go back. Delete. Can't remember how.

The footfalls creep closer. Loud in the quiet space. Confident.

His head pulls up involuntarily. He stares into the shadowy spot where the hall leads to his bedroom door. Sees just the faintest stirring in the gloom there.

Savage backpedals from the sound, from the swirling murk.

He tries again to focus on the glowing phone screen. On the backspace key. On the numbers above it.

His thumb jerks. Slaps the button. Deletes the digits.

Yes.

A figure steps out of the dark hallway at the back of the apartment. That roiling gloom going solid all at once.

Savage gapes. Whimpers. Drops the phone.

The little plastic box skitters away from him. Skids face-first into the beer puddle.

But his eyes stay locked on the figure in the distance.

It's Tyler Huxley.

CHAPTER 61

Hissing sounds fill the void. Sucking and then venting.

Vinnie Savage's consciousness spirals to the surface to that soundtrack. Even sizzles. Faintly wet. Familiar.

He places the noise before he's awake: his own breath in his nostrils. A little ragged.

He rises toward the waking world. Eyes bobbing open. Head lifting from a tilted forward position.

It's dark. Lights off again.

But it's his living room. He can tell that somehow even with just the partial light from the moon and stars filtering through the window. The feel of it. The smell of it.

At first he can only make out contours. But then he blinks a few times, and his eyelids seem to squeeze everything into focus.

He's looking down at his own lap. Seated in the office chair near his corner desk. Legs bent at the knee, body bent at the waist.

It takes a second for the odd detail to register: his arms aren't part of the image.

He squirms. Feels the restraints pinning his arms to his sides then. Some muffled sound coming from inside of him.

He sees the line there. Gray strips wound over and over his chest, shining where the moonlight touches the surface.

Duct tape.

He's taped to the office chair in his living room. Stuck.

He writhes again. Like he might be able to rip free of the ribbons of cloth-backed tape. Shimmies back and forth.

The wheels of the chair rock backward out of the indentations in the carpet but only move an inch or two.

Another muffled sound gets caught in his throat, in his mouth. Deadened there. Unable to get free.

And then fresh awareness arrives. That tight sticky feeling clenches his face as well. Wrapped around his jaw, around that cleft where his spine and skull meet.

Oh, Jesus. My mouth. He's taped my mouth.

It's only then that he remembers how this scenario came to be, who is here, who knocked him out and put him in this chair.

Huxley.

He remembers the bulk coming for his dome. Some blunt object he couldn't make out sending him to the dream world all at once.

He snaps his head to the side, and he's there. Just a couple feet away.

Huxley's eyes look black and wet in the dark. His smile glows the shade of a bruise in the moonlight.

Savage tries to scream. But the duct tape holds the sharpness of it in, grips his lips like fly paper holding insect wings flat to its surface.

"It's your lucky day, Vinnie. This is your big break," Huxley says, voice a little soft. "The role of a lifetime, you could say."

Savage screams again. Rocks the chair back and forth. Feels it start to wobble.

Huxley's smile fades.

"Keep still now. We've got important things to do, you and I."

Savage thrashes harder. The chair teeters up like it's about to tip.

Huxley's hand lurches out of the dark. Catches one of the office chair arms. He holds it there at an angle for a second and then sets it back down in slow motion.

And then he steps back into a box of light and Savage sees the dark bulk in his other hand. A gun — a Glock — held close to his belly.

Savage stops fighting. Body gone still save for that harsh breathing heaving in and out of his nose.

He stares at the gun. Frozen. Unable to look away.

The barrel looks darker than everything else in the room. Blacker than black.

"Good," Huxley says. "See? We're going to get along just fine. But there are a couple of things I need you to do. Look at me now."

Savage's eyelids flutter. The words wash over him, but they won't register at first.

"Vinnie. Look at me."

The reporter blinks again. He manages to pry his vision away from the gun, sweeping it up and up.

He gazes into the dark eyes there, that purple smile once again glowing beneath them.

"You'll work with me. Won't you? I thought that's what your invitation meant."

Breaths roll in and out of the reporter, the tape squeaking a little as his chest expands. Huxley goes on.

"I need you. Or maybe it's better to say that we need each other."

Another breath sucks into Savage's chest, but this one holds there for a beat. He blinks. And Huxley's words once again rattle around in his head a while before they make sense to him. He holds still for another second.

Work with me.

Invitation.

We need each other.

Holy shit. If I work with him...

He nods vigorously, neck free enough to do that. Feels like a little kid agreeing to go for ice cream. He can hear relief in the breath rolling out of his nostrils.

Huxley's smile broadens. Flashes light as he steps forward again.

"I'm going to turn on your laptop, and then I'll free your arms."

The computer screen flares to life, white text flashing on the black screen as it boots. The glowing home screen casts a blue box onto Savage's lap.

And then a box cutter snicks in Huxley's hand, the blade jutting out of the sleeve. He brings it to the duct tape and swipes. Three strokes freeing Vinnie's right arm, two more freeing the left.

The bomber steps back, and then the reporter lifts his hands, one and then the other. He rotates his shoulders, some stiffness having already settled into the muscles there.

That purple smile opens in the shadowed spot where Huxley stands.

"I need you to post something."

CHAPTER 62

Midnight had come and gone, and still they searched for any sign of a clue in Trent Carter's mansion. Scanning. Sifting. Sorting. Cataloging. Fitch had even taken to knocking on walls in search of some kind of secret compartment.

They'd found nothing.

Darger braced herself for the bad news. Any second now, word would come down that the next bomb had gone off. More grisly details would filter in, fodder for nightmares if she ever got to sleep again.

But it was almost 2 A.M., and so far the bad news hadn't arrived. She didn't know what to think of that.

They kept searching and re-searching. Going over the same rooms over and over.

Darger had given up on finding anything hours ago. She knew there was no clue here, that Huxley had changed the game again. Cheated, as Rohrbach had put it.

Still, she had to keep looking. She wouldn't be able to forgive herself if she gave anything less than all she had.

She and Loshak were working their way through Trent Carter's closet — bigger than Darger's bedroom — for the third time when Loshak's phone blipped.

Darger's belly sank right away.

This was it. It had to be.

The agent dug the phone out of his pocket, swiped the screen. Then he squinted at it, some touch of confusion furrowing his brow.

"What is it?" Darger asked, rising from where she had been

squatting to dig around in a rack of rare sneakers.

He glanced at her and then back at the phone. Shook his head.

"I… Maybe it's the exhaustion, but I'm not sure what I'm seeing."

He held the phone up, and Darger took it from him.

A photo filled the screen. At first Darger could only see two necks and torsos there on the iPhone. Some kind of extreme close-up shot. Nonsensical.

After a second, she realized that Loshak had zoomed in on the picture, so she did the opposite, and then the image made sense.

Two familiar faces hovered on the screen, close together, both smiling, looking right into the camera. It was a selfie, Darger noted. Something casual about it, something light.

Tyler Huxley was the one holding the phone or camera. His dark hair looked shorter than it had been before, and all those hard lines the plastic surgery had added to his face came off all the creepier up close like this.

The person next to him sat in an office chair, from the looks of it. The gray hair swooped back from the forehead, voluminous as always. Vinnie Savage.

"I still don't get it. I mean… is it new?" Loshak asked.

"Posted minutes ago," Darger said, her voice sounding hollow in her ears. "Probably taken tonight."

The picture was the top story on *The Daily Gawk,* probably being viewed by thousands this very second. The six-word caption formed the entirety of the text of the post.

"Look who's working together. Stay tuned."

CHAPTER 63

The glass door glides out of the way, and the night air swirls into the apartment. Damp. Substantial. Like the darkness itself carries weight.

The cool trickle of a breeze touches the reporter's sweaty neck and forehead. Icy smears that make him shiver.

And then Huxley is behind him. Hands on the headrest. Rolling the chair toward the opening.

The wheels of the office chair catch on the threshold leading out to the balcony. The ride gets choppy. Wheels butting against the metal track for the sliding door.

He's lifted. Bumping. Free at last.

As soon as the chair is fully outside, Savage thrashes against the fresh restraints — new layers of duct tape plastered right over the old in a mummy wrap.

"Please! I did what you wanted."

Huxley chokes out a little sound that might be a laugh.

"This is your big moment. You wanted to be famous? You're about to become more famous than you could have ever imagined."

He stretches his hand out toward the empty sky beyond the balcony before he finishes the thought.

"A shooting star."

Savage wheezes. Breath sizzling between his teeth. The sounds come out as whimpers more than anything.

And then the chair lifts off the concrete balcony floor. Hovers in empty space. Makes the reporter weightless. Floating. Quivering just a little as Huxley's legs strain to support the weight.

Oh Christ. Oh Jesus Christ.

Savage rises toward the open air where the balcony shears off into emptiness. Ascending to clear the barrier there.

The front wheels batter into the wrought iron railing and catch. Lock the chair in place, right on the precipice.

Savage hangs there, angled in a recline. Weight still firmly over the balcony for now.

He is frozen. Too scared to move. Too scared to even breathe.

He's just trying to scare me, that's all. If I hold still and stay quiet, he'll see I'm being good. That I'll do whatever he wants.

But then Huxley changes his grip and lifts. The angle rotates.

The chair pushes forward again. Pivoting from that spot where the wheels stick the top of the rail.

Savage watches the camera in his head pan away from the sky. Sees the city lights come into view, first the tops of the skyscrapers in the distance.

The city opens up before him. Looks small from the 26th floor.

His field of vision keeps moving. Tilting lower and lower. It sweeps down past the lamps over the parking lot. Keeps going until the asphalt and concrete smothering the ground below fill most of his view.

He feels the gravity shift in the flesh of his face. Cheeks tugging forward with every inch of rotation. Sees those long strands of silver hair shake into the foreground.

His front half drapes over the empty space below, only the tape holds him to the chair now.

No. No. No. Please no.

He wants to scream, but the sound is stuck in his throat like a lump of dry bread.

His weight strains. Tries to rip free.

Somehow the wheels or chair leg still hold him there at that impossible angle. Gripping the iron rail like a hawk's talons, like even for the chair this is life or death.

Savage's breathing comes out in little woofs and yips now. Something animal overtaking him.

At last the wheel slips. The rail surrenders.

Gravity rips the chair out into nothing.

CHAPTER 64

Darger scanned the background of the photo again, rolled up close to Trent Carter's gigantic flatscreen in an office chair, nose pressed right up to the glossy screen. Her eyes flicked over the background, what little of it there was — a white wall, the edge of a casement window, and what looked like a green ribbon jutting into the left side of the frame.

She blinked. Twice. Then her finger hovered up to the screen, tracing along the greenery.

"Is that a house plant?"

Loshak squinted.

"Could be. I mean, it's a reasonable assumption, I think."

"Looks like one of those, what do ya call it, spider plants," Detective Rohrbach said.

But their words barely registered. Darger's mind was already racing to the next thought. Frenetic. Words pouring out of her lips just as they occurred to her.

"Does Vinnie Savage live in a high-rise apartment?"

The conversation paused for a beat.

She wheeled back to look at the others. Rohrbach fished a little notebook out of his breast pocket and started flipping through his notes.

"He lives in Skyview Towers, Building B, Apartment number 2613."

Loshak typed and swiped and pulled the location up on his phone.

"Yeah. It's a 30-floor high-rise. Based on the apartment number, he probably lives on the 26th floor. Are you thinking..."

Darger pointed to the edge of the glass pane visible in the photo. Windows burned bright in the distance, rectangular slabs of glowing yellow.

"That slice of the cityscape out the window looks like a view from up pretty high, doesn't it?" She took a breath. "I think they're at Vinnie's apartment. Both of them. Like right now."

Loshak's phone shrieked and rumbled against the desktop where he'd just set it down. A notification.

Then everyone else's phone blipped one after another. Six miniature sirens in a row. The cavernous movie star's living room gone suddenly shrill.

All those glowing screens rose to hover in front of their faces. Loshak muttered to himself.

"Oh shit."

The video loaded on Darger's phone — Tyler Huxley's face suddenly filling the small screen, that smug smile curling just the corners of his lips.

When he spoke, his voice sounded deep and relaxed. Almost sleepy.

"I'm adlibbing now. Pulled off-script. So it goes. A project like this eventually takes on a life of its own, doesn't it? The narrative pulls you where it wants to go. If it's any good, the story starts to tell itself."

His smile grew. Brightened. Darger could see a flash of his old features, the old Huxley, in that grin.

"But we're getting toward the third act now. We needed another action sequence, no? A set piece with some kind of spectacle. Violence to get the audience's blood up headed into the finale. Well, I came up with something. You'll see."

He slow-blinked before he went on, something thoughtful

overtaking his features now.

"This end was always coming. Starting way back with the little package in Gavin Passmore's kitchen, it has all built to this. Destined. Surprising yet inevitable."

He blinked again, his eyes looking wet, his pupils looking big and black.

"The final spectacle arrives at first light. We ride at dawn. The last reel. The climax. The point where it all comes off the tracks.

"Bigger and better than all that came before. More. More and more."

Another blink.

"Eventually the villain comes on-screen. For better or worse. Well, here I am."

He smiled again. Something wolfish in it now.

"I can only hope you're all thoroughly amused."

The image of Huxley's face cut out then. Something choppy, jarring, in the transition to the next scene.

Dark figures struggled in front of a wrought iron rail. The edges of a door frame occupied the sides of the screen — a sliding glass door.

From there, it came to Darger in pieces.

Balcony.

They're on the balcony.

Her vision snapped to the gaping nothingness beyond the rail, eyes going wide. Then she studied the figures.

Savage and Huxley. Of course.

Duct tape coiled around the reporter's chest, adhered him to an office chair. He squirmed against the seat, sharp squeaks erupting from where his body writhed on the leather.

And the bomber wrestled with the chair. Got it over the

threshold and onto the concrete balcony. Then his knees bent, and he lifted.

We have to do something. Someone has to stop this, Darger thought, though she knew it was already too late for that.

The chair rose up, the grating sound of the wheels on the cement guttering out. Only a breathy wind came from the speakers. Hollow.

The chair floated toward that rail edge, toward the nothingness beyond.

Another smash cut. Somehow stimulating in its abruptness, its crudeness. The image of the chair balanced on the rail cut out all at once, cleaved into something new.

And now a dark night sky filled the screen. The towering building rose up to block out some of the view.

Again, it took Darger a second to make sense of the image there.

The building sat at an angle in the frame. Reminded Darger of a Zoom call with the webcam pointing straight up someone's nostrils. The camera must be on a tripod tilted up toward the balcony.

She swallowed. Felt the lump in her throat jiggle.

Something stirred in the darkness above. A swirl in the shadows. A flitting gloom blacker than the rest. Hovering outside one of the balconies way up high, the silhouette of the rail visible like a bit of lacework beneath it.

And then that dark spot plummeted. Diving. Falling.

It blotted out brightened windows all the way down. Inked them black for a fraction of a second each. Made them blink in sequence like a busy string of Christmas lights.

And words played in Darger's head, even before the horror came clear:

This is everywhere.

Plastered on social media.

Being viewed by millions right now.

Shared and liked by thousands.

The shape of the chair winnowed into focus. The broad meshwork of the back tapering into the seat, the stick-like metal frame protruding beneath that, fanning out like spokes to support the wheels.

Tumbling. Rotating.

The duct-taped figure grew as it fell. Rapidly inflating from a speck into something bigger.

Vinnie Savage himself became visible as he entered the orbits of the street lamps closer to the ground. Yellow light cast over his sweat-slicked face.

Eyes gone wide.

Silvery hair tossed out into the air. Rippling and whipping against his scalp.

Body wriggling against the seat.

The chair blurred as it drew closer to the ground. Racing across the screen too fast to stay in focus.

Darger braced herself. Hugged her free arm against her chest.

The blur slapped the concrete with a single crack that cut off at once.

The chair splintered. Seat flattening to match the angle of the back. Wheels popping off like champagne corks.

All the downward momentum stopped dead. Silent.

The body within the piece of furniture seemed to pound flat into the cement. A bashed piece of chicken breast.

And then the blood slowly seeped out of the broken thing. A black puddle growing outward in all directions in slow motion, shiny where the moonlight touched the pool's dark surface.

CHAPTER 65

By the time the C-IED dogs had cleared Vinnie Savage's apartment building, the sky was going gray, that predawn light already creeping over the horizon. Darger couldn't believe the night had fled them so quickly. All those hours gone, drained searching Trent Carter's mansion to no avail, the darkness vanishing just like that.

She stepped out of Rohrbach's Camry and crossed the street heading toward the high rise apartment building. Her eyes felt gritty, and some filmy layer lacquered the inside of her mouth.

But at least she was out of the car. Upright and striding through the cool morning air.

The bulk of the task force and all of the techs had been waiting in their cars until the dogs made their way through and cleared the place. Darger wasn't sure how long it'd been, but it felt like an eternity.

Her lower back had gone sore in the backseat, and that slimy feeling had slowly overtaken her mouth. The lively conversation that had crackled within the Camry when they'd first arrived on the scene guttered out within ten minutes. Snuffed like a torch. Somehow, the quiet and the discomfort intertwined to make the wait nearly unbearable.

It smelled like the ocean here, clean and a little salty. Darger supposed it made sense — the beach wasn't so far away — but she didn't like it. Considering the video she'd watched of this very building, Vinnie Savage tumbling out of the sky to his gruesome death, it seemed wrong for it to smell so good.

Loshak jogged to catch up with Darger and then walked

alongside her. She couldn't help but notice the way his head angled toward the high rise's parking lot, and then her own gaze matched the angle of his.

Though police had removed the body and office chair, the bloody spot lay just there where Vinnie Savage had landed. A stain. A dark puddle, thick and shiny on the asphalt like chocolate syrup.

Darger forced her field of vision back to the street underfoot. Watched her knee lift higher as she stepped up onto the curb.

They fell in with the procession of law enforcement filing through the front doors, and they crossed an apartment lobby so quiet it was eerie. Tense. Overwhelming. Darger felt sick as she listened to the muffled footsteps echo around.

This time, at least, they managed to catch one of the first elevators going up. The ride sent a fresh wave of butterflies aflutter in Darger's stomach. Twenty-six floors later, the stainless steel elevator car belched them out just two doors down from Savage's place, the one with the door hanging open.

Darger ran back through snippets of Huxley's video speech again as she crossed the hall.

First light.

We ride at dawn.

They'd quickly deduced that he meant for something, presumably the next attack, to happen in the morning. Probably very soon now.

She jumped to other bits they'd discussed on the ride over.

Comes off the tracks.

Thoroughly amused.

Loshak had been the first one to suggest an amusement park. With *tracks, ride,* and *amused* all mentioned, everyone was on the same page there.

And then there was the worst bit to consider.

More and more.

Bigger and better than all that came before.

Multiple bombs this time. It had to be.

That left them just one problem. Which amusement park? There were over a dozen in the Los Angeles area.

She cleared her thoughts again as they crossed the threshold into the reporter's apartment. She needed to focus on searching with an open mind. If they were lucky, there'd be another clue here.

Something.

Anything.

Darger walked the apartment first. She wanted to make her way around the perimeter, get a feel for the floor plan, and see if anything jumped out at her before she went down any rabbit holes.

Her first impression: Oddly plain, given Savage's dyed silver hair and loud personality. Clean and modern. Almost suburban or even rural in its understated decor. More like an old Sears catalog than Lumens or even IKEA.

Aside from the broken beer bottle on the kitchen floor, there were no signs of a struggle. If you took away the couple empty cans and bottles on the counter, you might not know that anyone even lived here, Darger thought. It was that clean, that sterile.

The bedroom gave off more of that antiseptic feel. Blinds drawn taut plunged this area in shadow, but one of the techs turned on the bedside lamp just as Darger entered the space. Its bulb cast a soft glow over the room. A plain blue bedspread covered the California king mattress, and the understated, even generic, decor read somewhere between hotel room and hospital room. The only sound was the whirring of the air conditioner and the low murmur of the tech's bootied footsteps as she crossed the room to shine her flashlight into the closet.

By the time Darger made it back out into the living room, the sun was partially up. Daylight leaked into the windows, and the splash of orange creeping over the casement frame made Darger uneasy given Huxley's talk of riding at first light.

Before the fear could really take hold, commotion near Savage's laptop pulled her that way.

A tech had something there. A ruddy square pinched between her nitrile gloved fingers.

A red sticky note had been stuck under the lip of the reporter's desk. Two lines scrawled on it in black ink. Darger recognized the spiky handwriting at once.

Life's ultimate choice: Get thrilled to death or find paradice.

Why can't we have both?

Darger immediately recognized the misspelling of "paradise" as another reference to the Zodiac ciphers.

She found herself talking, something automatic working her tongue, her jaw.

"This is the clue to which park. It has to be."

Loshak nodded like a bobblehead just next to her. Then he pulled out his phone.

"I made a list of all the local parks. Hang on."

He swiped the screen with his finger. Squinted at it.

"Here's something… Galaxy Studios has a ride called Thrillactica."

"Maybe," Darger said, but it didn't feel right. The clue would have alluded to outer space if that were the target.

She huddled closer, looking at the list herself.

"Is there anything with 'paradise' in the name?" she asked. "Or maybe something similar. Heaven. Wonderland. Utopia."

Loshak's eyes bulged.

"Wait. Wait. That's it."

His eyes lifted from the phone screen. Met Darger's. Finally he said it.

"Thrilltopia."

CHAPTER 66

A single rotating beacon spun red light over the dash of Detective Rohrbach's unmarked car. The bulb looked like a snow globe tinted blood red.

Darger and Loshak were crammed in the backseat of the Camry, which suddenly felt a bit claustrophobic to Darger. Chief Cattermole joined Rohrbach in the front seat.

They rocketed down the highway, headed for the Thrilltopia theme park, everyone in the vehicle already armored in Kevlar vests, a detail that gave the proceedings a weighty feel going in. Important. Urgent. A little grave.

Rohrbach drove like a lunatic, hunched over the wheel, a smoldering cigarette tucked into the crook of his mouth. Darger could see his eyes narrowed to slits in the rearview mirror, squinting to keep the spiral of smoke away.

He darted in and out of lanes to advance their way through traffic. I-5 felt like a ladder, and they were climbing past the civilian vehicles one by one, the dashed white line gone blurry from the speed.

Chief Cattermole sat in the passenger seat barking commands into his cell phone. Tactical fragments spilled out of his mouth as fast as he could think them, the words spluttered and blurted in haphazard chunks. He interrupted himself, trailed off, doubled back to repeat key phrases.

Darger wondered if the person on the other end of the call might be doing the same thing. Both of them just yammering at each other, red-faced, without listening to the other or even pausing to take a breath. Either way, she found the babble exhausting to try to follow so she quickly gave up on listening, letting the burble fade into background gibberish.

In any case, it was clear enough that the task force's operation had suddenly ballooned in both complexity and urgency. A look out the window showed her that.

Sirens screamed around them, cruisers jockeying for position on the freeway. A hulking SWAT truck rode along on their left flank, and another of the monstrous black things blazed the trail out in front of them, hurtling along. It looked like it might just run over any smaller cars that didn't get out of its way.

She knew these weren't the only vehicles racing for the park, either. They had another couple SWAT crews coming in, courtesy of the Los Angeles County Sheriff's Department. A slew of officers were making their way up from Glendale in a volunteer capacity, at least based on what she'd overheard Cattermole saying. She knew there'd be more than that, too.

With so many units mobilized now and everyone geared up in bulky armor as though headed into battle, it almost felt like a military operation. Part of her hoped they could overwhelm the park with sheer manpower and root out the bombs that way, but even thinking about the next step weighed down her belly something awful, that leaden bloat gripping her abdomen and not so gently squeezing.

Better to blaze forward for now. Just focus on getting there. She could worry about the rest later.

She fingered the Velcro on the side of her vest. Wondered if the Kevlar squeezing her ribcage was helping keep her calm at all just now, like those jackets that hug dogs and make them less scared of thunder and fireworks. If so, she couldn't detect it.

Cattermole rotated the phone away from his mouth for a second.

"You should take the next exit," he said to Rohrbach, his voice still loud. "Switch over before we get caught up in traffic."

The driver didn't say anything back. Just kept driving.

Cattermole furrowed his brow and curled his lip.

"You hear me? Take the next exit."

Nothing inside the car moved for a second. Then Rohrbach huffed and flipped on the right turn indicator aggressively, hand and arm flicking that way in a flourish.

The click of the blinker rang out over the quiet, keeping time as the awkwardness swelled for a few seconds, and then Cattermole went back to yelling into the phone.

"No. Uh-uh. Not good enough. I told you we need the park cleared now. Right now. Fucking immediately, if not sooner."

Darger resumed tuning him out. Went back to messing with the straps on her vest.

She looked over at Loshak in the spot behind the passenger seat where he studied his phone. He'd slid his sports jacket over the vest, making him look oddly bulky up top, almost like he was wearing one of those foam muscle suits under his clothes.

He glanced up at her then. Blinked.

"What?"

"Huh?"

"You're staring at me like some kind of weirdo. And it kinda looks like you're about to laugh."

Darger did sniff out a laugh at that.

"It's nothing. Just thinking."

"Well, I found a map of the park. Want me to send it?"

She nodded.

Loshak smeared his finger around his screen, and a second

later her phone blipped.

The map took a second to load, and there it was. A color-coded representation of the park filled the phone screen. She zoomed in and started looking around.

The color splotches represented the main areas of the park, each with their own cutesy name, and thick black lines veined the thing, marking out the walkways.

The biggest blob by far, in pale pink, was labeled Coaster Village in some garish font. The next two largest, The Magic Realm in purple and Waterslide City in sky blue, were probably less than half the size of the coaster area each. A red and white striped swatch represented the food court area, Grub Town, and a few matching striped areas throughout the park showed where the restrooms were.

Her fingers scanned around the little map over and over, and she couldn't help but wonder where the bombs were.

Coaster Village? Grub Town?

And she couldn't believe that these were real questions she was asking herself, that these were real thoughts she was having, that any of this was really happening.

She tried to swallow, but that valve at the back of her throat seemed stuck open. Rigid. She choked on saliva and coughed into her fist.

Loshak stared at her, eyebrows raised. Just when he was about to say something, the front seat went quiet all at once, and he snapped his head that way instead.

Chief Cattermole's babble of yelling chatter cut out. He still had the phone pressed to his ear, but his lips held motionless now.

And the tension swelled in the car as soon as his yelling ceased. The silence felt charged. Electric. Important.

All heads turned to face him. Bodies leaning in. Everyone waiting.

Did something happen? Was it already starting? Word coming over the line that — what? Bombs going off? Something else?

Darger's jaw clenched. Molars scritching against each other.

She could just faintly hear the burbling voice in Cattermole's ear. Deep-toned and talking fast.

A sigh puffed out of the chief's nostrils.

"Look, I'm not yelling!" he yelled into the phone. "No. You'd know if I was yelling. Believe me."

He was definitely yelling. Darger didn't think that point could even be debated.

Anyway, the *not yelling* exchange seemed to ease the tension in the Camry. It wasn't starting after all. At least not yet.

When Darger looked back at Loshak, he was pointing out the window. She followed the trajectory of his finger.

Skeletal shapes seemed to sprout out of the horizon. Towering coaster hills rising and swooping, curved lines of steel bent into contoured arcs and loops. The metal supports crisscrossed beneath the tracks, the geometric beams and struts angular and inflexible against the serpentine twists of the track itself. A jarring contrast.

This was it. Thrilltopia. It was really happening.

The rides grew bigger as they got closer, and the color of the metal came clear. The biggest ride sported red tracks and supports. A smaller one, in the foreground, was cobalt blue, the lines twisting up into corkscrews in a couple of spots. The next biggest revealed itself to have an amber tone going gray in spots like a deck that could use a fresh coat of stain — and Darger remembered that one of the biggest wooden coasters in the world made its home here.

A chill ran up her spine and down her arms. She shivered.

Any second now, it will all happen. For better or worse.

CHAPTER 67

Steve Cooby jammed the button on the intercom with his middle finger. Then he leaned into the microphone, and his deep voice crackled over the sound system throughout the park.

"Attention, all guests. Because of a security threat, the park must be evacuated immediately. Please proceed to the nearest exit in an orderly manner. Your fee can be refunded at a later date. Thank you for visiting Thrilltopia."

Cooby sniffed. Looked over at the other security guard at the console, Dan Childress, who was scratching behind his ear with a capped BIC pen while he chattered into a walkie-talkie. Cooby wanted to wait a few beats before he recited the lines again.

The script kept the sentences short and declarative. Authoritative. Almost made him feel like a real cop for once.

He let his eyes shift over to the bank of monitors that dominated one wall in the park's security suite. He scanned the screens, tried to make sense of the totality of the images.

The cameras nearest the front of the park told him the story he'd expected. Some of the guests cleared out right away, filing down the cobblestone aisles toward the exit ramps that led out to the parking lot. Their body language reminded him of a herd of cattle, shoulders slumped, gait slow, the whole throng seemingly only half aware.

But the throngs on the other six cameras seemed largely unperturbed by the message. Walking. Clustering around booths and rides. Eating huge elephant ears and snow cones.

He read the message again. Heard his voice ring out over the entire park. He couldn't help but be a little impressed with himself for not tripping over any of the lines. Real professional stuff.

Some of the heads in the crowd turned up toward the speakers themselves as he spoke, like the horn-looking things hung up on poles might offer further explanation or clarity.

When he finished, a few more bodies started filing for the exits, but most of the crowd remained listless.

Childress slid the pen out from behind his ear and pursed his lips. He set the pen and walkie-talkie down, grabbed a pack of Twinkies from the counter and tore it open while he talked.

"Dang. Sure looks like a bunch of 'em don't wanna skedaddle. Guess I don't know how I'd feel, paying over a hundie for a ticket and then getting run out of the place. Not great, probably."

Cooby shrugged with one shoulder.

"They'll get refunded. I read that as part of the message."

Childress turned his head. Gaped at his coworker. He took a big Twinkie bite.

"Well, maybe read that part again, and, like, put some stank on it. No pussyfooting. Really give 'em the business."

Cooby looked down at the script, eyes jumping to those final lines that focused on the refunding of tickets. Part of him felt like he shouldn't parse the script, like its power over the crowd would somehow be broken if he changed the wording up at all.

"It's not… I mean it wasn't written to be… broken up into chunks… like… uh… what do you call it… piecemeal."

Childress's eyes got big. He almost choked on his Twinkie, and then he hissed out a laugh — a mean-spirited laugh to

Cooby's ears.

"Piecemeal? Jesus Christ, buddy. We just want to get these people out of the park before the po-lice get here. I mean… piecemeal. Lord have mercy."

Cooby sighed. Felt his face go warm.

He leaned forward until his lips were almost touching the microphone and read just the part about the refunds. He could hear a trace of irritation in his delivery, but it was subtle enough that he didn't think the masses out there would detect anything.

He leaned back when he was done. Turned his head to watch the reaction.

Not much changed on the monitors. The crowd didn't seem swayed by the words.

Childress swallowed a mouthful of Twinkie and then sucked his teeth.

"Dang. Should we hit the siren?"

He hovered his free hand over the big red button on the right hand side of the console.

"Wait."

Cooby closed his eyes. Took a deep breath. He could already hear the air raid siren blaring in his imagination, that shrill warble reaching out over the park. He knew what the sound would bring.

"If the herd panics, there'll be a stampede, right? Chaos. Injuries. Let's try to clear some of the mob kind of low key style, then hit the siren if and when we need to. We have a little time, right?"

Childress's meaty hand pulled back from the red button and went back to crinkling the plastic around his snack cakes.

"OK. That's smart. But we shouldn't wait too long."

Cooby blinked and then nodded. He could feel his pulse battering away in his neck. When the voice in his head spoke up, it sounded more confident than he felt.

All right, Coob. Time to change gears a little bit here.

Gotta put some fear into 'em. Just a touch.

Another deep breath sucked into his chest and rolled out slowly. A clock ticked out the seconds somewhere behind him, stark in the silent room. He pressed his face close to the mic again.

This time he barked the commands over the loudspeakers. Rasped out something verging on a growl. Bit off the words at the ends of the sentences.

When Cooby sat back this time, Childress looked at him with eyebrows raised, mouth open, cream and yellow sponge visible in the hollow between his teeth. He gathered himself after a second and talked through the snack cake.

"Dude. That was wicked. Cripes. I mean, I got goosebumps, man." He shook his head. "Didn't know ya had it in ya, Cooby."

Another big mob broke off from the rest and moved for the exit on the monitors, a cluster of humans looking like a gliding bit of bacteria on a microscope slide, the shape constantly morphing and flexing as it advanced. They shuffled down the wide aisle leading to the exits, a few hundred people, maybe a thousand.

Cooby felt some kind of warmth inside his chest, a glow there that reminded him of the feeling he got whenever the Rams won on Sunday. Victory, he guessed.

But the mob on the screen slowed as they reached the gates leading out to the parking lot. The individual members of the crowd kept looking back, heads swiveling atop shoulders.

Cooby read meaning in the body language:

Some see that others are staying, still clustering in the food court row with milkshakes and corn dogs, and they wanna turn back.

The mob started to disintegrate — that amoeba splitting, splintering. A large portion turned back as Cooby had sensed they would.

"That right there is peer pressure in action, man," Childress said. "They think if the others are staying, well hell, they can stay, too. Monkey see, monkey do type-uh deal. Mob mentality, brother. It ain't a pretty picture."

Cooby slammed a hand on the edge of the console.

"God damn it. Hit the siren."

Childress slipped the last half of Twinkie into his maw and slapped the big red button.

After a beat, the air raid siren shrieked out over the speakers. Loud. Sharp. The voice wavering like an injured gull.

Everyone in the park froze, and all the heads looked up into the sky in unison. All necks craned. All eyes wide and staring into the heavens like they might be able to see something there… but what?

Bombers?

Nuclear missiles streaking across the sky with thin white trails of smoke behind them?

But no. Nothing like that. Empty heavens.

Cooby felt his eyelids twitching now. He angled himself into the microphone, barked another round of commands, this time with the siren singing the high harmony part.

And still the crowd hesitated. Milling. Unsure. Gazing at the speakers again, at the sky again.

What the fuck?

"See? Mob mentality. It's a freakin' epidemic, man."

"You'd think with the bomber on the loose, everyone would be wary."

"Human nature. No one ever thinks the bad thing will happen to them until it does, until it's too late."

Finally, the crowd on the monitor showed signs of life. Another mob, bigger than the first, moved for the exit. Slowly. A herd of grazing cattle spurred along at last. Not terribly motivated, but moving.

Cooby's eyes snapped around from screen to screen. Most of the crowd now seemed to be exiting, but not all. At the food court row, a few people still sat at picnic tables eating burgers and elephant ears and paper cups of ice cream. At the platform just outside the Bronze Dragon, a red-faced guy argued with a park employee over the ride being shut down.

"You reached out to all the ride operators?" Cooby said, his voice flat as he mostly focused on the screens.

"Yes, sir. Just talked to the Mountain Blaster dude a second ago. He'd just sent a couple of trains out, so that's like, what, three minutes and they'll be shut down along with all the rest. Took us, I don't know, seven or eight minutes to get the whole park locked down? Not too shabby."

Cooby nodded. He couldn't look away from that raging customer on camera nine. As his rant extended, his face slowly veered from red into a purple territory, some kind of merlot color. Cooby couldn't see flecks of spit flying out of the guy's mouth, but he knew they were there.

He was just about to press the button to get sound on that camera.

And then something flashed on camera three. Bright white filled the frame for a second.

Cooby punched that button instead.

Childress's words came out in a harsh whisper.

"Holy fuck."

On camera three, the Mountain Blaster exploded at the top of the hill. Bits burst outward from the skeletal peak. Looked like bright motes flitting in a bar of sunlight.

The metal track splintered, thick steel ripped into impossible angles. Sundered. The bars bent away from each other. One huge section of track plummeting, banging all the girders and struts on the way down.

And all the while, the rumble of the initial explosion growled in the little speaker, a fluttering exhale filling the security control room. The thunder plumped goosebumps up and down Cooby's arms.

And then the sound cut out. Silent. Nothing.

The line of carts arrived at the broken bit of track just then and wrenched free from the rails. It tipped forward just like it would at the top of the hill normally, but then it veered hard to the left, following that last bit of track that had blown outward like an exploded cigar.

The small train tumbled out into the open, out into nothing.

The little string of cars fluttered on the screen, rippling in the wind, and the security control room held so still. The space suddenly made cold. Ghostly. Cooby couldn't breathe.

And then the screams started.

The terror went tinny in the speaker. Shrill sounds torn from all those throats. Needles pricking Cooby's ears. Piercing.

The train looked like a floppy centipede in the air, each car a segment quivering on its own, yanking against the connecting piece tying it to the cart behind it and the one in front of it. The whole thing writhing. Squirming.

The passengers screamed all the way down. The thrashing centipede fell out of the frame, building speed.

And then, somewhere off screen, the cart banged to the asphalt. Cracked. The screams cut off.

Both security guards jumped in their seats, and the quiet got huge all at once.

CHAPTER 68

The crowd thrashed around Darger, a panicked sea of people pressing into each other. A stampede trying to crush its way through the exit.

She bent at the knees and waist and weathered the storm at first. Fended off bodies with her forearm.

Keep going.

Get through this.

Waves of humanity crashed into her. The mob flexed and dumped its weight on her again and again. And people toppled to the ground all around her, caught up in the swells and thrown down to the asphalt. All those feet pressing and pounding over the fallen forms, the shadow of the horde blotting them out.

But Darger kept her balance, kept her feet. Shuffled backward when she could to stay out of the worst of it.

The scene flashed through her head again. Standing in the parking lot, staring through the turnstiles at Thrilltopia beyond, those loops of rollercoaster track rising up over everything like dinosaur skeletons in the distance. She and the rest of the gathering storm of law enforcement had seen the park's efforts to clear the park slow to a trickle, the people clogging the exit lanes like hardened arteries, moving in slow motion, some turning back, reluctant to leave.

So the SWAT teams and other police had rushed into the void. They could help clear the park. No problem. Something about a heavily armored cop screaming at you through a face shield of a riot helmet had a way of appealing to a person, in

Darger's experience — maybe it was the AR-15 crossed over their chest that so quickly changed the hearts and minds.

The cops had run in like sheepdogs and started herding the mob out the exit. Some of the SWAT officers sprinted deeper into the park, probably to cajole the laggards along the food court — Grub Town. Darger and Loshak got in behind the milling mob and helped funnel them out.

Then the bomb had blown. That boom like thunder up above. All heads turning to that metal track trying to puncture the heavens, the crowd watching in unison. The coaster track splintering in the distance. The strand of carts tumbling to the earth.

The blast still echoed in her ears, dulled her hearing, made it feel like someone had fished a couple of those long strands of cotton out of a vitamin bottle and shoved them deep into her ear canals.

Sirens had warbled over everything earlier, but Darger realized those sounds were gone now. Turned off.

Now, awash in the sea of panicking masses, it was the sound of fear that filled the air. Moaning. Whimpering. Screaming. It rang out over the park. Those normal amusement park sounds twisted into something dark, something wrong.

She fished her hand down into the throng of bodies. Grabbed the arm of a skinny kid who'd just been swept under the surge in front of her — dark hair, angular face, maybe 12 or 13. She pulled with all her might, could feel his forearm stiffen as he tried to lift himself.

But she couldn't wrench him free of all that weight.

His wrist slipped out her grip. She had him around the knuckles for a second, pinching his fingers together in hers, and then that ripped free as well, and he was gone. Lost.

Swallowed up.

The mob trampled onward. Choked into the narrow gaps that formed the row of exits. Human figures wedging themselves into a standstill there, somehow bringing to mind the image of a clogged meat grinder.

Darger knifed back into the rush now. Turned her body sideways and hurled herself into the gaps. Tried to swim upstream.

Huxley was here somewhere. In the park now. His video practically told them that outright — *eventually the villain comes on-screen* — and besides that, she could feel it, that dark presence here, something familiar about it — another psycho wanting his moment in the spotlight.

Slow and steady progress inched her through the pack. She shoved her way to the edge of the mob, and then she spilled into the open all at once, falling onto her hands and knees on the cobblestone walkway and practically flinging herself up onto her feet again. Instinct not wanting her down on the ground. At all.

But she was in the clear. Free.

She heaved for breath then. Felt sweat leak from her pores, greasing her face and neck, a thin film of salty moisture likewise adhering her shirt to her upper back.

The heat and exertion seemed to catch up with her all at once. Overwhelming. She stared down at the stony path and sucked wind.

And then Loshak was there at her side, breathing heavy on his own and shaking his head.

"The words *holy fuck* spring to mind," he said, his baritone surprisingly audible given the throbbing screech of panic just a few feet away. "Almost got stomped back there."

Darger tried to think of words but none came. She nodded.

Her breath fluttered in her throat. Too dry, but it was cool, at least.

It would get worse from here. She knew that. This was only the beginning.

Loshak started to speak.

"Do you think—"

But he never finished the sentence.

The bombs along the exits blew, four in a row, one after another. The blasts sounded flatter up close. Impossible. Violent cracks and roars her ears couldn't fully comprehend. Some kind of compression in her head smashing the sounds.

Darger saw the fireball of the first and shielded her face by instinct. The back of her left hand sweeping up over her brow. The carnage visible in the gaps between her fingers.

And the front row of bodies flung skyward. Cascading from left to right, one group at a time, like something choreographed for a junior college cheerleading competition.

That closest cluster came to pieces as the blast wave threw them straight up. A whole row of legs liquefied. A bloody spray rising along with the torsos.

Others toward the front of the mob looked to be cut in half. A whole mess of people just dropping out of sight in unison. Felled trees. Bags of potatoes.

The blast wave knocked Darger back even as she watched. Her legs splayed one in front of the other like she was trying to keep her balance on the deck of a listing ship.

She righted herself. Stood up straight again.

The scene fell strangely quiet. The explosive sounds cutting out fast and hard.

And then the patter of all that wetness slapped down in

dribs and drabs. Red rain smacking and slurping at the asphalt. Stark wet sounds in the quiet.

The bodies thumped down as well. A waterfall of them plopping over each other. Heavy. Flopping. Dead weight.

And then everything thrust into motion again. Screams lifting out of the mob, rising in pitch like a tea kettle.

Before Darger could think, the bodies crushed around her again. The mosh pit cinched into her shoulders, into her waist.

She could feel a hand close on her elbow, looked over just in time to see that it was Loshak's, and then he was ripped away from her. Lost in the mess. She got swept up in the tide suddenly gushing the other way.

The stampede had reversed course. The wave of humanity washed back into the park.

CHAPTER 69

Loshak jammed his arm into the crush of bodies. Wrenched it hard to the side. He tried to lever a gap into the throng, tried to make some space, tried to fight against the current and get back to Darger.

But it was useless.

He gritted his teeth. Ripped his arm out of the tiny crevice of wriggling body parts, all those torsos and limbs constricting against his elbow like a python. He felt his watch rip free from his wrist as he pulled his hand into the open.

God damn it.

His jaw muscles squeezed harder. He tried to scan the ground but saw only body parts in the way, got a glimpse of a shadowy layer along the crush of knees and ankles. The dark there blotted everything out.

The watch had been a gift from Jan. He'd had it with him daily for over a decade, fastened to his body, almost a part of him. But now it was gone.

And then he laughed at himself — just a single sniff of laughter — at the absurdity of caring about a $120 watch at a time like this, in a hellscape like this. Blood and bodies and bombs all around. Death pressing closer than ever.

The watch didn't mean anything now. Not here.

The mosh pit shifted directions slightly. A swell in the ocean of torsos tottering the other way.

And he could see Darger again some thirty or forty feet away now. The green of her eyes somehow startling, just a flash of them seeming to fire out over the crowd like a lighthouse beam.

But then she was gone. Swallowed up by the crowd again.

Loshak let the crowd carry him. Drifting. He felt the bulk of bodies cinch so tightly around him that it lifted his feet off the ground, swept him along.

The whole mass seemed to sway then. It rocked a little to the left and then swooped hard to the right. Smashed into the wooden fence along the walkway there.

Shoulders dug into Loshak's ribs on both sides. A pointy elbow lanced into his spine, the prodding bone jiggling back and forth there like it was trying to trigger some nerve response in a particular vertebra.

But the agent ignored the pain, blocked it out. He kept his gaze fixed over the top of the thrashing mob.

And he looked for Violet Darger's face there in the teeming swells, scanned for any flash of her hair or those eyes opened too wide.

But he didn't see her.

CHAPTER 70

One side of the churning mob thudded up against a wooden fence, all the bodies jamming there like something gummed up in the cogs of a machine. The roving amoeba seemed to slide along the barrier, the people hurling themselves into it over and over, the mass still slowly plodding deeper into the park even as it clotted.

Darger found herself thrust into the obstructed area. Her body sandwiched between two thick lumberjack-looking guys for a second like two sides of beef clapping together around her.

The force squirted her out the side a second later, and she came back into the light pressed into the wooden beams of the fence. She braced her hands against the tallest of the cross pieces, which stood about chest high. The weight of the crowd seemed to flex in pulses, smashing her into the wood and releasing over and over.

Her eyes darted everywhere. Her breath gone shallow. It took her a second to realize that open land stood just on the other side of the barrier.

She hiccupped once. Her pulse punched in her temples.

Then she fished her fingers into the open space between the beams, finding wire mesh strung up there like a spider web. The filaments felt sharp against her skin.

Another obstruction.

Fuck.

But she knew there was another way.

She gripped the top of the beam and thrust herself upward.

Kicked out her feet for that middle beam, both legs pistoning against the swirling mob instead.

Her right foot found something solid and pushed off.

She rose. Heaved upward. A shaky lunge up the fence.

She lifted one knee up onto the top beam. Balanced there. So close to freedom. Her forward momentum slowing.

She kicked out again with her free leg. Tried to push off. She could feel her momentum slipping, gravity trying to rip her back into the writhing horde.

Her foot slithered off everything it touched. No traction. No help.

She dug her fingernails into the grainy beam. Clawed and leaned forward. She could feel her jaw spasming as she clenched her teeth.

An accidental push from the crowd chunked her from behind — someone running face-first into her butt from the feel of it — and then she was falling.

That balanced knee and the heels of her hands skidded off the coarse wood. Her weight tipped over the breach.

She tumbled over the fence face-first. Plummeting.

She kicked out again. Threw herself forward, launching toward some bit of green in the blur of landscaping coming at her.

And she landed in a bush. The branches catching her like so many arms. Green feathery bits brushing at her cheeks and chin and neck. Its shadow encircled her, enfolded her.

She twisted. Rolled free of the shrub, sinking to the ground as she turned, spilling free onto her hands and knees in soft grass.

She stayed like that — on all fours — and breathed. Cool wind surrounded her, filled her.

It felt incredible to be out of that crush of body heat. Empty in a good way. That familiar hollow stretching out around her. The endless space that made up the vast majority of the universe returning now like an old friend, replacing that claustrophobic panic that had engulfed her in the swarm.

She breathed. In and out. Her throat seemed to hitch at the apex of each inhale. And she could feel how flushed her face was, fevered blood engorging her cheeks and forehead.

Finally she tilted her head up. Looked back the way she'd come, watching the throng of bodies through a screen of wire mesh.

The mob had broken in half. The free bodies streamed toward the back of the park while a mess of them still thrashed against the fence, pounding into each other.

She looked for Loshak in both groups, but she couldn't see him.

CHAPTER 71

Rivulets of sweat drain down Tyler Huxley's back. He holds still. Watches the chaos rip through the park.

Violence. Panic. All the people running amok.

And squirming feelings lurch in his belly, bubble in his skull, dance on his skin. Moths and butterflies and dragonflies, all those wings flitting everywhere, flitting everywhere, inside and out.

He pounds down a flight of wooden steps. He'd watched the proceedings from one of the highest points in the park — the platform next to the Screaming Maiden. Felt the whoosh of the explosions as they vented over the grounds. Their warm breath on his skin. Intoxicating.

At the bottom of the steps, he takes a hard right, catches a fragment of his reflection in the sheet of glass over a bulletin board there. His arms pumping as he passes himself by.

A neon yellow shirt swaddles his chest, a highlighter shade of stretch fabric that cups him funny in the chest and hips. It looks about two sizes too small, somehow makes even his skinny frame look almost paunched, but it has served him well enough.

With employee gear on, sunglasses, and a ball hat pulled down low on his brow, no one has confronted him at any stage as he plotted and planned and placed his little toys throughout the park. He'd been able to skip right through all the lines, get access to parts of the grounds that were supposed to be off-limits, even fumble with tools and a toolbox in areas that might not make sense given any scrutiny at all.

He'd even had exquisitely detailed explanations ready to fly every step of the way, but no one had ever said anything to him. As far as he could tell, they hadn't noticed him at all.

Even the most wanted man in the country can become invisible in working-class garb.

It'd been disappointing in a way at the time, their lack of notice — all that work on his backstory for naught. A waste. It would've been such a thrill to lie to someone's face and get away with it. To see the trust form in their eyes.

But watching the bombs blow, up close and personal, he'd forgotten all about those pangs of regret. The scale of the display was hard to fathom.

For once, something in life had exceeded his expectations.

He speed walks toward the back of the park, and the memories wash over him in waves. Violent pictures opening in his head, the visual spectacle laid over a soundtrack of moans and whimpers.

Goosebumps roil on his skin when he remembers. The track at the top of the Mountain Blaster splintering. That row of carts shooting off into the sky, tumbling to a hard landing.

The screams on the way down had affected him more than he ever thought they would. All those piercing sounds of terror, spiky in his ears, thin and screeching.

God, it had sent a quiver through him. Slicked his body in sweat. Held his chest so tight it had been hard to breathe.

And fireworks burst in his head. Striking. Vivid.

Little motes floated over his field of vision. Pink splotches that tremored in time with his pulse. He'd thought he might pass out.

Rapture.

And then he'd turned and set his sights on the exit chutes.

Watched the mob race there just like he knew they would. Maybe he'd gotten a little assist from Harris and Klebold on that one, that part of the plan an oldie but a goodie.

The bodies had mashed up against the gates, a blazing every-man-for-himself panic winning out over all other impulses.

And then he'd triggered the devices. Four out of five went. One dud, which hurt for a second.

But the results overshadowed the technical failure. Many times over.

Bodies thrown in the air. Legs reduced to a slushy spray.

The red mess drenching everything like the first few rows at a Gallagher show.

Another couple rows of them chopped down all at once. Pierced by shrapnel. Torn wide open. Flopping down in heaps.

So many people blown to bloody bits.

Adrenaline floods into his limbs as the replay unspools in his head. Turns his hands icy and numb in a matter of two seconds.

And those pink blobs fill his eyes. Strobing along with the rhythm of his heart.

A big breath rushes into him, quivers in his chest. He holds it for a second. Thinks maybe it will help erase those flickering lights in his eyes.

He blinks a few times. Watches the coral spots die back to a fainter shade.

In the distance, he can see the thrashing mob running nowhere fast. A big mob crashes into a fence. A few break free and stream away, but where to go?

Off to his left, he can see a slice of the food court area — Grub Town — through a gap in the obstacles. It looks like the people are hiding under picnic tables there. Cowering figures balled up on the concrete, those grated tabletops forming grids above them. Too funny.

And then the wind, that held breath, shudders out of him. Leaves a vacancy in his chest again, but it's OK.

He's free now. Free of all the tethers that chain one to the ground in this world. Free of the pain and doubt that cage so many, a life sentence of insecurity, of alienation, of bitter disappointment.

Free, at last, to pursue whatever his heart desires — once and for all.

He sprints toward the next catastrophe.

CHAPTER 72

The whirlpool of humanity spiraled around Loshak. Wailing. Choking. Thrashing. Throbbing. The bodies swirled around and around like he'd get sucked down a drain sooner or later.

The agent balanced in the eye of the storm, arms splayed to fend off the swells. Ready to block the odd fist or forearm that launched his way.

He surveyed the situation in all directions. Found several yards of tightly packed mosh pit between him and any kind of open space, all the way around.

From his taller-than-most perspective, he saw a sea of writhing skulls all mashed together and wriggling. So tightly packed he imagined he might walk right over them if only he could hoist himself on top of the teeming mass.

Damn. He'd really gotten washed out into the center of it all, the whims of the currents pushing and pulling until he found himself here, far from any exit. Not unlike a riptide catching a swimmer and propelling them like a Jacuzzi jet out into the endless deep.

But he'd also found himself in a relatively loose pocket of the mob for the moment. His chest was free enough to breathe deeply — something that wasn't the case where the bodies jammed together in gridlock.

He sucked in air while he could. Breathed and watched and tried to strategize his next move. He felt like a hurt boxer just trying to survive the round.

And for this moment he'd surrendered to the whims of the crowd. Accepted that he was at their mercy, at least for now.

Better to roll with it, accept it, and try to keep his head clear. His chance would come if he let it.

Around and around the mob went. A thoughtless panicking mass. Shrill and flailing.

He could smell their sweat now, that piss and ammonia stench of panic coming through. And he realized that he was soaked as well, perspiration glossing his body in a greasy film until he looked like a pork roast on a spit.

And some flare of hysteria shot through him then like a frigid bolt.

What if the way out never comes?

What if I get pulled under all those stomping feet?

But he pushed the fear away. Shoved it back down into the dark part of his brain, that sub-basement where his eyes couldn't go.

He scanned that sea of skulls again. Swiveled his head to take in the panorama.

He'd gotten a few feet closer to the edge of the mob, the shortest path to what was now on his left. He could see a clump of decorative grass sprouting out of a bed of pea gravel there. A clear expanse of green grass beyond it.

OK.

OK.

This could work.

Deep breath.

And go.

He jammed his arm into a gap again. Thrust it in like a blade.

And he pressed himself in after it, wedging his shoulders and hips into the crevasse. Shoving into that flexing gorge among the limbs and torsos.

But the gap disappeared. The bodies snugged tighter, a sphincter squeezing.

He got rejected, ejected, pushed out with some force like a cannonball. The sweat helped lubricate his egress. Spilled him back from whence he came.

He wobbled backward. Choppy steps. Off balance.

Something kicked hard at Loshak's shin as he stumbled back. Felt like a steel rod shot out of some machine catching him in the outside of his calf, though he knew it must be someone's foot.

The impact jammed his leg funny, sort of torqued the knee sideways.

And now he was falling.

He reeled. Spun. Plowed into some lady's shoulder first and hugged his arms around her like he meant to tackle her. They both bobbed downward and popped back up. He just managed to keep himself upright.

And he felt something pop in his ankle.

A bolt of pain flared up the length of his leg, tendrils of it writhing like pinpricks in his foot.

And then the pain turned to heat. A surge of boiling liquid climbing the nerves in his ankle, his shin, his thigh. Prickling all the way up.

He wobbled on the bad leg, the joint feeling like some mushy thing that couldn't hold him up, but he righted himself.

Holy shit.

Gotta keep my feet.

Gotta keep my feet or…

He drifted again. Surviving and nothing more.

He kept his weight off the bad leg and let the mob carry him. It spun him slightly, like a toy boat redirected by every little whim of the water's surface.

And he drew in great lungfuls of air. Tried to get his breath under control again. Regrouping. Bracing himself for the next disaster.

The seconds wept past. His confidence slowly swelled.

He could do this. He just needed to stay patient. Needed to—

The body he was leaning on collapsed. Sucked under the mob all at once. Gone.

His prop knocked out from him, he pitched into the void to his left where that support had been.

Tilting.

Falling.

He stabbed the bad foot into the ground. Felt the fresh shock of pain jolt through him. That halted his fall for a second, stood him up straighter, but the ankle wouldn't hold.

And he thrashed like a drowning victim. Grabbed at some of the bodies around him.

His hands slid over sweat-soaked blouses and t-shirts. Fingers clawing at anything they touched. Noses. Ears. Ribcages. Elbows. All of them smearing past. He couldn't get a hold of anything.

He finally grabbed a handful of something and his grip found purchase.

He yanked to hoist himself. Rose a few inches back toward standing.

Still didn't realize what he was hanging onto until he felt the cluster of hair give, ripping, a handful of salt and pepper fluff coming away in his fist.

He faced the ground fully now. Zoomed in on the writhing mess of limbs there. Saw the textured outline of the asphalt through the gaps.

Gravity pulled, hungry, sucked him into the gloom.

And he sank into the darkness at the bottom of the crowd.

CHAPTER 73

Darger walked a few steps deeper into the field of sod to get away from the screaming and yelling. Her legs felt wobbly beneath her, the soles of her boots squishing into the grass and dirt in a way that felt strange — wrong — after all that stomping about on the cobblestones. A plush carpet shoved into the midst of a horror scene.

She scanned the park in all directions. Let her eyes drift past the streaming parkgoers and the few vested members of law enforcement she could now see splayed among them, none of them Loshak.

She fixed her gaze on the gaps, the darker places that trailed away deeper into the park, and part of her pictured that colorful splotchy map as she did.

The screams and moans still pricked in her ears, awful sounds that kept her hackles up and her breath shaky. She needed to block them out. It was the only way to help anyone.

Panic was a social phenomenon. She knew this. It elicited a sympathetic response, spread through a crowd like a forest fire during drought season, lighting up everything around it.

Right now she needed to push down the panic and flip herself into Huxley's point of view. It was the only way.

She took a few more steps over that spongy green carpet, and the screams got smaller, tinnier. The thump of her own heartbeat swelled to fill the fresh quiet, something urgent in the rhythm.

She closed her eyes. Listened only to the beat of that crooked drum in her chest.

He's here.

He's here right now.

But where would he be?

Veins throbbed in her neck, and the muscles in her jaw rippled. She trained her ears on the empty space beyond the beat. Listened.

Empty.

Nothing.

No words came to her. No pictures.

Just that sucking nothingness beyond the here and now. Space. The void that surrounded us always and sometimes found its way inside.

Her neck craned without her telling it to. Tilted her chin toward the taller rides in the distance. She opened her eyes.

Skeletal frames filled the lower portion of the sky. Curved contours trying to puncture the clouds.

And a lightness rushed to fill that emptiness in Darger's skull. Something fizzing inside her head, prickling over her scalp.

Up high.

You'd want to be up high.

To see. To watch.

A spectator. Your own biggest fan.

She blinked. Squinted.

Are you filming this now? Ready to broadcast the grand finale?

As if on cue, a chuffing sound pierced Darger's quiet space. Something chopping at the wind.

She recognized the mechanical din. Turned around to verify it.

A pair of news helicopters floated not so high above.

Zooming toward the bigger rides to try to catch the next action sequence. Probably competing networks, the pilots fighting for position to get the superior footage, some producer screaming in the speaker in their ear.

No. You didn't need to film it. Between the security cams and the media, you knew the footage would leak.

One less thing for you to worry about.

Darger strode forward now. Instinct seemed to aim her shoulders toward the back of the park.

She pictured the map blots again. The biggest rides occupied the rear of the park, a pack of brontosauruses grazing there eternally. But what else?

The food court. Grub Town.

She bet a lot of the crowd was milling there, a blind impulse moving them as far from the exit chutes as possible. They might even feel some false safety in being away from the bigger rides as well.

Yes.

Yes.

So far both the coaster area and the exits had been hit. That left the food court as the last space that might feel safe, didn't it?

Darger picked up into a run.

CHAPTER 74

Huxley glides toward the back of the park, the wind breathing on his face. Chilly against the wetness coating him, though it cannot touch the heat inside.

He smears the back of his wrist over his forehead, feels fluid drain down the side of his face. His pores wide open now. His skin itself weeping openly.

Close.

So close now.

His eyes flick back and forth. Consciously avoiding the rides up above and keeping his focus low.

He takes in the buildings in the middle distance. Lets his focus winnow in on the small structures — a general store and a saloon. Both places have a faux old-timey look — rustic clapboard siding and beams in the front, the font on the signs looking properly of the Oregon trail or Deadwood or some shit. Cartoonish. A Disney World version of the old West slapped here in the middle of the coasters and arcades. Just another way to separate fools from their money.

But right now they look beautiful to him. Striking and strange. Steeped with importance, with intense meaning that borders on religious or profane or both at once.

He obsessively snaps his gaze from one building to the next and back.

General Store.

Saloon.

Saloon.

General Store.

His vision traces the cleft between the two. A shadowy slit between the buildings set about shoulder wide. Darkness creeps out of the gap, tries to reach its black gauze out over the park itself, but the gray light streaming through the clouds above beats it back into its cave.

He squints. Tries to see the little receptacle in the opening there. A green mesh thing. Stooped like a vulture in his memory. But either the angle is wrong or the gloom is too thick to make it out.

Still, he knows that what he seeks lies just there. The reason. The purpose. The solution to all his problems. The end. It rests just there. Hidden away. Waiting for him. Waiting his whole life long for this moment, *his* moment.

Yesss.

It has always been headed this way. The point. The confluence. The trajectory of every choice shuffling him closer and closer to this. He can see that now, how all the pieces fit together, how his life did accumulate to something, something singular, something meaningful, even if it so often felt otherwise, felt pointless.

Looking back, he can see the shape. The progression. It had always been baked in. Something in his DNA. Something in the air.

He grimaces. Refocuses on those buildings slowly growing closer, growing bigger in his field of vision. Goes back to trying to pierce that shadowy fissure with his gaze.

Something squats there at the corner of the alley. He can't make out the details yet — can't see the steel cells that form the cage around what he seeks — but he knows it's there now.

Fresh adrenaline tingles in his limbs at the sight of it. He's been anxious. Nervous that in his agitated state he could somehow miss the spot, run right past, lose time. That it all could go wrong somehow at the last minute.

But now that fear is past, is over. The visual confirmation eradicates it, replaces it with a new appetite.

He swerves to his right and shoots through a gap in the fence. His feet clap over the brick walkway here for a second, the sharp reports echoing back from the hard surface, and then he cuts through another expanse of grass, and the sound is gone.

The buildings rise higher now. Sprouting from the horizon to stand over him. Closer and closer.

That clammy feeling has overtaken his body again. His skin a soggy membrane, so slick it's as though it's been oiled.

He shivers when the breeze kicks up and touches the moist places. Frigid. Excited. Unable to stop himself from squirming.

And then he's racing across another walkway, and the buildings seem to zoom toward him, and the shape and color of that object in the alley come clear all at once.

The forest green meshwork of metal jails the black plastic sheet on the other side of the bars. The mouth of the garbage can gapes at the sky, always hungry, always ready.

He strides the last few paces. Towers over the thing.

His tongue knifes out. Licks his lips. Tastes the salt.

And then he goes to work. Rips the lid off the garbage can, that perpetually open mouth removed and tossed aside.

His fingers pry along the edges of the black plastic. And then the garbage bag itself is removed, a gloomy wraith floating over toward the lid, weighed down by only a paper plate and a few empty Coke cups.

He shuffles back to the green metal cage. Stares down into the thing.

There's another bag nestled at the bottom of the can. White plastic this time, a big department store bag wrapped tightly around another bulk.

Silvery lines of duct tape wind around the thing and somehow give the shape beneath the plastic a sense of dimension, of volume, of density.

This is it.

This is it.

He'd hidden it here, under the garbage bag, tucked up against the side of the saloon where no one could see.

And now its time has come.

Sound and movement behind him. Footsteps crunching.

He whirls around. Panic shrieking in his skull.

One of the parkgoers goes sprinting by, heading for the back of the park, for the food court. The footfalls trail away as quickly as they'd come.

He gapes another second at the vacant path before him. Giggles a little. A laugh that sounds crazy even in his own ears.

It's no one. Nothing. Just another victim to be.

He moves to a bench just along the alley's edge. Places his packet there like it's an altar. Kneels before it like this is worship.

And then he pulls a pocket knife out of his left hip pocket. Unfolds the blade from the handle.

One hand holds the package. The other performs the surgery.

The knife's metal tip dips under the edge of each flap of duct tape. Slices right along the seam. Clean cuts. Easy.

And then the plastic comes loose in his hands.

He takes a deep breath and lets it out slow, shaky. Unwraps the bag. Keeps a light touch as he does.

When the bag is stripped away from its contents, he tosses the white plastic in the general direction of the lid. Watches it float that way out of the corner of his eye.

His vision stays trained on the silvery pipes and red wires attached to them. All of it strung together with straps.

He stands. Sheds the too-tight neon shirt. Feels the moisture of the stretch fabric sop against his neck and head like a soggy sponge.

And then he picks up the vest and pulls it over his moist torso, onto his naked flesh. The straps feel rough. The wires smooth. The pipes heavy.

He straps the bomb to his chest. Pulls the Velcro tight and locks the teeth side to the carpety side. Then he moves his arms out to the sides.

The weight of the C4 in the pipes tugs toward the ground. But the vest holds it to him.

He knew it would. Had practiced this many times alone in his room. Looking at himself in the mirror, at that gaunt face he didn't really recognize as himself anymore.

Back at the trash can, he takes a black hoodie out of the very bottom. Pulls it on over the bulky chest piece. Zips it up almost to the chin.

It's new, the hoodie. Too big. A little stiff.

But it'll work. The size might even play to his advantage. Might cover, at least a little, twenty or so pounds of explosive strapped to his sweaty chest.

He pivots. Runs for the food court.

One shining moment, he thinks.

And then he smiles a little to himself once more.

Shining so so bright.

CHAPTER 75

Darger's hand clutched at the radio, pressed it to her lips as she ran. The words streaming out of her seemed oddly calm compared to the lurching fever of thoughts in her head. She was pretty sure they made sense, even if she could only kind of follow them herself.

"The food court. We need to clear the food court. I think it's the next target."

Faintly distorted voices babbled back. She couldn't keep them all straight, neither the speakers nor the sentences, but she got the gist: Everyone was on board.

Some of the C-IED agents and SWAT officers were already herding people out of the picnic table area. She could hear their hard voices giving commands in the background on some of the transmissions.

Something about the aggression in their tones lifted her spirits, gave her hope. They seemed to be taking control, being proactive. Attacking the problem instead of merely being the victims of it.

Good.

Good.

Maybe there's still time.

The sounds on the walkie only filtered into her consciousness as an afterthought, somehow secondary. Softer sounds, the moans and whimpers of children, threaded through the crowd. When the reality sunk in, it made her shiver.

She weaved around an abandoned ice cream cart and got

back on the walkway. Then she picked up speed. Sprinting. Feet springing off the brick that lined this part of the park's paths.

Storefront windows flitted by on both sides of her. A menagerie of gift shops, every tourist's dream. Novelty t-shirts. Shot glasses. Fanny packs. Saltwater taffy. Fudge. Posters and pamphlets in all colors of the rainbow. It all pulsed along the edges of her vision.

She took another left, a gentler angle this time, and the food court row opened up before her. Smooth asphalt coated the walkway here, the path broadening out to nearly the width of a city street.

A series of food stalls occupied most of the real estate beyond the blacktop here — elephant ears, French fries, snow cones, corn dogs, burgers, even deep-fried Oreos.

It immediately reminded Darger much more of a county fair than the rest of the park — something a little old school, a little rinky-dink about it all. Only the bigger restaurant at the end of the row betrayed that impression.

Darger's feet shuffled beneath her. Stuttered as she prepared to change directions and head into Grub Town.

She let her gaze go past the fair food to the sea of picnic tables beyond. Wooden planks. Gravel paths. Green grass. Her heart sank right away.

People still milled there. Huddled masses like refugees. Frightened faces and stooped shoulders. Sitting, standing, clogging the picnic area.

Too many people.

SWAT officers worked to clear the area, their black-clad bodies looking more angular and upright than everything around them as they stalked through the throng.

But there were hundreds of people. How could they clear

them all? Where could they all go? Was any place here truly safe?

Darger hurled herself that way. Picked up her knees again.

The fryer grease smell hit two steps later. Hot oil wafting everywhere, stinking like French fries. She thought about the fat vapors hanging in the air here, ready and willing to adhere to her face and clog her pores, knowing it mattered not at all just now and thinking about it anyway.

Fresh screaming in the distance shattered that thought. Ragged. Piercing.

And Darger's free hand snaked down to her side without her telling it to, without her slowing. Instinct taking over.

She unsnapped her holster and drew her Glock.

CHAPTER 76

The shadows engulfed Loshak, the crush of bodies blocking out the sky above. He flopped downward into darkness, sank through a whirl of knees and shins and ankles. Landed flat on his belly on the cold stone of the walkway.

And that blanket of gloom pulled taut over top of him, tried to smother him.

He froze like that for the length of three galloping heartbeats. Wild eyes swiveling, swiveling.

Inky shapes throbbed everywhere. The many-limbed blur churning all around him. A mindless, restless creature clapping at the sidewalk, out for blood.

He scrabbled. Hands clawing at the seams between the cobblestones like hamster paws probing at the lip of the cage.

He pushed himself up onto hands and knees. Weathered the clubbing feet and elbows that mostly seemed to glance off his hips and back, a few fleeting blows catching the top of his head.

Again he froze for a beat.

He felt the mass of humanity mash into him and lean away over and over, moist bodies stamping him with their sweaty imprints like postmarks. The body heat flared around him like a broken furnace stuck on full blast, the heat rolling off in waves.

He stilled his panicked mind. Winnowed everything down to one stream of thought.

This next bit would be the hard part. How to get from his knees to his feet with that endless surge of body parts roiling around him, kicking and kneeing and elbowing and punching, whether they meant to or not.

One clean breath rushed in. Muggy in his throat. Heavy in his lungs. That seemed to steady him further.

He pushed off with both hands, thrust himself skyward. His spine stiffened, angled upward a few degrees toward vertical.

But then a heel stomped into the center of his back. Felt like the kick of a Clydesdale. Pain radiated outward from the point of impact, a sizzle of agony that arced around his curved ribs and into his chest.

He couldn't breathe. Couldn't think.

He crumpled back to the cobblestone. Felt his head go lighter as his forehead thumped rock.

And that person, the Clydesdale, was on top of him now. Heavy feet trampling on his back, one and then the other. Digging into the meat of him, grinding muscle against bone, pulverizing his form against the textured cobblestone like it meant to grate him over the grout lines.

Trapped. Smashed. Cold rock smearing and clawing at his face, at his body.

He tried to force himself to breathe, but he couldn't. Wind knocked out. Some overwhelming paralysis clutching his lungs.

One of the feet left his back. All that pressure returning to one point just under his right shoulder blade. Again he could only picture a fluffy horse hoof puncturing his back, twisting a little.

He bucked and rolled to the side. Some instinct taking over.

The Clydesdale lost his or her balance. That foot sliding off as Loshak hurled himself sideways.

And then the big lug came crashing down into the gloom just next to the agent.

He couldn't see her, not really, but he could tell somehow that it was not any large breed of livestock after all. It was a woman, older he thought, a little heavyset.

The crowd shifted around them, a trickle of shifting light spilling down to them from the outside world. That was something. Maybe with the two of them down here together they'd carved out a little more space.

The words popped into his mind unbidden and seemed absurd just as quickly: *Wiggle room.*

He threw himself upward again. His upper body sprang harder this time. Fresh adrenaline, maybe.

He got his torso most of the way toward upright, but then the momentum started to shift. Gravity wanted him back.

He reached out into the half-light. Grabbed a belt cinched around a doughy dad bod. Hooked his fingers around the leather and held on like this was a bucking bronco instead of a guy who looked a bit like Ron Swanson.

He climbed the belt like the rung of a ladder. Pulled himself up enough to get his feet underneath him, and then he was rising again. Standing. Rushing through the last layer of shadows.

His head broke the surface. Reborn into the brightness. He gaped at the domed sky above and felt funny, the heavens open again, the vast universe yawning over him.

The hollow felt cool against his wet face. A relief from that sweltering humidity below.

Some of the fight had gone out of the mob, or so it felt to him. The stampede was breaking down as he supposed they always did eventually.

He breathed and sweated and breathed some more.

Then he reached back down into the dark to help the lady

with horse hooves for feet.

CHAPTER 77

The helicopters *whomp* overhead. Rotors slicing the sky. Louder now.

He ignores them at first. Racing for the food court. Faster, faster.

But then he feels their wind sweep over him. One of the choppers right on top of him, the twirling rotors blowing air like a box fan jammed in a window.

He cranes his neck to see them, two different news helicopters, one and then the other coming clear above him. Jagged things. Stark against the drab clouds.

The first chopper is smaller, sleeker, aerodynamic, darting around. A black thing that flits like an insect in the height of summer. The fly that keeps landing on the potato salad, spiraling away, coming back for more.

The second aircraft looks stiffer, bigger. The more angular of the two. It's white and glossy. The big "Channel 7" in gold on the side, glowing against the dark blue background of the logo.

He can see the camera apparatus leaning out the side of this one. The thing bolted there, the silhouette of the person manning it just a dark shape behind, the camera panning so smoothly toward the back of the park.

They both keep swinging around each other. Jostling for position. Trying to flank either the damaged coaster track or the food court with a sweeping shot. Something dramatic.

It occurs to him that he might be on TV even now. A tiny figure like an ant hauling ass over the brickwork as the camera swoops by. Probably looks just like any of the other terrified masses. Running scared.

It calls to mind so many memories. Watching riot or chase footage on TV. Seeing cars smack into each other, the fleeing perp getting out and running on foot. Darting through yards, between houses. Something frantic in every step.

The police climbing out to give chase. All of it culminating in some spectacular tackle and then just a mob of police beating the utter shit out of the perp who can only cup his arms around his head.

That's him now. He's the running figure on all those screens out there. Broadcasting live, probably worldwide.

Crazy.

Crazy.

And new heat flushes his face. Fluid that sloshes along with his gait, pulls his cheeks funny, makes his face feel like one of those rubber hot water bottles from one of the old cartoons, thick-looking things the same shade as the brick walkway under his feet.

The choppers veer out of sight, a few treetops now blocking the way, and he turns his vision back fully to the area along the ground. Scans for movement.

A few more stragglers in the distance sprint along, flitting in and out of his view. Arms pumping. Legs churning. Red and blue t-shirts flickering in the gaps between the rides, between the buildings, between the trees.

Invariably they head for the food court. The false safe haven.

Funny.

Funny how predictable groups of people truly are, how the behavior of billions ultimately slots into just a few sociological or psychological buckets, how the only ones who stand out are the truly insane.

Funnyyyyy.

He can see the signs for Grub Town all around now. Little cartoon burgers and corn dogs emblazoned under the white lettering and arrows.

And he knows, from his research trips, that the row of food carts and stalls is just over the next gentle rise, starts at the place where the brick walkway gives way to smooth asphalt — another way to demarcate the various regions of the park, he supposes. He races for the line where the red brick bleeds into black.

It's here.

This is it. His big moment.

The role of a lifetime.

CHAPTER 78

The screaming girl looked to be about fourteen, give or take a year or so. She thrashed in the arms of one of the SWAT officers. Legs kicking, arms flailing. Her face glowed a crimson shade, glaring a little where the daylight touched her sweat-lacquered skin. The sounds coming out of her made Darger's arms pucker into goose flesh.

The officer absorbed the girl's blows and hugged her closer. His face held mostly blank save for something somber in his eyes.

Darger slithered through the outskirts of the crowd and ran right up on them, trying to read all the cues in the body language before her, trying to make this make sense.

Was the girl hurt? Injured? Had Huxley set off some other kind of device here?

A memory flashed in Darger's head from the first Huxley case, a luxe apartment in New York. An actress had opened a gift box, and acid had sprayed her in the face. Flesh melting like pizza cheese. Skin smoking a little as it vacated the cheekbones and wept down from the jaw like candle wax.

The image of that ruined face had been seared into Darger's memory forever.

And she saw the same kind of damage on the girl's face now. Blistered skin like a charred red pepper. Features morphing as flesh and cartilage liquefied.

But then Darger blinked and the injuries vanished. Just a red-faced girl. Clearly upset but seemingly unhurt.

The agent pulled up a few feet shy of the SWAT officer and

the girl, Glock pointed at the trampled grass between her and the two of them. Suddenly she didn't know what to do, what to say. She swallowed. Blinked. Found herself yelling unintentionally, adrenaline wrenching control of her vocal cords.

"Is she… is she hurt?"

And then another SWAT officer was there at Darger's shoulder, speaking softly just near her ear.

"The explosion by the exits. She lost her parents. Both of them."

Darger blinked again. Felt the information kind of roll into her brain and slowly settle into place there.

Both parents.

Holy shit.

The girl was probably exiting the initial stage of shock, maybe just coming out of that numbness the mind somehow draped over trauma like a warm blanket, at least for a short while. The enlarged pupils and rapid breathing seemed to fit that diagnosis.

The screaming cut out. The rigidity in the girl's body seemed to sag all at once. She crumpled against the SWAT officer, finally let him hold onto her. And the big flat-topped lug rocked the girl lightly, cooed words Darger couldn't make out, his eyes wet and crinkled, comforting this stranger like she was his own daughter.

Darger swallowed. Looked on for a few seconds. And then she turned away.

She slowly swiveled around and scanned in all directions, staring out at the distant pieces of the park, taking in all those pathways trailing off into the horizon and the rides rising over everything. The goose flesh crawled over the backs of her arms again.

Huxley is here. I know he is.

But where?

She walked back through the picnic area. Eyes sharp, darting.

She watched bits of the mob stream toward the front of the park as she did, SWAT officers barking commands everywhere like drill sergeants and the herd mostly obeying. They were making progress quickly now.

Perhaps the screaming girl had spurred the herd into action some, shook them out of their lackadaisical state.

The helicopter rotors whined right overhead. Two distinct mechanical voices. The harmony changing pitch with every movement. Louder and louder. The sheer volume made Darger clench her jaw.

She holstered her Glock and strode back onto the blacktop and moved toward one of the burger stands that seemed to be walled off on three sides by pine trees. The sounds of the choppers dulled a touch as she drew herself into the cluster of spruces, those chopping sounds losing their edge, their brightness.

She closed her eyes and tried to clear her head again. Let her ears drift past the rotor sounds and reach out into the space beyond them, the emptiness. Her breath rolled in and out of her, rising and falling in steady waves — a placid sea even with all the chaos around.

The stillness came over her slowly, cautiously. She could feel the shift in the flesh of her face somehow, some subtle ache sinking into her cheeks.

She drifted. Let herself get swept up in that tranquility, pulled into the gentle waves.

And then the vacancy inside, the lack of thought, seemed right. The space, inside and out, became more real than the physicality, than the objects. More real than the concrete world. It thrummed with the bright voltage of life.

She directed her awareness again toward where Huxley might be, toward what he might want. Pointed the stillness in that direction.

The wind picked up. Exhaled. Blew cool across the bridge of her nose.

And the voice in her head seemed to speak up from that stirring breeze. A whisper like stones scraping against each other.

I'd want to...

The helicopter whine changed pitch again overhead. Another breath rolled in and out of her.

I'd want to be there at the end.

She sat with that a moment. Let it tumble in her empty head. Then the whisper came again.

I'd want to be there at the end. The grand finale.

The choppers would swoop overhead. The eye in the sky showing the whole world what I'd made.

The big final shot would be me, center screen, would be as dramatic as possible.

Her mind leaped forward, a bolt of intuition skipping steps and grasping for the logical conclusion all at once. The words sprang to mind as if from nowhere: *blaze of glory.*

And then she replayed snippets of his earlier speech, from some of his journals.

The plan will cost me everything. I know that now.

The villain comes on-screen. For better or worse.

And now, finally, I can finish my work here.

She opened her eyes. Blinked a couple times.

He wants to martyr himself.

Of course.

And the helicopters are already here, already broadcasting live.

She stepped out of the copse of pine trees and heard the sharpness come back in those chopping rotors overhead. She shifted her view to the pathways leading into the food court. Scanned that strip of asphalt again.

Two streams of the crowd blazed trails toward the front of the park. The SWAT officers walked along the fringes of the foot traffic flows, coaxing the herd like sheep dogs.

She pulled her vision back from those focal points. Made herself look at the big picture instead. Almost let her eyes go out of focus to see what didn't fit.

New movement caught her eye. A black shape, a shadow, that cut against the grain. Something that swam upstream compared to all else around it.

Her eyes snapped to the mote of darkness.

And he was there.

Tyler Huxley.

Clad in black. Red-faced. Moon-eyed.

The bomber jogged with something bulky under his hoodie, running for the biggest mob.

CHAPTER 79

Huxley crests the final hill. And then the back of the park gapes before him.

Food carts. Black asphalt. The cowering herd. It all lies open at his feet, at his mercy.

This is where I leave my mark. This is what the world will think of when they hear my name.

Deliverance.

Damnation.

He sprints down the slope. Head going light, going airy. Little pops firing off in his skull like a sheet of bubble wrap.

His calves and thighs have likewise gone numb beneath him. But the beat of his footsteps controls him now, owns him now, the established rhythm a perpetual kind of motion that seems to function on its own.

His body merely obeys the beat. Pounds onward.

Breath scrapes over his teeth. Cool on the way in, hot on the way out.

And his eyes whirl over the spoils before him. He takes it all in again.

Food carts. Black asphalt. The cowering…

But then he looks closer at the mob. Really looks.

No.

That airy feeling flees him at once. His breath hitches in his throat. Dry.

And that rhythm fails him for a moment. Beat disrupted. Footsteps thrown off. Lost balance wobbling him off course. Ankles flexing to their limits to keep him upright.

The horde isn't crowded around the picnic tables like he'd expected. No ducking. No huddling. No hiding.

They're streaming out of Grub Town instead. Two long lines of them like worms inching back toward the front gates.

Mass exodus.

Shit.

He's drifting to the left. Body tilting. A listing ship.

He sticks a foot into the ground. Pushes off as hard as he can.

That sets him upright again. Gets the beat thumping on time.

He keeps going.

Too late to quit now, isn't it? He'll have to improvise. Make the best of it.

He examines the roving herds. Two groups. One bigger than the other. Maybe twice the size of its counterpart, spilling into the widest of the brick walkways, and moving a little slower for its breadth.

Well, that settles the first decision.

He runs for the bigger mob. Picking up speed. He tries to picture how he'll work this.

If he runs out into the middle of the group, he can still plausibly wipe out probably the entire pack, a thought that brings a half-smile back to his lips.

Yeah. Thirteen pounds of C4 can do a lot of good if you use it correctly. Much bigger than the charge he set off by the gates. That's for sure.

And of course, he's peppered it with a little something extra this time. Saved the biggest special effects sequence for last.

He can't help but imagine the spectacle.

A whole crowd of people chopped down in a single second.

Ripped. Perforated.

Limbs and heads removed in a flash.

Stumped necks jetting arterial spray.

All of it broadcasting live worldwide.

But then he pictures it again. This time only about a third of the mob goes down, one or two segments of that worm ever-lengthening along the brick walkway.

Maybe that's more realistic. The line of people stretches too far from end to end, will pull too many of them out of the blast zone.

He clenches his jaw. Feels his chin quiver.

They were supposed to be hunkered among the picnic tables. A tightly packed throng he could dispatch altogether.

He needs to think. Like now.

Christ, it's all happening soon. One way or another.

A voice speaks up behind him. Loud. Harsh. Strident enough to cut through the chopper noise.

"Hey Huxley."

A woman. Familiar.

And that beat of footfalls cuts out beneath him. Vanquished.

He stops dead. Turns.

It's her.

The wind from the helicopters whips her hair around her face. She stands there with both her hands up. A pose like she's been waiting for him to catch her all this time.

The FBI agent. Darger.

Sweet Jesus.

He's seen her face plastered on all the magazines, strewn far and wide on the internet. Something like a folk hero, this one.

But she looks different in person. Smaller.

He doesn't hesitate. He runs for her. His scowl veering into a smile once again as he does.

Excitement bursts like fireworks in his head.

This is it. This is it.

The improvised finale. Not the mark I thought I'd leave.

Something better.

His sweaty thumb readies itself on the detonator. The smooth plastic gone warm against his body heat, against his skin.

He doesn't even need to get all the way to her. He just needs to get close.

Maybe he can't take out a big chunk of the herd like he wanted to, but here's another celebrity that can go down on live TV.

Both of them are celebrities, he realizes. Him and her.

And now they'll die together.

It's perfect.

CHAPTER 80

Darger ripped her Glock out of her holster again. Swept the gun up to sight Huxley.

She swallowed. Focused. All of her consciousness sucking up into her head, save for the grainy feel of the Glock's grip in her hand, the cool of the trigger against her finger.

She stared down the length of the gun. Unblinking. The barrel leveled at Huxley's chest at first.

But no.

No.

He's wired to blow.

Darger brushed the muzzle higher. Lined up the head shot.

Her wrist dipped and swayed along with the minute variations in Huxley's gait.

And she felt some distant gurgle in her belly. A rumbling emptiness somehow part of her and still so far away.

Wait.

A few seconds more.

Let him get away from the crowd, and then take the shot.

He lumbered for her still. Looked bigger now. Thicker. Heavier. Grinning like a jackal running down something helpless, something weak.

Her tongue flicked out over her lips. Her hand shook just a little.

Can't miss now.

Can't miss.

The grip of the Glock suddenly felt like a two-by-four snugged into the web of her hand. Chunky. Harsh. Unwieldy.

Awkward. Her whole hand slicked by the sweat leaking out of her palm.

But she knew it wasn't real. None of it was real.

Just nerves.

She cleared her head. Pictured a target at the range, just like the ones she'd put thousands of rounds into over the years to meet the Bureau-mandated shooting quotas.

It's routine. Just a shot like any other.

She lined up the barrel again.

Exhaled and felt the looseness spread through all of her being. Neck and shoulders settling. Back releasing all the way down the length of her spine, the vertebrae like chain links going slack one by one.

Her hand steadied along with her will.

The wide part of her forearm jumped and flexed. Her hand tightened.

She squeezed the trigger.

The Glock bucked in her hand, spouted flame.

And the bullet thwacked into the bomber's forehead. Punched a clean red hole there, some pink foam lining it right away.

Huxley stumbled forward. Momentum carried him two more steps.

And then he fell down in a heap all at once. Face-first. Planted flat.

His baseball cap fluttered off to the side as he landed, exposing the dark hair cropped short.

One tendril of blood spouted out of that hole in the forehead. Then the body lay motionless.

Spent.

Dead.

And everything fell quiet. Tension rolling over the whole scene like a silent wave, somehow blotting the drone of the rotors above out of Darger's ears.

She braced herself for the explosion. Puckered her mouth. Backpedaled.

Her eyes stayed locked on the fallen figure. Tyler Huxley reduced to a dark lump on the ground. Inert. Lifeless.

And part of her sensed the mob spurred to life in the distance. Each swell crushing into the aisle, a high tide surging up onto the beach. They raced now. Frantic. A silent movie.

They knew.

Everyone knew what would happen next. Here and now.

The big bang.

Huxley's form lay funny. His belly cupped on top of whatever blend of explosives he'd strapped to himself.

It arched his back in a way that reminded Darger of a dead sewer rat she'd seen in the gutter once. A bloated black thing with all four legs outstretched as though it'd somehow died mid-hurdle, fur all soggy and slicked to the bulging body.

Darger took a few more steps backward. Blinked for the first time since Huxley had gone down.

And still, he didn't move. Not so much as a nervous twitch.

Maybe the bomb wouldn't blow. They could call in the C-IED team to dispose of it. Use the robot and the containment vessel again.

She licked her lips. Let her free hand drift down to her side. Carefully she unhooked the radio from her hip like any sudden move could lead to catastrophe.

The black box drifted up toward her face. And all the while she stepped backward, stepped backward, eyes never leaving that black-clad torso draped over the ground.

Her finger pressed the button. She spoke into the radio. Fragmented thoughts pouring out of her. The words ebbing and flowing. Jumbled rushed parts punctuated with pauses.

But her own words didn't register in her head now. Not really.

With the conscious part of her mind, she watched. Waited.

Huxley's body flexed on the ground. Shoulders lifting and then sagging again. The single fish flop made it look like he'd just lurched in a big breath.

Darger instinctively brought the hand holding the radio up to shield her face. Her wrist and forearm angled in front of her eyes.

And she caught just a glimpse of Huxley's body coming apart. That black torso jerked taut and then burst outwards into a powder, into particles.

And the flash blew out Darger's vision then. Impossible radiance everywhere all at once. Too bright.

Glowing white filled her field of vision. Burned itself into her retinas. Scorching. Gleaming.

She stumbled back. Half surprised to find the ground still there underfoot, though it quaked like Jell-O against the tread of her boot.

And the blast came whooshing at her. A ripping heat that seemed to pass through her as much as around her. Felt like something solid, knocking her straight back.

Staggered. Legs kicking out from under her. Falling. Her spine suddenly perpendicular to the ground.

And the glow swelled brighter, brighter all around her. Searing. Blinding.

Light that filled the sky, filled the universe. Blistered her eyes.

The roar boomed out from the spot where Huxley had been. A rumble like thunder spreading outward. Aggressive.

The heels of both hands rushed to cover her eyes, even as she fell. Tried to block the brightness out. She could feel the Glock touch her brow, realized the radio was gone now.

She screamed into the endless white.

She couldn't hear herself, but she could feel her vocal cords shredding themselves to ribbons in her throat.

And then the brightness was gone. Extinguished. Sucked out at once. The black rushing to replace it seemed a mercy at first.

An absence. A void.

The nothingness yawed above and below. The big nothing opening wide.

And Darger fell down, down, down into the dark.

CHAPTER 81

When the explosion hit, Loshak was still bent at the waist, head hanging down, sucking wind. Dark spots strobed in the corner of his left eye.

It felt like his heart would never slow, like his breathing would never catch up to that galloping muscle, like he'd be stuck here forever just trying to survive, struggling, all of his consciousness reduced to its simplest form — one breath at a time.

But then bright white flashed like lightning off toward Grub Town at the way back of the park.

That telltale *boom* ripped over the grounds, the shuddering sound wave sweeping past him, and he was up and running all at once, legs twitching to life without him telling them to.

He jogged toward the food court like a magnet pulled him that way, bricks clapping under his feet. Only after he'd gotten up to full speed did it occur to him that he was running toward the explosion. The realization brought him no comfort, but he didn't question the instinct. He went with it.

He fixed his gaze on the distance, the little lip of that hill where the bricks seemed to melt into the horizon, where the land sloped down out of view. Kept trying to see something there. Anything.

He replayed the explosion in his head. The sound had been different than the earlier explosions. Muffled in some way. But was that good or bad?

The horde formed all at once in the distance, two fat rivers of humanity washing over the hill. Flushing out of the food court area. Thrashing and lurching. Two more stampedes headed right for him.

Christ.

This time he made sure to give the mob a wide berth. He hopped a gated barrier to his right and hustled well off the pathway into a green area — a grass swath interrupted by a few saplings.

The streams of humanity rolled up on both sides of his grass field. He couldn't help but picture all those people spilling over the fence, like that hurricane footage he'd seen so many times — waves washing up over a concrete barrier and flooding some city street, the ocean itself unleashed, loosed upon the urban sprawl.

He could hear hips and elbows pinging against the fence. Mostly the ringing of grazes with a few heavier thuds now and then.

The bulk of the crowd brushed past quickly enough. A few stragglers pumped their arms with exaggerated fury, faces all wadded up in scowls like Halloween masks, unable to keep up and apparently panicked at the prospect of being at the back of the pack.

Then that trickle, too, moved on, and Loshak found the way open before him again.

He jumped the fence and ran for the daylight. He thought he could smell smoke — an acrid stench that reminded him of liquefied polyester — but he didn't see any rising up from the hill before him, at least not yet.

The walkway tilted upward underfoot. He rushed for the top of the hill. The bricks transitioned to asphalt.

And then the land opened up before him. The food court sprawled to fill the bottom of the hill.

He swiveled his head to take in the full width of the view. Blinked.

One of the food carts looked cratered. Blackened. Shredded metal bent at impossible angles back from where the front of the thing used to be.

He ran. His eyes followed the darkened marks on the ground — blacker than black — toward the epicenter of the blast. A spot where the asphalt had been rent, a cavity there, blacker still than all else around it.

He rocketed closer. Trying to think.

The middle of the aisle didn't make sense for a detonation spot. Did it?

He tried to imagine the steps that led to this result. Huxley wouldn't have planted the device there, out in the open.

And then he saw it in his mind's eye.

Huxley with the explosives strapped to his chest, rushing out into the crowd. It followed, somehow. It made sense.

But if he managed to take out any victims, there was no sign of it here. No shredded corpses. No wounded down and bleeding. Nothing.

He noted that there was no sign of Huxley, either. Nothing left of him, of what he'd done here.

Just that empty stretch of broken land. Asphalt scorched and fractured and dug out in the middle.

He gazed up at the choppers circling overhead for a second. The news cameras would have captured it all.

The footage would show him exactly how it went down. It'd be the only way left to confirm that Huxley had done himself in, and Loshak expected full confirmation.

He sat with that a moment. Tried to process it.

It was over. The whole thing was over.

He sucked in a big breath and let it out slowly. But the tension in his back wouldn't let go.

His eyes snapped back to a spot in the grass further to the right. Something discolored there.

No. Not a spot.

A person.

A person laid out on the ground. Half on their side, half face down.

He changed directories. Raced for it. For her.

It wasn't until he hovered right over the body that he could recognize the fallen figure.

It was Darger.

CHAPTER 82

Loshak followed the EMTs up the hill. Their orange-clad backs faced him, Darger laid out on the odd yellow plank hovering between the two of them.

The spine board bobbed over the uneven walkway, tilted funny as they lugged it up the hill. The figure strapped to it didn't move.

The back of the ambulance waited at the top of the slope. Back doors open wide. Light glowing within the chamber. Ready to race back across the park to the nearest hospital.

Fever flushed Loshak's cheeks as he ascended toward that line where the black asphalt changed to red brick. The heat inside made his thoughts cut in and out. Some shrieking panic blotting the words out now and then, violently thrusting nothing into his head instead.

And something about that searing intensity inside reduced his view of the world around him to impressionistic flashes. Exaggerations. Distortions. All bright colors and bold shapes like he was seeing the park around him rendered in cave painting smears.

Darger was a lumpy thing, a wadded-up rag, laid out on a plastic slab roughly the shade of lemon peel. Her complexion was ashen. Her form motionless.

The tapered backs of the paramedics became ape-like. The V-shaped musculature inflated, intimidating, strange.

Gray clouds smudged the sky. Dirty cotton stretched out into curving fibers. Somehow overwhelming.

He mostly stared at the ground and blinked. Saw the

texture of the asphalt take on vivid detail. Every dip and divot somehow discernible to him now, like he could see the loops and whorls of the thing's fingerprints.

And the EMTs were loading Darger into the ambulance, her limp figure wobbling as they shoved the stretcher home. They slammed the doors, one then the other. And then one of those orange-suited figures jogged around to climb into the driver's seat.

A lump bobbed in Loshak's throat. His eyebrows slowly scaled his forehead. He wanted to say something, to tell them to wait for him, to demand to ride along.

But his voice held silent, didn't follow through on the impulse.

What would his waiting at the hospital serve?

He could still do good here. Some part of him knew that.

The brake lights flared and the flashers came on, painted ruddy ovals on the ground, the smaller of which blinked off and on. And then the ambulance jolted to life, picked up speed as it moved.

Loshak followed it back toward the front of the park, jogging along behind, lifting his head to watch it. The wind felt cooler on his nose and cheeks now, his whole body sheening with sweat.

The vehicle slowed as it transitioned over the narrower thresholds separating the different sections of the park. It likewise lost speed when it got near any straggling foot traffic.

He couldn't block out the words that came to his head as he stared at the back of the ambulance: *Meat wagon.*

But the white and orange thing slowly receded from Loshak's view nevertheless. It grew smaller and smaller until those flashers and taillights were tiny red pinpricks creeping toward the horizon. Eventually it rounded a distant bend and fled his view entirely.

He swallowed hard once it was gone. Felt that little bit emptier, that little bit more alone.

He no longer seemed to be doing something constructive, just racing into empty space.

But the heat came over him again and shoved the feelings down. Magma spewing in his brain pan, some molten urgency erasing all other impulses.

Still, he jogged. Ran for where he knew the bulk of the people would be now.

His feet pounded the bricks. Footsteps echoing funny off the clapboard gift shop siding.

He finally rounded that same bend where the ambulance had melted into the scenery. Watched a new slice of rides and buildings slide into view.

He sucked in a breath when he saw it.

Where empty land had mostly stretched before, people blotched the horizon now. Clusters of them here and there as far as he could see.

Some were down. Laid low on the pavement, in the dirt, in the grass.

Kneeling. Sprawling.

Hurt. Dead.

Some were paramedics trying to gather up the wounded, save those they could. They scuttled around. Hoisted people on stretchers. Their reflective gear shimmering when the light caught it right.

More ambulances squared off toward the front of the park. The vehicles sat at obtuse angles from each other, clogging the aisles, flashers blinking red.

Loshak ran for it, for all of it, his throat constricting. He wondered what horrors and wonders lay on the path ahead, wondered how he might help.

That last thought spurred him on.

Sometimes, in moments of crisis like this, he felt old. Weak. Useless.

But not today.

Today he could help. He would help.

And a memory blazed in his skull. He could see the skyward point of view he'd momentarily had as he climbed his way out of the crushing mob and back to his feet. All those heads and shoulders, and the endless gray gauze hung up above them all. And he remembered the first thing he'd done — reached back down into the mess of limbs and helped someone up.

The horse lady. He'd helped the horse lady.

And he'd help more.

Here and now.

He'd help.

The first bodies he came upon were too far gone for any such assistance. A pair of them a few feet apart. Torsos punctured. Lying in bloody pools.

He stopped to check both even though he knew. Cold to the touch.

They must have been right up against the exits when the blasts went off. Caught shrapnel of some kind.

Then they'd crawled here and bled out. Panicked. In shock. Alone.

He swallowed again. Harder this time. And he marveled at the will expended at the end, at the way people kept going until they couldn't, because… because what else could you do?

He ran on, and from there the pieces of the morning started to blur together. His mind seemed to fast forward, pushing him from trauma to trauma.

He aided a pair of paramedics in getting a heavier guy in a neon pink t-shirt up onto a stretcher, probably offering more psychological support than muscular. The guy writhed around, fought the paramedics off, seemed in a terrible panic despite not showing any external wounds. Loshak overheard some chatter about a possible heart attack.

He knelt close and offered up his hardest police voice. Told the guy to hold still now, that they were helping him.

The guy blinked hard and complied immediately. Lying back.

They hefted him onto the stretcher, and then they were rushing for the ambulance and gone all at once.

Loshak kept moving. Helping more. Seeing more deaths up close. His head going light, going tingly.

He called EMTs over to a wild-eyed ten-year-old kid hiding in some bushes. She had a badly lacerated arm, something that would definitely need stitches, but she would live.

He held another girl's hand as she was loaded into the ambulance. This one looked dicier. Major blood loss. Skin and lips gone pale blue. Maybe seven or eight years old.

She didn't want to let go of his hand as they lifted her through the loading doors. He had to kind of rip free of her fingers. And then he stumbled back and the doors slammed, and they squealed out into the parking lot and away.

He realized he'd crossed the entire park. And he stood a moment at the front gate looking out into the lot.

The sky felt enormous above him. The world felt endless and empty.

He walked out onto the asphalt.

CHAPTER 83

Drifting. Nothingness.

Darger floats in the emptiness. Only vaguely conscious of herself now and again. She wakes, internally, to moments of confusion that she can never quite hold onto for more than a few seconds.

Where is she?

Sleeping?

Waking?

Alive?

Dead?

The bewilderment slips free of her grasp over and over, the scarf turning to smoke in her fingers no matter how tightly she clenches her fists.

And her mind glides back into the stillness. Reverts to blankness, to that barren tundra. Cold and empty.

Dark hours drip past like that. Eternity rendered only in charcoal shades.

The dark sprawls around her. Endless.

☾

Distant beeping seems to slowly coax Darger to the surface. A steady rhythm, loping, something relaxed in the mechanical tones.

She wakes up confused. Warm. In the dark.

She can tell by smell somehow that she's in a hospital. Some antiseptic tang hangs in the air here. Sharp in her nostrils.

She picks up her head. Swivels it to try to scan the room.

She can't see.

It must be late — the middle of the night — but she should still be able to see *something.*

The shadowed outline of the doorway.

A rim of soft light glowing around the curtains.

The lights on that beeping machine, wherever it is.

Something.

But no. She sees nothing. The gloom dominates the room.

She reaches her right hand across her body, fingers the forearm on the opposite side. Slides her touch down to where the IV enters her skin.

Yes. The hospital indeed.

Something about the confirmation comforts her. An easing of that tension of not knowing. The hospital. At least she has that.

She drifts back to sleep.

☾

Dreams rise up to squelch the darkness for a time. Ever-changing images mash themselves together and project the results on the inside of Darger's skull, the bulb of that internal projector fluttering and lurching, flooding her brain with light.

Another part of her brain tries to link the disparate pieces into some kind of narrative, adding wants and needs and conflict to try to cohere the flickers into scenes, to make it all make sense, but the imagery will never quite obey the dramatic structures placed upon them, always veering off script.

Grub Town sprawls in front of her once more. The food carts. The asphalt walkway. The streams of the dispersing mob roving toward the front of the park.

And there's Tyler Huxley, something bulging funny under his black hoodie.

The bomber runs for Darger, sprinting through the food court just like he had been. Something in his posture speaks to a horror movie villain. Shoulders stooped. Arms pumping. Lips curling into a smile.

She lines up her shot. Squeezes the trigger.

But she's holding some kind of paintball gun instead of the real thing. The thing *whoomps* in her hand, some t-shirt cannon noise venting along with the projectile, the plastic stock bucking against her shoulder.

Blue paint splats on Huxley's forehead. A Smurf smear where the wound should be, where the blood should be.

Nevertheless, he flops face down. Looks like he's belly-smacking off the high dive.

And then Owen is there with one of those paper boats full of curly fries.

"You gotta try these," he says, and he tilts his head back and injects a coiled-up bit of fried potato into his mouth in a way that looks like a robin slurping down a worm.

He bends down and tries to feed Huxley a fry. Presses the tip right to the dead lips, which don't budge.

Then he shrugs.

"More for me."

He swipes the fry in that paint smear on Huxley's forehead — now ketchup red — and eats it.

"Me! Me!" Loshak yells, suddenly there at Owen's side. The agent seems small. Childlike. He bounces up and down in excitement.

Owen swipes another fry through Huxley's wound and feeds it to Loshak, who chews it with his mouth open like a

German Shepherd. Then Owen boops the agent on the nose.

Darger shudders and shakes herself out of the dream into a higher plane of sleep, though she doesn't wake.

She sleeps on in dreamless murk.

☾

When Darger wakes again, she can hear the faint bustle in what must be the hallway outside her hospital room. Foot traffic stomps past, some faint sense of whooshing accompanying the footsteps. The pit-a-pat slowly brings her to the surface of consciousness.

She opens her eyes. Blinks. Twice. Three times.

She still can't see.

The dark holds strong in all directions. The opaque black of nothingness hung up around her.

She brings her hands up to her eyes this time. Feels the tubes in her left wrist pull taut as she does.

And she touches the thin skin beneath her eyebrows. Cold fingers confirm that her eyes are open, that they are still there.

She closes her eyes and prods at the lids. She hopes to see those little bursts of pink light that this sometimes produces, but there's nothing.

She breathes funny for what might be a minute or two. Panting. Almost panicking.

I'm blind.

☾

Another dream sloshes warped images in Darger's head.

At first, she sees only bending beams of light. Tracers like she's taken a hallucinogen. Flares like flames catching a camera lens.

It stays abstract. Smeary contours and lines. Glowing shapes flitting over her mind's eye.

Then the blotches congeal into something concrete all at once.

Sunlight glints off the sea of asphalt in the foreground, off the pale cement strip of the sidewalk in the distance. The scene strikes Darger as familiar, as somehow urgent.

You're in a parking lot.

Something important here.

Something...

She needs to get over to that sidewalk, even if she doesn't fully understand why. Needs to hurry, too.

She strides across the blacktop, and she feels slow. Arms and legs impeded like she's walking underwater.

Determined, she pushes herself harder, faster. Wills speed into her limbs. Hurls herself against that invisible force slowing her down.

But it's no use. No good.

She looks up at the building there, the brick thing that seems to sprout out of the edge of the sidewalk. Hulking. Muscular.

Jagged fragments of light refract from some of the windows cut into the brick. The sunlight sparks and spits off a different pane of glass every time she takes a step, a flint throwing orange glitter.

She presses herself that way. Still moving in slow motion like she's wading through a pool full of chocolate pudding.

And then he's there.

Justin Leffew appears in that fourth-story window. The top of his skull hangs in shards around his face, still connected to the rest of him by flaps of scalp. Shiny white bone that shimmers in the sunlight, dangling in a way that reminds her of both a broken eggshell and Christmas ornaments at the same time.

His lip snarls. His brow furrows. He's yelling but she can't hear him, can't understand.

And then he's lifting the baby out over the rail of the balcony. Suspending her over empty space.

Darger hurls herself forward. Puts all of herself into it. Straining.

Leffew flicks his arms. Flings the baby over the edge.

The pale bulk plummets like a falling star. Sinks toward the concrete with gusto.

Darger grits her teeth. Jams her feet into the ground one after the other. Pushes off as hard as she can.

But she can't. She can't.

She's too slow. She won't make it.

That streaking object rushes for the ground. Faster, faster.

And then Darger shakes herself awake.

That antiseptic smell stings in her sinuses again. That murmuring beep joins in a fraction of a second later.

Back in the hospital room.

Her breathing is ragged. Noisy. Strange. Dry.

She rasps for a while like that. Listens only to her breath. In and out.

Finally, she opens her eyes. Lolls her head to the left and then the right. Looks all the way around.

The black nothing still hangs around her like a curtain.

☾

The next time Darger wakes, Loshak is talking to her. He's

close, just next to her right side, but she can tell he's basically yelling. He sounds closer than the beeping, but not by much.

"You hear me?"

She swallows before she replies.

"Yeah."

Her voice sounds hollow in her head. Her hearing must be fucked up, too, but at least she *can* hear.

"You saved a bunch of lives. You know that?"

She swallows again.

"I can't see."

He goes quiet. Stays that way for what feels like a long time. Finally, he responds.

"I know."

The quiet stretches out again. A vacuum somehow occupying the hospital room like it's some cavernous space.

Then he's talking again, but she can't hear him, can't stay awake.

She drifts back under the surface.

☾

Another dream paints kaleidoscope smears across Darger's imagination. Colors that blur into one another. Shapes that melt and morph and sprout and bloom.

No Huxley this time. No Grub Town. No blood.

No asphalt. No Leffew. No falling bundle of babe.

Just blobs. Splotches that can no longer rise to the level of meaning. Color and movement without any narrative substance.

She can hear that hospital beep, but it's miles away now. A brittle sharpness that cuts through the dreamscape somehow, tiny as it is.

And then the blush starts to drain out of everything. All the reds and yellows and oranges fade first. The palette goes cooler and darker, dissolving into cobalt blues and purple shades that remind Darger of plums and eggplants.

Wilting. Dying.

And soon even those cool tones leach away as well.

Darker and darker.

Dimmer and dimmer.

The black bleeds into everything. Swirling, coiling shadows encroaching.

Until the darkness becomes total.

☾

Brightness. Indistinct.

The next time she wakes up, she can see something.

The world looks like she's looking through smudged glass. Colors, yes. Shapes, not so much.

For a second, she thinks she's still dreaming, but no.

That telltale beep is louder. Fuller.

She can hear the endless shuffling in the hall, the soles of shoes scuffing, scrub pant legs swishing. The bustle persists.

She swivels her head, pans her cloudy field of vision from right to left. Tries to sharpen her focus, to make all the soft lines and blots tighten into solid shapes again.

And then she can make out the rectangular brilliance that must be the window. A fuzzy glare to her left, cloudy and smeared, but in this moment it is made beautiful.

The frame of reference somehow takes her breath away.

Soon, she can discern other shapes.

The black sheen that must be the TV screen, presently off.

The blond plank that must be the wooden door.

Loshak is there again at her side. A gray smear that is talking.

"I can… I can see now. Sorta," she says.

"Well, the doctors said that recovering your eyesight would be about fifty-fifty, so you're lucky, you know?"

She hears paper crinkling and realizes that he must be reading a newspaper as he sits with her. Probably has a paper cup of coffee, too. She's almost surprised she can't smell it.

"Yep," he says. "You're not out of the woods, but they're optimistic you'll make a full recovery."

The newspaper flaps as he turns a page. Then he goes on.

"Like I said. Lucky."

EPILOGUE

The doctors at UCLA Medical Center kept Darger under observation for several days before finally discharging her. Her vision was still blurred and doubled from the damage her optic nerve sustained during the head injury.

"You're very lucky," Dr. Tran, one of the neurologists, told her.

Darger let Loshak help her into a wheelchair, per hospital policy.

"So everyone keeps telling me," Darger said. "But I still can't see shit, unless you count blurry, doubled blobs."

"That's not unusual with a TBI. People often overlook the fact that our eyes are only part of the equation when it comes to vision. The brain is responsible for processing what the eyes see, for controlling their movements, and ensuring they work in tandem. The visual processing system is very complex. I suspect the initial loss of vision was a form of cortical visual impairment, a result of injury to your occipital lobe. The persisting blurred vision and diplopia may be lingering effects of the CVI, but it also might mean there was damage to one or more of your cranial nerves," Dr. Tran said.

"OK, but how long before it goes back to normal?"

"That's impossible to say. For some people it's days. Others, weeks or months. And then there are those who never recover full visual acuity and function."

Darger tried not to panic at the notion of being stuck this way forever. Tried not to think about the strict vision requirements for FBI agents.

"I recommend finding a neuro-optometrist when you return home, who can give you a more thorough evaluation and suggest appropriate vision therapy techniques. I'm generally more knowledgeable about providers here on the west coast, but I'm sure I can come up with a few names if you can't seem to find anyone. Just give me a call."

Darger thanked Dr. Tran, and Loshak wheeled her to the open door, which looked like a big, blurry white rectangle. She squinted and fumbled for the sunglasses perched on top of her head. Her increased sensitivity to light was another fun symptom she'd been experiencing since her vision started to come back.

Head injury, she thought. *The gift that keeps on giving.*

Fitch had the car waiting for them at the door to the parking garage. Loshak helped Darger into the backseat and climbed in front.

"Thanks for volunteering to drop us at the airport," Loshak said.

"No biggie," Fitch said and glanced at Darger in the rearview mirror. "Least I could do for my guardian angel, who saved the day. Again."

Darger grunted a noncommittal reply.

The truth was, she was angry it hadn't turned out better. That they hadn't saved more. They'd saved many, yes. But it never seemed like enough. Not when every time she passed a TV, she heard some snippet of a news anchor updating the casualty toll — 82 confirmed dead, 647 injured — or announcing that they'd found a new, never-before-seen angle of the Thrilltopia attack or the Vinnie Savage death, going on to warn viewers that, "The video you are about to see contains graphic, disturbing content which may be unsuitable for children. Sensitive viewers are encouraged to leave the room or change the channel."

It was everywhere. A 24-hour churn, rehashing the whole grisly affair. They were giving Tyler Huxley exactly what he'd always wanted.

Darger argued with herself internally that it didn't matter. Huxley was dead, a fact which prevented him from enjoying the fruits of his perverse labor. But someone else would come along eventually to fill his shoes. To see death and destruction as their path to infamy. The media blitz was only sweetening the pot.

And there was yet another part of her that still couldn't quite believe Huxley was really dead. That it hadn't all been another trick.

She knew without a doubt that she'd shot him. That she'd watched him explode.

But the lack of a body left her feeling the vaguest sense of uncertainty.

☾

Darger kept a tight grip on Loshak's arm as he guided her through the bustling airport. He paused before the escalator that led up to the security checkpoint, then pulled them to the side so they weren't blocking the way.

"Hmm… this is gonna be dicey," he said. "You probably can't see the lines between the steps, can you?"

Darger lifted her sunglasses to peek at the churning conveyor.

"Nope. It's one big black blur." She settled the glasses back on the bridge of her nose. "Just do it like 'Mother, May I?'"

"Mother who what?"

"You don't know that game? Kind of like Simon Says. One

kid plays the mother and everyone else lines up across the room or whatever. And then Mother gives each person a command like, 'Take three bunny hops' or 'two giant steps' or 'five duck waddles forward.'"

Loshak nodded.

"OK, yeah that does sound familiar." He peeked over his shoulder. "Well, there's no one coming right now. Let's do this."

He scooted them so they were squarely facing the perpetually moving stairway.

"Alright... uh... one giant step."

Darger stretched out her right leg and placed her foot on the escalator. As soon as she settled her weight on it, she felt the pull of the forward momentum.

"Scoot backward just a little. Your toes are just over one of the seams," Loshak said.

Darger inched her feet back.

"You're good," he said. "Although you didn't say, 'Mother, may I?'"

"I thought you didn't know the game."

"It's coming back to me now."

Loshak gave her a warning as they neared the top of the stairs.

"OK, you're going to do a little bunny hop in 3... 2... 1... now."

Darger landed on solid ground and was relieved to be back on stationary land.

They'd moved a few hundred yards down the terminal when Loshak chuckled.

"What?" Darger asked, unable to make out anything but muddled amoeba shapes swaying around her.

"We just passed an elevator. Could have spared us the

whole escalator debacle after all."

Darger was always thankful for the fact that, as federal agents, they were not subject to the same TSA screenings civilians were. She was doubly grateful for it today. She tried to imagine fumbling about her luggage for her liquids and electronics. Just getting her boots on and off was chore enough when she could barely see.

They reached their gate and found an open section of seats. Darger chose one facing away from the windows looking out on the tarmac. Loshak sat across from her, picking up a newspaper someone had left behind.

"Is it rude of me to read the paper in front of you when you're half blind?" he asked.

"Why would you want to read that? It's just going to be more drivel about Huxley and the bombings."

The newsprint rustled as Loshak flipped through the pages.

"Not in the Sports section it isn't."

"Well then, knock yourself out."

Loshak's head disappeared behind the paper before popping up two seconds later.

"I could read aloud, if you'd like."

"I'm already blind. Please don't make me wish I was deaf, too."

Loshak sniffed out a little laugh, and his blur melded with the paper again.

Darger slouched in her seat and tried to engage in her favorite airport past-time: people-watching. The problem was everyone looked mostly the same, blurred past all recognition as they were. If Darger tilted her head just right and really focused, some of the doubling seemed to resolve, and she could even make out the vaguest facial features. Enough to tell if she was looking at a man or woman or someone young or old, at least.

After a few minutes of that, she started getting a headache and figured that was enough straining her senses for one day. She was about to settle back in her seat, resigned to simply watching the indistinct colored daubs float by, when she spotted a familiar build.

Black hoodie. With a strange bulge in the front.

Darger scrambled upright, heart racing.

The flat expanse of blurry newspaper across from her was whisked aside.

"What is it?" Loshak asked.

Darger leaned forward as the black-clad figure came closer. She concentrated hard, as if she could will her vision into clearing. She could not, of course, but the figure passed near enough that Darger was finally able to make out a few details.

It was a woman. With short spiky hair.

The bulge was a baby carrier strapped to her chest. It wasn't even black, either, but dark blue.

Heart still galloping away like a stampeding buffalo, Darger sat back in her seat.

"Nothing. I thought I saw…"

She shook her head instead of finishing the thought.

"Huxley?" Loshak said.

She whipped her head up to face him.

"How did you know?"

He shrugged.

"Pretty common PTSD response."

"Well yeah, but… it's more than that."

"What do you mean?"

Darger knew it sounded silly, but she didn't care. She had to say it out loud.

"It's just… what if he isn't dead?"

The pair of dark arches above Loshak's eyes stretched skyward. He dropped the newspaper in his lap.

"You saw Huxley vaporize himself with your own two eyes. And I know they aren't working so well just now, but I think you were seeing fine then."

Darger picked at a loose thread on the pocket of her jacket.

"I know that. But what if it was some kind of trick again? He's done it before. Faked his own death."

"Darger, he used a very rudimentary ruse the last time that only worked because A., it was entirely off-screen, and B., we were more worried about finding and defusing his bombs than figuring out whether the dead body he'd left us was actually him. If he hadn't come out and told us it was all a sham, we would have figured that out anyway with a simple DNA test. Faking his death this time would have required a level of sleight of hand and special effects that Tyler Huxley had neither the talent nor the resources to pull off. I'm sorry, but the guy isn't David Copperfield."

Darger's mouth puckered.

"Criss Angel would be a slightly less dated reference, just FYI."

Loshak snorted and moved to pick up his paper.

"Besides, you can rest assured that there are bits of Huxley's DNA strewn all over that park."

"That's not the same."

Loshak released his grip on the paper again, and even though he was blurry, Darger could tell he was staring hard at her now.

"OK, what then?" he asked. "You want a body? You want Huxley's pale corpse brought before you so you can poke it with your finger? Would that satisfy you?"

She huffed out a breath. It was annoying, having a partner

who was so rational all the time.

“No. I don’t want to poke his corpse with my finger,” she said, crossing her arms over her chest. “Obviously I’d use a stick.”

COME PARTY WITH US

We're loners. Rebels. But much to our surprise, the most kickass part of writing has been connecting with our readers. From time to time, we send out newsletters with giveaways, special offers, and juicy details on new releases.

Sign up for our mailing list at:
http://ltvargus.com/mailing-list

SPREAD THE WORD

Thank you for reading! We'd be very grateful if you could take a few minutes to review it on Amazon.com.

How grateful? Eternally. Even when we are old and dead and have turned into ghosts, we will be thinking fondly of you and your kind words. The most powerful way to bring our books to the attention of other people is through the honest reviews from readers like you.

ABOUT THE AUTHORS

Tim McBain writes because life is short, and he wants to make something awesome before he dies. Additionally, he likes to move it, move it.

You can connect with Tim via email at tim@timmcbain.com.

L.T. Vargus grew up in Hell, Michigan, which is a lot smaller, quieter, and less fiery than one might imagine. When not click-clacking away at the keyboard, she can be found sewing, fantasizing about food, and rotting her brain in front of the TV.

If you want to wax poetic about pizza or cats, you can contact L.T. (the L is for Lex) at ltvargus9@gmail.com or on Twitter @ltvargus.

LTVargus.com

www.ingramcontent.com/pod-product-compliance
Lightning Source LLC
Chambersburg PA
CBHW020257030826
48979CB00026B/1344/J

* 9 7 8 1 9 5 4 2 0 3 1 5 0 *